# PRAISE FOR

"Joy Callaway never fails to bri_____ This
book has it all: the lush mystery _____ solve
of a woman at work, and the b_____ something
that will last for generations. I absolutely loved it."

—AMY JO BURNS, AUTHOR OF *MERCURY*, FOR *WHAT THE MOUNTAINS REMEMBER*

"A stunning portrayal of the building of the Grove Park Inn that reveals not only its grandeur, but also the struggles of the laborers tasked with its construction, Joy Callaway brings the famed Vagabonds to life with immaculate research and rich details in this intriguing, elegantly written historical fiction that readers are going to love!"

—MADELINE MARTIN, *NEW YORK TIMES* BESTSELLING AUTHOR OF *THE KEEPER OF HIDDEN BOOKS*, FOR *WHAT THE MOUNTAINS REMEMBER*

"Callaway is back with another insightful rendering of a place and time in history, bringing her trademark attention to detail, warmth, and heart to a story centered around one of the nation's most beautiful and fabled hotels, the Grove Park Inn in Asheville, NC. Readers will root for Belle as she uncovers more than she expected and discovers herself along the way."

—MARYBETH MAYHEW WHALEN, AUTHOR OF TEN NOVELS AND CO-FOUNDER OF *THE BOOK TIDE*, FOR *WHAT THE MOUNTAINS REMEMBER*

"For anyone who has ever had to find their voice in a crowd shouting to be the same as everyone else, Sadie Fremd will be your hero. With lush gardens so generously described that one feels as if they can pick the flowers, *All the Pretty Places* is immersive, engaging, and full of wonder."

—PATTI CALLAHAN HENRY, *NEW YORK TIMES* BESTSELLING AUTHOR OF *SURVIVING SAVANNAH*

"Joy Callaway's *All the Pretty Places* is a fascinating, heartwarming story that brings to light a time and place where only the wealthy had access to the beauty and restorative power of gardens. Callaway draws us into Sadie's world with gorgeous prose (you can practically feel the rich, damp soil and smell the sweet lilacs) that transports readers to the lush landscapes that Sadie will go to any lengths to protect."

—ADELE MYERS, AUTHOR OF *THE TOBACCO WIVES*

"Masterfully written with elegant prose and exquisite detail, Joy Callaway crafts a story as sumptuous and colorful as the Gilded Age gardens she transports readers to. *All The Pretty Places* is the story of a young woman fighting for personal and professional integrity and freedom, as well as a searing social commentary on poverty, privilege, and class discrepancy. I found myself cheering for Sadie with each page and tearing up at the emotional and nuanced ending."

—YVETTE MANESSIS CORPORON, INTERNATIONAL BESTSELLING AUTHOR OF *WHERE THE WANDERING ENDS*

"Callaway's dialogue captures the cadences and concerns of the American upper crust, and the society drama is sure to please fans of such aristocratic historicals as *The House of Mirth* and *The Gilded Age*."

—PUBLISHERS WEEKLY FOR *THE GRAND DESIGN*

"A beautifully written historical romance novel. Joy Callaway has impeccably researched the life of Dorothy Draper from her days as 'Greenbrier' debutante to her return as the hotel's decorator. Five Stars!"

—CARLETON VARNEY, PRESIDENT OF DOROTHY DRAPER & COMPANY, INC., FOR *THE GRAND DESIGN*

"*The Grand Design* is a spellbinding tale of a woman's quest to escape the confines of upper-crust society and make her own way in the world. With vivid characters, illuminating prose, and perfect pacing, this novel is as captivating and confident as the heroine at its center."

—KRISTY WOODSON HARVEY, NEW YORK TIMES BESTSELLING AUTHOR OF *THE WEDDING VEIL*

# WHAT THE MOUNTAINS REMEMBER

## ALSO BY JOY CALLAWAY

*All the Pretty Places: A Novel of the Gilded Age*

*The Grand Design: A Novel of Dorothy Draper*

*The Fifth Avenue Artists Society*

*Secret Sisters*

# WHAT THE MOUNTAINS REMEMBER

## JOY CALLAWAY

HARPER MUSE

Published by Harper Muse,
an imprint of HarperCollins Focus LLC.

ISBN 978-1-4002-4431-7 (TP)

ISBN 978-1-4002-4430-0 (epub)

ISBN 978-1-4002-4432-4 (audio download)

**Library of Congress Cataloging-in-Publication Data**
Title: What the mountains remember / Joy Callaway.
Description: [Nashville]: Harper Muse, 2024. | Summary: "International bestselling author Joy Callaway returns with a story of the ordinary people behind extraordinary beauty–and the question of who gets to tell their stories"– Provided by publisher.
Identifiers: LCCN 2023053129 (print) | LCCN 2023053130 (ebook) | ISBN 9781400244317 (TP) | ISBN 9781400244300 (epub) | ISBN 9781400244324
Subjects: LCGFT: Novels.
Classification: LCC PS3603.A4455 W45 2024 (print) | LCC PS3603.A4455 (ebook) | DDC 813/.6–dc23/eng/20231115
LC record available at https://lccn.loc.gov/2023053129
LC ebook record available at https://lccn.loc.gov/2023053130

*Printed in the United States of America*
24 25 26 27 28 LBC 5 4 3 2 1

*For Jed, Hannah, and Reece—*
*May you always realize the importance of your story*
*and the light you shine in the world.*

# CHAPTER ONE

APRIL 15, 1913
ASHEVILLE, NORTH CAROLINA

Women of elevated social status did not camp nor spend more than an hour or two in the elements. It was unnatural. There were silks and comfort and odor to consider, after all, and when one had the choice to recline on goose down and remain warm next to a coal fire stoked by servants and have a bath—infused with rose oil—drawn at her bidding, the notion that she would choose to freeze while sleeping on a canvas cot was preposterous. Scandalous, even.

Marie Austen Kipp, daughter of Augustus Kipp, my stepfather's favorite cousin and inventor of some sort of polymer that Henry Ford was using in his autos, was clearly of this mind. We had been each other's closest companion for years—some families required proximity even if it provoked madness—as well as these last four hours riding in one of Mr. Ford's blue Model T Town Cars. Marie Austen kept giggling and whispering about living in the elements as though it was something incredibly naughty. Instead of rolling my eyes, I played along as I had for the last six years, feigning the heiress innocence required of the stepdaughter of gasoline magnate Shipley Newbold, and grinned and giggled with her.

"Hi! Hi, all of you lovelies! We're going camping! We're sleeping out of doors," Marie Austen proclaimed through the closed rear window to the gaggle of ordinary folk gathered in front of what appeared to be a clapboard general store. From the moment we'd disembarked at the train station in Johnson City, Tennessee, and were situated in autos behind the procession of our fathers, who had been traversing the open country since mid-March on the camping vacation Mr. Ford called the Vagabonds Tour, we'd encountered thousands of onlookers. The paper men had done their jobs well, alerting every small town along our route to Asheville that Mr. Ford, Mr. Firestone, Mr. Edison, and their friends were coming for a breeze-through visit.

"Don't just sit back and ignore them, Belle. Give them a little wave. It'll be the high mark in their day," Marie Austen said, nudging me. Believing that a glimpse of herself was enough to set a person's day right was the reason Marie Austen was in such an agreeable mood. So long as she was secured in her rightful place— the sun to the rest of us simple planets—she was merry.

"Don't you agree, Mr. Leslie?" she asked our driver, who stoically nodded. He was a perfect chauffeur. He said absolutely nothing.

Marie Austen raised her arm and slightly twisted her gloved hand from the wrist as though she were Queen Mary and the gawking onlookers—who were mainly entranced by the autos—her subjects.

"I doubt it'll be the high mark of their day," I said. "Unless, of course, Mr. Leslie would like to pull over and give one of them this fine machine in exchange for one of their mules and buggies." Marie Austen laughed and Mr. Leslie pretended not to hear me. I leaned forward just slightly as we passed a rail depot nearly hidden by felled logs ready to ship. A crowd of men in flannel shirts and well-worn overalls stared. I waved and then settled back against the tufted leather seat.

I'd been avoiding the view on purpose since Tennessee. I hadn't bargained for the way my heart startled and buckled at the sight of the spring-green hills cloaked in cloudy smoke, the way my soul seemed to scream and fall to its knees at the earthy-sweet smell of home. We weren't anywhere close to home, to the hills and hollers of Red Dragon, West Virginia, but to a girl who'd been living on the unending flat of an Indiana plain since Mother married Papa Shipley, the particulars of where the mountains were didn't matter.

There was a chance I'd cry my way through the week, that the hills would draw my father out of the recesses of my and my mother's hearts where we'd hidden him. Or perhaps I'd find a way to continue in this parallel world where Belle Coleman had died completely and risen Belle Newbold.

"What do you suppose we'll do if a bear comes upon our tent in the night?" Marie Austen asked abruptly. "Father said it'll just be the two of us covered in a sheet of canvas. I don't figure that's much protection. I think I heard someone say that you should play dead or perhaps run away. I'm terribly nervous." She bunched her fingers in her midnight-blue satin skirt, likely imagining the need to gather the fabric in her hands before running wildly through the woods.

"You should be. They prefer red hair, I've heard," I said, barely keeping from laughing. I needed the comic relief as much as she did. "The color is reminiscent of salmon, you know, and —"

"Stop it, Belle," she said, slapping my arm. "Truly. You know how I get, and to agitate me at a time such as this is highly unkind."

"I apologize." I'd known Marie Austen for over half a decade and still found it difficult to determine her moods. At times she preferred her fears to be thwarted with merriment and at others, like now, she demanded earnestness. "If a bear nears our camp, which it is apt to do with all the cooking and the like, and it comes upon you, simply stay still. If you're standing, slowly wave your arms so it knows you're a human."

The mention of bears took me back to fishing on Elk Run with Father. It was dusk and I could see his weathered hands, stained black from coal dust, as they froze on the trout he was cleaning. *"Still, Belle. Still,"* he'd whispered, nodding to an enormous black bear that had just come down the hill to the creek. *"If he comes closer, just lift your hands and wave them real slow. Remind him you're a girl, not a predator."*

"And how would you know?" Marie Austen charged. Her fear had been stoked into anger, displayed in the wash of blush across her nose.

I thought fast. "Worth told me . . . in one of his letters."

Mother had forbidden me to speak of the particulars of our former life the moment I met Papa Shipley. No one in my current acquaintance, save Mother, knew my true history, and they never would. I could say that I'd been born in West Virginia. I could say that my father had been in the mining business and perished in a roof collapse. I could not say he was a regular coal miner and not a manager or operator.

All of Red Dragon had watched Boss Elkhorn, the coal mine operator, turn out his first wife and banish her from town when he discovered that she'd grown up impoverished. He'd then swiftly married a rail magnate's daughter. Several months later, his first wife's emaciated body was found beneath a fallen tree she'd been living under eleven miles from town. She hadn't been able to survive the harsh mountain winter. When Boss Elkhorn refused to allow her burial in Red Dragon, the miners who found her buried her in the dirt below the felled tree, left forever alone. Though she never spoke of it, I knew Mother worried we'd endure the same fate if our past was revealed. It was one of my greatest fears too.

Mother hadn't meant for Papa Shipley, a millionaire who owned the majority of the gasoline wells in Indiana, to assume she was well-to-do; it had just happened that way. She'd been modeling a dinner dress for Hadley's Department Store's spring fashion show for extra money and was taking a break for water on the sidewalk when Papa drove through Red Dragon on his way to vacation at The Homestead and noticed her. He'd stopped and asked her to dinner. When she'd said she lost her husband the year before, he commented that the mining company was likely lost without his leadership. She didn't correct him because the paper had just called Father a leader in his obituary.

Nevertheless, it occurred to Mother that Papa Shipley wouldn't have stopped if she'd been wearing her threadbare cotton gown and apron. The fashion show dress had made her seem like she was used to fine things, like Papa and Mother were a sensible match. After he'd whisked her off to dinner nearly an hour away in Beckley—a distance that allowed Mother to keep Papa secret from all of our friends—she immediately made arrangements for us to visit him in Gas City. The visit was made permanent by their swift engagement. Mother and Papa were married only a month and two days after their first meeting. We never returned to Red Dragon.

"Worth told you? Don't you suppose that makes it worse? It's his land we're using for this camping experiment. Now it's confirmed, Belle. There are bears." Marie Austen's voice squeaked on the last word, bringing me back to her fear. I reached to hold her hand. Despite being only eight months younger than me, at times she reminded me of a child. She'd been formed feral and desperate in the wake of her parents' frequent disinterest and, as a result, clung to and repelled affection in a chaotic, unpredictable manner. I felt a particular responsibility for her well-being. She was my cousin, after all.

"I know it looks rather foreign here, completely unlike the terrain we've left in Indiana, but our fathers have been in the wilderness these last weeks with no incident," I said. This seemed to calm her, and she heaved a breath and took her hand from mine to touch my lace sleeves. Papa Shipley had me fitted for fourteen new costumes for this trip alone on account of my seeing Worth Delafield for the first time in five years.

"He's absolutely going to swoon when he sees you," Marie Austen said softly, appraising my gown. It was made for a fine drawing room, completely inappropriate for a camping outing, but Mr. Ford told Papa that the ladies dressed just as well when their quarters were outdoors. The bodice was of bloused Brussels net with a blue taffeta jacket outfitted with ribbons over the breast and waist. When Father took me to sleep in the woods as a child, I wore trousers and long socks to keep the ticks from biting and whatever stained garment I could fashion into a shirt. This was a different sort of excursion.

"Worth doesn't swoon," I said. "At least he didn't the last time I saw him."

Marie Austen sighed.

"He did seem to be a serious sort at your stepfather's birthday celebration that year, but he was only nineteen and the two of you barely knew each other then. You've been writing these last months and now you're . . . well . . . whatever you are."

"We have been writing here and there, but nothing romantic in the slightest. He simply tells me of his daily schedule, and I do the same."

"And yet you've agreed to marry the man upon his proposal this week. You love him. You have from the start, all those years ago. You have to, to accept something as asinine as this," she said.

It wasn't the first time she'd questioned my arrangement with Worth—or my desire for a match based on sensible things instead of love. Marie Austen couldn't fathom settling for anything less than both. But then again, she'd never known the ache of starvation or seen the effects of a deadening heart when it broke.

At first I'd regretted telling her about Worth at all. She'd responded with a strange sense of outrage—perhaps it was because when last we'd seen him, he'd appeared pleasant enough for some to deem handsome, and she couldn't bear the possibility of my settling with a suitable, attractive man before she did. But now I didn't pay her comments any mind.

"I don't love him. I don't really know him. But his values are the same as mine. He wants a family and his fortune will support us," I said. We careened to the left, veering off the main road, and I startled, lurching into Marie Austen's shoulder in an attempt to hide as we sped past a young man with near-white hair carrying a tin lunch pail.

"Are you all right?" Marie Austen asked, gently pushing me back into my seat. My heart was racing. The man looked just like my former neighbor in Red Dragon, Willie Smith, and that lunch pail was identical to Father's, handmade by old man Cato, who'd taken to collecting scrap metal in his elderly years.

I heaved a breath and nodded as we started down a narrow sort of trail canopied entirely by trees. Mother and I were safe. No one we'd known back home would come upon us here—Asheville was nearly three hundred miles from home, from the little holler where the Smiths lived. It was only the familiar sight of the mountains washing my mind in memories, tricking me. I lifted my hand to the roof of the auto to prevent jolting as we bounced over roots.

"Marriage shouldn't be a transaction, Belle," Marie Austen said, bringing me back to her critique of my relationship with Worth. "You're setting yourself up for misery. Perhaps I haven't found my match, but I refuse to settle—regardless of what Father says."

Both Marie Austen and I had been out for three seasons as of last year and neither of us had received any proposals—her because she refused to agree to a marriage that didn't include both love and immense wealth and me because I was only part Newbold, without the advantage of inheritance that came with blood. The moment I married or Papa died, I would lose the support of his pockets. Somehow, everyone in town knew the particulars. Mother would have some sort of stipend, but the majority of the fortune would go to my much older stepbrother, Hartley, to satisfy a promise Papa made to Hartley's mother on her deathbed.

I was glad for my suitors' trepidation and relieved when Papa called me into his study to discuss "an arrangement," as he called it, with his late best friend's son, Worth. Though I'd hardly voiced it aloud—save to Marie Austen—I did not want to marry for love. If it wasn't for my desperately wanting security and a family so I would never be left alone, I would have refused Papa's offer to sponsor my coming out at all.

I'd vowed the moment my father died and Mother took to her bed for eight long months, leaving me to grieve alone, that I would never love a man the way Mother loved my father. True love created such a bonded family that its separation felt like tearing limb from limb. Fondness, instead, could foster love and affection, but the sort that won pleasant remembrances instead of a wound that never healed. Mother and Papa Shipley had a comfortable sort of marriage. From what I recalled of Worth, he would provide me the same steady life free of the charm that could capture a heart.

"As I said when last we discussed this, it is your decision to wait for love, just as it is mine to accept a more practical union." I cast my eyes out the window at the forest. The late-afternoon sun dappled the ground, eluding the shadowy tree cover. Here and there pink-purple sprays of wild redbuds shocked the new-life green of the grass and trees and the brown of last year's leaves. The sight caused a strange sensation—an anxious churning in my stomach, a hollow grief in my heart, and an elation in my soul that made me feel weightless.

I turned away from the window and pressed my palm against my chest, but the pressure couldn't stop the tightness now clutching my lungs. I took a slow breath, glad Marie Austen had shifted her back toward me in her frustration.

"I disagree that my marriage will be miserable," I said. It was easier, better, to focus on Worth. "In fact, it is exactly what I've hoped for."

Worth had approached Papa asking if he knew of any young women agreeable to a sensible match. He was looking for a companion, a mother for his future children who didn't require the wooing of a lovestruck suitor—something he said he hadn't the time or the energy for after inheriting his father's land holdings. He was away from home often, buying and selling land from coast to coast, but he understood his time was short.

Already twenty-four, Worth knew if he didn't marry soon, he never would, and the Delafield name would ultimately render itself extinct. Papa had inquired of me for two reasons. He wanted me settled with a kind man with sizable pockets, as he couldn't ultimately finance me, and he was eager to have Mother to himself. Even so, he had approached the conversation with tenderness, allowing me the option to decline, but I had practically begged him to write Worth and accept straightaway.

"You're going to leave me in Gas City all alone." Marie Austen turned to me and her eyes filled. This was the real reason she'd challenged my match. Prior to my arrival in Indiana, Marie Austen hadn't been able to claim a single friend. She'd repelled all the other Gas City debutantes long before she was presented. When I arrived, a sudden cousin with a dubious past, equally snubbed by our societal contemporaries, Marie Austen decided to embrace me—primarily because standing next to me, the least suitable match for any discerning Gas City gentleman, she hoped her worst qualities would be forgotten.

"The wells are drying up—of course we all know it, though your stepfather has tried to keep it quiet. That's why he's come alongside Mr. Ford, hoping he'll support the initiative for the drive-up gasoline stores. He's not ready to slow down, but what choice will he have when it's all gone?" She wiped the corners of her eyes. "It won't affect his fortune or Father's, but everyone else is going to leave. You first and then the rest of the world." Marie Austen suddenly burst into tears.

Mr. Leslie, clearly sensing a drastic turn in our conversation, held a handkerchief over his shoulder as the auto lurched and stumbled over the bumpy path. Marie Austen took it and blew her nose.

"You could visit Worth and me in Charlotte. Perhaps your match could be found there? I'm sure Worth wouldn't mind, and—"

"Father says the Delafields have land all over the country. Why Worth would settle in such a small town is baffling. I'd wager there are fewer prospects there for me than in Gas City. Perhaps I'll just marry ugly old Ronald Swingle and take a lover. That would satisfy everyone, don't you think?"

I gasped.

"Ronald Swingle's breath is horrendous. Not to mention he's terribly conceited for a man with such an unfortunate look."

My first season out, I'd taken interest in any unattractive man I could find. I'd assumed I could find an amiable match quite easily that way, but I'd been wrong. It seemed that the ugly, wealthy men in Gas City often had a personality that matched their appearance. If it wasn't their temper, it was their manners. If it wasn't their manners, it was their pompousness. "I forbid you to marry Mr. Swingle."

Marie Austen grinned and then laughed.

"Despite my fury at your abandonment, I've never loved you more than at this moment. You gasp at my ill-fated match with a suitable but disgusting society man, while you don't bat an eye at my proclaiming that I'd swiftly soil the union by taking up with a lover."

I stared at her, my mind flipping through the men I'd caught her kissing over the years—the French lawyer, the postman, the Chicago banker, the auto mechanic, the newspaperman. She was addicted to the thrill of a man's adoration, to the way their touch made her feel. She'd told me as much, which was why she was holding out for a man with both pockets and allure. Marie Austen's cheeks flushed as though she knew what I was thinking, and she leaned in close.

"I only loved the one, you know, and nothing went farther than I allowed."

"Of course not," I whispered back.

The auto made a soft clacking noise as it began a steep descent, and then a chorus of Klaxon horn *ahoogas* permeated the air.

"We've arrived, ladies," Mr. Leslie said. I looked over his shoulder, over the roof of Mother and Mrs. Kipp's auto descending in front of us, and at once felt my nerves settle. We were situated in a vast valley, nothing like the sky-scraping hills and center-of-the-earth hollers of home.

"It appears that the servants have already set up camp, right on time," Mr. Leslie continued. "I declare I'm greatly impressed each time I see it. At the beginning it was just Ford, Edison, Firestone, and Burroughs—and their servants, of course. Now, with the families all coming and with various guests each year at the excursion's midpoint, the operation has become a veritable moving town." He sighed. "This is such a lovely place. Some of the locations the men choose in the weeks before and after the families come are not suitable for camping—swampland, hillsides, swollen riverbeds, and the like. This beautiful valley will be to everyone's enjoyment."

Mr. Leslie was right. The landscape was delightful, and the camp was enormous, situated in a large rectangle, likely the size of two or three city blocks. From this angle it actually resembled the American flag. Two sizable tents billowed in the breeze side by side on the left end of the valley, anchoring three rows of a dozen smaller tents stretching across the flat expanse. At least twenty autos—half looked to be roadster pickups—were parked in an orderly fashion in a large circle below the tents. In the middle burned a massive fire. The flames licked the bottom of several pots hung on metal chains from an A-frame.

"I imagine you're all hungry. In an hour or two, you'll take dinner in those large tents to the left. Chefs begin preparing almost immediately after setup is complete, and by the looks of it, they've been ready for some time," Mr. Leslie said.

"Thank heavens," Marie Austen said. "It's always unfortunate to encounter my mother when she's been too far between meals. This auto ride will have put her much behind her schedule."

Mrs. Kipp scheduled her life around food. Eight in the morning, twelve in the afternoon, five in the evening, and a sweet at nine before bed. She'd had a bit of a sandwich at the station, but that was hours ago, and judging by the sun, it was nearing six. I felt sorry for Mother, who had likely had to endure her sniveling for the last hour. Then again, I'd had to endure Marie Austen's sniveling for four and I doubted Mother felt sorry at all for my misfortune.

Mother didn't seem to feel much of anything anymore. She had once been my confidante, but now we never spoke of our triumphs and sorrows. Now her expressions were muted but pleasant, her tone always even, her embraces stiff. Perhaps it was the burden of the secret we kept. She'd been vibrant, always laughing back in Red Dragon before Father died, but she was a society woman now, a different person, like me, and had absorbed the role of Papa's wife seamlessly.

She must have learned the proper ways of doing things from the Jane Austen novels she always read. Though I had been trained to say "yes, sir" and "yes, ma'am" and was versed in the table manners needed to prevent a tablemate from being repulsed at my position next to them, I had not been taught that there were right friends and a correct manner of speaking to those below your class as though they were just a little bit less important than you. Somehow, Mother had learned those things quickly. The Kipps were right company.

The Leftlings were right company. But Charity Simpson, the milk-man's daughter, was not.

When I was seventeen, Mother had asked me to close my eyes to the past and forget the person I'd been, but now the mountains were dredging and sifting, unearthing memories of my life as a miner's daughter and the father I left behind. The auto sputtered and stopped behind the circle of the others. Mr. Leslie stretched, clicked his door open, and offered a greeting to Mother, who had just been helped out of her auto by her chauffeur. Mr. Leslie opened my door and I stepped out. The spring chill was evident in the light that had begun to disappear over the distant hills, and I shivered.

"Do let me give you my jacket," Mr. Leslie said immediately, and before I could decline it, he had fit the wool snugly over my shoulders. The excited chatter of the newly arrived guests and the clicks and slams of auto doors echoed in the crisp air. Mother stood unmoving next to the auto, her gaze trained on the hills in the distance. Mrs. Kipp charged past her toward the cooking fire with Marie Austen close behind, but Mother didn't seem to notice.

I reached for her arm.

"Mother, it's—" I'd started to say it was going to be all right, that I felt him too, but she jerked back. Her gray eyes settled on mine. They used to look bright, like a cloudless blue sky when she wore any sort of matching shade. Her traveling gown was a spring plaid of navy and cornflower, but the color in her gaze didn't change.

"You are in tent number fourteen with Marie Austen," she said. "You young girls are on the south side while the young men are on the north." Mother had begged Papa to hire a dialect instructor to give her lessons when they were first married, and now the familiar drawn vowels, the flattened *i*, the clipped *-ing* were gone. Mine were too.

"Very well," I said.

"Papa and I are situated in six, next to Henry and Clara and Augustus and Sarah." Mother nodded to a servant as he pulled several trunks off a neighboring auto, confirming two were hers. "Your hair has come loose of its figure eight. I'll send Sylvia over to plait it before dinner," she went on, appraising me. "And do freshen up as well in case Mr. Delafield arrives earlier than planned."

"Where do you suppose I could find the nearest creek?" I asked as Mr. and Mrs. Burroughs walked past us toward the tents.

Mother threw her head back and laughed heartily.

"Oh darling, can you imagine? Reclining in a creek."

I stared at her, waiting for the couple to pass.

"Where else do you propose I wash the stink of exhaust from my body?" I asked pointedly.

"In the washbasin in your tent, of course," she said under her breath. "There's lavender oil on the stand too, just like at home. My goodness, Belle. You haven't washed in a creek in six years. What would possess you to think you'd do it again now?"

I looked around, taking in the forest. This. This was what possessed me to assume that a bit of my former life was welcome, that for a week I could remember and reclaim a bit of what I'd lost. We'd always bathed in the creek in Red Dragon.

"We are not *there*," she whispered as we walked toward the tents and into the crush of inventors and their families, thrilled at the thought of camping, though true camping wasn't at all this elaborate charade of servants and finery. Mother's hand clamped onto my elbow and pulled me back to her. "We are not *them* anymore. We have never been them. Do you understand me? Our lives depend on it. I shall not be shamed. Papa shall not be shamed. You are a Newbold."

At once I heard an echo, the same determined tone. "*We will not starve. We will not give up. Do you hear me? Do you hear me, Belle?*" And at once I saw her face as it had been the day before the fashion show, the day before Papa. Her cheeks had been hollow. One hand holding a piece of stale bread while the other forced bits into my mouth. I'd been up for two days straight mending clothes for extra money without food. My vision had been hazy and my body weak.

"Belle! Come along! Come see our tent!" Marie Austen pushed

past the Firestones making their way to the other side of the compound. She grasped my hand and the memory faded. I looked back to find Mother gone.

Marie Austen twirled, her lampshade tunic billowing out as she did.

"I don't care about the bears. I've never felt so free!"

# CHAPTER TWO

The reason for Marie Austen's merriment wasn't the feel of the mountain air or the vast wild that separated our camp from civilization. It was the realization that Peter Thorp was the reporter Mr. Ford had selected for this part of the voyage. He was a known features writer for many national and local papers, including the *Star Press* in Muncie.

He was five or ten years our senior. It was hard to tell his age, really. In truth, it didn't matter. Mr. Thorp was charming and handsome and inquisitive—these were, perhaps, his greatest gifts and the reason he was so accomplished. He made readers believe—and by *readers*, I mean primarily society ladies—that they were the loveliest, the wittiest, the most interesting, and thereby every secret a woman was keeping was gladly revealed in his company.

This was simply an observation. I didn't abide charmers. They had been plentiful in Red Dragon, and charm, more often than not, was a cover for some ominous flaw. I'd warned Marie Austen, but she adored flirts and encouraged Mr. Thorp to an inappropriate degree. Only four months ago, during Papa Shipley's annual Christmas soiree, I'd gone up to my bedroom for a moment's peace from pleasantries and caught them alone, reclining on my fainting sofa. Her bodice had been unbuttoned to the corset and he'd been kissing her, his long curls tousled by her fingers. She claimed she loved him. Perhaps he loved her too. But nothing had ever come of the night. Mr. Thorp had left for a story in Sacramento the following day and he never wrote. Neither did she. She was too proud, and he was too poor, besides.

"This must be the smallest, tiniest of worlds," she proclaimed, yanking at the canvas flaps of our tent that had been opened for welcome and light. I stilled her hand.

"Don't shut them. We won't be able to see. The lamps haven't been lit." I gestured to the glass oil lamps on a small mahogany bedside stand between two cots laden with bobcat pelts and down blankets. A porcelain washstand complete with towels and a small vial of lavender oil occupied the right side of the space, while a generous carved cherry armoire stood to the left. The tent was nearly as comfortable as my room in Gas City, nothing at all like the bed of leaves I was used to when I slept out of doors.

"Fine," Marie Austen huffed. She walked to the washstand, plucked the lavender oil from its place, and uncorked it with a small *pop*. I took Mr. Leslie's jacket from my shoulders and set it on one of the cots. "I'll simply keep my voice low. I saw him across the camp, near the gentlemen's tents, with Mr. Burroughs and a striking Black man I didn't recognize. They were passing 'round a large earthenware jug and drinking straight from the mouth of it. It was quite a peculiar sight."

She tipped the end of the vial on her neck and then on both wrists.

"It's likely local moonshine—spirits made in the mountains here," I said. When I was growing up, the local shiner would bring his buggy down the mountain to the edge of the Red Dragon town line each week and sell out of jugs in a matter of minutes.

"Do you really think so? Father said North Carolina has outlawed alcohol these past five years. In any case, I've never heard of moonshine, though I gather it was quite known where you're from in . . . Oh, how terrible of me. I don't recall at all where it is you were born." She whirled around and snapped her fingers. "Virginia."

"West Virginia," I said, not at all surprised that she couldn't recall my origins. "And yes, I do believe alcohol has been banned here, but we are situated well away from anyone who would sound the alarm. I'm sure there will be imbibing regardless." I knew enough of my company to know that no one would last long without wine.

"If that's so, I'll have to prevail upon the men to let me try the mountain spirits this week. Now, about the matter of Mr. Thorp. Suppose he took the assignment knowing I'd be here," she said quietly, lowering herself on the edge of a cot.

At first, I said nothing. Of course it wasn't the truth. The man had come because he'd been given a gift by Mr. Ford, an exclusive honor of covering the voyage of the Vagabonds, as Mr. Ford liked to call his camping group. Each year they explored a different section of the country. First they'd toured the Everglades, then the following year, the Panama–Pacific International Exposition in California, and the year after that, the New England Adirondacks and Green Mountains. This year, they were planning to canvas several states. They'd already camped in Tennessee before arriving in Asheville. The Vagabonds trips were always of tremendous interest to readers across the nation. No stable-minded writer would think for a second about turning down this assignment.

Thinking of the opportunity brought Father to mind. An appointment like this had been his dream as a young man. He would have been both a prolific writer and a gentleman—a combination Mr. Thorp could never claim. Before Red Dragon swallowed him up in destiny, before he realized he had no choice but to become a miner like the three generations before him, Father had wanted to be a journalist.

When he was a young boy, a writer for the *Charleston Gazette* had come to town to cover the acquisition of a new mining company, and his stories, his adventures, had been an intoxication for Father. Even after Father was grown and the dream of writing for a paper long-lost, he continued filling notebooks and telling his stories—even if only to his family and friends. He'd gifted me a blank volume the moment I learned to write, and I'd begun cataloging and unraveling my thoughts by his example. Writing had once been my time of solace, but I hadn't picked up a notebook since his death. I couldn't bear it.

I swallowed and turned my attention back to Marie Austen. It wouldn't do to dwell on what I couldn't change.

"Suppose he did take the post for you," I said. "What shall you do?"

She smiled. "I'll tell him there's absolutely no chance we can continue on this way, and then I'll kiss him."

"And if he proposes marriage in front of your parents and mine and the Edisons and the Fords and the Firestones and the Burroughs?"

Marie Austen swatted my arm.

"Don't be ridiculous. It wouldn't get that far," she said. "I'm absolutely crazy for him, but as soon as a man with pockets and a face as fair comes around for me, I won't be anymore." She sighed. "I suppose the alternative is that I settle for someone hideous but tremendously wealthy and keep Peter on. I can't decide." Her eyes met mine. I couldn't understand how she could live this way without her heart getting maimed. I was too sensitive, too afraid to feel anything at all. I hoped I would never fall in love.

Outside, a group of lady's maids hastened past our tent. In the distance intermittent whoops were echoing in the valley.

"Shall we go see what that's about?" I asked Marie Austen. She nodded and stood, casting her gaze toward the mirror one last time.

"You and Worth Delafield are both pretty," she said, still looking at herself. I didn't know what she was after. "At least he was when last we saw him. Remember how his picture kept turning up in the papers? Of course, that was partly because his family is important, but mostly because he's attractive. And you're a natural beauty like your mother."

Mother was stunning, but I had never considered that we looked alike. I had her hair—thick chestnut with golden strands from tow-headed childhood days—and perhaps her delicate features, but my eyes were hooded and deep brown like Father's and I was tall, five feet eight inches.

"Thank you." I glanced in the mirror. My figure eight was indeed in shambles. I pushed the fallen strands back into the updo as best I could and wandered out of the tent. I could stay and wait for Sylvia to do it back up as Mother had instructed, or I could see what all the yelling was about. I preferred the latter.

"Your father must have been handsome too," Marie Austen said, catching up to me as we made our way down the aisle of tents toward the noise. Most of the tents on the female side were servants' quarters. They were equipped modestly—a cot with a quilt and a metal water basin for washing—and were all vacant. The hour was likely the cause. Dinner was approaching and Mrs. Kipp and Mother and Mrs. Ford and the like would need tending or the tables would need setting.

The idea of servants had been completely foreign to Mother and me before. No one had employed any in Red Dragon except for the Elkhorns, the mine operator's family who lived in a large brick home I'd once thought of as a mansion. I suppose that was who Papa Shipley thought Mother and I belonged to. Not the Elkhorns specifically, of course, but to someone in charge. Papa hadn't even inquired of our last name until he proposed to Mother. She'd told him we were Montgomerys, her people, whose name had died out with her parents twenty years before. It wasn't entirely false, and the knowledge was incidental regardless. All that mattered was that we'd come from someone important and that the woman he loved was his.

"Was he? Handsome?" Marie Austen pressed as we skirted the final tent and made our way toward the cooking fire. Right beyond the crush of parked autos was the source of the merriment—a grouping of our fathers and the other men surrounded by most of their families, five photographers, and Mr. Thorp. I couldn't quite make out what they were doing, though Mrs. Firestone was squawking encouragements at her husband every few seconds.

"He was, though what is your point? Appearance is superficial," I said.

"I'm trying to figure whether children with an ugly man could still be beautiful." Marie Austen raised her gloved hand to me to stop my reply. "Before you call me vain, do think about the advantage of beauty in your youth. People are attracted to pretty in marriage, in business, in life. It is quite a benefit to be born with a pleasant face." She shielded her eyes from the setting sun, now beaming bright gold over the western peak in the distance. "I'm considering my options. If I decide to keep Peter, I'll need to find a suitable husband."

We reached the gathering in time to see Mr. Ford and Mr. Edison burst from the nearby woods with handfuls of dead leaves and sprint toward the crowd with the vigor of ten-year-old boys despite their white hair and three-piece suits. Edsel, Mr. Ford's son, stood beside Toots, Mr. Edison's daughter, and upon seeing their fathers' advancements, they shouted a series of hurrys. The two men beelined for one of the large stumps—there were seven, I suppose intended for seating—and the *click* and flash of the cameras began.

Wooden spindles and flat notched-wood planks sat next to each stump, and as Mr. Ford abandoned his leaf pile, set a piece of bark beneath the wood plank, and turned the spindle vigorously in the plank's notch, I couldn't help but laugh under my breath. Papa was never going to win this contest—if a contest was what it was.

"Does your father know how to make a fire in the forest?" I asked Marie Austen. I doubted Papa Shipley had ever set foot in the wilderness before this outing.

"Here come Mr. Burroughs and Mr. Carver," Edsel commented to someone, perhaps the whole of the group. "I was betting on either of them to win this contest. They're the environmentalists after all."

George Washington Carver was undoubtedly the man who had caught Marie Austen's attention earlier. He was dressed in a smart blue double-breasted suit, and though I'd never seen a photo of him, I'd heard his name plenty. Other than gasoline, Indiana was known for farming, and I'd heard his name mentioned often at parties and around the table on account of his work with soil regeneration.

"I'm sure you're wrong. I'll allow your blunder on account of your youth, but see here? My father is going to win," Toots said on his other side. Despite Mr. Edison's and Mr. Ford's swift rotations with the spindle, their efforts hadn't yielded even a whisper of smoke. The wood was too wet or the notches were too generous. Given the chance, I would have bested all of them.

"I suppose I know who is not going to win," I said to myself, shielding my eyes and looking toward the woods where Mr. Kipp and Papa hadn't yet emerged.

"Don't be too hard on your father, Miss Newbold," Edsel said, apparently hearing me over the constant popping of the photographers' cameras. "It's his first time doing this charade. Our fathers find it great fun to initiate contests of wilderness know-how when they camp—especially when some of their guests aren't quite as versed." He began to laugh as Mr. Edison flung his spindle to the ground in frustration.

I thought the whole thing fun but strange. There was no need for these men to know how to start a fire when they'd brought such a staff of servants along. It must have been for the papers, which was why the cameras were going off with such fervor. It was advantageous for the everyman to assume they had much in common with this group of inventors and industrialists. If Mr. Ford and Mr. Firestone were actually common men and not only men of high society, surely the goal of a Ford Model T with Firestone tires was in reach for the loggers and miners and factory workers.

Finally Papa burst from the woods carrying his fistful of leaves. His hair, which only grew on the back and sides like a halo, had somehow been volumized in its inaugural trek through the trees and stuck out. Mr. Kipp was still absent.

The shouts around me grew louder as Mr. Carver's plank began to smoke and then Mr. Burroughs's.

"Do you suppose your father has taken a wrong way?" I asked Marie Austen, who hadn't uttered a sound since our arrival to witness this spectacle. When she didn't answer, I looked at her. She was gazing longingly at Mr. Thorp.

"He hasn't felt me staring," she whispered. "I need him to look."

The reason for Mr. Thorp's ignorance was his focus on the contest.

He'd folded his lanky frame on the ground in front of the spectators, to the right of the participants, and was writing furiously in his notebook, only pausing a time or two to push his eyeglasses back up on the bridge of his nose.

"Miss Kipp is going to look for Mr. Kipp. She's quite concerned he's been lost!" I shouted and pushed Marie Austen forward into the open. She startled but then nodded at me and crossed the semi-circle, striding past the men toward the woods. Mr. Thorp stopped writing then. His entire countenance drooped in shock and then enlivened as he watched her walk past.

As Papa approached, I realized no one was shouting his name. I glanced around for Mother but found her absent. Perhaps Sylvia was doing up her hair.

"Come on, Papa! You've not lost yet!" I yelled. He shook his head and grinned as he took his seat on a stump. He was different from Father in nearly every way, but he was a good man who cared for us well, and I truly loved him.

Mr. Burroughs and Mr. Carver were attempting to stoke the ember they'd captured from the wood. They'd both dropped and buried it in the pile of leaves they now held in their hands and were blowing into their palms.

Finally, a lick of flame lapped the crisp air from Mr. Carver's hands, and Mr. Thorp, now released from the shock of Marie Austen's appearance, lifted a thin silver whistle from a cord around his neck and blew. The shrill note elicited a groan from the losers— though not, of course, from Papa, who clearly had never thought he'd emerge the victor.

"Mr. Carver is the winner! And if I need a fire stoked tonight, I'll know where to go," Mr. Thorp proclaimed. Mr. Carver smiled and set the bundle of leaves on the ground, then stomped the flame out with his boot.

"It was a close race, a close race indeed," Mr. Carver said, extending his hand to Mr. Burroughs, who shook it heartily.

"There will be more contests before we're off to the next stop. Many more so I can win," Mr. Ford said, chuckling. "Now, Mr.

Thorp, when you write this up, do recall that I was the one to invite you to this fine excursion." He stood from his stump and clapped Mr. Thorp on the back.

In the distance, Mr. Kipp had finally come out of the woods, and Marie Austen, her gaze still fixed on Mr. Thorp who had suddenly turned to look her way, was smiling.

# CHAPTER THREE

Aside from the mountain breeze billowing the enormous walls of the tent and the absence of the three dozen Newbold family portraits, the dinner was exactly like the gatherings in our dining room in Gas City. The servants wore the same sort of black-and-white livery, the guests all wore the same beaded silks and fine tuxedos, and there was music, though this time it was Mrs. Firestone, draped in reindeer hide, singing an original number instead of me fumbling my way through "Let Me Call You Sweetheart" on the piano.

I yawned into my palm, took a small sip of wine, and then stared down the endlessly long, starched white tablecloth at Marie Austen, who'd been placed next to a newcomer who'd arrived just before seating. The arrangement was obviously predetermined. The man was Mr. Robert Gibbins, a congress hopeful from Bloomington who, I'd overhead from Mr. Kipp, had been introduced to Marie Austen when she was visiting her aunt and uncle a month ago and had just happened to be passing through this remote stretch of country outside of Asheville on his way to business in Washington, DC.

Worth had referred to this area particularly as Swannanoa in his letter, but I doubted Mr. Gibbins had any inkling where he actually was. Mr. Kipp had clearly telegrammed to invite him to join us. There was no reason for Mr. Gibbins's presence other than to force Marie Austen to consider him. It was clear in the bits and pieces of conversation I was overhearing from the other end of the table—Mr.

Gibbins was speaking mostly to Mr. Edison and Mr. Carver—that he knew nothing of autos or science or nature while the other men of this party had gathered specifically for these shared interests.

Marie Austen, who had selected her Maison Margaine-Lacroix pale-pink satin dinner dress with a slender silhouette to attract the eye of Mr. Thorp, was obviously pouting in his absence. She barely looked at Mr. Gibbins when he addressed her.

"I wonder what's causing the delay. They've been working on preparations since our arrival at four," Mr. Ford mused across from me. He cast a glare toward the tent entrance where the servants had appeared with our green turtle soup nearly half an hour ago. Now all of the white china bowls sat empty, some receiving longing glances.

"Perhaps the fish were overboiled," Papa Shipley suggested beside him. "It's quite an art, boiling fish. Overdone they are chewy and inedible."

"Indeed," Mother said. How difficult was it for her to remain silent in moments like this, when the subject matter involved something she'd once known so well, something that had once been a part of her every day? We had never had extra money for food, so each week Father and I fished in Elk Run from sunup until we caught enough catfish or trout to fill our basket, and then Mother would prepare them for us. Sometimes she'd fry them, but most of the time she boiled them and topped them with a pat of butter—if we had any.

"I suppose we can't do anything about the meal, so we may as well fill our cups again," Mrs. Kipp said next to me and snapped for a waiter, who hastened from his post to uncork another bottle and deposit the contents into her glass.

"Hear! Hear!" Mrs. Edison said. "We can toast to a beautiful day in absolutely gorgeous country. Have you ever seen such a striking landscape?"

"I admit I haven't, but the fact of it doesn't surprise me. Worth Delafield has the smartest eye—I daresay even smarter than his father's. In fact, I'd buy any land he recommended," Papa said.

He was telling the truth. Papa had bought a ranch in Wyoming from Worth last year, one he'd never seen.

"I don't doubt it," Mr. Edison said. "He's not an inventor like us, but he thinks like one. I noticed it the first time we were introduced. Miller brought Worth down to Fort Myers to appraise some land there over a decade ago. Worth was only thirteen or so but asked the smartest questions. Now he's one of the savviest businessmen of the next generation, and quite amiable too."

"I suppose it's good fortune that our Belle has made his . . . acquaintance then," Mother said. "Do you expect him this evening?" The particulars of my arrangement with Worth made discussing it quite difficult. We were practically engaged; both of us had agreed to the match, but he'd insisted that the actual proposal be done in person. He'd written that he thought a proposal made by letter unnatural. Though he hadn't said it, I also suspected he'd suggested a face-to-face proposal as a courtesy in case we found each other repulsive.

"Tomorrow morning, I believe, though I do wish he were able to join us this evening, before we men adjourn to toddies around the fire. He tells an engaging ghost story. Scared the life out of Burroughs once, but Burroughs won't admit it. He's quite a fellow. A fine addition to our motley crew." Mr. Edison extracted his napkin from his lap, folded it again, and placed it back. He'd done the same thing three times already. Perhaps it was a tactic to avoid screaming out in hunger.

Mother suddenly squeezed my hand under the table. It occurred to me in that moment that she could be relieved. Despite knowing I wholeheartedly thought Worth the right match for me and that Papa thought highly of him, she'd only exchanged a few words with Worth herself when he'd visited for Papa's birthday years ago. The knowledge that he was known as a respectable, kind man outside of our circle was more than welcome.

"I'm looking forward to Mr. Delafield's arrival as well. I feel immensely fortunate to have caught his eye," I said. It was a tender statement, one that would encourage others to think I was in love. Shouldn't they think that? And anyway, though it wasn't really true—I had no reason to believe I'd captured his attention, considering his letter to Papa hadn't asked for me specifically—I meant it. I did feel fortunate. He wanted something and I wanted something, and we were both able to find the person willing to give us what we desired.

"Indeed," Mr. Ford said. "I don't believe I'm speaking out of turn when I say he believes himself equally blessed to have turned your head, Miss Newbold. In fact, I ran across him at the train station in Detroit about three weeks back, and he looked brighter, near as happy as he was before the tragedy, thank God. He'd mentioned he was going to be in Charlotte after, speaking to an architect about expanding his estate." His eyes met mine and his eyebrows rose in an expression I took to mean he knew I was going to be receiving a proposal imminently.

Instead of thinking of my impending match, my mind fixed on Mr. Ford's comment about a tragedy. Papa hadn't mentioned such a thing and neither had Worth in his letters. Then again, our letters read like the weather forecast in the papers. They were purely informative, a near listing of our daily goings-on and nothing more. I would find out about this tragedy in due time. It wasn't beneficial to speculate, though I imagined it had something to do with the sudden passing of his parents three or four years back. I only recalled it because Papa had departed at once to attend the funeral. I turned my attention back to the conversation and tried to look pleasant.

"Charlotte is a fine town, but if I were Delafield, I'd settle right here. This area in general is becoming quite prosperous, known for healing. I can feel it, can't you?" Mr. Kipp said, intentionally turning the conversation away from talk of matches. Marie Austen received her vanity from both parents, but particularly her father. To the Kipps, life was a contest to be won. If talk of romantic entanglements left out his darling daughter, Mr. Kipp often made it his mission to steer the topic elsewhere—never mind that he barely acknowledged Marie Austen's presence otherwise.

"He's keen to keep this land natural. Says he has no interest to turn to Asheville permanently." Mr. Edison took a sip of wine.

Worth had never mentioned any affection for this piece of land in any of his letters. Now that I was here, I was heartened to know he viewed it as he did any of his other holdings. In this valley, the echo of heartache wasn't as strong. It wasn't like home. But if we were to reside here, I would have to venture into the woods, I would have to become reacquainted with the memories, and they would consume me. It would be better in Charlotte.

"He almost settled here once, but that was long ago, and I know for certain he'll know no other home but Charlotte," Papa said.

"Still, being here among the trees and hills and fresh air is such a balm. Don't you all feel it too?" Mrs. Kipp asked.

"Of course, that's why we suggested a stop here. Edwin Grove"— Mr. Ford turned to Papa—"You have heard of the man, of Grove's Chill Tonic renown? He is building a grand hotel called Grove Park Inn here along with his son-in-law, Fred Seely, the inventor of a genius pill cutter."

"I've heard of Mr. Grove. His tonic was a miracle to some I knew in childhood. It kept the mine running," I said, instantly wishing I'd remained silent. Mother gripped my kneecap.

I recalled the Chill Tonic well—the bitter taste that lingered, despite it being heralded as tasteless, the way the crystals would settle in the bottom of the bottle in a swampy muck, leaving the dark liquid at the top. There had been several cases of malaria in Red Dragon the summer I turned six.

A group of forty men had just arrived from a small mine in northwest Georgia when several began to emerge from their shifts in the sweltering mines shivering. At first Doc Morgan had diagnosed them with flu and sent them to bed, but when some of them began to seizure and perish, when most exhibited jaundiced eyes, he had drawn blood and found malaria under the microscope. Boss Elkhorn had panicked then, despite Doc's insistence that malaria was spread primarily by infected mosquitos—of which we had none.

A large coal shipment was due to Canada in short order, a shipment that if forfeited could result in a large deficit and layoffs. To ease Boss Elkhorn's fears of an outbreak, Doc ordered cases of Mr. Grove's Tasteless Chill Tonic for the entire town because it claimed to ward off malaria infection. After several weeks of choking down the chill tonic while Father worked shift after shift to make up for the population of miners who were ill, the temporary infirmary set up in Red Dragon's town hall closed. Most of the miners had been healed and returned to work in time for the deadline, yet the tonic remained a popular beverage for those who claimed its curative effects. I, thankfully, would never have to drink it again.

"Yes. It's quite a wonder. I take it daily while traveling in the Deep South and haven't fallen ill yet," Mr. Edison said to me. "Mine, you say? Whereabouts? I operated an iron mine in New Jersey for a time."

"Belle's father was a fine coal man in West Virginia," Papa said. I smiled at Mr. Edison, confident in Papa's accurate description of Father.

"Well then, I do believe you'll be especially thrilled by tomorrow's surprise excursion, Miss Newbold. Those who have an appreciation for geology will be absolutely gobsmacked, I'm told," Mr. Ford said, lifting his glass to his lips.

The blood drained from my face. I'd always heard there wasn't coal in North Carolina. Surely I hadn't been mistaken. Surely we weren't visiting a mine. I could barely endure this week if it was only the woods I had to face, but I could not stand and survey the tipples, watching men disappear into the pitch-black mouth of a mine. Perhaps they were planning to make it one of their wilderness games for the papers, the eight of them competing to see who could harvest the most coal in an hour.

The thought made me nauseous. I knew Mr. Ford was known for his spontaneity on these excursions, at times surprising his guests only upon arrival at the day's destination. I couldn't risk the possibility of panicking. I reached for my wine, nearly toppling the glass before my fingers found the stem. I took a long sip and set it down. Mother was staring at me, but everyone else had turned their attention to the servants, who were finally making their way into the tent with five enormous platters of salmon à la Chambord.

"Do you suppose you could share what this surprise will be?" I asked. My voice was strained. "I only ask because I'll need to have Sylvia press my costume tonight, and—"

Mr. Ford smiled and stood from his chair. He tapped the bottom of his spoon against his now-empty crystal wineglass.

"Excuse me, all! If I could have your ear for a moment." His voice boomed over us, a voice clearly practiced in commanding attention.

Marie Austen, who had been talking to Mr. Gibbins, stopped at once. Not because of Mr. Ford's pronouncement but because of the gigantic salmon platter deposited in front of her.

"Miss Newbold here kindly reminded me that there are ladies present on this leg of the Vagabonds excursion and that the fairer sex might prefer to be let in on the happenings of the following day in order to adequately prepare their costumes." Snickers were heard from the men. "I know it's not quite as exciting for us gents, but it's a worthy price to pay when we have so ardently desired to show our wives and daughters the wonder of our ways." Mr. Ford stepped back as a servant placed one of the platters on the table in front of his place. The salmon's head, eyes bugged out, mouth slightly open, was facing me, and in the moment, as my stomach churned with nerves and my skin flushed hot and cold, I thought I might vomit.

"Mr. Delafield, the owner of this fine property, has kindly notified our friends Mr. Edwin Grove and Mr. Fred Seely that we are in town. They are building a most extraordinary hotel—a hotel built atop a mountain called Sunset, constructed almost exclusively of boulders harvested from the mountain itself. Worth has commented that it is a wonder of a build, a craftsmanship completely unique to anything we've seen anywhere else. Though Grove and Seely were planning to be departed on business in Atlanta by now, Worth has convinced them to stay for a few more days to give us a tour of the facilities. Half of us will go along on a tour with Seely and Grove, while the others will be introduced to the hotel by the foreman, Oscar Mills, and Seely's temporary business manager, Thomas Pierce."

My shoulders slumped and I sat back in my chair, feeling as though I'd been brought back to life. The table erupted in cheers.

"We'll leave at eight in the morning, sharp, and will enjoy a picnic lunch on the hotel's recently constructed patio," Mr. Ford concluded before sitting back down.

"Made of boulders, you say?" Mrs. Kipp said. "I can't quite imagine it. Built like the pyramids, I'd wager."

"Quite," Mr. Ford said.

I felt eyes on my face and looked up to see Papa staring, not at me but at Mother. He was grinning widely, and she returned the affectionate stare.

"Salmon, crawfish, sole, truffles, fish salad, or all?" a servant asked Papa, leaning over the table with tongs.

"All, please. This is a special meal, and it warms my heart that you've happened to serve it tonight," he said.

The servant nodded and extracted a crawfish that had been speared into the side of the poached salmon, then removed a fillet of sole checkered with black truffles and placed it on Papa's plate.

"Cook Serano served it the night Belle and I arrived in Indiana, the night—"

"I proposed to the love of my life," Papa said, interrupting Mother.

At once I remembered the meal. I hadn't at first because I hadn't eaten it. Everything that whole first week had seemed like a dream or a nightmare depending on the angle, depending on the moment. We had left Red Dragon wearing our finest homemade dresses, carrying two bags, and boarded a train in nearby Whitesville bound for Indiana. I knew Mother had made an impression on Papa and we were going to visit him, but I'd thought we would come home after—at least for a while.

Instead, during our first dinner in Papa's palatial dining room, Mother had started crying and said she couldn't bear to return home, that she was sure the memories would suffocate her. I recalled the way her face pinched the same way it had when they'd told her Father died, the way my head spun with the implication of her words. My thoughts had been disjointed as Papa soothed her—he'd lost his first spouse, too, to cancer—and she spoke of how miserable she'd been at home. I'd wondered if she'd decided we'd never return before we packed or if being at Papa's home, faced with the luxury of everything we'd never had, made her desperate to make it our own.

Returning to Red Dragon meant hard work, poverty, and the painful, ever-present reminder of Father's death. I'd had a bite of mint sorbet, a palate cleanser I'd mistaken for ice cream, when Papa Shipley fell to one knee in front of Mother's chair. "*I don't want you to go back,*" he'd said. "*Will you marry me?*" She'd whispered yes, and I said nothing. Neither of them had remembered I was there in the moment anyway.

I'd stared at the faces portrayed in the Newbold family portraits lining the walls and wondered what would become of our things we'd left behind, of the picture of the three of us we'd had taken at the Red Dragon parade the day before Father died, of the box of my notebooks detailing the wonders I'd noticed around me all my life, of my father's notebooks and journals—hundreds of them—filled with his stories.

In the midst of my thoughts of losing Father's volumes and thereby his voice, the salmon à la Chambord had been served, and though the dish was laden with butter and herbs, all I could make out was the pungent stink of imported salmon.

"What if you hadn't taken that long drive through the hills?"

Mother's question startled me back to the moment. It was the same one she'd asked that night, after accepting Papa Shipley's hand.

"We would have been distraught forever, Belle and me," she kept on.

I stared at her, watching the familiar tenderness play on her face. Mr. Ford said something about second chances, but all I could remember was what she'd said to me later that night, after the proposal. *"I'm very fond of him, Belle. I know it has probably come as a shock to you, but I'm doing this for us both. He is kind. We will never want again."*

"I'm convinced that drive was destiny, my dear, that there was magic in those hills just as there is magic in these for our Belle," Papa Shipley said. He smiled at me and I grinned back, despite the pang of missing Father.

Mother had been right. He would never be my father, but he was kind and he loved us. If I could find the same with Worth, I would be content.

# CHAPTER FOUR

Marie Austen was finally asleep. Her soft snores broke the rhythmic cry of the crickets, the gentle flapping of the canvas in the breeze, and the faraway howl of a lone wolf. We'd both been restless tonight. Her, because she'd suddenly recalled the threat of bears as she was drifting off, and me, because the mountain sounds were deafening. They'd started in earnest what I imagined to be an hour ago, after the men had stopped their drunken singing of "A Home on the Range" and retreated to their tents, and had only grown louder.

Every time I pulled the hide around me and closed my eyes, the yip of a coyote or the rasping scream of a barn owl startled me from the brink of sleep. The noises were familiar, like a loved one calling my name, and with each awakening I assumed momentarily that I was in bed in Red Dragon.

I'd slept on the floor on a trundle that was brought out from under my parents' bed each night. The situation of it had been directly beside the window that was open most of the year—for cool air in summer and to balance the heat of the coal stove in winter. I hadn't realized I'd missed the sounds until now.

Memories were interesting that way. Sometimes you didn't realize how much you ached for something until it materialized again. Back in Indiana our windows were locked up tight and the only sounds that broke the silence were the low hum of the furnace or a distant train whistle from the track across town.

I turned on my side, fluffed the down pillow, and shoved it forcefully back under my head. Marie Austen was mumbling something. Whatever it was, it was clear she was angry. Perhaps she was dreaming about her solitary walk with Mr. Gibbins around the campsite. After a round of strong coffee, champagne jelly, and pistachio éclairs, everyone had begun to depart the dining tent—Marie Austen one of the first. I'd noticed Mr. Gibbins's look of alarm when she stood, his glance down the table at Mr. Kipp as if he could stop her retreat. When it was clear she would be lost to the night if he didn't make an advance, Mr. Gibbins practically ran after her.

She'd returned to our tent half an hour after me, furious. Mr. Gibbins had apparently made her aware that Mr. Kipp had recently advertised among our peers a sort of incentive to woo Marie Austen this season—his father-in-law's elaborate Bloomington mansion on top of her one-million-dollar dowry. The sixteen-bedroom Italianate home, called Rues D'Or, had been funded by invention— flaked corn—and was a showpiece. It would undoubtedly lure a great number of suitors to Marie Austen's side and also greatly complicate her desire for true love.

*"How am I to know if a man loves me anymore or if he just wants the keys to Rues D'Or?"* She'd slammed her fist on the bedside table, nearly unsettling the oil lamp that had been set aflame. *"I don't even find Mr. Gibbins pleasant, so clearly I'm not in danger of falling in desperate love with him, but what if I become enamored with a man and he isn't at all taken with me? Or what if I decide to be practical and marry someone I can tolerate and find love elsewhere only to discover that my husband is a terrible brute? Rues D'Or is coveted and Father knows it. Why is he so desperate?"*

Her face had hardened even more then, as though she'd answered her own question, and she pointed at me. *"You. That's why. You and your neat match with Worth Delafield. Now that you're nearly settled, Father is clearly in a panic. If I don't marry, they'll be stuck in Gas City alone while your parents travel about. They're desperate to get rid of me."*

I'd started to disagree, to say something heartening instead, but she held up her hand and proclaimed she didn't wish to speak to me.

I forced my mind blank and tried to listen to the crickets. That was what Mother had always told me to do when I was little and couldn't sleep, on the nights when the day had brought the ground-shaking *boom* of an explosion and gut-wrenching screams. I'd lived through six accidents. Back when there were only five, Father said that was an impressively low amount in seventeen years, but the sounds of my friends' heartbreaks, the shrill wail of a child just told their father wouldn't be home again, would burn in my head for days.

A shriek sounded and I bolted upright, the melding of my thoughts and reality too much to ignore. It came again, louder this time—a vixen's cry, a red fox. Goose bumps prickled my arms. My father had a fox as a pet when he was a boy—not the sort of pet that slept inside but the sort that endeared itself to the person who fed it, because it trusted them.

He'd told me often that communion with the fox, a wild species, made him realize that fear was just the natural reaction to something foreign. Each time I developed a fear—of water or darkness or bugs—he'd beckon me toward it, and in the course of days or weeks, my fear would subside. Perhaps I'd been awakened on purpose. Perhaps Father wanted me to face the way the mountains knotted my stomach and made me weak.

I peeled the hide back from my body and stood. I walked to the armoire, opened the carved door slowly, and withdrew my new wool cape. The garment fit perfectly. All of my costumes fit perfectly. I fastened the pearl button against my neck and stepped out of the tent into the crescent moonlight. I'd forgotten my boots. My toes curled in the dewy grass, becoming reacquainted with the feel of it as I padded down the aisle between the tents. When I was growing up, no one wore shoes unless it was snowing. In part because some people didn't have any, but mostly because for a child set free in the wild, shoes were a hindrance. They got wet or muddy in the course of a wrong step, while feet were easily cleaned with a dip in Elk Run.

I trained my eyes to the shadowy, faraway horizon where the

mountains loomed, forcing myself to stare at them, to let the magnitude of being back in a place that felt so much like home sink into my soul. My stomach clenched and my heartbeat quickened, but I didn't balk at the sensation. I welcomed it, just as Father had instructed when he'd dipped me into the river or placed a centipede in my palm.

Snores, some loud, some soft, permeated the night sounds, and the smell of woodsmoke from the cooking fire still hung heavy in the air, mingling with the sweet crispness of a spring night. I burrowed into my cape as I skirted the dining tents. The breeze, once obstructed by the swaths of canvas, now whistled in my ears and made my satin nightgown tangle around my legs.

The woods stood in front of me, and my skin washed hot and cold, a warning to turn back, but I wouldn't. After each of the five disasters before the one that took Father, a group of men would turn up in our small front yard. They'd sit there together, speaking of the friends they'd lost and the worth of their lives. Father would write their stories in his notebooks—sometimes I'd write them in mine, too, if I overheard—and then turn the conversation to what had transpired. Some would swear they'd never work in the mine again after what they'd experienced, but what else could they do?

There were tears as the tragedy was recounted—an overturned lantern that set a trestle ablaze, an influx of water that caused a roof collapse—and Father would write that down too. The next morning he'd go to Boss Elkhorn, a man feared by so many, and suggest ways to make the mine safer. At times he would listen, and Father would reassure his friends. Other times, there was no change at all, but Father would face the fear, clasp the trembling shoulders of another man, and lead him forward until the sharp stab of tragedy healed to a scar. I needed to allow his memory to do the same.

I entered the woods, pausing to run my hands over the tree bark, to inhale the earthy aroma of fallen leaves. The tightness in my chest persisted as I walked deeper and deeper. Ahead, the moonlight seemed brighter, and I kept on toward it until, suddenly, the trees fell away and I found myself in a clearing. It wasn't a natural arrangement. Roots, still bound tightly in the soil despite the absence of trunks, riddled the expanse and the ground dipped slightly in a rectangular configuration. I thought of Papa's comment, that Worth had once considered settling here, and wondered if this had been the location he'd selected. It would have been a bit of a strange place, considering the naturally clear valley, but perhaps he enjoyed the cozy feel of a house tucked into the pines.

I sat on the knobby knee of an exposed root and wondered what had changed his mind. Overhead, an owl hooted. I stretched my legs out and poked my toe into a small hole in a neighboring root. Something crawled onto my foot and I yanked it back, silently cursing my curiosity before I realized it was a centipede, the same sort Father had made me hold long ago.

"*You are frightened because you feel threatened,*" he'd said as the bug crawled around my palm. "*And perhaps sometimes you truly are. In those moments, your instincts serve you well. But I must warn you, Belle. Fear is greedy. If you let it, it will expand and grow until it steals your joy, your wonder too.*"

Those last words rang out in my mind, his voice as clear as the day he said it.

"Very well, Father," I whispered. "I won't allow it to overtake me."

I held the centipede, letting it twist and turn across my hands, feeling the tension drop from my shoulders and unfasten itself from my chest. The crickets sang and the sweet breeze rustled the new leaves, and I smiled, allowing the echo of home to bring gladness instead of sorrow.

# CHAPTER FIVE

By the time I made my way past the autos and the still-smoking fire and into the aisle of tents, my eyes were heavy. Our departure to the new hotel would come swiftly, Sylvia's rousing even earlier. I would look a fright for Worth, but there was nothing to be done now.

I sighed and walked through the row of servants' tents until a body struck mine. My tongue curled around a scream, and a hand clamped over my mouth.

"Mr. Thorp?" I breathed against his palm. He removed his hand and let me go.

He looked disheveled and smelled worse. His white linen shirt was untucked, and even in the moonlight I could see that his eyes were glassy with drink.

"I . . . I'm sorry to have startled you," he whispered. His gaze darted past me to my tent. "I . . . I thought I heard a bear. In fact, I couldn't sleep. Miss Kipp spoke of how fearful she was, and then I heard a noise. I . . ."

"I assure you it was only me," I said softly. "There are no bears about right now. I used to live in West Virginia in the mountains."

"Oh," he said, though he didn't move away or seem relieved.

"Is there something else you needed?" I asked. I stepped toward the tent and Mr. Thorp shook his head.

"No. No, that's all," he said quickly, then tipped his head at me and disappeared into the night.

I opened the tent flap and let it shut behind me before removing my cloak and practically falling onto my bed. I stretched, tucked the hide around me, and closed my eyes.

Beside me, I heard the cot creak, felt the wisp of air as the canvas lifted and fell.

"Peter," I heard Marie Austen whisper. "Peter?" Then there was a low chuckle, the soft click of lips parting, and a sigh. "Come on." She giggled, and the gentle rush of barefoot steps faded into the night.

I tried to settle into sleep, to let Marie Austen handle her own affairs without my meddling, but my mind would not slow. It conjured images of Mr. Thorp atop Marie Austen on my sofa the night of Papa's Christmas party. I knew without a doubt that if I hadn't interfered, she would have allowed him more liberties. If something were to happen tonight, if Marie Austen were to let her intoxication with Mr. Thorp muddle her sensibilities, she could ruin her chances of a proper match, and I had no doubt the Kipps would let her drown in the modest life Peter Thorp could offer.

I threw off the hide and reached for my cloak once again. The grass felt colder this time as I emerged from the tent. I pulled the edges of my cloak around my neck and wandered to the right, passing the last few servants' tents before turning back and making my way down the north row where Mother had mentioned Edsel and the other young men were staying. Although Mr. Thorp might enjoy a rendezvous in the woods, I knew Marie Austen's fears would keep her close to camp. I listened for whispers, for the sharp intake of breath or the rustle of fabric, but heard nothing more than owl cries and soft snores as I neared the tents that held the older set. Perhaps Marie Austen and Peter had taken to the woods after all.

"I told you I do."

I froze at the sound of her hushed voice coming from a tent just ahead of me.

"Very well, but I—" Mr. Thorp's soft reply was silenced by something and followed by a guttural groan. My heart quickened. Perhaps I was too late. I paced to the tent and threw back the curtain. Marie Austen screamed, a short shrill note immediately dulled by

Mr. Thorp's hand cupping around her mouth. A whisper of cool air struck the back of my neck as the fabric fell back into place, trapping me in the intimate space, in front of Marie Austen lying on a cot beneath Mr. Thorp's naked chest. She feverishly began to pull her nightgown back over her drawers as he lifted himself from her.

"I woke and you weren't there. I was worried, so I set out after you," I said, attempting to keep my gaze on her face and my tone even. My cheeks burned, my mind filled with equal parts embarrassment at finding them this way and irritation at her carelessness. If I had delayed even a few more moments, I have no doubt she would have allowed him anything he wished.

"Well, as you can see, I'm quite all right," she snapped, her glare apparent even in the dark.

Mr. Thorp didn't look at me but lunged for his discarded white nightshirt and threw it over his head.

"What is this about?" The tent flap behind me was yanked back and Mr. Kipp materialized, his face red with anger.

Marie Austen scrambled from the cot.

"You are a disgrace," Mr. Kipp snarled at his daughter.

"Father, I . . . Father, we love each other," she attempted.

"You," Mr. Thorp breathed barely above a whisper, his eyes boring into mine as Marie Austen continued her plea to her father. "You alerted him."

"I did not. I—"

"Take your cousin back to your tent," Mr. Kipp said to me, his voice rising slightly as he lost control of his temper. He snatched at Marie Austen's elbow and yanked her toward me. She was sobbing, and despite my utter irritation with her, I wrapped an arm around her trembling shoulders and started to lead her out of the tent.

"Come along," I said calmly, but she jerked free of my embrace and glared at me.

"No." She tried to turn back toward where Mr. Thorp stood beside the cot, but he stopped her.

"Go. Please. You must," he said.

She wailed, and I feared she might collapse, but I held her fast and directed her out of the tent. She stumbled toward the exit alongside me, casting longing glances back at Mr. Thorp, who kept his stare fixed on Mr. Kipp.

"You will tell me exactly what went on here," Mr. Kipp growled. "You've clearly seduced my daughter, but I must know to what degree you've compromised her."

"That's not at all what happened!" Marie Austen cried, twisting out of my grasp toward Mr. Thorp. "He's not to blame, Father. I—"

"I take full responsibility," Mr. Thorp interrupted, his voice suddenly strained. He stared at Marie Austen, forbidding her to come closer. "You're right. I should not have been alone with Miss Kipp, but I promise you nothing sordid transpired. Miss Newbold was misguided in her assumption and alerting you was unnecessary. Miss Kipp and I were only—"

"I am not a fool nor blind, Peter," Mr. Kipp said evenly, not bothering to address the claim against me. "We will not discuss these matters further in the company of the young ladies. Marie Austen, you will go back to your tent with your cousin. If you do not comply, your every breath will be chaperoned the remainder of this trip."

Marie Austen whirled toward me, swallowing a sob, and paced out of the tent ahead of me.

"I didn't wake your father," I whispered to her back. "I came alone and I'm glad I did."

"Of course you're glad," she grumbled under her breath, turning to face me. Tears ran down her cheeks, but she didn't wipe them away. "And I don't believe for a second that you didn't wake Father. From the moment you arrived in Gas City, you were determined to steal my shine. Isn't your perfect match with Worth Delafield consolation enough? You have made Shipley and your mother proud, and you will be settled. You have won, Belle, and you know it. Tonight was torture, an awakening to my fate. I'm doomed to marry someone like Mr. Gibbins. I thought you understood that and would at least allow me Peter, the desire of my heart."

"I've never thought of our fates as a contest. You're my cousin, my friend. You deserve the life you've always dreamed of—the love and the affluence." I hastened to catch up with her and our strides matched as we walked around the far edge of the tent row toward our quarters. "I was worried you'd compromise with Mr. Thorp and that in doing so you'd vaporize the possibility of having your every wish realized."

She stared at me for a moment, then lifted the flap of our tent and laughed, a haunting sound that matched the utter hatred on her face.

"You're not truly my cousin, you know. Our relationship was built entirely on my charity. I despise your false sincerity. I can see through it to who you really are."

My body went cold and the woods along the edge of the valley seemed to close in. A cool wind swept across us, and I thought I heard the groaning jet of air across the mouths of the caves in the distance, the warning cry of Boss Elkhorn's wife. I'd told Mr. Thorp I was from West Virginia when I ran into him outside our tent. He believed I was to blame for Mr. Kipp's appearance. If he was angry enough, he could investigate my past and seek vengeance against me. He'd been to Gas City. He could have heard the whispers about Mother and me. Then again, Mr. Thorp was likely subject to few, if any, repercussions from being found with Marie Austen—Mr. Ford needed him to write his stories. There would be time for any possible annoyance he felt toward me to pass, and I would be sure to make it plain that I hadn't had anything to do with Mr. Kipp coming upon them.

Marie Austen walked into the tent and I followed, my heartbeat drumming in my ears. I took a deep breath and forced myself to calm down.

"You can think me insincere, although I am not, but you will not make me out to be a liar. I promise you, Marie Austen. I didn't tell your father. Mr. Thorp has to know that too. And regardless of what you think of me, I have never wished for anything but your happiness," I said, hoping the desperation wasn't obvious in my voice.

She exhaled softly and wiped the tears from her eyes, then her face changed, displaying only misery.

"I know. You're perfect that way, aren't you?"

The sentiment was expressed in a soft, polite manner, but the words speared my heart. Nevertheless, it was as close to an apology as I would ever receive, and she believed I had nothing to do with waking Mr. Kipp.

"We should get some sleep," I said.

"Yes. Very well." She collapsed onto her cot, pulled her hides up around her, and turned away from me. I did the same and forced myself to sleep to the sound of Marie Austen sobbing.

❧

When I woke, the pink-gold of morning was just beginning to shine through the tent flaps and Marie Austen's cot was empty again. The sight of the bobcat hide crumpled at the foot of her cot jolted me from drowsiness to absolute panic regardless of how she'd treated me the night before. I stood suddenly, not bothering to rub the sleep from my eyes or call for her.

She'd gone out in search of Peter Thorp and hadn't returned. It wasn't late enough in the morning for the possibility that she'd gone to fetch something from her parents or to beg a drink from the dining tent. The sun had just risen. I lunged for my cape, hanging cockeyed in my armoire, and fitted it around my shoulders.

There was also a chance Marie Austen had run away. It was exactly the sort of dramatic thing I knew she would do given the presence of Mr. Gibbins and her father's disapproval of the man she thought she loved. But not Mr. Thorp. He'd been given the opportunity of his career, and an ordinary man with the world at his fingertips didn't throw it away for a girl he'd abandoned twice. I was keenly aware that he hadn't told Mr. Kipp he loved Marie Austen in the wake of his confrontation last night.

If she hadn't run away on her own, perhaps she'd sought him out and they'd gone into the woods to rendezvous. I knew for certain they'd not risk being discovered by those in camp again, but surely they would have sneaked back by sunrise. They could be lost, or perhaps they'd gone into the woods and been attacked, mutilated by a bear. The irony and horror of that possibility were too much to consider. I thought of the thousands of acres of woods surrounding the expansive valley. They could have entered from anywhere — behind the autos as I had or north to the far end or east behind our parents' tents or south following the entry road.

I started to walk out of the tent, but my feet were still bare. I turned back for my boots, situated at the bottom of the armoire. I snatched them out and jabbed my toes in one. They were Russian vamps with tight patent leather and gray-and-brown buckskin. They'd been heralded for their ease of wear because they buttoned at the top rather than the side, but there was nothing at all easy about the way the unforgiving fabric refused to cinch together enough for the black pearls to slide through the loops. I was used to old oil-tanned leather and laces and had never had to do these up myself. I never had to do much of anything myself now that I had Sylvia. I was paying for my indolence. I pulled the leather with vigor, finally securing the first of twelve buttons before the tension gave and it popped free.

"Damn," I said under my breath, wishing I could scream it. "Damn it." My voice was louder this time, breaking strangely on the last word. I pinched the taut leather and yanked it with all my might, my teeth bared, my eyes blurring.

All these years, I'd remained stiff and pleasant, swiftly burying any swell of emotion the way I'd watched Mother do, but now in the wake of a sleepless night and the panic that came with the possibility of a sudden loss, I had no strength to dig the grave required to conceal it. As ridiculous as it seemed, I couldn't lose Marie Austen — not to the woods or a bear. She was pompous, irritating, and selfish, nothing like the loving friends I'd left behind in Red Dragon, but she was the only person I had. My first soiree in Gas City had been at her home, and while the others whispered about me and Mother coming to take advantage of Papa Shipley, she had claimed me not only as her cousin but also as her friend — her best friend, in fact.

Now I understood why she was angry with me for my arrangement with Worth—for leaving her alone. It was hard to comprehend the sense of betrayal when I was the one going. A person abandoned a place, most of the time anyway, for something better, to grasp hold of something they'd been lacking, and the thought of it was enlivening. You couldn't help but assume everyone around you would feel the breath of relief too.

"Damn you, Marie—"

A horrible, guttural sob silenced me. Then Marie Austen appeared in the tent opening, the whole sight of what she'd become—the torn nightgown, eyes swollen to slits from crying, her cheeks splotchy with hives, her hair damp and stringy—visible only for a moment in the misty morning light before the flap fell shut, concealing the nightmare in the dim.

She collapsed onto her bed, and I hastened to her side. Relief washed through me, and I wrapped my arms around her, feeling the rise and fall of her shoulders as she cried.

"I know something terrible has happened," I whispered. "But I suppose I was imagining the worst."

"What? That I'd died? That would be better," she said forcefully and pushed my arms away. She sat up and stared past me at the open armoire.

"Whatever heartbreak has befallen you, it will pass. I know it doesn't seem so now, but—"

"You don't know!" She practically yelled the words. "You don't know at all. You have never loved a man and you claim you never will, so don't . . . don't presume that I'll ever get over it."

I sat on my cot across from her. She was right. There was nothing more to say. I could still hear Mother's wails, calling out for Father in the night, whispering his name over and over in the morning as she stared out the kitchen window at one more day without him. Mother's heartbreak would never pass. It was with her even now, and given an inch it would consume her again.

That was why, I figured, she'd let societal expectations harden her, why she never spoke his name. She could say it was for Papa, that a good man like him deserved better than to live with the ghost of his wife's true love, or that speaking of Father put us at risk for someone to find out who we really were and set in motion the consequences of a match made in half-truths. They were both necessary deceptions, reasoning made in that animalistic, subconscious need for survival. Love had ultimately ruined her and now, perhaps, Marie Austen too. The thought of it made me ache for them and reinforced the steel I'd forged around my own heart.

Marie Austen didn't bother to wipe her eyes. She'd long since reached the point where they ceased to flow.

"What happened?" I asked.

Her gaze shifted to mine and then dropped to her hands. She picked at her fingernails.

"Before I went out to meet him the first time, I heard you leave," she said, avoiding my question. "Where did you go?"

"Nowhere interesting," I said. "I couldn't sleep. I just wandered in the woods a bit. You have to tell me what hap—"

"Alone?" Marie Austen asked, her tone more accusing than question, as though my absence meant I'd attempted to meet Mr. Thorp for a tryst too.

"Yes. You forget I'm accustomed to the forest." This seemed to satisfy her and she nodded. "Mr. Thorp ran into me outside our tent, quite literally actually. I knew he had come for you. I should have stopped you both."

"I never would have forgiven you if you had. It turns out it was my last . . . my last night." She stumbled over the words. "After you brought me back to the tent and fell asleep, I laid awake, my heart shattered, and decided right then that I didn't care if he was poor. I'd been foolish to think I'd only want to entertain him as a lover later. I wanted to marry him, only him. I snuck to his tent and woke him, and regardless of his initial protesting, he agreed to walk to the edge of the trees with me to talk.

"When we reached the shadows, I confessed my love for him and he kissed me but said nothing more. I thought he didn't feel the same, but after we were through talking and kissing, we walked in silence back to our tents, and right before he said farewell, right in front of his tent, he got down on one knee and asked for my hand. I suppose I accepted too loudly, because Mr. Ford peered out of his tent and spied us and then immediately hastened to wake Father again." She sobbed, clutched the front of her dirty cotton night-gown, and fell from her cot to her knees on the ground.

"They sent him away," she said through her tears, now suddenly plentiful. "I told Father we were engaged, but he took a look at me, at the state of my nightdress soiled more severely from our walk to the woods, and asked if I'd been compromised after all. I said no, and Peter echoed the same. Then he smiled—he *smiled*, Belle—and told Peter he was to leave immediately, and that was the conse-quence of speaking to me again after he caught us earlier. Mr. Ford had his things packed and loaded in an auto in a matter of minutes and then two servants were pushing the auto containing Peter . . . my Peter . . . toward the road so as not to wake anyone with the mo-tor." She punched the ground.

"I ran after him, but Father held me back. Peter has lost his post. We have lost our love." Marie Austen crumpled, her body bending at the side and resting on the grass in a heap.

A wave of heat prickled my skin. Any sympathy for Marie Austen was washed away in my panic. Mr. Thorp was gone. I wouldn't have time to explain myself or smooth things over. Of course, I hadn't been involved this second time they were caught, but perhaps he saw his dismissal as my fault regardless. If they hadn't been found out on the first occasion, this last instance would have been the first and perhaps there would have been mercy.

"What will I do?" she cried. The question matched my own. My answer was clear—I'd need to pray and forget about the omi-nous possibility hiding just around the corner of each moment. If I didn't, I'd go mad, and nothing could be done regardless. I recalled my walk in the woods, how I'd let Father's words guide me to peace, how I'd triumphed over fear. I would do the same now.

"Perhaps give it time. After we return home, your father will have softened to the shock of it, and Mr. Thorp can call to beg for your hand," I said, my voice soft and calm. There was no point in pushing her down further. The reality was, of course, that Mr. Kipp would never abide his Marie Austen with anyone but practical royalty—whether royalty of pocket or actual blood.

"You're right," she said with a sniff, sitting up. "Our love hasn't been snuffed out and there's no sense in giving up hope." She pushed her hair back from her forehead and met my eyes. "No word of this to anyone. Father and Mr. Ford have vowed to keep it quiet, and I think you're on to something—I'll be the most obedient daughter the world has ever seen. When we return to Gas City with my angelic behavior still fresh in his mind, I'll write to Peter and have him come by."

I sat on the ground and reached for her hands.

"A perfect plan," I said, mostly to hearten her.

"Ladies, you're already up." Sylvia burst through the tent flap with steaming china mugs on a silver tray. Her eyes were tired, but her gray hair was done in a neat chignon like always. "Did the blasted ruckus wake you? I daresay it's quite uncouth to be chattering at all before sunrise, but those two footmen of Mr. Edison's were up stoking the fire and laughing long before the light broke. I suspect they're likely nuisances in his house too."

"No, but I'm sorry you were roused before you were ready," I said. She shook her head and handed me a mug full of coffee, then gave the other one to Marie Austen. Sylvia balked when she saw Marie Austen's state, but then turned, busying herself with organizing the hairpins she'd brought in her apron along the washstand countertop.

I took a sip of the coffee. The smell of roasted beans heralding the enlivenment I desperately needed warmed my spirit.

"I envy you two today," Sylvia said, looking at my reflection in the mirror. "Some of the local servants Mr. Ford employed have spoken so highly of Mr. Grove and Mr. Seely's new hotel. They say it is the eighth wonder of the world, it's so grand."

Marie Austen picked at the grass in a veritable trance.

"What high praise," I said. "I'll be sure to describe it to you in

49

colorful detail upon my return." I rose and Sylvia turned from the mirror and smiled.

"Thank you. Now let's set to creating the ninth wonder of the world—you. Your beauty must rival the hotel today, Miss Newbold, which won't at all be a challenge. Mr. Delafield will be speechless."

For a moment, I had forgotten about Worth, but now, in the wake of Marie Austen's heartbreak, I was tremendously grateful for the simple arrangement we'd made.

"You're kind, Sylvia," I said.

"But honest." Marie Austen looked up at me from her position on the ground. "Like I said before, you're both pretty." Her eyes filled again. "The perfect tidy match for a perfect tidy girl."

# CHAPTER SIX

The morning, it seemed, had found everyone in a bit of a fog. It could have been last night's wine or the fact that breakfast was as delayed as dinner had been. It could have been Papa Shipley's near row with Mr. Ford over the location of the drive-up gasoline stores he was proposing. Mr. Ford was of the mind that the inaugural locations should be in Michigan, run by his men, close to his factories, and expanded from there, while Papa argued for the first store to be placed in Indiana, close to the gasoline wells and run by *his* men. Or perhaps the foul moods were a result of the fact that in Mr. Thorp's absence no one was present to record and report on the fun of the camping venture. Regardless of the reason, we had all boarded the autos bound for Grove Park Inn in relative silence.

"At least the sun is shining." I attempted optimism as Mr. Leslie drove Marie Austen and me down a tree-lined brick street.

We'd just caravanned through the town of Asheville, which had been quite busy at this early hour with residents hoping to catch sight of the auto parade—clearly our every movement had been advertised—and reminded me of Gas City. The usual brick buildings were organized in blocks—city hall, a church, a convention auditorium with a pretty marquee, a bank, and an opera house—but the highlight was a darling square with lush trees, grass, and an impressive obelisk monument in the middle reminiscent of the one dedicated to Washington in DC.

"Look at the way the rays come through the morning haze and dapple the forest floor just there. Doesn't it look like heaven?" I tried again, pointing out the window into the woods as the autos turned up a hill.

"It certainly does," Mr. Leslie replied, his voice sounding forced as he was likely torn between his duty to remain absolutely quiet and the awkward silence that had met my dozen or so questions since we'd left camp. Marie Austen hadn't so much as uttered a sound since our departure. She hadn't even lifted her hand at the onlookers this time, though many shouted and waved at us. Instead, she'd stared straight ahead, over the vacant seat next to Mr. Leslie. She was angry at everyone for Mr. Thorp's absence—including me for my untimely interruption the first time they were found—but there was little I could do about it.

She'd seemed to brighten after Sylvia helped her select a deep peach costume to match the flame of her hair, deeming her a great beauty as she tied the gold beaded belt in a knot about her small waist and smoothed the paste diamonds arranged in a Grecian design around her long neck. She'd even smiled at me and told me I should have been in the fashion magazines when I emerged from behind the dressing screen in a new dainty yellow dress made of figured voile and cotton crepe and finished with two elaborate gold silk bows at the back of my skirt. The mood was so amiable at that moment that Sylvia had even extracted a pot of rouge from her apron and offered to apply it to our cheeks and lips. Marie Austen and I laughed as she swept it across our skin and fell silent at the way it cloaked her misery and my sleeplessness in beauty. She'd been in a foul mood ever since.

"Paradise incarnate isn't only out the windows. It's also apparently sitting next to me too—in soft crepes and creamy skin, in dainty nose and full lips," Marie Austen said suddenly, startling me. She'd been pointing out my apparent beauty for the past day and I couldn't figure out why. She was equally as striking as me.

"Stop saying things like that," I said, meeting her gaze. "I don't understand how I deserve your scrutiny or how any of my features have anything to do with you. I've done nothing but care for you, and—"

"You're right. You haven't done a thing but interfere with my one moment of happiness." She stared at me. "Do you know how often my parents instruct me to model my behavior after yours? Father reminded me just this morning. And why would he not? You're perfect in temperament and appearance. You do not get flustered or out of sorts; your countenance doesn't wilt into something grotesque when emotion overtakes you." She was speaking quickly. "I am jealous of you. Terribly so. Even over Mr. Gibbins, a man I find repulsive. I watched him at breakfast, staring at you without so much as a glance at me, all the while hearing Mr. Edison singing the praises of your Mr. Delafield."

"My match with Worth was not a contest won by my beauty," I said evenly. I was tired of Marie Austen's airs. "He hasn't laid eyes on me since I was eighteen. He would have been satisfied with anyone. I simply heard of the arrangement first."

"Peter departed without a glance back, without a fight, just like last time. If he cared, if he truly intended to marry me, he would have refused to leave me," she whispered as though she hadn't heard me.

She wanted me to say I was sorry for her, to gush about her hair and her vivacity and the way she transfixed men, but I'd already reassured her of all that countless times before. She couldn't be permitted to treat me this way. Soon I would be gone and she would have to learn to temper her disappointments without me.

The autos kept climbing upward and the air that now seeped in through the slight opening at the top of the windows—Mr. Leslie had cranked them down a few inches so we wouldn't overheat—was increasingly sweet. I breathed it in, thankful my soul had made peace with the memories, with the mountains. The rhododendron grew wild and heavy in the woods on either side of us in shocks of pink and white, and then up ahead, sunshine seemed to stream unbidden like the forest was a tunnel and we were nearly at the end of it.

Mr. Leslie whistled as we drove into the light. I blinked, blinded for a moment, and then my eyes fixed on the granite rocks stacked five stories high. It seemed at first like an immense rock cairn, the sort the O'Connors had built at the mouth of the mines. I couldn't take my eyes from the structure as Mr. Leslie followed a dirt road around the front of the hotel, past crates of what appeared to be red-clay tile lined up near a ramp and scaffolding affixed to the roof.

At first I couldn't fathom it, how the stones had been fitted this way, how they stood in perfect order stretching all the way to the sky. They hadn't been dulled or finished; they hadn't been polished into slabs and neatly sealed with concrete. Instead, they were jagged, colored white and gray and black depending on the minerals that made them.

"It looks like they're making good progress," Mr. Leslie commented as we stopped momentarily behind the other autos. We were now situated on a drive that curled toward what I assumed was the front entrance to the hotel. In front of us was a barren swath of dirt housing, a chugging steam shovel and piles of wood beams, and a perfect view of the building, which had been formed in three parts—the middle being a story taller than the sides. The left and center portions looked nearly complete. A team of men walked along the contoured roof of these two, affixing a web of some sort of steel rod across the smooth cement. The right side of the hotel was still being constructed, just a frame of four rock walls.

"I've never seen such artistry," I said finally, once I'd glanced over the hotel three or four times. "Sylvia said some of the local servants called it the eighth wonder of the world, and no doubt why." I was suddenly struck with a familiar but long-forgotten feeling. I looked beside me, desperate for a notebook and pencil. I'd always carried them in Red Dragon like Father, writing down in great detail the things I found remarkable in case I forgot the wonder someday— the first electric light shining from Boss Elkhorn's house, the recipe for Mrs. Keeley's banana ice cream. Father had given me my first notebook because he'd done the same thing.

*"One of these days, you'll need to read about something wonderful or share a marvel with a friend to pass a hard time. You'll be able to open one of these and remember."* I took a breath, settling myself.

My memory of today would have to be enough. My notebooks were gone. His notebooks were gone. Even so, he would have loved this hotel.

"Look at what they've done to form the windows," Mr. Leslie said, pointing toward the building. Each window's top rail was marked by an enormous stone, creating an interesting visual that broke the monotony of the smaller rocks. Somehow they had managed to situate each rock perfectly and come upon enough boulders to build something this magnificent. However they had accomplished it, one thing was certain: these craftsmen had built a palace.

"I admit I discounted my interest in this," I said. "I suppose I didn't realize how breathtaking it would be, and now I can't wait to be inside. I have a million questions."

Mr. Leslie chuckled. "So do I," he said.

I was thankful that a bit of his formality had eased—especially in the presence of Marie Austen's silence. I didn't know if she'd even glanced out her window. She was currently looking down at her lap.

"What will you ask first?" I fiddled with the tight belt of yellow at my waist.

"Oh, I won't be permitted to stay for the tour, Miss Newbold. It's only for the group of you. And anyway, there's been quite a hubbub about last night's dining delay, so the whole of the staff has been asked to assist in preparing dinner this evening. We're expected to return to camp straightaway and will drive back to collect you at one." Mr. Leslie smiled despite this disappointing news.

"Well, the very least I can do is ask your most pressing question for you. I'll deliver the answer upon your return," I said.

The autos started moving forward again, and as Mr. Ford's shiny black Model T Touring sped past us absent Mr. and Mrs. Ford, a jolt of excitement passed through me. In moments I would be standing inside the hotel. Given the material, it would likely be cool inside, almost cave-like. It was warm today and I hadn't brought my cape, but I'd never minded the chill.

"I want to know where and how they're harvesting the stones for this endeavor," Mr. Leslie said. "I suppose that's really two questions."

"You can hardly answer one without the other." I inched forward on the seat as Mr. Leslie let up on the brake and we glided to a new position on the edge of a small hill that led to the entrance. I watched Mr. Carver and Edsel Ford emerge from the back of their auto and cross the dirt drive to a wide opening in the middle of the center portion of the hotel, beneath a bit of scaffolding.

"I assume they're going to construct an overhang above the main doors there," Mr. Leslie said, nodding to the wooden beams jutting over the doorframes.

Mr. Carver and Edsel had reached a group of men standing outside the entrance in the scaffolding's shadow. A man in a gray overcoat and bowler hat stepped forward to shake their hands, followed by a burly man in a pinstriped suit and a short, slight gentleman in a blond costume often called a Palm Beach suit. The auto lurched forward but not before my eyes leveled on the man at the very end of the line.

He was tall, nearly a foot taller than Palm Beach, and I barely noticed what he was wearing because of the way he moved. He stepped forward to greet the men, and the strength in his stride and the squareness of his shoulders, the way he clasped the guests' hands with both of his in greeting, exhibited an earnestness I found enchanting. We moved forward again, four car lengths this time, and at once I saw his face and couldn't look away.

I'd seen him before, naturally, but Worth had aged. The pillowy softness of a young man's jaw had been replaced by the chiseled set of a man's. The full lips that had before given him an almost feminine beauty were now lined with gold-brown hair that matched his eyebrows, which were drawn together, exhibiting a fierceness I didn't recognize. His eyes were the only things that remained the same. Blue and hooded, the corners turned down just slightly. When I recalled seeing him at Papa's party, I remembered that his eyes seemed kind.

"Ah, Mr. Delafield's here I see," Mr. Leslie said helpfully.

"Yes." I forced out the word, shocked I could make a sound at all. I glanced at Worth again, hardly able to help it, and thought to myself just then that someone who looked like him asking for a match like ours was about as incomprehensible, as ridiculous a notion, really, as a hotel made of balanced stone.

"Whyever would he initiate such a thing?"

I hadn't realized I'd spoken aloud until the door clicked open and Marie Austen replied dryly, "It's quite perplexing. The ninth wonder of the world, perhaps."

I took Mr. Leslie's hand and stepped out of the auto. My heart lurched into my throat and my pulse pounded in my temples. My gaze swept the row of men now greeting the Firestones. I followed Marie Austen toward them, intentionally focusing on the inn's entrance instead of the men—instead of Worth—as I went. I hadn't been nervous about meeting him again until now, but my former steadiness had swiftly given way to a jittery sensation upon seeing his face.

I felt quite like I was walking a tightrope over a great ravine. Perhaps Worth was as stirred as I was. I pressed my palms to my skirt and hazarded a look to the men as we neared. My eyes met Worth's and his lips turned up. I smiled back despite my nerves and Worth abandoned his position at the end of the welcoming party, taking the place at the head of the group. Dizziness consumed me.

"You go first," Marie Austen said, pushing me around her.

At once Worth was in front of me, his eyes lingering on mine, his hands enclosing my small ones.

"I've been looking forward to seeing you again, Miss Newbold," he said simply. "After all this time." The timbre of his voice was low, much lower than I remembered, and for a moment I was able to say absolutely nothing. In the fleeting silence, I was vaguely aware of Marie Austen huffing and skirting around us, and just as Worth's left hand withdrew from the back of mine still clasped to his right, just as he lifted my fingers to his lips, he smiled. The expression transformed his face, warming and settling me somehow.

"I've been told the shock of my ugliness wears off in due time," he whispered.

We laughed and I found my voice.

"If not, I suppose there are always masks, Mr. Delafield." It was a strange tone, not quite my own, but thankfully calm, and after it passed my lips, he squeezed my hand. "I can hardly believe you're in front of me right now."

He smiled. "I feel exactly the same." Worth let my hand go. "I'll find you inside."

I peeled myself away from his gaze and continued down the line, greeting Mr. Grove, Mr. Seely, Mr. Mills, and Mr. Pierce.

"Come, Miss Newbold. Let us join the others in the lobby. We're excited to tell you about the inn," Mr. Pierce said after I'd made his acquaintance. I followed him in his blond Palm Beach suit toward the inn's entrance, eager to see the magnificence of the hotel's interior.

As I was ushered into the lobby, my eyes fixed on the back of Worth's smart black suit at the front of the group, on the broad shoulders and the handsome profile, and the peace that had so swiftly emerged in his company suddenly abandoned me.

# CHAPTER SEVEN

**M**arvel upon marvel. If I had any say in the matter, that would be the advertising slogan in all the papers for Mr. Grove and Mr. Seely's Grove Park Inn. It would be luxurious—that went without saying—but the true attraction was the craftsmanship.

I was transfixed by what Mr. Seely called the Great Hall—in part because I was forcefully, frantically, if I was honest, determined to cast my thoughts from Worth. The task, which I was certain would have been nearly impossible on an ordinary day, was eased significantly by the way we'd been swept from the entrance to the cavernous lobby.

The whole place was teeming with workers, and it was no wonder why. The construction of the hall alone would have been a conundrum for an ordinary construction crew. While Mr. Grove and Mr. Seely climbed up on a bit of wooden scaffolding that skirted the concrete pillars lining the one-hundred-twenty-foot room and bellowed an introductory speech over the echo of voices and hammers and the clang of metal chains, I settled at the rear of the group—away from the view of Worth at the front—and watched the workers.

One side of the hall was being used for material storage, likely because of the sheer size of the space, and men of all ages and ethnicities hauled lumber, tile, windows, and stacked glass doors in and out of immense entryways that framed a sweeping panorama of the Blue Ridge Mountains. On the opposite end of the room, three Italian men wearing stained overalls stood by an impressive pile of granite rock outside the mouth of an enormous fireplace. A matching hearth was on the opposite side of the lobby. The men were clearly stonemasons, their skills likely forged from generations of the same sort of trade in their home country.

They painstakingly studied each stone, crouching and turning them over, then standing to consider the rock they'd just affixed to the concrete wall before instructing one of the men idling nearby with a plaster bucket to muddy the next spot. The entirety of the walls inside and out had already been constructed in this fashion. They must have worked continuously to have accomplished so much. Mr. Seely mentioned that they'd only broken ground in the fall.

"It was heartwarming to watch you reunite with Mr. Delafield today." The soft voice startled me, and I turned to find Mrs. Burroughs beside me. I hadn't noticed her presence. Then again, she was tiny, one of the smallest people I'd ever seen, and nearing eighty, which caused her already slight figure to bend even lower.

"Yes, thank you," I whispered, though the reminder was not welcome. I could still feel the echo of my nerves, the sensation of his lips on my fingers.

"You laugh. That is something Mr. Burroughs and I never shared," Mrs. Burroughs whispered, bringing me back to the moment as Mr. Grove went on and on about how honored he was to have such esteemed visitors. "We only had attraction. Love requires both."

My gaze snapped to hers, her words a resounding alarm in my mind. I could not risk achieving the outcome I'd so desperately wished to avoid. Amiability was one thing. That could hardly be avoided. But attraction could be extinguished swiftly given the right set of circumstances. I thought of Mr. Hardee, the way his statuesque looks were overtaken by the horrid stench of his sweat, of Mr. Johannesen, who was considered very handsome save the unfortunate frothing of the mouth when he spoke too quickly. I hoped Worth had such a revulsion. In any case, it was most likely my nerves upon meeting him again that had caused the sensations I'd mistaken for attraction, not actual captivation at his pleasant appearance.

"No reason to be alarmed by my plight," she said, patting my hand, now curled into a fist. "Mr. Delafield isn't the sort of man Mr. Burroughs is. He looked into your eyes, not over your body, when he addressed you. He is not the sort who swears his life to a woman only because he wants to take her to bed." I gasped, and she chuckled, but she was right. I was thankful for the reminder.

I looked over the crowd gathered in the entrance and found Worth's gaze fixed on the presentation. My nerves settled. The sort of arrangement he sought—marriage to an agreeable woman without any specifications as to her personality or appearance—indicated he wasn't interested in love either. I was safe with him. He was safe with me.

❧

After nearly a half hour of listening to Mr. Grove and Mr. Seely thanking us for coming, we were instructed to break into two groups. Mr. Grove, Mr. Mills, and Mr. Seely would lead the men through the "boring particulars" of the hotel—particulars I was very interested in—while Mr. Pierce would take the women to see the amenities they were constructing specifically with the fairer sex in mind. As the groups were announced and their focus revealed, I couldn't figure how anyone in this group was deemed more delicate than the others. It wasn't as if Augustus Kipp was miles away from someone like Ursula Burroughs or rugged and tough like the men I'd known in Red Dragon. Society men were pampered and catered to, their muscles generally unformed and useless.

"Suppose I wanted to go with the men, to see something other than the view or the pool or the rocks," Toots Edison commented to someone, perhaps Mother or Mrs. Kipp, as the group broke up and the women made their way toward Mr. Pierce as he waved from the last of four doorframes, the view behind him exhibiting a cloudless blue sky over the indigo-tinged peaks in the distance.

"What rocks? Where?" I said, laughing, as we converged in front of Mr. Pierce. Toots glanced at me, unamused, while Mother shushed me and started whispering to Mrs. Kipp and Mrs. Firestone about when we would be served lunch. Never mind that it was only nine thirty judging by the ragged grandfather clock in the corner of the room.

A group of men, some in faded dungarees, some in overalls, shuffled around us carrying a wooden beam at least twenty feet long. I stepped toward Mother, hoping my action would encourage the others to remove themselves from the path of the men hard at work. I was at once engulfed in the waft of soft green leaves and lemony notes of Coty's Lilas Blanc, a perfume she'd chosen for her wedding to Papa.

"You know, they say this is the prime altitude and climate in which to find them." I turned to find Worth behind me. He had a bemused expression on his face. "Rocks," he said, and I smiled, heartened to find my earlier jitters completely relieved.

"Why, Mr. Delafield, whatever are you doing here?" Marie Austen asked. She'd been hiding in her mother's shadow and under the generous overhang of her hat, but at once pushed it back a bit to address Worth, her eyes wide and doll-like. She always did that—made that ridiculous face. It was her trick to enrapture men and make them believe she was a naive little heiress who needed rescuing or teaching or kissing. "This tour is for the women. You're not a woman."

I glanced at Worth. He laughed.

"Thank you for noticing," he said. He smoothed his immaculately pressed black suit jacket and gestured to Mr. Pierce, who was now engaged in conversation with Mrs. Burroughs instead of initiating our tour. "I thought I'd join you ladies and Mr. Pierce today. I've crawled all over this hotel, and I've heard Grove and Seely's side of things. Now I'm here to give Pierce a listen, see if he'll tell me anything I don't know."

Mr. Pierce broke free from his conversation with Mrs. Burroughs and shook his head.

"I doubt it, Delafield, but if I forget a beat or two, you pipe in now, won't you?"

"I am thrilled you've decided to join us," Mother said, reaching around me to touch Worth's arm. Her tone was meek, the way our language coach had instructed us to address men, and she looked diminutive. "I've been so eager to get to know you, and—"

"Now we'll begin, ladies, in the north wing where the pool and the bowling alley and the finest guest rooms—all the merriment— will be housed. It is under construction right now. In fact, the roof is not entirely finished," Mr. Pierce began, shouting over the hammering coming from the hearth face across from us. He began to walk backward down a narrow hallway.

"I've been eager to become acquainted with you as well, Mrs. Newbold. Do you suppose you would mind escorting me through the tour?" Worth asked, holding his arm out to my mother.

# CHAPTER EIGHT

By the time we reached the atrium, we'd been shown the room of concrete slabs drying vertically in sheets for the walls, the half-finished tile pool in the basement, and the newly laid alleys for bowling. Everyone was tired—tired of my questions, tired of looking at luxuries that couldn't be enjoyed, tired of contending for Worth's arm that had kindly escorted at least ten women—and begged to forgo the remainder of the tour to lounge in the rocking chairs on the makeshift terrace outside the Great Hall.

No one noticed when I remained in the atrium as they departed, the hems of their dresses making slight shuffling noises that echoed in the hollow four-story silence as they hastened out the door that led from the atrium to the stairwell. Besides the artistry of the rock walls, this was the most impressive feature in the hotel, and they'd all rushed past it.

Floating rectangular walkways—parapeted galleries—circled the space, boasting doors to private rooms on one side, while the other displayed an overlook to a beautiful glass ceiling and a gathering space where I now stood. Currently, scaffolding stretched all the way from the floor to the glass above, and buckets for plastering tile decorated the wood at each level. I stepped onto the lowest bit of scaffolding platform, sighed, and sat.

I closed my eyes and spread my palms across the rough plywood, breathing in the smell of new lumber with a hint of dusty plaster. I could see the majesty of this place. It was easy to fathom, even at this point in construction. The Great Hall would be noisy always, a boisterous gathering place where friends who'd traveled a far distance to see each other again would reunite. The fireplaces would blaze as guests reclined in wicker rocking chairs in front of them, servants would bustle to and fro with cocktails and hot cocoas and coffees, and perhaps there would even be music—I thought I'd heard Mr. Seely say something about music during his presentation.

Here, however, beneath this glass ceiling, it would be quiet. Here, the loud celebrations would drop to whispers. Mr. Pierce said Mr. Seely was planning to employ a group called Roycroft to craft handmade furniture that would allow guests the luxury of simple comfort. I could imagine the expanse, arranged for intimate conversation before guests retired to the adjacent bedrooms—an old couple reading together on a couch crafted of cherry with straight lines and deep brown buttery leather, a young couple sitting across from each other in matching armchairs, a game of chess between them, a chance for their fingers to brush and then tangle.

I opened my eyes, removed my hat, and lay back against the wood to stare up at the perfect blue sky. No one else was around. There was such peace in my heart here. From the moment I set eyes on the building, I'd been struck with awe, and then as we were guided through the halls and shown the magnitude of it all, a feeling like pride welled up and warmed me through. I couldn't figure the reason. I had no claim to this place or this town. I didn't know a soul working here. Perhaps it was because the men looked like home, because they were mountain folk like me, and they'd built something splendid. To the rest of the world, the hotel would be attributed to Mr. Grove and Mr. Seely, and of course that was right, but to me, this hotel palace built of stone and steel and skill was also theirs.

"Are you all right, miss?"

I jerked upright, nearly hitting my head on a beam as I got to my feet. A man my father's age stood in front of me holding a plaster bucket.

"Yes. Yes," I said when I settled. I reached down to retrieve my hat, fit it back on my head, and smiled at him.

"You sure? Saw a pair of buckskin boots and that fine yellow skirt just lying slack and near had an attack," he said. He spoke like Father, annunciating his *t*'s, but his accent was a bit slower, a hair more Southern. Though he hadn't asked outright what I was doing, why I'd been lying on the scaffolding, he was asking. His eyes narrowed, surveying my face for any sign of illness or peculiarity.

"I wanted to see what the sky looked like from there." I smoothed my skirts and stepped down from the scaffolding. "Some friends of mine arranged a sort of tour—"

"I know. We all know. You're with the camping group initiated by Mr. Ford, Mr. Edison, and Mr. Firestone. That man who writes about nature too."

"Mr. Burroughs," I said.

A lone ladder-back chair was occupying a vacant corner, and I walked toward it and sat down. I would return to Mother and Marie Austen eventually, but the moment I did, they would all be watching me, praising or criticizing the way I interacted with Worth. I was quite peaceful right here.

"Unfortunately, they broke us into two groups, and I was placed with the women, though I'm quite interested in the particulars of this hotel. The others tired of walking by our third destination— the bowling alley—and passed through here rather quickly on their way to the rocking chairs on the veranda. I wasn't finished looking around. I'm quite impressed with this wing of the hotel."

"Thank you. You might be the only one. The stonework is more interesting." He put his bucket on the ledge where I'd just been sitting.

"It's fascinating, too, but it's wonderful in here. Serene," I said.

"Today it's quiet. Tomorrow twenty-seven men will be crawling all over these here beams glazing the tile."

"Have you been working here since the beginning of the project?" I asked.

He nodded. "Yes. Thankful for it. They pay well, and it's steady work, but hard. When we're full up, there are four hundred of us working ten hours a day, six days a week. Mr. Mills is clear—Mr. Seely wants the whole place finished by July 1."

"It appears to be on pace," I said.

"Right now, it is," he said. "But lose any men to anger or sickness and that can change. A man died the other month. Got hit in the head with a beam. He was from South Carolina and had just come up for work. Was staying in the workers' quarters on the side of the mountain over there." He gestured beyond me, then paused. "You wouldn't have seen them. They ain't the sort of attraction I'm sure they're keen to show you fine people."

I forced my lips into a tight smile, forbidding myself to tell him I didn't need to see the housing to know what it was like.

"Anyway. My point is that there was an outcry from those hundred or so workers over there. They were scared to come back, and losing a quarter of our men would set us back at least a month or two. But Mr. Seely went down there himself and talked to them. Gave that man's widow a nice amount of money too."

"The money can't bring him back," I said without thinking, and the man looked at me.

"To be sure, but it was nice of Mr. Seely anyway. There's a risk we're going to die when we take a job like this, miss, but it's a job, see? And I'd rather have a job where I might die than waste away watching my family starve."

"I know," I said softly. He didn't question me, though I'm certain he wanted to. Here I sat in my French gown, my contemporaries the families of the great inventors of our time. What would I know about a life like his? I cleared my throat.

"How long have you been a tile setter?" I asked.

"Don't know. Thirty-one years, I suppose. My papa was a setter before me. Worked in Virginia mainly. I moved down here eighteen years ago to work on Mr. Vanderbilt's place and then just stayed." He climbed up on the scaffolding, the assortment of small tools hanging from his dungarees chiming as he moved.

"Hey, man, have you seen a young woman in a yellow dress?" Worth's voice boomed through the doorway from the hall. He materialized moments later, his eyes fixed on the tile setter, his posture rigid, his countenance a picture of panic. The tile setter looked down at Worth and then pointed to me.

"I'm right here." His gaze jerked to mine, and his face softened.

"Thank God," he breathed. "I'm not quite sure how we lost you. Miss Kipp was rather talkative going down the stairs, and when we reached the veranda she continued to inquire about the number of bears found on my land. When I looked around and realized you weren't among us, I admit I thought the worst."

"As did I when I saw her body lying on the scaffolding," the tile setter said. "My heart might have stopped. I was sure there'd been a terrible accident."

"Did you fall? Are you hurt? Whatever were you doing, Miss Newbold?" Worth paced toward me, his eyes once more crinkled in concern, and I laughed.

"Of course I didn't fall. I know I cannot scale much of anything in these boots. I can hardly walk in them. I was lying on the scaffolding because I wanted to see how the sky looked through the glass ceiling."

I stood when Worth reached my side. He looked down at me, amusement playing on his face.

"I stayed back because I wanted to see more," I explained. "Perhaps the rest are so accustomed to marvels like this that they don't feel the wonder anymore, but I find this place fascinating, and I'm interested in it all. I want to know how it is made, where the granite is harvested, how it is brought here, how it is placed, how the tile is selected by Mr. . . . . Mr. . . . ."

"Woods," the man said. "George Woods." Mr. Woods was spreading plaster now, the movement of his hand a flawless stroke that rendered the material absolutely smooth.

Worth pushed his hands into his pockets and stepped out from under the overhang of the floating walkway above us into the light from the ceiling. The sun washed the blond in his hair gold, contrasting the somber black of his suit. Then he stepped onto the first platform of scaffolding in one long stride. Mr. Woods, who had just set down his bucket to clip a section of tile with some sort of plier-like tool, turned to face him.

"Mr. Woods, I'm Worth Delafield. It's an honor to meet you. Thank you for keeping Miss Newbold company." He stuck out his hand and Mr. Woods nodded and shook it with his free one.

"Just relieved she wasn't dead, to be honest," Mr. Woods said.

Worth chuckled, stepped to the edge of the scaffolding, and gestured to the wood.

"Would you mind?" he asked. Mr. Woods shrugged, likely as confused as I was. Then Worth dropped to his knees and lay on his back, threaded his arms beneath his head, and tipped his face to the sky.

"It is radiant today. Not a hint of a cloud," Worth said, his voice low. "You know, you can't get this sort of blue just anywhere. Only in high elevations and only where there aren't factories nearby. I haven't taken notice of it in some time." He glanced at Mr. Woods. "I know we seem like we're absolutely out of our minds. Even so, have you ever taken a moment to look at this?"

Mr. Woods looked up and grinned.

"Yes, sir. My wife and I have a little yard and on a nice day, we lie on the grass and look at the sky and doze when we feel a rest coming."

I looked at Worth lying on the scaffolding in his tailored suit, the gesture done in an instant to understand me, and imagined myself next to him on a patch of grass. It would be easy, comfortable. He must have been thinking the same, because he edged up on his elbow and met my gaze.

"Do you need another look?"

I shook my head, despite the sudden urge to accept, and he rose and stepped off the scaffolding.

"Come, Miss Newbold," he said, holding his hand out to me. "I have something to show you."

# CHAPTER NINE

I'd never held a man's hand before, other than Father's, but it felt nice, natural, to hold Worth's. His fingers were long and his calluses hardened—something that greatly surprised me for a society man—and his touch immediately filled me with such an extraordinary sense of contentedness I hoped he'd not let go.

"We're almost there," he said in front of me. We had scaled some makeshift stairs behind the atrium wing and were now on the sixth story above the Great Hall in the dim of boarded window sockets, wandering through what he said would be the top floor of guest rooms. The space was relatively undone, the rooms only framed, and when I squinted, after my eyes had acclimated to the dark, I could make out the opposite wall on the other side of the hotel. Above us, workers hammered and iron rods scraped across the cement ceiling.

"They're making a web for the clay tiles they'll begin affixing to the roof tomorrow." Worth had to shout now, as the sound grew louder.

He turned toward the west side of the structure where the roof narrowed and bent low. The ceiling rattled overhead, and I instinctively reached forward, my free hand skimming the top of his head as if my fingers could actually shield him if it fell in. At once, the familiar tightness curled its way around my lungs.

"You don't suppose it'll collapse, do you?" I yelled. I thought I heard him laugh, but I couldn't be sure. "No" was the only clear answer I could make out.

Suddenly, he sat and pulled me down beside him. My breath

was coming in short gasps, the vibration of the roof seeming to get louder. I was thankful it was dark. I knew if he could see me, he'd see the pink splotches rising up my neck. A *boom* rang out and I jolted and must have screamed because Worth pulled me toward him.

"Are you all right?" he said in my ear. His lips and the prickle of his hair touched my skin. A tingling materialized in my stomach and departed as quickly. I thought to move away in case it happened again, but my fear held me fast. I forced a ragged breath, feeling his heartbeat against my shoulder.

"No." I turned to face him. There was something sacred about darkness, something honest. "My father died in a roof collapse." The words were clear, not the scrabble of noises I usually made when I said it. This time, my throat hadn't tightened. Perhaps it was the sensation of being held, the sensation of being safe—however untrue it really was.

"I'm sorry. How terrible. I didn't know. We'll go." He moved away from me but continued to grasp my hand. He rose, still crouched, and started to pull me out of the small space, but I stilled him.

"What did you want to show me?" I asked loudly. For a moment, the hammering and pounding stopped, and the echo of my question lingered.

"It doesn't matter," he said.

"I want to see it." I remained planted where we'd been, refusing to allow the fear to move me. "I can't stay afraid forever. In any case, it seems like the battering has stopped for now."

He ran his free hand across his face and shook his head.

"They're changing crews to give the first a break for an early lunch. They'll take it up again in ten minutes or so. I can show you another time. I got ahead of myself . . . I didn't think, but we're up here by ourselves, Miss Newbold, without your mother or your friend, Miss Kipp, and I don't—"

"Belle," I said. "And you thought I was lost. You came to find me alone. Our solitary moment can hardly be seen as a scandal in that case."

Worth stepped toward me and folded himself back into the

space at my left side. "I suppose you're right. In any case, we're —"
He stopped dead as though the reality of our arrangement wasn't
known by us both. Even so, I understood that voicing that we
were to be engaged this soon after reuniting could be uncomfortable.

Worth cleared his throat, leaned forward, and jimmied a large
board back and forth until it slid out of place. Light spilled over us,
and a panorama of the mountains took my breath before a rush of
elation washed through me.

"You can see almost all of it from here, all the goings-on," he
said. "This window — well, it will be a window when it's all said and
done — is the exact center of the hotel, the highest you can be."

"This view makes me feel weightless," I said. The sun was still
yellow in midmorning and high above the blue mountain peaks in
the distance. Right below us in the distance, a few groups of men in
knickers and caps gathered 'round a flagpole on a golfing green. It
must have been some sort of country club. Papa went off to one golf
club or another at least once each week.

"I know." Worth glanced at me. "Lightens your heart a bit."

"I grew up in the mountains but never really on top of them. My
view was the forest and the rivers, the dusty wash of clouds. When I
arrived here yesterday, it was almost too much to bear. The road to
your land reminded me too much of home. I've gotten past that. I'm
glad to be here now, no matter the view. But this, this is different."

"It is," he said. "Do you know I haven't been to my land here in
over three years? I stay with Seely when I'm in town, and I don't
make a habit of visiting all of my holdings often anyway, so there's
really no need, but . . ." He heaved a breath. "I bought that land for
myself at first. I don't think I told you that. When I offered it to Ford
and the others for camping, I hadn't planned to be in town. I hadn't
considered that offering it to them would encourage my going there.
You might have much to teach me about forgetting if you're willing."

Why was he so hesitant to visit his land? What did he want to
forget? I wanted to ask but didn't want him to ask anything of me in
return. I knew in this moment I'd be apt to tell him the truth.

"Father used to help me face things I was afraid of," I said. "He knew fear crippled and paralyzed, and he wanted me to live a life full of joy. When I got here, I compelled myself into the woods, required the deep breaths of the sweet mountain air, touched the tree bark, listened to the call of the animals. I remembered that before . . . before the bad memories, the forest was my heart."

"I like that. Perhaps I'll try it." Worth smiled, his white teeth and crinkled eyes transforming his face. "I recall West Virginia, though I've only been to the central part of the state and not the southern region where Shipley told me you're from. Even so, I can see why being here would feel like being there."

"I hadn't seen anything but plain since we left six years ago." I waited for Worth to ask me something about the particulars of that leaving. Over the years I'd said something occasionally at a debutante soiree or other gathering of how long I'd been in Gas City, and the mentioning of it was like a dam breaking. Straightaway a suitor's pressing questions about my origins, my father, really my suitability, would emerge.

"You must have felt like you were starving in those years," Worth said instead. I nodded. He was right in some ways. The hollowness, the desperation in the pit of my stomach, came from a different place but was much the same sensation.

We stared out the window. A hawk called and we watched it circle above the golfing men, then swoop close to us. In that moment I realized that we were still holding hands. It was a pleasant sort of touch, and I relished it.

"Mr. Seely comes up here often," Worth said. "It's easier to see things from a bird's-eye view if you're in a hurry, I suppose, than having to walk from one end of construction to the other. That's why I thought you might like to see it." He edged forward, pulling me with him toward the opening. It wasn't a large window. Only two feet tall at most.

"Come just a little closer here. It's the only way to see," he said. "I know you said you were interested in the boulders when we were touring with Mr. Pierce."

I nodded and pushed forward. "I hope you don't find it terribly irritating—all of my questions, my compulsion to know more regardless of whether it truly matters to me. It's how I've always been, I'm afraid—fascinated by how things work and the people working behind them. Father and I used to keep notebooks full of observations and stories about the pattern the coal seams made as they followed the river or how our seamstress, Mrs. Pennington, was taught to sew by her great-aunt, who sewed the first American flag for our town. It was almost like we were writing the sorts of news stories we wished were published."

"To be frank, Belle, I'm relieved to hear of your interests. I wasn't sure how we'd get on in person. All I could truly remember of you was that you had a pretty face. I know we didn't speak much when I visited those years ago," he said. "Father had just become sickly, and I wasn't myself, but the truth is that I have the same sort of mind as you do. Only my interests lie in land—why and how it was formed, the beauty of life in each part of the country, how to maximize the soil and all that." He paused. "Speaking of soil, do remind me to speak to Mr. Carver about his peanut findings."

"I will," I said. "And I'd like to hear all about your travels, Mr. Delafield." I studied his face, the way his blue eyes had widened just slightly and sparked with passion when he spoke of his interests.

Worth made a dismissive sound and let my hand go.

"Worth, please. For the love of God. If it were up to me, I'd do away with formal addresses once people have been introduced."

He moved forward a hair more, his knees folding nearly flush to his chest, and then gestured for me to come closer.

"Here, look over the edge of the south wing and you'll be able to see the wagon train."

Worth pointed out the window to my right, and I saw a parade of wagons puttering down a serpentine pathway to what I assumed was a depositing station at the foot of the hotel. In the absence of the roofing noise, I could hear men shouting, though what they were shouting about, I couldn't tell.

"What sort of machine is operating this train?" I asked. Of course, it wasn't an actual train. There were no tracks. I supposed it was just called a train because the wagons were somehow configured together.

"Packard motor trucks." Worth gritted his teeth. "Seely asked me not to mention it to Mr. Ford. The Packards were a bit of a deal, see."

"I understand." I turned my attention back to the train. The wagons were loaded with boulders. Thousands of them.

"You don't have a notebook. Here." Worth extracted a sheet of folded paper and a fountain pen from inside his jacket. He held them toward me, and I took them. "There's a letter from a buyer on the one side, but the other side is blank."

"I haven't had a notebook since I left home. West Virginia, I mean. I . . . I stopped writing when we moved to Indiana."

"Perhaps you stopped writing this way, but you didn't stop altogether. You wrote letters—at least to me—and I was transfixed by them if I'm honest. Your prose made even your reports of the weather or your dinner menu seem interesting." He grinned. "Shipley told me when I visited that year that you were quite gifted at writing. He mentioned that you'd written a letter to him and your mother upon their marriage and it moved him to tears."

I turned the pen over in my fingers. I'd never quite grasped how to respond to compliments and hadn't had any idea that Papa had reacted at all to my letter. At the time I'd thought the well wishes expressed in that letter hollow and insincere. Despite being immensely thankful for Papa, I was in deep mourning for Father.

"Waterman's sterling silver. Papa prefers these," I said, directing the conversation to the pen in my hand.

"You don't have to use it. I only thought you might—"

"I do. I want to write this all down," I said quickly. "And I love Papa. He's been good to us."

"To me too." The corners of his mouth lifted. I thought he might say more, but then he nodded toward the view. The train had stopped momentarily.

"How does it work? Where are the stones coming from?" I asked.

"All of the rock is harvested right here on Sunset Mountain. You can't see them, of course, but at the end of that makeshift road up there are nearly one hundred men. They extract the stones from the mountainside with their own strength and pulleys. Sometimes they hitch a donkey to one of the stones if it's stubborn. Then they load up a wagon—Seely's using six-foot Birdsells—and the donkeys pull it to the road. I'm not sure how much your father allowed you around the coal fields, but it's much the same process, only above the ground and without axes."

I nodded and scooted back to gain room to write, pressing the paper against the wood floorboards.

"Mr. Leslie will be glad to know the answer," I said.

"Mr. Leslie?"

"Our chauffeur. He wondered and since he has unfortunately been assigned to me and Marie Austen, I thought the least I could do was obtain the answer for him. The poor man has had to endure so much already, and it's been less than a day."

"Miss Kipp's carrying on isn't restricted to bears?" Worth asked.

I laughed. "No. Though she did spend most of the ride from the station fixed on the idea that she could be mauled to death."

Worth smiled.

"Despite the hysterics, she's quite entertaining and makes life exciting. Just this morning, the reporter Mr. Ford hired to document our venture was turned out on account of the fact that he and Marie Austen went into the woods for a solitary conversation, and she emerged saying she wanted to marry him."

I clapped my palm over my mouth. "I shouldn't have said anything. I was just talking to you as though—"

"Even if I hadn't heard of it—which I had; Edsel told me during the presentation in the Great Hall—I wouldn't say a word. I will keep everything you say to me in confidence always. I promise you that." He pressed his lips together and shook his head, then his eyes found mine. "Love makes a terrible mess of things. I'm glad we've chosen practicality and risen above it."

"Yes," I said. Something shifted then. The earlier laughter hid and the air seemed to still. Worth stared out the window, and the chiseled lines of his face sharpened. I thought to rise and depart, letting my last word punctuate an extended silence, but I still had questions, and he'd brought me all the way up here to have them answered.

"How are the wagons fixed together, and how much weight can one bear in a single load?" I asked.

"Much like a freight train," he said, his voice low and even. "They pull about six feet of a pole out of the cuff and then couple the stub pole to the extended reach of the next wagon fastened with a pin." He yawned. "Each load is around forty tons. A group of thirty men down at the foot of the hotel are waiting for the new granite, and they unload it—takes about six hours or so—and then the wagons return for the next load."

I wrote the answer on the paper. The train was still idling in the same position. My eyes shifted from one wagon to the next. I was fascinated by the strength of the steel trappings. Common sense suggested that a load that large would cause the wagons to buckle and fold, but these had been engineered to handle this sort of project.

"What about the clay tiles?" I asked. Worth didn't look at me, instead continuing to stare out at the mountains.

"They're affixed to the roof with wire, cement at the edges." He squinted. Something about his expression troubled me.

Overhead, the hammering and pounding suddenly resumed. This time it sounded louder, and a shrill whine of what I assumed was bending steel accompanied the noise. I inhaled deeply, reminding myself of Worth's words—we were safe—but noticed he hadn't moved at all.

"Perhaps we should go." I rose to my feet and straightened my skirt, but Worth remained still.

"Worth." I said his name loudly and leaned to touch his arm at the same time he lunged to pull the window board closed. His jacket sleeve slid up his arm with the swift motion, and my fingers grazed burning heat, my eyes catching sight of a puckered purple scar on the underside of his forearm just below his elbow. He jerked the sleeve down and yanked the board back, leaving us in darkness.

"Are you—"

"Yes, I'm fine. It was a long time ago," he said quickly. He stood, and my eyes began to adjust to the darkness. Worth held out his hand, the perfect hand attached to the scarred arm, and watched my face, doubtless considering whether my fingers would still find his. I clasped his hand, and the warm sensation of his touch washed through me.

"It is ugly," he said simply. I started to tell him I didn't mind, that I had my own, albeit invisible, scars, but before I could, he began to lead us down the corridor of frames once more. I watched the stretch of his long arm ahead of me as we walked and wondered how much it had been damaged, how much it had damaged him.

# CHAPTER TEN

By the time Worth and I made it back to the Great Hall and out to the makeshift terrace, the men were done with their tour.

"I hope your curiosity hasn't deprived you of luncheon," Worth said as we made our way across the leveled dirt to the group of women in wicker rocking chairs and men reclining on spread blankets situated toward the mountain view. I'd asked to see the wagon train up close after we descended the stairs, and the diversion had taken at least fifteen minutes.

"I don't mind if it has. I'd trade my luncheon again to watch," I said, raising my voice a little to be heard over the much more muted but still present hammering of the roofing men, the shouts of the stonemasons from inside the hall, and the lively chatter of our group. As we approached, I saw that Worth was likely right. We'd missed the meal completely. Empty white china plates boasting nothing but crumbs and discarded starched napkins sat atop several personal tables situated in front of the rocking chairs.

"The way those men have figured their system of pulleys and chains is mesmerizing," I went on. The group of workers was nearly as mechanical as a bicycle gear. Unfazed by even the largest boulders, the men would secure the weight in sizable straps and then lift them into the air using an enormous A-frame structure that whined before depositing the stones in a pile beside one of the towering, unfinished walls.

"I hope you haven't forfeited *your* sandwich to accompany me, though. You've been terribly kind." I withdrew my hand from Worth's and smiled at him.

The conversation hadn't warmed again since that turn in the rafters. It had been easy before, almost as if the understanding of who I was and who he was had come instantly, depositing friendship at the foot of our hearts without effort. Not so now. Now, the blithe spirit who'd lain down on the scaffolding and joined me in my wonder had retreated into formal stoicism.

"I wasn't hungry to begin with," he said, returning my grin with a close-lipped one of his own. "Seely's cook makes a hearty breakfast."

Marie Austen noticed us first. Breaking away from her conversation with Toots, she set her teacup on the small table in front of her and gestured at me.

"Where in the world have you been, Belle? We thought we'd lost you." Her eyes drifted to Worth before landing back on me. She'd removed her hat at some point in the hour I'd been away. She'd come out of hiding for someone. Perhaps she'd warmed to the prospect of Mr. Gibbins, or perhaps it was Edsel. He was sitting across from her with Mr. Ford, but then again, he'd never given her much attention. Or maybe it was Worth. Maybe she thought she'd attempt to woo him away from his devotion to me. We weren't engaged yet, after all, and at this juncture it likely wouldn't take her much effort.

"She was keen to see more of the hotel, and I was glad to show her around," Worth said. I watched the way he looked at her and wondered if he found her enchanting after all. Despite her being perfectly done up at the moment, the picture of a proper young woman, he knew she was rebellious. Rebellion was a society man's Achilles' heel.

"I'm glad to know you didn't perish beneath a boulder," she said, fiddling with a small curl of hair that had come loose behind her ear. "But you've missed the brie-and-fig-jam sandwiches, and I know how much you love brie."

"I've got a bit of tarragon chicken salad and lemon poppyseed pound cake you can have, dear," Mother said. She was sitting three chairs down from Marie Austen between Mrs. Kipp and Mrs. Firestone. Papa Shipley was situated on the ground in front of her, his back leaned comfortably against her knee. They had an easy way about them. Despite Mother's being much more buttoned-up than the vibrant woman she'd once been, her marriage seemed quite easy and idyllic—better than the passion she'd shared with Father, the sort that, once found, seemed to be required for breath.

"Don't worry about me," I said, leaving Worth's side and making my way toward them.

"Delafield. Come over and tell me about the land Fred said you're buying out near your other holdings here." Mr. Grove, his white hair now tucked beneath a neat bowler, was leaning against a pile of wooden beams on the edge of the group with Mr. Seely, positioned directly in front of Mr. Carver and Mr. Burroughs, who were seated on a blanket.

I watched Worth walk toward them, his long stride measured and sure. I watched the way the men around him enlivened in his company, the way he bent to meet their gazes and clasped their hands in greeting. Had they seen the man I had, or were they enraptured with the polish of who they thought him to be?

I walked around the row of rocking chairs and up the narrow dirt channel between the ladies and the men on their blankets.

"Here, take my plate." Mrs. Burroughs, who was sitting next to Mrs. Firestone, stopped me. She leaned forward, plucked her full plate from her table, and held it out to me.

"But it looks like you haven't touched it," I said, taking it from her.

"I haven't." She looked smugly at her husband, who was now in deep discussion with Worth and Mr. Seely. "I've lost my appetite."

"Don't let him trouble you," Mrs. Firestone said softly, patting Mrs. Burroughs's hand. "He could have been speaking of building *you* a new home in this manner."

I looked down at the plate of neatly arranged tea sandwiches— cucumber and herbed cheese, roast beef and arugula, tarragon chicken salad—trying to determine if I should leave the ladies to this conversation or if departing suddenly when I'd inadvertently been engaged in the commentary was rude.

Mrs. Burroughs scoffed. "He's been carrying on with her for twelve years and still acts as though I haven't a clue. She's younger than our son. He hides her in his little hermit's retreat a mile from Riverby—our home on the Hudson."

"Let's turn our thoughts to something more lively, shall we?" Mrs. Firestone attempted. She looked a bit panicked, as though Mrs. Burroughs might suddenly incite a scandalous scene and confront her husband right here on the Grove Park Inn's terrace.

"Thank you again, Mrs. Burroughs. If you'll excuse me," I said to them both, tipping my head and walking toward Papa and Mother. My stomach growled as I lifted the cucumber sandwich to my lips. I hadn't realized I was hungry, but now I was thankful Mrs. Burroughs had lost her appetite. The bread was soft, the herbed cheese delicate and creamy.

"One of the servants said the cheese is made fresh from Mr. Vanderbilt's farm," Mother said, watching me eat the sandwich.

"It's delightful."

"I would summon a servant to bring you a chair, but it seems they've all departed," Papa said. He leaned away from Mother's legs to glance down the aisle of occupied rocking chairs. "Did you enjoy yourself today?"

"Yes, very much," I said. "Worth was an obliging tour guide."

Mother and Papa looked at each other and smiled. It was telling when a woman began using a gentleman's given name.

"We're quite glad," Mother said.

"Come sit with me, Belle. I'll scoot," Marie Austen said. She pushed her small frame to one side of the chair, folded her skirt over her legs, and patted the white cushion. I walked toward her and took the seat.

"You're more cunning than I ever imagined," she whispered when I was settled beside her.

"What do you mean?" I took a bite of roast beef.

"Staying behind so Mr. Delafield would be compelled to come look for you," she said softly, glancing at Worth standing only a few feet away. The other men, save Mr. Firestone and Papa, had now risen from their blankets and were gathered together talking. "You won't admit it, but you've learned a thing or two from me after all."

I laughed. "It wasn't intentional. I—"

At once, five servants in white livery emerged from the expansive doorframe carrying silver platters.

"If everyone wouldn't mind sitting, dessert will be served." The first servant, a giant of a man whose height rivaled Worth's, made some gesture to the group of men and most of them complied, finding their seats on the blankets in front of us. Mr. Seely, Mr. Grove, and Worth remained standing.

The servants came around with éclairs and strawberry trifles, setting them on each small table with care. When they made their way to Worth, he waved them off politely.

I looked down at my plate of sandwiches.

"I'll be right back," I said to Marie Austen.

I skirted the table laden with desserts and then nearly tripped over Mrs. Kipp's feet, which were decorously crossed far out beneath her table.

"Excuse me," I said to Mr. Seely and Mr. Grove when I reached the three of them. I looked at Worth. "Mrs. Burroughs gave me her whole plate of sandwiches. I've already had all I can eat." That part was a lie, but the part of me still longing for chicken salad would be satisfied by an éclair just as well. I held the plate out to Worth. He hesitated for a moment, and I thought he might refuse it, but then he nodded and took it from my hands.

"Thank you," he said. I started back to Marie Austen.

"Miss Newbold," Mr. Grove said, and I whirled to face him. He was a kindly looking man, balding, with round spectacles and a full mustache in the shape of a horseshoe. "Every time we expose someone new to this place, we ask what they think. We've asked plenty of men, but it would be nice to hear a woman's opinion."

"It's absolutely majestic, a true wonder of the world," I said, smiling.

"That's high praise, Miss Newbold," Mr. Seely said.

"She isn't simply saying it to say it, Fred." Worth took a bite of the chicken salad and leaned toward his friend. "Belle is quite interested in the craftsmanship here and finds the entire project marvelous."

"Worth is exactly right. I'm in awe. I'm sure you're tremendously proud of how your design is turning out," I said.

"Thank you. I am indeed." Mr. Seely looked over our heads at a boulder being hoisted four feet in the air to settle at the top of one of the unfinished walls.

"It will be an asset to the whole city, a landmark that will proclaim Asheville a tourist destination. Speaking of— Please excuse me for a moment." Mr. Grove broke free from us and walked to where Mr. Ford was enjoying his second éclair and a glass of sherry.

"Darling, here. We wouldn't want you two to miss dessert as well." Mother appeared at my right shoulder holding a plate of desserts with Papa at her side. I was well aware that the desserts were a ploy to come over and speak with Worth again.

"I do love a trifle," I said, plucking the small crystal glass from the plate and extracting a dessert spoon from her hand. "Worth? Mr. Seely?"

"No, thank you," Worth said, raising the sandwich plate just slightly. "I admit I'm one of those strange people who prefer savory to sweet."

Mother looked at me pointedly, as though this were some tidbit I should store, before remembering herself and smiling. Of course I wouldn't need to know the foods my husband preferred and how to prepare them. We had cooks for that.

"I'll take an éclair," Mr. Seely said, reaching for the chocolate-covered pastry. He started to take a trifle as well but was diverted by a cloudy-looking Mr. Grove who had just rejoined our group.

"The reporter, Peter Thorp, has been sent away," Mr. Grove whispered to Mr. Seely.

"Is something the matter?" Worth asked.

"Somewhat," he said. "It's not anything of a devastating nature, but we had asked Henry to lend us time with his reporter this week to catalog and document the minutiae of the building of our hotel—those remarkable things you spoke of, Miss Newbold. The way the granite is harvested and set, the way the roof is formed, the way the architectural plan was constructed, et cetera. We had hoped for a story of sorts that could be sent 'round to newspapers across the country to drum up some excitement for the grand opening and later made into a book. Peter Thorp is quite a writer with a great eye to detail. We were rather excited to hear it was him along." Mr. Grove shook his head.

"I suppose we could ask one of the local writers or someone from the *Georgian*," Mr. Seely said. "I know we've sold the paper to Hearst, but I believe he's retained a few familiar names."

Mr. Grove shook his head. "We need someone who can write a narrative, not just a good news piece," Mr. Grove said. "Peter Thorp has been writing a novel. He's skilled in both newspaper and long form. We were looking for a melding of the two."

"Belle could do it," Worth said. His words shocked me, and I stared at him. Surely his hunger had encouraged this foolish suggestion. I'd never written for a newspaper and certainly had never drafted a novel. "She's a wonderful writer. Her letters are compelling and well-crafted and they often read like a story. Not to mention, she has interest in this hotel in spades, and interest is what makes a narrative come to life."

I laughed, hoping to dispel the warm flush I felt on my face.

"I agree that she's a wonderful writer," Mother said quickly. "Has been since she was a small girl, but surely it wouldn't be a suitable option for her. In order to draft such a piece, she'd have to go interview men in the woods where they're harvesting the stone and then interview the masons and the plumbers and the like alone here at the inn." Her cheeks were pink, possibly because it was against her new nature to disagree with men.

"He was only speaking in jest," I said to Mr. Grove and Mr. Seely. I could tell they weren't sure whether to take Worth's suggestion seriously.

"I don't think he was," Papa interjected. "Though, Worth, I—"

"Thank you, Shipley. I wasn't." Worth, who was now finished with his plate, set it down on the edge of a wooden beam and pushed his hands into his pockets. "As I said, interest is the catalyst for success, and she's curious about the building of this place. So much so that she already began writing notes on it. We missed luncheon to watch the workers unload the stones from the train." Worth laughed and glanced at me.

"Yes, I am interested, but Mr. Grove and Mr. Seely are surely looking for a professional writer, one who can command the attention of the nation's papers. That is Mr. Thorp, not me." Worth's insistence made me feel uncomfortable, and I couldn't understand why he was doing it.

"They need the story, not the papers. We have plenty of connections to those," Worth said. "Consider, Edwin, Fred, that I am who I am because I'm inquisitive about the land I love. Edwin, you have earned great success because you are passionate about treating malaria. And, Fred, you are an inventor through and through, and your inventions from pill cutters to this hotel are wildly successful because of your love for creation." He turned to Papa. "Consider, Shipley, if you didn't boast your continuous wonder. Would you have spent the funds to drill anyway? Would you have the motivation to begin a new venture, these gasoline stores you're thinking about, at your age?"

Papa chuckled. "You didn't say Edwin or Fred was old," he said.

"We do need an account of it all before the walls are finished, and with any luck that will be in the next couple of weeks," Mr. Seely said softly to Mr. Grove.

I smoothed my dress and tried to focus on Marie Austen, who was now flirting with Edsel Ford, but it suddenly occurred to me that I desperately wanted Mr. Grove to tell me I could write the piece. My palms were sweating and my heart was galloping with nerves. I could be a terrible disappointment, but something inside me refused to say I'd rather not. Perhaps it was the questions burbling up even now: How was the concrete poured so smoothly? How many pieces of furniture had been ordered to outfit this place and from where? How often did the crews shift?

"Miss Newbold, perhaps do try your hand at it. That is, if you'd like to and if you have the time," Mr. Grove said. "If you don't take to it, we can search around for someone else next week."

"I'd like to try." I felt nearly as light as I had in the rafters with Worth. My thoughts shifted to Father. Perhaps in some small way this piece was meant for me. Perhaps in writing it, I could fulfill his dream of writing for a newspaper. I wouldn't fail.

"Then it's settled. We'll toast to the arrangement tonight at my dinner party." Mr. Grove clapped Worth on the back. "Thank you for the suggestion."

I could feel Worth looking at me and found him smiling. I grinned back, barely able to look away from his face. It was one of his true, honest smiles and the sight was as captivating as a flame.

"She'll need a chaperone," Mother said, clearly uneasy about this arrangement but unable to do anything to stop it. She might be thinking of Father, too, the idea that I could write a piece for the newspaper reminding her of how much he'd wanted to do the same.

The men nodded, the idea of my requiring a chaperone while in the company of unfamiliar, working-class men an obvious necessity.

"I suppose I'll be able to spare Sylvia in the afternoons until dinner," Mother continued.

"No need to spare your maid," Worth said, his gaze still fixed on me. "I'll accompany her, so long as you would find my doing so appropriate. We're to be engaged, after all, and my business in town only requires a few short meetings over the next week. It was my idea, in any case."

I was stunned at the ease with which he expressed the particulars of our relationship, considering he'd been unable to voice it at all in the rafters only an hour before.

"I suppose you're right," Mother said to Worth. "You don't think it will be too much for you, dear?" Mother attempted. "Ladies require a certain amount of rest and only delicate activity."

"I don't imagine it will be too much for her at all, and she'll be safe with Worth," Papa said.

"That's quite right," I said. "I think it will be a great adventure."

# CHAPTER ELEVEN

No one had spoken a word about my new endeavor since the moment it was proposed. Perhaps they would all forget about it. I prayed they wouldn't.

When we'd returned to camp, the men had departed for another contest—a gathering of edible plants this time—while the women were left behind. I'd tried to take up my sewing, an inconsequential sampler intended for a five-year-old, while Marie Austen resumed crying over Mr. Thorp, and Mother, Mrs. Kipp, Mrs. Firestone, and the rest of the older set went to nap in their tents.

The laziness of the afternoon wasn't unusual. I, too, had taken to napping after luncheon these past six years, but now the act of reclining for hours seemed terribly dull. Now I was back in the mountains and there was work to be done. The part of my mind that wondered and spun with possibility had been woken from slumber, and I couldn't stop thinking of the hotel.

"Miss Newbold?"

I jolted at the sound of my name, my fork jabbing unbecomingly into the turbot draped in lobster sauce. We had been situated in Mr. Grove's dining room since eight, and whether it was the heavy red-velvet brocade that covered the windows, chairs, and walls making the room feel like it was wrapped in a blanket or the droning sound of Mr. Kipp's voice talking about the latest polymer he'd invented, I had fallen into a sort of trance.

"Yes," I said quickly, not entirely certain who'd called my name.

"Have you given much thought to your father's new gasoline

stores? I only ask because I know you must be interested given your curiosity in innovation." Mr. Grove spoke from the head of the table. He'd finished his course and drawn back from the plate for conversation, his hands wrapping the elaborate gilded scrollwork on the arms of his chair.

"They've exhausted the topic of polymers, thank God, and will now move 'round the table and discuss each man's latest endeavor, starting with Shipley's," Worth said under his breath beside me. Marie Austen turned to glare at Worth from my other side, likely at his insinuation that polymers were boring, though she'd spent the entire discussion moving pieces of turbot from one side of her plate to the other.

"I find them utterly genius, Mr. Grove. It simply makes sense," I said. "We have markets for food and department stores for clothing and housewares, but as it stands, if one would like to take a voyage in their Ford auto, they must stop and ask around for gasoline."

Across the vast table, I met Papa's gaze. He was smiling, beaming, in fact, as though he was proud of me. I returned his grin, surprised I could make any sense of Papa's endeavor at all, but the concept was straightforward enough. Truthfully, I hadn't spent a second thinking of Papa's new venture, and I'd visited his wells only once. Now, given my awakening, it was odd that I'd just looked over the towers of scaffolding that stretched all the way to the horizon and then departed for our home without a single question. But then, I had been grieving, and despite Papa's kindness I'd wanted nothing to do with him. I'd missed the mountains and I'd missed Father.

"I daresay I think the presence of these gasoline stores will show the country that it is easy to travel by auto and train isn't the only way. You have to plan trips around the rail schedule with trains, but if you own an auto and if gasoline is widely available, you could depart and arrive and depart again whenever you desire," I went on. "If I can be permitted to be so bold, Mr. Ford and Mr. Firestone, I believe the stores would advance your own endeavors as well."

Mr. Ford looked up from his wineglass and nodded.

"Yes, I believe they would," he said.

"Shipley, you should engage your daughter in every discussion on this topic from now on," Mr. Firestone said, chuckling quietly. "She is quite clear without all the talk of finances and logistics that muddle our conversations."

I wasn't certain if he was making me out to be an unintelligent simpleton or if he was earnest.

"A sincere, straightforward opinion outlining the benefits and drawbacks of our ideas is what we all require to understand our markets," Worth said, his tone not indicating that he was scolding Mr. Firestone or agreeing with him. Despite Worth's continued formality, the polish of his outward facade, the truth of the gentleman he was remained unaltered in this state.

I appreciated the way he stood up for me, the way he saw value in who I was beyond a vessel that would someday bear him children. When I'd agreed to marry him, I had made peace with the notion that he may view me forever as a useful appliance like a stove or a lightbulb. After all, our arrangement was made to fulfill our mutual want for family and comfort and nothing more. But from the moment he greeted me today, he'd cared for me, treated me as a true friend. I'd grown unaccustomed to that sort of affection after moving to Gas City. The friends I'd known and counted on my whole life had been replaced by the solitary dysfunction of my relationship with Marie Austen. I hadn't realized how much I needed a confidant until now.

"I agree, Mr. Delafield. And on that note, Miss Newbold, do you think the average consumer prefers brass over steel in the ornamentation of the autos? I know Mrs. Ford is of the mind that they do—Mrs. Firestone too—but what say you?" Mr. Ford asked. Mr. Firestone and Mr. Gibbins were staring at him as though he'd gone mad. Mother and Evelyn Seely, who had the same kind eyes as her father, Mr. Grove, were whispering about something on the opposite side of the table from us, while Mrs. Kipp's face was turning red on account of me, the unfit stepdaughter of Shipley Newbold, stealing attention from her Marie Austen.

I hesitated, but Worth nudged my arm and tipped his head forward, encouraging me to respond.

"Brass is more handsome, in my opinion," I said. "From a manufacturing perspective, I imagine it's beneficial too. It shows less wear than steel, it's more malleable, and it's wonderfully rust-resistant." I knew what I did because of Father's ammo, the way he'd saved up to buy brass casing over steel for his hunting rifles.

"Don't be ridiculous, all of you." Marie Austen suddenly dropped her fork, letting it fall to the china with a clatter. "None of us women know anything about the goings-on of commerce, Miss Newbold included. It is well beyond what we're intended for. Just look at us all done up in silk and lace. We're outfitted for the home, not in suits for exploring the world. You didn't ask me about Father's polymers, Mr. Grove, because you know it is not my place."

I glanced down at the top of my bodice draped in red roses along the décolleté and then at my skirt, its hand-embroidered lace panels adorned in pearls and gold spangles. In some ways, she was right. We were living art just waiting for a place on the proverbial wall. I'd been content with that. I'd craved that steadiness before today, and still, if given the choice between writing the story about the hotel and securing a proper home, I'd pick the latter.

"I don't agree," Evelyn said. She was sitting next to Mother and Mr. Seely, who was seated at the other head of the table opposite Mr. Grove. "Perhaps I don't deal in figures or architecture, but I have a capable mind, same as Fred and Father, and my opinion has been consulted on nearly every decision for the interior decoration of the hotel. I have looked at hundreds of bathtub designs, thousands of linen brands." She beckoned the servants to come in with the third course.

"Not to mention you were the one to first bring to mind an alternative for Asheville, dear," Mr. Grove said to his daughter. "You see, if we hadn't settled on another economic course for the town, it would have become a veritable leper colony within the year. The town is already awash with tuberculosis sanitoriums, teetering on such a fate as it stands. It would have soon fallen completely the way of the sick, avoided by travelers altogether, but Evelyn mentioned the idea of a grand hotel. Now, if all goes as we plan, the hotel will open to great acclaim, we will continue to systematically eliminate the sanitoriums, and Asheville will be known the country over as a place for the well to come and rest."

The sentiment seemed odd for a man whose whole life had been about the business of creating remedies for the sick. I stared at the roast quarter of lamb served on a bed of rosemary in front of me, willing myself to stay quiet.

"It's going to be just lovely," Mr. Gibbins said from beside Marie Austen. He'd been looking at her throughout the meal and did so again now. Perhaps he thought his contribution to the conversation would award him a glance from her, but I knew his efforts were futile. She had no interest in his profession, his personality, or his looks—which were, unfortunately, lacking. He was balding and his teeth, though straight, were considerably stained.

"Do you suppose you'll develop any remedies for tuberculosis, Mr. Grove?" The question was out of my mouth before I could stop it. "I only ask because you say there's a need, and I recall so many in my youth who were saved from the perils of malaria by your tonic." I said the last bit hastily, hoping he'd think my question sprang from admiration and not criticism as it truly did.

"I'm glad your peers were helped by it," Mr. Grove said, cutting into his lamb. "I swore I'd find a cure after I lost . . ." His gaze drifted to his wife sitting beside him.

"My mother and my sister from the disease," Evelyn said, finishing his sentence. "You can still speak of them, Father." I watched the way her gaze fixed on Mrs. Grove. I couldn't recall them speaking all night. Perhaps there was tension.

"But no, neither of us—Seely or me—knows what to do to fight tuberculosis," he said, leaving Evelyn's charge unaddressed. "I'm sorry for those poor souls, but there's nothing we can do. Malaria is caused by a parasite, and quinine, the primary property used in our Chill Tonic, is effective to either kill the parasite or prevent it from growing. Tuberculosis, on the other hand, is bacterial, transmitted person to person through saliva when an infected individual coughs or speaks or sings. It is quite a different disease."

"Father has been incredibly concerned about its prominence among the residents here," Evelyn said.

"Yes," Mr. Grove said simply.

It occurred to me then that his eliminating the sanitoriums and altering Asheville's focus might not be solely for the successful future of the town but also for the safety of his family. I recalled the scream that erupted from my mouth upon the death of my father. It was part animal, uncontrollable and fierce, and it had echoed through the holler. In the next moment, as I watched the other men walk down the holler, toward the hole that had just captured Father's life, I'd shouted in a voice too ragged to be understood, *Shut them down! Shut them all down!*"

"That's why your story will be such an asset to us, Miss Newbold," Mr. Seely said. Shifting the conversation to the hotel, to something merrier, was a good decision. During our exchange about tuberculosis, everyone save Marie Austen had stopped eating.

"I do hope my words will do your inn justice. That sort of masterpiece should be celebrated the world over," I said. At once my mind fixed on the workers I'd seen hauling boulders at the hotel. They would likely never visit the palace they'd helped build, but they deserved to be acknowledged all the same. I hoped my story would serve as a small recognition of their contribution. I would ensure I captured not only the work of their hands but also the work of their hearts. Neither Mr. Seely nor Mr. Grove had given me any sort of guideline besides that they wanted a catalog of how the hotel had been crafted—that could include personal bits on the workers too.

"What story are they talking about?" Marie Austen asked, dabbing her mouth with her napkin.

"Oh. Mr. Grove and Mr. Seely have asked me to write a piece on the building of their hotel." I'd forgotten that she hadn't been privy to our conversation when this was decided, and in her sulking state after luncheon, I hadn't mentioned it to her.

"Why? You're not a writer." The rest of the table had moved on now. Mr. Ford was speaking with Mr. Carver about utilizing plants to create a rubber substitute in case the material was rendered scarce one day, while Worth was discussing the beauty of the Rocky Mountains with Mrs. Firestone.

"I haven't been as of late, but I used to be," I said.

"Really? For what papers?" Marie Austen asked. She cut a piece of lamb, placed it in her mouth, and chewed daintily. She lifted her hand to her hair, done up in a low coiffure inlaid with pearls to match those sewn in a floral pattern on her lavender bodice.

"You know I wasn't a professional." I cut a slice of meat and inhaled the rosemary as I lifted it to my mouth, hoping its calming properties would work wonders on my patience with Marie Austen. "I simply enjoyed it as you enjoy sewing and playing the piano."

"I suppose your lack of proficiency with the needle makes sense then." She smiled at this and for a moment I thought she might transform into the enjoyable version of the girl I knew. "It's because Mr. Thorp has gone, isn't it? They're out a writer." She took a long sip of wine, set the glass down, and looked at me. Her eyes filled with tears, and she shook her head and blinked them away. "It doesn't matter." I patted her arm lightly and she turned. "How in the world did you get involved in the assignment? I hadn't any idea you wrote a thing, and I've known you for six years."

"Worth suggested I step in," I said.

"Why? How would—"

"I've read her letters this past year. She is a talent. Shipley agrees," Worth answered. Marie Austen nodded and turned to Mr. Gibbins abruptly. Something about facing a man like Worth, a man so kind and sure and handsome, often silenced even the most ardent tormentors.

"She is jealous of you, and it is unfair and horribly unbecoming," he murmured. He took his last bite of lamb and set his fork down.

"Perhaps," I replied. "But her question is one I've wanted to ask you too. I know you must be aware of other writers, professional writers, but the moment the opportunity presented itself, you suggested me. Why?"

His gaze trained on mine and stayed. Being beheld by him like this unnerved me. I thought to look away, but then he spoke.

"Exploring and writing were once your source of wonder and you stopped," he whispered. "Grief or fear or perhaps both stole it from you." His hand found mine under the table, and I wrapped my fingers around his palm as warmth rushed through me. "I hear what you say, Belle."

The comfort I'd felt in his company earlier today returned, and in this moment I knew I was sitting with the man he was, not the man he thought he should be.

"You said your father was adamant that fear not pilfer your wonder, and I don't know . . . I watched the way you wrote today, covering the small space you had, and I remembered how I'd always been transported by your letters. I couldn't let you forfeit such talent. Your father would want you to revive it, to steal it back. You found peace with the mountains again. You can do the same with this."

Tears burned my eyes and I looked away, trying to focus on the half-eaten lamb in front of me. How he knew me so well so quickly, I couldn't comprehend. How I'd stumbled into such a friendship with a man like him was nothing short of miraculous.

"If I spoke out of turn, I apologize," he said. "And if you don't wish to write the story at all, I will tell them I made an error in suggesting it."

"No. I want to write it. I've never wanted to do something so much in my life." It was a bold statement, one I'd not intended to make, but after it emerged from my mouth, I knew I meant it. A servant reached between us to remove our plates, and I let Worth's hand go. "You're right about my father. We shared a passion for writing. Before . . . before he went into mining, he considered journalism. Writing this story will be a gift."

Worth smiled and nodded. "I'm glad."

I thought of what he'd told me today as I scoured my brain for some ounce of merriment I could give him in return. He'd said little about his family, his own heartbreaks, though the distance he kept from his land here and the presence of the terrible scar offered hints.

"Perhaps it's time you visit your land again," I said. "Surely Mr. Ford could procure another tent. You once loved it, and it's beautiful country. If you didn't intend to return, you would have sold it by now. Whatever drew you away doesn't matter. I'll be there with you."

He took a deep breath that raised his shoulders, then shook his head and looked at me.

"I'm not sure I'm as brave as you are. At least not yet," he said simply. "As to keeping hold of the land, it isn't by choice. I can't sell it."

"Are you casting a line with us tomorrow, Delafield? Vanderbilt plans to join us," Mr. Ford said, bringing Worth back to the table's conversation, but my mind remained fixed on what he'd just said. I wanted to know exactly what was broken, what had happened to him, but in the midst of all of these people, it was impossible. "I suppose we'll go down to the French Broad unless you think there's any biting in the streams around your place."

"There are plenty in the streams—trout, walleye, bass—especially in the north streams, but their swimming patterns aren't consistent. You'll have more luck behind Biltmore on the French Broad," Worth said. A servant deposited flaky Neapolitan pastries in front of us, and Worth quickly transferred his next to mine. "Here, have both."

"I couldn't if I wanted to." Seven-course meals had taken getting used to, and even now I could barely finish five.

"I won't be joining you tomorrow. I promised Miss Newbold I'd accompany her on her research for the Grove Park story," Worth said to Mr. Ford and nodded for a bit of coffee.

"I don't want you to miss the fishing," I said. "We can go when you return."

Worth chuckled. "You wouldn't want me to go with you after a fishing expedition. We're all worse for the wear, and Mr. Burroughs always brings a pungent botanical whiskey." He poured a small stream of cream in his coffee, then whispered, "Don't tell them, but I don't want to go anyway. Most know how to bait a line and dismantle the fish, but others don't, and—"

"Are you sure you can't delay going with Miss Newbold?" Mr. Ford called from across the table.

"She can't go alone, and I'm happy to show her about," Worth said.

I started to say I didn't require a chaperone. I hadn't for seventeen years. But now, of course, that wasn't true. I was Shipley Newbold's stepdaughter and therefore must be watched at all times—especially around men of less fortunate breeding. It was odd that freedom depended on the importance of one's father, as if the possible peril of a miner's daughter was somehow acceptable while an industrialist's daughter could not be spared.

A sob erupted from Marie Austen next to me.

"I can't take it. I can't take it," she said breathlessly. "I had it in my grasp, and now you have it, the match I always dreamed of, and I . . ."

I reached for my napkin and pressed it into her hand to dry her tears.

"It's not been twenty-four hours," I whispered. "Mr. Thorp will surely return. You must give him more time to work things out." Suddenly the idea that Mr. Thorp could return not only for Marie Austen but also for revenge, armed with the knowledge of who Mother and I truly were, reemerged. I forced the fear away.

"No," she hissed, dabbing her eyes with my napkin. "I tried to believe that, but it is unrealistic. He left. If he had any intention of loving me, he would have refused to leave without me, and now I'm stuck in any case. Father took me aside at Grove Park and told me he would disown me unless I—"

Mr. Gibbins stood abruptly. He lifted his empty wineglass and struck it gently with his dessert spoon. His face paled and his gaze fixed on Marie Austen.

"I was planning to ask later, but it . . . now . . . now seems right," he said, fumbling over the words. Political office likely wasn't the best course for him. It required a great deal of public speaking, and this was unimpressive to say the least.

"No, Mr. Gibbins," Marie Austen whispered pointedly, but he seemed to ignore her.

He dropped to his knee beside her chair, and I gasped.

"I must have you . . . I must have you as my . . . my wife. Marie Austen Kipp, will you marry me?" His countenance bloomed from ghost to tomato the moment he asked, and as he stared at her, I waited for Marie Austen to positively explode. She would either reprimand him or sink to the floor in tears. Either way, she would decline.

"Yes," she said.

Shock struck me through. I reached for her arm, hoping to dispel whatever trance had come over her. She'd been holding out for a great love affair, and this was not it.

"Yes," she said louder. "You will have me and Rues D'Or. What a prize." She rose, evading my touch, and pivoted away from her quivering fiancé to look at her parents. "Did you hear me, Father? I said yes. I suppose this means I'll remain in your will?"

Mr. Kipp's face burned and he cleared his throat to say something, but Mrs. Kipp's hand clasped hard around her husband's and he remained silent.

Mr. Gibbins finally seemed to compose himself enough to beckon Marie Austen close to him, and the dinner party guests came to their senses and began to clap and wish them well.

In the midst of the noise, Mr. Gibbins whispered something in Marie Austen's ear and lifted her hand to his lips. She remained stoic but poised as he beamed at her and petted her fingers.

"What a peculiar engagement," Mrs. Firestone remarked softly beside Worth.

Despite being with Worth nearly all day, I'd forgotten that sometime this week, I would be in Marie Austen's position. Worth and I were much more suitably matched, and I genuinely liked him, but the thought of a public proposal made my stomach turn. I looked away from the disturbing sight of Marie Austen and Mr. Gibbins, who were now seated again, his body twisted toward hers while she sat rigid in her chair, and took a sip of my coffee.

"That was horrific," Worth replied to Mrs. Firestone. "Entirely improper. To propose among peers like this, to coerce a woman into an engagement this way, is shameful."

My nerves suddenly steadied and I felt as though I could breathe again.

"Are you surprised I've decided to marry? Of course, I'll take a lover," Marie Austen whispered in my ear. "How horrible, how desperate am I? It was you who made me do this terrible thing. It was you—your match and your startling me last night—and Peter's abandonment and Father's ultimatum prompted by your awful fortuity."

"I did not make you do anything," I snapped under my breath, the velocity of my sudden emotion nearly toppling my coffee. I would not be made the scapegoat for her horrid decisions. "Perhaps it was *your* misery or *your* jealousy, but whatever it was, this decision was yours alone. It has nothing to do with me."

"I . . . I feel . . ." Her face went slack and her body went limp, and before I could stop her, she fell, lifeless, from her chair.

# CHAPTER TWELVE

Nearly twelve hours later, I was still reeling from Marie Austen's fainting spell. The shocking scent of ammonia still stung my nostrils from waving the smelling salts beneath her nose and mine, and the vision of Worth's face etched in concern, the way his arm had wrapped 'round my waist and held me close to him as we tried to revive her, kept intruding into my mind. Despite the way my nerves still raged with adrenaline, it seemed that Marie Austen had forgotten about the whole thing the moment she was brought back to consciousness, which, though highly irritating in theory, had been a benefit to me.

"Thank you so much for letting me come along," she cooed, scooting closer to me as the auto emerged from the forest and turned onto the road that would lead us into town to meet Worth. "I know I was terribly naughty last night, and I know I will have to bear the attention of Mr. Gibbins . . . I mean, Robert, sometime, but I simply couldn't today."

She looked at herself in the rear window's reflection and straightened her flat cap. She'd selected an ambitious costume today, something we would have chosen for the opera back home—a sky-blue skirt and matching fitted jacket trimmed in fancy white braiding. I could tell she was determined to make an impression on someone. I had a feeling it was Worth.

"I'm glad I can provide a diversion," I said, though I'd selfishly brought her along as a distraction for me. It wouldn't do for Worth and me to be alone together today, to continue the proximity that encouraged my frequent thoughts of him.

"You selected the most hideous costume in your armoire." Marie Austen scrunched her nose, appraising the pastel-pink walking gown I'd had for two seasons. "The color washes you out completely." She shrugged, not at all considering I'd worn it for that very reason. "I suppose it's your decision, though, and what does it truly matter now anyway? You have Worth."

"I could say the same of you," I said. "You have Mr. Gibbins."

"Don't be ridiculous. I told you he disgusts me and that has not changed. Perhaps I could hire someone to stand in for me . . . intimately." She whispered the last bit. "Or perhaps I could feign some dreadful deformity."

Mr. Leslie cleared his throat.

"Mr. Delafield has asked that we meet him at a farm he is considering for purchase. He'll drive you to town. Mr. Seely has arranged your visit with his architect, Mr. McKibbin, at the temporary office of Southern Ferro Concrete, and I will collect you at one so you'll both be back at camp in time for luncheon."

"Very well," I said.

We turned down another dirt road, this one full of potholes from rain in the spring and ice in the winter, paralleling a railroad track. A valley stretched out from Marie Austen's window.

"Where in the world are you taking us, Mr. Leslie?" Marie Austen asked.

Up ahead, porches were being constructed on an immense brick mansion. A weathered sign reading *Blue Ridge Terrace Sanitorium* was mounted on two vertical poles between the construction and the tracks.

"It's just up this way he said." Mr. Leslie leaned over the dash and slowed, then resumed his speed.

Marie Austen began to wave at a group of men stacking lumber on the rail platform who had stopped to stare at our auto.

"Suppose you were born to one of these men," she mused. "Or

perhaps married one. Would you appear as worn as they? People say the poor age much quicker than we do."

"I'm not sure." I'd never thought of our peers in Red Dragon that way, though it made sense. Worry and poverty and hard work were taxing on a body. Then again, there were also variations in how each person aged. Mother's face had always been luminous.

With the auto windows shadowed by mountains on my side, I could see my reflection. My skin was perfect beneath my sailor's hat adorned with a simple pink ribbon, my lips soft and full. Last night Sylvia had spent nearly an hour applying lemon extract to my face to lighten my complexion, followed by Nyal's Face Cream and a rough lip scrub that she claimed would bring out the natural rosiness of my lips.

"Oh, look at that poor woman." Marie Austen went on waving, her gaze now fixed on a woman in an old-fashioned bonnet and filthy brown skirt sweeping the unfinished upper porch of the sanitorium. "It's proof that they're right. She's likely our age, but she looks sixty."

"I'm surprised Mr. Grove hasn't put a stop to the building of this one," Mr. Leslie said. "When Mr. Delafield was going over the directions last night, he told me it's the one hundred and twenty-eighth facility in town. Mr. Grove has purchased and removed near thirty of the largest sanitoriums, though many refuse to sell to him."

"I can understand why Mr. Grove is worried for this town," Marie Austen said. "I don't suppose I'd want to live here knowing the streets are roamed by those with consumption. My aunt Mary died of it before I was born. Father said it was a horrible way to go."

"Indeed," Mr. Leslie said. I'd never seen anyone with tuberculosis —at least that I knew of—but I read the papers enough to know of its perils. "One of the other chauffeurs, one of the local men, said they try to contain the sick to their own facilities, but the disease is creeping into the town's population. It's affecting the working-men and some companies are finding it difficult to maintain their businesses as they can't locate workers who are well enough. And then there's the worry that men are hiding their illness and working regardless. Not to mention there are no facilities at all for Black citizens if they fall ill. There's a boardinghouse being built now somewhere or another for the Black sick, but none as it stands."

"Of course, a man wouldn't admit his infection unless he was in utter peril. A man out of work means his family cannot eat. Are they free? These sanitoriums?" I asked. I thought of my father's friends who often found themselves sick with what Doc called coughing flu. Despite the breathing treatments Doc offered and his advice to remain home until they'd recovered, they rarely did either. The treatments cost a significant amount, and the Elkhorns didn't compensate a man for convalescence.

"I'm sure they are quite expensive," Mr. Leslie said.

"What fortune that we are tucked away from the population here," Marie Austen said. "Perhaps Mr. Grove and Mr. Seely should have located their fine hotel elsewhere."

"And leave the town they love to wither? It is breathtaking here," I said.

Mr. Leslie slowed again and directed the auto up a steep hill. Scraggly tree branches slapped and scraped across the metal, and I gritted my teeth to keep my spine from quaking at the sound.

When the landscape finally planed, we found ourselves in a small clearing. Ahead was a ramshackle barn, a clapboard home nearly overtaken by some sort of vine, and a handful of cows roaming freely in the high grass. A strange auto that looked a bit like a walrus head had been affixed to a fine sailboat with wheels sat vacant and out of place between the house and barn.

"Ah. That must be Mr. Seely's Panhard et Levassor his chauffeur was telling me about last night," Mr. Leslie said as he navigated our auto toward it.

"It's quite ugly," I said. The vehicle had a long nose, round eyes, and metal hooks protruding from the front bumper. Two curved tufted-leather seats had been fitted into the polished mahogany body and there were no doors.

"Don't say so to Mr. Seely. It's the first of its kind, a skiff design handmade by Jean-Henri Labourdette in Paris to be windproof and aerodynamic," Mr. Leslie said.

I glanced out the rear window. Worth was nowhere to be found. Mr. Leslie stopped behind the other auto.

"I will not get out in this," Marie Austen said, her nose scrunching at the veritable prairie around us. The scent of manure hung heavy in the air.

"Perhaps Worth is looking at this land for Mr. Gibbins, a gift for your wedding." I couldn't help but laugh thinking of Marie Austen emerging from the rotting door of the home to tend the cows.

"Mr. Gibbins is welcome to live here. In fact, I'd celebrate it. I'll be living at Rues D'Or." She tipped her chin up.

"You found it. I was beginning to worry." Worth's voice sounded and I looked past Mr. Leslie to find him coming around the side of the barn. He was in a black suit similar to the one he wore yesterday, and as he waded through the grass toward our auto, he tipped his bowler. Marie Austen sighed.

"To me, he's Jane Austen's Mr. Darcy made manifest," she said. "Traipsing across the moors."

I looked at her, sure she would come to her senses and laugh. She did not.

"Yes," I said. "He's quite handsome." My throat was strangely tight.

Mr. Leslie started to remove himself from the auto, but Worth held up his hand.

"I can open her door." He strode around the front of the vehicle and past Mr. Leslie to my window. He smiled when our eyes met. "What do you think of the land?" His eyes shifted to Marie Austen beside me, and a look of confusion played on his face.

"Beyond the barn and the house, it's quite beautiful," I said. "What do you think of it?"

"It has nice trees, a few streams, no view, however. Could be of benefit to a sawmill or one of the dreaded sanitoriums Mr. Grove loathes," Worth said. "Lovely to see you, Miss Kipp."

"And you as well, Mr. Delafield. I hope you don't mind my

coming along. I begged Belle to let me. You see, I was so rattled by the happenings of last night, I didn't want to be left alone," she said. She drew her lips into a pout.

"Of course not," Worth said, but his expression said otherwise. He clicked my door open and held his hand out to me. I took it and stepped out into the tall grass. The blades slid under my skirt, prickling my skin. I must have made some movement to indicate my discomfort, because in the next instant, Worth swept me into his arms and carried me toward the walrus boat masquerading as an auto.

"Why did you allow her to come along?" he whispered. I could feel the warmth of him against me, the thump of his heart, too, and an echo of the elation I'd felt when he held me the night before. I'd made the right choice in having Marie Austen come along. She was needed here. Absolutely required. At least until I was comfortable, used to his proximity, and could feel around him the way I felt around a dear friend. "She is going to cause a scene and distract you from your research."

"I felt bad," I said finally. "She's had such a rough few days, and—"

"Caused by her own folly," he said. "She hasn't weathered a hurricane, Belle. She is one." He set me down in the front seat of the auto.

"I brought you something." He smiled and reached behind me, extracting a new leather portfolio fitted with notebooks and two Waterman's fountain pens, the same as the one he'd lent me the day before. He placed them in my lap.

"I don't know what to say." I ran my fingers over the smooth leather, barely preventing myself from opening it and holding the new paper to my nose. "You're the most thoughtful."

"I'm glad you like them. I knew you couldn't procure the items necessary for your story out at the camp."

"Not unless I took to writing on great pieces of bark with berry ink like I did as a child."

"I did the same. Which berries did you use? We always used Mother's blueberries."

"I'm not entirely sure. Some blueberries, wild blackberries, elder-berries." I smiled and grasped one of the fine silver pens. "This is much better. Thank you."

"You're welcome." He stood there for a moment, looking like he wanted to say something else. He ran his hand along the pol-ished wood and finally met my gaze. "I want to make you happy. You're . . . You will be . . . the only family I have. I've been alone these last few years, and I've had no one to call home."

His eyes were so earnest, so full of sorrow, and my heart under-stood it. I was certain in that moment that his family was exactly who I was meant to be.

I cleared my throat.

"Here," I said. "I'm the only family you have here. The others still live, and though you can't see them, they're—" I reached up and rested my palm on his heart. His hand reflexively lifted to the back of mine. "They may not be here physically, but they love you still." He looked away. "You treasured them as I will treasure you."

Worth's fingers tightened lightly around my hand, and he shook his head.

"I did treasure them, but if they were here now, I know they couldn't possibly still love me."

"Are you going to leave me in the auto?" Marie Austen yelled.

Worth jerked as though her voice had shot him, and I took my hand from his chest. He blinked and turned away from me to go help Marie Austen from the auto. His words echoed in my mind. I hadn't any idea what had become of his family. Papa hadn't said a word about the circumstances that led to his parents' deaths.

"Oh, Mr. Delafield, put me down. Put me down this instant." Marie Austen squealed and shrieked and threw her arms tighter around Worth's neck as he carried her through the long grass to-ward me.

He set her in the back seat, walked around to the other side, and stepped into the auto behind the steering wheel.

"We're set, Mr. Leslie!" Worth shouted. Mr. Leslie nodded and turned the auto the direction we'd come from.

"We'll head downtown now, ladies," Worth went on. The bench seat was small, suitable for Mr. and Mrs. Seely, but not at all constructed for a man Worth's size. Our legs were nearly touching, my skirt settling against his black trousers.

He'd become rigid in the moments since he gifted me the portfolio and pens. It was the same sort of shift that had happened in the rafters. I knew the feeling well—the way the memory of something terrible faded to the point where you could breathe again only to emerge in a word, a look, an object, and shatter your soul anew. I hated that I'd brought it to mind two days in a row—whatever it was.

We rode under the trees, dappled by the early sun, following Mr. Leslie. This auto was open air without a top to shield us from the wayward branches, and I ducked while Marie Austen chattered about how whoever owned this piece of land had neglected their duties.

"I suppose that person is me," Worth said.

"I thought you were only considering it." She made a sound of disgust as she swatted a thin dogwood branch I'd just avoided.

"The man was eager to sell it, and the price was so low that to pass it by would have been foolish," he replied.

The trees gave way to the wider dirt road and Worth turned right. His body was absolutely straight, his eyes trained on the road, his jaw clenched.

"Let's wave," Marie Austen said from the back seat as we passed the new sanitorium. She lifted her arms and shouted greetings at the bewildered workers still stacking lumber on the rail platform.

I clutched the portfolio and closed the inches between Worth and me, leaning close to him.

"I'm sorry," I whispered, hoping he could hear my voice above the engine and the wind and Marie Austen's shouts. "I know what I said prompted a painful memory, and I can see it must be unbearable."

His eyes shifted to mine briefly. I watched him swallow and he finally shook his head.

"You've done nothing wrong," he said softly.

The road snaked down a small hill and we were on flat ground again. Ahead, another set of railroad tracks crossed the road and on each side were two great factories. Dark smoke puffed from pipes on both sides and an intolerable rotten, metallic stench tinged with firewood began to settle over my nose and mouth.

"Here." Worth extracted two silk handkerchiefs from inside his jacket pocket and handed one to Marie Austen and one to me. "Put them over your face or you'll not smell anything else for the rest of the day."

"I know," Marie Austen said loudly. "It's a different sort of smell, but just as pungent as Mr. Newbold's wells."

"These are machinery and lumber," Worth said, gesturing to the right and then the left.

The factory on our right boasted two enormous barnlike structures. Train cars full of what I imagined was steel idled at the entrance to the first building in front of a ramp that stretched two stories high to an open loft. *Carolina Machinery Company* was painted in red across the top.

"I sold that land to the English Lumber Company over there a few years ago. They're doing quite well." Worth tipped his head to the factory on our left, a larger operation than the machinery mill with six rectangular buildings that looked like they each occupied at least a quarter mile.

Less than a mile past the mills were several rows of small residences made of concrete block. Some were painted white, but the majority remained a lazy concrete gray. The mill operators must have employed the same architect, because their homes across the street from each other were nearly identical, both done in a Queen Anne–style that looked almost like a Christmas gingerbread house.

"However did you come across this town? Beyond the few men we know taking to it, you must admit it's quite unknown. You must like it a great deal to have such a vast personal holding," Marie Austen said.

I stared at the residences lining the streets so Worth wouldn't notice my interest in his answer. The number of white frocks I saw hurrying into work at what looked like tuberculosis boardinghouses was shocking. No sick lingered on the porches, however. Perhaps it was required that the patients remain in bed until midmorning.

"Beyond the land I sell, I have personal holdings in twelve states, most over one thousand acres." I turned at the sound of his voice. It was strained and his knuckles were white on the steering wheel. "I invest in areas poised to boom. Asheville is convenient to much of the country and was well on its way to much growth before the influx of sanitoriums. If Grove and Seely's hotel works, the town will be back on track." He paused and squinted. Marie Austen seemed satisfied with his answer and tipped her head toward the blue sky and closed her eyes.

"I discovered Asheville because of my father. He was at risk of respiratory failure due to acute severe asthma and his doctor advised a high elevation to remedy it." This was said in a much lower tone, intended just for me it seemed, but he didn't turn his head to see if I'd heard him.

"Papa said your father was a fine landholder too." I knew there was a chance I shouldn't reply, that I'd already said something that encouraged the remembrance of sadness, but he'd been the one to bring him up.

"Yes, and the reason I can't claim I'm from anywhere. I was born in Cleveland, and in my early years he manufactured carriages, but by the time I was six we were traveling the country, staying in a place for a few months at most so Father could go to the next town, buy the next land. Mother and I were lonely. When I was eight, Father bought some land in Gas City, land Shipley bought from him." Worth turned right when the next road intersected. I could see the town up ahead, the courthouse flag flapping. He looked at me.

"And now, the man traveling 'round the country is me. I cannot keep it up, and I am established enough that I no longer must. I've set roots in Charlotte, and though I will travel at times, I will not subject you to the life I have lived." He cleared his throat. "You were nervous to ask me about him. Don't be afraid to ask questions. I might not want to discuss the answers right away, and I might find myself retreating, but I will hear you and I will reply to every one when I am able."

"I was born in the wrong place," Marie Austen suddenly proclaimed. "I loathe little towns like this, like Gas City. Don't you ever long for the thrill of New York or London or Paris? The possibility of what it means to be surrounded by thousands of strangers, no one paying you a bit of mind, no one able to track you down?"

Worth pulled the auto to a stop in front of a two-story brick building with rock-faced stone lintels, an arched window in the center of the second story, and cast iron piers. The side read W. H. Westall Building Supplies.

Marie Austen suddenly clutched my shoulder and pleaded, "Please don't let him take me. I can't bear it." I followed her gaze across the street to see Mr. Gibbins, who was wearing a grin and occupying a stone park bench alone. "I've fled from him, but he's found me out with ease. I want him gone."

"He is your fiancé," Worth said. He silenced the engine.

Mr. Gibbins crossed the street.

"I don't want her to faint again," I whispered to Worth.

"If she does, we'll find salts." He smiled.

"But I find him despicable," Marie Austen snapped under her breath. "Please."

"A marriage proposal is an offering of what a man is willing to give, and its acceptance is sealed by the lady. It is not a prison sentence in which you have no choice," Worth said.

"I didn't have a choice," Marie Austen said. "My father was planning to disown me if I did not accept this horrid troll."

"As horrible as the alternative would be, you've chosen Mr. Gibbins, and I suppose making his acquaintance will be required at some point," I said, though I did feel terribly sorry for her.

"Good morning, Mr. Delafield, Miss Newbold." Mr. Gibbins's attention fixed on Marie Austen still languishing in the back of the strange-looking auto. "Your mother told me where you were heading, Marie, darling, and I thought perhaps we could go for a walk. I don't care for fishing."

"Marie Austen," she said, staring down at her skirt instead of at her intended. "It's a double name, Mr. Gibbins, and I'm afraid I don't have the shoes for a walk."

"Take Seely's auto here for a drive. He won't mind," Worth said, stepping out of the auto. Marie Austen's head jerked up and she glared at him. "Belle and I will be here for several hours." He walked around to my door and helped me out.

The morning's conversations had remedied my earlier reservations about being alone with Worth. It was clear now that our intentions had always been the same, that any sort of magnetism I'd felt had actually been elation that we had both found family again.

Worth clasped my hand.

"I'll return it in perfect order, Delafield," Mr. Gibbins said, taking his place behind the wheel. He turned in his seat and held out his hand. "Would you care to join me up front, dear?"

"No, I don't suppose I would," Marie Austen said. The engine roared to life and Mr. Gibbins steered the walrus boat down the road, leaving Worth and me on the sidewalk.

# CHAPTER THIRTEEN

"How do they find anything in here?" Building supplies—nails and hinges, lumber and rebar—littered the sizable room along with a heavy amount of dust. I'd already sneezed four times and we'd barely walked through the door. Worth handed me the handkerchief I'd used passing the factories.

"They don't. Not anymore," he said. "Mr. Westall is older now and had a fall several years back. He thought he'd return to the shop, but I suppose he's given up that thought." Worth started walking down an aisle, the only clear space in the entire room. "He's a friend of Seely's and lent Mr. McKibbin and Southern Ferro Concrete a space in the back to use as their home office."

We reached the back of the shop and Worth knocked on one of the etched double doors. The scrollwork was stacked with dust and the small brass knobs were tarnished.

"Come on in. I'm just switching out the plans." I'd never heard an accent so Southern but knew immediately it originated somewhere in Alabama or perhaps Mississippi.

Worth turned the knob and a spill of light blinded me.

"Good to see you again, McKibbin. It's been a piece," Worth said. I blinked, my eyes adjusting to the sudden brightness. The back section of the store boasted a sort of greenhouse look, though of course, there were no plants. Instead, long weathered tables lined the windowed walls displaying pages and pages of blueprints. In the middle of the room stood an enormous banker's desk and Mr. McKibbin behind it.

"It certainly has. It was down in Atlanta, wasn't it? You were with your father at Seely's old place." Mr. McKibbin was a slight man with wiry curly gray hair and a remarkably wrinkleless face that bore no mustache or beard. Worth reached out to take his hands.

"Yes. Right before Seely sold the paper and moved." He turned to me. "This is Miss Belle Newbold, Shipley Newbold's—"

"Yes, yes. I've heard all about her from Seely when he came by to tell me about her project this morning. Lovely to meet you, Miss Newbold. I find it unusual and refreshing that a woman of your status has taken up the pen."

"Thank you. I have always loved to write and am tremendously thankful for the opportunity." I smiled. I practically had to. The sun, hidden so much in the winter months, was now shining unhindered through the glass ceiling and the glass walls. As ridiculous as it was, I felt much like a caterpillar suddenly unveiled as a butterfly, shedding the darkness of winter, the shackles of a gentlewoman, to fly into the light, into a new purpose.

"How long have you been in the business of architecture?" I asked. I glanced at the renderings on the tables, longing to look them over.

"I suppose since I was fifteen or so. My father had a machine shop in Calhoun County, down in Alabama, and my brother Lucius and I worked there from the time we could walk. Neither of us were interested in the machine business, unfortunately, and about that time, buildings started popping up around town. I'd spend the time I was supposed to be helping with fabricating staring out the window at a structure that had just been built and drawing what I imagined should go beside it."

I opened the portfolio, folded the front against the back, and clicked the top off one of the pens. The origins of a person's passion were always interesting, and I wanted to document everything I could, not only about the hotel but about the people who built it.

"How did your father feel about your passion being architecture and not machines?" I asked as I wrote his first answer.

"He was mighty disappointed that I didn't want to take over

the business. Especially because Lucius had the same interests as me." Mr. McKibbin chuckled. "Then again, it was my father's fault that I have the skills I do. If you consider it for a moment, it's much the same thing. When he thought of his machines, he saw them in parts and figures at near the same time he envisioned the finished product. He gave me not only creativity but a precise mind."

"In that way his business continued on after all," I said. "When did you begin your career in earnest? Was there anyone particularly instrumental in giving you your start?"

"Indeed. I'd come to Atlanta in '92 with my brothers hoping for work in architecture, but there was none to be had, so I found a job as a carpenter with Woodward Lumber Company. It was a fine post, nothing I'd dreamed about, of course, but it paid. I worked there for ten years. By that time, I'd nearly written off architecture as something I'd never do when I happened upon Willis Denny at a meat counter of all places. He'd just broken ground on the Piedmont Hotel, and all of the city was abuzz about it." Mr. McKibbin shook his head.

"Ever have a moment that you see as a stroke of luck, pure and simple? Well, this was mine. I told him how much I admired his work and that I was an aspiring architect. He told me he needed a draftsman and that if I could come down to his office the next day and draw a sample for him proficiently, he'd hire me. I did and he kept his word." He smiled.

"Nearly lost the post the next week, though. Unbeknownst to me, I'd been hired over a more seasoned architect whose father was in the news business. He was mighty angry about being overlooked and had his father go to my hometown to dig up anything scandalous he could find—and he succeeded. I'm named after my grandfather, see, who was a bank robber of mostly petty amounts. I suppose the reporter didn't understand that we weren't the same person. When Willis called me into his office to discuss my previous role as a thief, I nearly collapsed. Thankfully, it was all sorted in a matter of moments, and we had a good laugh about it." Goose bumps prickled my arms. "Here's a lesson for the two of you—be wary of newspapermen. They are often unscrupulous."

I suddenly felt faint, the fear of Mr. Thorp returning with the intention to ruin me—and Mother inadvertently—intruding once again. Panic gripped my neck and paralyzed my lungs.

"Willis Denny trained several prominent architects, correct? I thought I heard that Eugene Wachendorff and Neel Reid studied under him too." Worth's voice sounded, and I swallowed, coming to my senses enough to record Mr. McKibbin's answer. I forced the prospect of peril from my mind. Of course, there was a chance Mr. Thorp recalled that I was from West Virginia, but I'd never told him the name of the town we were from, and no one, not even Papa, knew our former last name. Surely the limited information he was privy to minimized the likelihood of our discovery or would, at the very least, delay him considerably.

"It's a terrible shame about the pneumonia taking him at such a young age, but what a tremendous legacy for such a short life," Worth continued. I took a breath and calmed.

"Yes. He was quite remarkable, a visionary," Mr. McKibbin said. "It was shocking when he passed, and the whole office sort of wandered around in a daze for months." He shook his head. "The world can be quite unfair. But for all the heartache, at least there's beauty too. I try to think of that when I feel the dim seeping in."

Worth had stilled, not only in voice but in face, in movement altogether. He stared above Mr. McKibbin's head toward the vacant back alley, but I was sure he wasn't truly seeing the scene in front of him. His expression was blank, and the vibrant blue of his eyes seemed to have darkened to gray.

"You're right, Mr. McKibbin. There is tremendous beauty to be had here. And if you can't find something to marvel at, you dream it up and build it. Isn't that right?" I smiled, thankful to find my earlier panic eased, and gestured to the blueprints lining the room. I wanted to ask Worth what troubled him, but given where we were, the best thing I could do was carry on without drawing attention toward his heaviness of heart.

Mr. McKibbin nodded and turned for a moment, I suppose to survey all the plans he'd created. I reached out and placed my hand on Worth's arm. My palm rested on his sleeve for a second at most, just so he'd know I recognized his pain. He blinked and his lips lifted slightly.

"Which project is your favorite?" I asked Mr. McKibbin, who had now rotated back toward us.

"That I'm currently working on?"

"Of your career," I said.

His eyes widened and he chuckled. "I don't have children, but I suppose that's much like asking a father who his favorite is," he said. "I also must apologize. I realized a moment ago that I should offer you both a seat, but I failed to bring additional chairs in from the supply store."

"I'll go get a few. I'm only here to be Miss Newbold's assistant in any case," Worth said.

Assistant. How easily he could have said chaperone, a term that would have made me feel both childish and incompetent.

"Thank you," I said. Our eyes met and he smiled, this time the sort that altered his face into something like sunshine.

Worth strode to the double doors and disappeared into the dusty supply shop.

"To answer your question, I suppose I should say Seely and Grove's inn," Mr. McKibbin said. He grunted and gestured for me to sit at his desk. "That's the point of your story, after all, is it not?" Ordinarily, I would have refused the seat. He was an older man and my legs were youthful, but today I was writing, and balancing the portfolio on the crook of my arm didn't make for neat penmanship.

"The point of the story is to give life to the construction of such a place. That includes the interests of its builders." I sat on the weathered cherry chair and smoothed my skirt before settling my portfolio on the tidy desktop. "I want to know which of your projects has meant the most to you."

Worth materialized in the doorway, carrying two ladder-back chairs.

"It took some looking, but I found these upstairs. I tried to dust them off as best I could, but I'm afraid we'll have the outline of the chair on our suits regardless, Mr. McKibbin."

Mr. McKibbin laughed. "For the first time in my life I've employed a maid, and she's grown quite used to the grime adorning my clothes," he said.

Worth set the chairs in front of the desk and the men sat.

"Actually, Miss Newbold, I do, in fact, have a personal favorite project. My parents' house. It wasn't a complicated structure, just four bedrooms and two washrooms, made of Alabama brick, but it's special because my father asked me to draw it." Mr. McKibbin paused and shook his head.

"For years after I moved to Atlanta, we didn't speak. He was angry with Lucius and me for leaving him, Mother, the business. But one day in early December '02, he walked into my office, apologized, and said it was clear that I was born to be an architect, that he would love for my brother and me to draw up a new home for him and Mother." He cleared his throat. "Professionally, of course, my favorite is this new hotel. It was an overwhelmingly large project, but a challenge makes the finished product that much more satisfying."

"Would you tell me how you went about it?" I asked.

"As with most structures I'm commissioned for, the client has an idea of the look they'd like. Seely and Grove had inquired of several renowned builders, but none were entirely right. You see, Seely went out to Yellowstone some five years back and saw the inn Reamer designed for the park."

"It's a magnificent piece of architecture," Worth said. "I was there last October when I came through to purchase a ranch in Montana."

"Yes, a testament to what one can construct using locally obtained materials. The entire place was built with lodgepole pine and rhyolite stones from the surrounding land. Seely wanted to do the same with Grove Park Inn, admittedly because he was reminded of his love for Yellowstone by Henry Ives Cobb, who was initially contracted as the architect for this project. I believe he submitted a much different design, though Seely retained Cobb's use of granite boulders and a red tile roof in his rendering. Both, I imagine, relied on the works and theories of William Morris, but with a naturalistic bent."

"I know we're all elated that you are the architect in Mr. Cobb's stead, but why did he depart the project?" I asked.

"I don't know, but I would assume it had to do with fees. Mr. Cobb is a New Yorker, a man used to obtaining rather large commissions for work that I'll do for significantly less." Mr. McKibbin smiled.

"I know you already knew Mr. Seely from Atlanta, but how did you obtain the post?" I asked.

"Seely knew his idea would require a great deal of strength in order to hold the heavy boulders. Southern Ferro, the company I am contracted with, is known for its reinforced concrete frames, and such a frame is vital for a design like this; it is the skeleton of the entire structure. Most buildings can be framed in steel, but in this case, the steel cannot carry the total tensile load, so both concrete and steel are required. We cast the whole of it in a single operation, the beams and the columns in situ, on-site. It is an important but rare skill that not many companies are versed in. If this sort of construction is attempted incorrectly, the whole building will be damaged."

"I can imagine," I said. The strength of the frame had to simulate the might of mountains. I thought of the poured concrete idling in sheets on-site. Those must have been internal walls, nothing structural.

"Here, let me show you my blueprints." He stood with some hesitation and walked over to the first table inside the double doors.

I picked up my portfolio and pen and followed. Worth did too.

"Do you mind?" he asked me as we walked toward Mr. McKibbin. "I'm interested, but if I'm in your way—"

"Of course I don't mind," I said.

It was clear at first glance that the plans had taken tremendous thought. The hotel was an enormous undertaking, after all, and

Seely and Grove's dream of transforming Asheville from a veritable infirmary to a traveler's escape was resting on the manifestation of Grove Park Inn.

"Before I show you all of these, I'll preface by saying that the central part of the hotel is four stories tall, four bays wide, with two stories in the attic. Those attic stories will feature eyelid dormer windows."

"Seely loves the middle window in the attic. It boasts a most magnificent view," Worth said.

The expanse of blue mountain ridges and coordinating sky was still fresh in my mind, and even recalling the sight filled me with peace.

"On the other floors, we'll have double casement windows. Granite lintels on the second and third stories. The ground floor boasts a three-bay porte cochere with a shed roof. Of course, you know, as I just mentioned, that the frame is reinforced concrete with native granite overlays." He cleared his throat. "Up top we'll have a double-story hipped roof made of clay tiles. Over the south wing, where the guest rooms are located, we've installed a glass ridge skylight from Tennessee."

"It is a gorgeous view there as well," I said.

"I thought I'd lost her yesterday, McKibbin, only to find her in the atrium. Before I arrived, she'd been lying on the scaffolding looking up at the skylight," Worth said.

"I don't suppose I blame her. It's a beautiful piece of glass and the sky up here in Carolina is a sort of blue they don't have down in Georgia—Alabama either," Mr. McKibbin said.

"I agree. I thought the same when I tried out the scaffolding myself." Worth laughed under his breath.

Mr. McKibbin pointed at the draft paper.

"Most of these are drawn floor by floor starting with the foundation here. This one isn't so interesting, but it shows the dimensions, lays out where the footers go, things like that." He transitioned to the second table.

"This is where the enjoyment for me truly begins. Here's the basement, which I believe Seely mentioned you toured yesterday, Miss Newbold."

The paper boasted an intricate sketch of exactly what I'd seen, though I hadn't noticed that the middle and south of the hotel were closed off—a boiler room of sorts. Precise lines indicated that the servants' dining room was on the north side of the basement, across the hall from the children's dining room, but we hadn't seen that either. It was only accessed through a small door from the grill room located directly behind the pool, or the plunge, as Mr. McKibbin had written, on the east wall of the inn. In front of the pool on the west side of the structure were the public baths and the barbershop. Farther to the south, the bowling alleys completed the points of interest in the basement.

"We thought to place the plunge and the dining rooms on the opposite side, the south side, but more support is needed in that area," Mr. McKibbin went on.

We went around the room, Mr. McKibbin talking, my fingers writing furiously, and by the time we returned to the blueprint for the roof, we were all the way around the small greenhouse room and I'd covered nearly fifteen pages.

"I'm amazed by you," I said when he concluded his blueprint tour. "I can't fathom the workings of such a brain. What if you'd decided to remain at your father's machine shop? Imagine the wasting of a talent like this, Worth."

I turned to Worth then because I knew that when one flattered men of an ordinary sort, they didn't know what to say. Ordinary men were used to being scolded, to being told they were disposable. They didn't smile knowingly and nod as men of Papa's ilk did.

"I'm certainly glad you were at that butcher those years ago," Worth said.

"So am I, though it occurs to me now and again that there were more times than I can count when I nearly forfeited this love of mine either because I'd tired of trying or because I was afraid."

"You persevered anyway. That's what matters," I said. "I'm doing the same. I haven't picked up a pen this way since my father died seven years ago. He was the one who always encouraged my writing, and then he was gone." I swallowed hard and looked down at my paper filled with notes. "It feels good to write again, especially about men like you. Without you, Grove Park Inn would never be."

Mr. McKibbin laughed. "I'm not certain that's true. I told you Mr. Cobb was hired before me, and I'm certain they would have found someone else if I couldn't do what they envisioned."

"Perhaps," I said, "but it wouldn't be *this* Grove Park Inn, your Grove Park Inn, this wonder of a place that people will marvel at for centuries."

He smiled. "I suppose you're right. You know, as time goes on, the architect is often forgotten on projects like this. It's always the financier, the originator, who is remembered for the structure."

"I know." I thought of my father and his peers. I thought of the many times he'd saved others with a kind word, an inspiring story, or an idea for mine improvement. I thought of the obituary that praised everything he'd done and the man he was. He had never seen it. If he was valued by Red Dragon Mining Company, he surely never knew it.

I looked at Mr. McKibbin, who was now going around rolling up the blueprints he'd laid out for me. He deserved to know he was important while he was still living, that his contribution wouldn't be forgotten. I closed my portfolio and a sudden sense of understanding washed through me. This story was meant for me.

"Are you ready?" Worth asked. He extracted his gold pocket watch and glanced at the time. "Mr. Leslie should be here."

"Yes," I said. "Thank you for your time, Mr. McKibbin."

"And yours, Miss Newbold," he said. "Good to see you again, Delafield."

"You as well," Worth said.

I followed Worth through the double doors and into the dusty supply store. I sneezed and pulled out Worth's soiled silk from earlier.

"Bless you," he said.

I sneezed again.

"Bless you. Belle?" Worth turned to face me mere feet before the door that would lead us onto the street and out of the dust. He opened his mouth and then shut it again.

"What is it?" I asked.

He looked down and then, as though he'd suddenly gathered some sort of strength, back at me.

"They've invited me for dinner at camp tonight." His voice sounded tense, and he shoved his hands in his pockets. "I have already declined on account of work, though you know it isn't the truth. I-I told you I haven't been back to my land in over three years, and even the thought of seeing it again makes my heart accelerate to the point I worry it may give out."

I grasped his arms. He withdrew his hands from his pockets and took my fingers in his. They were clammy and his body had gone rigid. My nose itched with an impending sneeze, but I sniffed to stifle it.

"Do you *want* to come for dinner?" I asked.

"No," he said. "I can think of nothing I'd like less. But I used to love that place. I used to crave the feel of it. Before . . . it was my favorite place in the world. I suppose hearing you and Mr. McKibbin has made me consider that I should come to terms with it."

Over Worth's shoulder, I could see Mr. Leslie pull the Model T to a stop outside. I wondered why he was here and why Mr. Gibbins and Marie Austen hadn't returned with Mr. Seely's auto.

"If you want to face it, I will be there with you," I said. "I'll not leave your side."

"If I come and depart suddenly, know it's not you, Belle." His face hardened and his brows furrowed. "Then again, perhaps I won't go at all. It's not the same as you or Mr. McKibbin, see."

"What happened there?" I asked softly.

"I can't speak of it. I can barely think of it. I promise you, I will tell you. Just give me a bit of time."

"Come anyway," I said. "We will confront it together."

"You don't know what you're facing. It's unfair to ask."

"You weren't asking."

The door behind him clicked open.

"Oh, Miss Newbold, Mr. Delafield. There you are," Mr. Leslie said. "I just wanted you to know I'd arrived." He paused and glanced at us. "And I'm afraid I come bearing some bad news. Mr. Gibbins let Miss Kipp take a turn at the wheel of Seely's auto, and I'm afraid she misread the edge of the road and ran over some large stones, bending two of the wheels quite badly."

"Are Gibbins and Miss Kipp all right?" Worth asked.

"Yes. I found them just as I was coming into town for some gasoline. I took them back to camp. Miss Kipp was quite irate with Mr. Gibbins, so I imagine she's retired to her tent," Mr. Leslie said.

"Whyever would she be angry with him? He let her drive," I said.

"I . . . Well, it seems . . . I shouldn't say," he said.

"We all know you overhear everything we discuss."

"Very well. It seems that Mr. Gibbins assumed she held some sort of affection for him, them being engaged and all, and he reached to hold her hand at the moment she lost control."

Worth laughed. "If she can't get up the nerve to hold his hand, what do—"

He stopped midsentence and looked at me, likely having forgotten he was in the company of a woman.

"I've gone by and alerted Mr. Seely's butler that the auto will need to be taken for repairs. Mr. Gibbins insists on paying for it, though if I were him, I'd allow Mr. Kipp to cover the cost," Mr. Leslie said.

"Mr. Kipp is giving him a palatial estate on top of Marie Austen's sizable dowry in exchange for him taking her hand. I suppose the cost of a wheel repair is much less," I said before sneezing once again.

"In that case, it's the least he can do. Fred is going to be terribly upset. That auto is quite a prize to him," Worth said. "Shall we depart before your sneezing turns you to vapor?" He laughed and opened the door and held it for Mr. Leslie and me.

Scattered clouds had rolled in, a pillowy one overtaking the sun. I shivered in the slight chill and held my portfolio to my chest as we made our way to the auto.

"Will you be going back to Mr. Seely's or will you be joining the rest for dinner, Mr. Delafield?" Mr. Leslie asked Worth as he opened the door for us. "I know they've all been hoping you can break away from your work for a little cheer. Mr. Ford has even designated a tent for you next to his in case you change your mind."

I gathered my skirt in my hands and stepped into the auto. Worth hesitated, then glanced at me.

"Fred and Evelyn, Edwin too, are due in St. Louis for the remainder of the week. They're planning a new manufacturing facility for the Paris Medicine Company there, so there's no one to notify of my plans here in town," Worth said. "I'll join the Vagabonds for dinner, perhaps for the night."

# CHAPTER FOURTEEN

I'd spoken to Mr. Leslie the entire way to camp. We'd discussed the weather—it was fine but chilly. We discussed the dinner—the fish were to be boiled over the fire. We discussed the new reporter Mr. Firestone had procured from the local paper to cover the happenings of the camping trip—he was quite old and lacked personality. Anything to distract from the fact that Worth hadn't uttered a word since he got into the auto. He'd barely moved. He sat straight, his head skimming the roof, his eyes fixed ahead, his hands fisted at his sides. I'd thought to take his hand, to say something encouraging, but there was no privacy here.

Out the window, the sky had lightened again, washing everything in optimism. Even the workers idling at the lumberyard train depot seemed happy. We turned left, onto the drive that marked the start of Worth's property.

"Have you been out here in a while, Mr. Delafield?" Mr. Leslie asked.

Worth's face had gone completely white. I scooted across the bench seat, situated my skirt slightly over Worth's hand to evade Mr. Leslie's eyes, and wrapped my hand around his fist. His fingers didn't move to clasp mine. His head didn't turn to meet my gaze.

"He hasn't been here in some time, Mr. Leslie. Work has kept him away," I said for Worth. "You'll have to excuse Mr. Delafield right now. He is prone to terrible migraines and it's clear one has come on." I hated lying, but it wasn't my place to tell Mr. Leslie the true particulars of Worth's pain. Few understood the way panic could silence one's voice and make one's brain swell and swirl to the point that little beyond the fear made sense.

"I'll send for the nurse the moment I park. I believe she traveled with several Zundra inhalers. They're quite effective, especially if the headache's source is a spring allergy."

"Yes. He has several allergies," I lied again, feeling the need to keep talking so Worth could settle his thoughts without worrying about conversation. "Everything's blooming, of course. The redbuds, dogwoods, tulips, princess trees, lady's slippers, Solomon's seal. Did you see those pinkshell azaleas in front of Mr. Grove's home? Weren't they lovely?"

"Indeed," Mr. Leslie said. "I tend to enjoy them blooming naturally in the forest. Look out your window just there."

Wild redbuds' purple-red sprays and small white dogwood blossoms broke the monotony of deep green and brown as the auto crested the hill and began its descent to camp.

"Looks like the men have just returned. Looks like they had much luck too." Mr. Leslie nodded.

Down below, a group of six Ford pickups were backed up toward the fire that hadn't stopped blazing for two days, and a group of men wearing new overalls and flat caps—they clearly intended to appear like the everyman but very obviously did not—were lifting buckets of fish to a crowd of servants. I saw a pop of light and then another as the cameramen cataloged the fruit of this excursion.

"I can't do this," Worth whispered. The words were so soft I barely heard them. We were midway down the hill now and for a moment, I felt the echo of my own panic at the view of the mountains—the unsteadiness, the racing heart, the utter terror of coming face-to-face with a nightmare I'd pushed away. And then the sensation was gone. I had made peace with my memories. Surely he could do the same.

I looked at him and squeezed his hand.

"You can."

His fist opened and his fingers laced with mine. The feel of his touch, even in this moment of disquiet, sparked a warm sensation that flowed from our fingers to my heart. What a gift it was to have found a confidant again, to understand and be understood this way.

The auto planed and eased toward the hubbub around the fire.

"Would you mind parking behind the dining tent? Mr. Delafield needs a moment to steady his headache," I said. "He doesn't want to appear aloof to the others."

"Of course," Mr. Leslie said. He turned the auto away from the festivities toward the dining tent where another small fire blazed. Servants gathered around it, hoisting pots over the flame. I was certain they'd been at the work of preparing the meal all day.

Mr. Leslie turned the engine off several feet away from where the servants were assembling.

"I'll go fetch the nurse for that inhaler," he said. His eyes met mine in question. I knew he doubted that a migraine, even a crippling one, could render someone as charismatic as Worth speechless.

"Yes. That'll do nicely," I said. "We can let ourselves out when we're ready."

Mr. Leslie nodded and departed, and I turned to Worth and grasped both his hands in mine. For the first time in nearly half an hour, he looked at me. He still appeared on the brink of fainting. Even his lips had taken on an ashen tone. For a moment the thought of a man this strong, this kind, losing consciousness made me feel dizzy, but then I took a deep breath.

"You're going to be all right. Everything is all right here," I said. "You've made it to your property without demanding Mr. Leslie turn around. Whatever is playing in your mind is a memory. It is not what's happening now. You are here with me, surrounded by men set on merriment."

Worth lifted one of his hands from mine and ran a palm over his face.

"I know it feels like whatever occurred is happening again. Let it," I said. "It's the only way to realize it's not the truth and to stop the fear."

His eyes suddenly shut. When he opened them, his face had

regained color and his posture had softened, but his expression was now one of anger.

"My parents died here. In their house in the woods. A fire." He yanked his sleeve up to reveal the puckered scar. "I haven't spoken of it since."

At once I recalled the vast depression I'd come across in the forest, the small clearing, the rectangle of sunken grass. There hadn't been a single beam left. Goose bumps prickled my arms, but I ignored the sensation and covered his gnarled purple skin with my hand. My eyes filled. I knew he was watching me as he had just yesterday in the rafters, wondering how I'd react to this news. It was clear he'd been there. He'd somehow survived, and they had not. I recalled the days Father had emerged from the mines without his friends, watching the widows and children grieve the loss of life while he remained unharmed. It had always haunted him. I couldn't imagine the way Worth felt, desperate yet helpless to save his family.

"I'm so sorry," I whispered. "I can't fathom your heartache." I lifted my palm and traced my fingers lightly down his arm. I'd watched Mother do the same to Father after an explosion or roof collapse. They'd sit on the porch saying nothing, but she'd stroke his arm. He always seemed to calm under her touch. Perhaps that was because they were in love. Perhaps this wouldn't work the same way for us, but it was all I knew to do.

"Thank you for staying with me, Belle." He looked at me. "I'm ashamed to let you see me this way. I know it's hardly the manner of a strong man, but it is a part of me. I thought if anyone would understand, it would be you, and as I said before, you're . . . You'll be my family soon, all I have left. I have felt for some time that I needed to be here again." He took my hand from his arm and pulled his sleeve down. "I can bear it here in the valley, but if the festivities take to the forest, I suppose I'll be stricken with a migraine again." His lips lifted. "It was a perfect excuse."

"I thought so as well." I glanced away from him and out the window. From here, the woods looked so inviting, so lush. There wasn't any sign of a blaze. There were no charred trees marring the wash of green, no holes in the blanket of forest. Perhaps the foundation I'd come across hadn't been the sight of their home after all. The thought of their home in flames, the thought of Worth's anguish when he realized his parents were gone, stilled my heart. I met his eyes.

"Let's go." He opened the auto door with a fervor that made the hinges whine and stepped out. The air held that sweet smell of new growth and the sun warmed my skin as I cleared the shadow of the model T's roof. I tucked my portfolio under my arm. Worth took my hand and I nearly had to run to keep up with his pace as we strode around the servants' cooking fire. He tipped his head at them as we passed.

"If it were only my parents, the memories would have been unbearable, but as it is, it is excruciating and enraging all at once."

The words *if it were only my parents* repeated in my mind. I couldn't recall him saying anything about a sibling—Papa had never mentioned one—but perhaps I'd overlooked it.

"What happened, Worth? Who else . . . Who else perished?"

He stopped just before the group of autos encircling the fire, where, judging by the noise, Papa and his friends were gathered for another contest of the outdoors.

"I wanted to wait until we had all the time in the world to ourselves to discuss this. You will have questions, Belle, and I—"

"Delafield! Delafield! Get over here." Mr. Carver was coming up the aisle between the sleeping tents and the dining tents. "The next challenge is set to begin in five minutes, and it's a team effort this time. Two men to a bucket of fish," he said as he approached us. "First team to fillet them all wins. Mr. Gibbins was set to be my partner, but the fiasco with the auto sent him to an early slumber. I bet you could clean a trout in a minute flat."

"I am rather proficient," Worth said, his face instantly brightening.

I wanted to ask him to wait, to say that what he was going to tell me was much more important than Mr. Ford's latest competition, but he had been revived right here on the land he'd been avoiding. Since our reunion, he'd done all he could to ensure I was comfortable, that I had all I needed in his company. The least I could do was offer the same to him.

"Go on and win," I said. "We'll wait to talk when the time is right."

He lifted my hand to his lips as the nurse hastened toward us.

"Mr. Delafield, I'm here with the inhaler for your headache," she said.

"I appreciate it, Nurse, but it's since departed. Forgive me for wasting your time," he said to her and then turned to Mr. Carver. "Let's go claim the victory."

Nearly an hour later, the contest still had not been won, though Worth and Mr. Carver were primed to be the clear victors. Mr. Ford knew how to clean a fish proficiently, but Mr. Firestone cut too deeply. Mr. Kipp and Papa had paired up voluntarily—who knew why—and had swiftly given up. Both just stood over the bucket of fish, talking. Mr. Edison and Mr. Burroughs were both capable but slow, and I overheard them talking about the color of the scales and the beauty of the fish many times before they began to fillet.

All the while, the photographers snapped photos, and the elderly reporter hired to replace Mr. Thorp sat nearby cataloging the progress of the competition.

I held my portfolio against my chest and stepped closer to the fire. Though hours from sunset, the sun itself had disappeared behind the mountain peaks, and without direct heat, winter tapped me on the shoulder.

"I don't know how much more I can take. It is altogether disgusting. Even watching Mr. Delafield is making me ill, and that requires something truly vile," Marie Austen said from beside me. I'd expected her to be in bed like her intended, but of course, Marie Austen thought nothing of ruining Mr. Seely's auto. After all, she figured it wasn't her fault. Nothing was. Which was why she didn't think commenting on my future fiancé's handsome appearance inappropriate in the slightest.

He did look striking. He'd shed his black jacket and was now in his white shirt like the others, though the other men were still wearing overalls and had rolled their sleeves to their elbows to prevent fish guts from soiling their clothes. Of course, Worth couldn't do the same. It would expose his scar.

My stomach swam with nerves when I thought of the conversation we'd left undone, but I pushed that thought away. Perhaps no one else had perished. Perhaps it was only his old life, the innocent life, he was referring to. If that was the case, mine had perished as well.

"It's a normal part of life, Marie Austen. Don't you suppose our servants are tasked with doing the same thing before each course that requires fish?" I'd been staring at Worth's hands, the way they worked mechanically and efficiently, like Father's used to, like mine used to. Cleaning fish was a daily chore in Red Dragon. We'd survived on whatever we could catch in Elk Run; the whole town had. Given the chance, I could best Worth at this contest despite his skill.

"I know they do, but I don't wish to see it," she said. Our mothers and Toots and the rest of the women were in front of us, intermittently yelling encouragements, but even those had waned significantly in the amount of time we'd been standing there. The competition should have required only half a bucket of fish at most.

"Would you like a hot cider, Miss Newbold, Miss Kipp?" A waiter materialized behind me wearing crisp white livery and holding a tray of steaming pewter mugs.

"Yes, I would. Thank you." I tucked my portfolio under my arm, then grasped the handle of a mug and wrapped my other hand around the warmth. Marie Austen did the same. The steam smelled heavenly, and the presentation was lovely—each mug was adorned with a cinnamon stick, star anise, and an orange slice with cloves.

I took a long drink and nearly spit it out. Marie Austen sighed.

"They've added rum. It will warm you up more swiftly than any fire," she said. "Make you forget about the worries of the day too."

I was surprised we'd been offered such a drink. It was an unspoken rule in society that ladies were permitted alcohol only in the form of wine and never more than a glass.

"Last fish!" Worth proclaimed, holding high a sizable trout. Mr. Carver laughed and set the fillet he'd just cleaned in a clay dish beside two wooden cutting boards on the small table in front of them.

"The rest of us might as well throw in the towel," Mr. Ford said. "Of course you had to join, Delafield. I was hoping for a swift victory."

The reporter, sitting nearly at the feet of Mr. Firestone, laughed so hard he nearly fell back against the ground. Perhaps he'd already enjoyed some cider.

"Where did you go with Mr. Gibbins?" I asked Marie Austen. The spectators were dispersing now, the women going back to their tents to ready for dinner, while the men would likely gather their rare cigars and trade them around the fire.

"Just through town. It was a terrible bore. He kept asking ridiculous questions, like where I wanted to get married and what meal I enjoyed most. I didn't answer a single one. Finally, when I couldn't take it anymore, I asked for a turn at the wheel to cure my boredom. It was all going well until he tried to hold my hand."

"You do know you'll have to hold his hand when you're married," I said.

"Why?" She tipped the remainder of her cider into her mouth. I had barely taken a quarter of my mug. "There isn't any rule that dictates I touch him at all."

"We're the winners!" Mr. Carver proclaimed, clapping Worth on the back. They held up their hands as the photographers' bulbs popped and then came around the front of the worn table, leaving behind the filleted fish and the empty bucket. Mr. Carver said something to Worth I couldn't make out and his head turned, just slightly, toward the southern range of forest before his face tightened and he shook his head.

Marie Austen snatched another mug from a servant as he passed.

"Perhaps I should have two more. I'm not forgetting my fate

yet," she said. "Will you procure another from the tray, please? I'll look like a terrible lush if I get another with one already in my hand."

"I'm afraid I can't," I said. "Drink disrupts your sensibilities and I—" Before I could finish my sentence, Marie Austen had grabbed another cider herself. "No amount of rum will change a thing about your engagement."

She glared at me and took a long sip from one of the mugs. "Stop acting like my mother, Belle." She threw her head back and laughed loudly. I looked around to find most of the men under fifty staring at her, including Worth, who was making his way toward us. She smiled at me, knowing full well what she was doing. "And it does change things. Not forever, of course, but for tonight, I'm determined to forget who Robert Gibbins is."

I walked away from her as Edsel Ford approached. It was strange to see him, to see all of them, dressed in ordinary clothes. I thought it made them appear more handsome, but then again, I'd been brought up by a miner and not an industrialist. Perhaps the clothes simply made me feel more comfortable.

Worth, on the other hand, had put his jacket back on and looked the picture of polish despite having just cleaned more than two dozen fish.

"I smell like fish innards," he said when he reached me. "I suppose I should ask Mr. Ford if I could, in fact, take advantage of the tent he constructed for me."

"Well done, my boy," Papa said to Worth as he and Mother made their way past us to the tents. "Miller sure taught you the ways of the land. I should have taken him up on that cross-country trip he proposed years ago. Perhaps then I wouldn't have embarrassed myself today." Papa chuckled.

"Shipley tells me your father could catch a fish with his bare hands," Mother said. She was nestled into Papa's shoulder, her face rosy from her proximity to the fire. Her statement, as though she'd never witnessed such a skill, was baffling. Father had often caught fish that way.

"Yes, he could. He was raised in the country. My grandparents were farmers."

Mother's gaze swept mine. I couldn't tell if it was a warning to remain quiet or a plea to take note that this man, this relative stranger who was to be my husband, wasn't entirely foreign after all. If it was the latter, I'd already taken it in. The knowledge of Worth's ancestry endeared him to me even more. He was a gentleman, a man of fine social standing, and yet he understood in some small way who I was. Perhaps years down the road, after marriage and children, I could tell him about my childhood, about my father.

"You should stay here for the duration of our time, win all of the competitions, and truly get under Ford's skin," Papa said.

"I'm not sure it would be wise to make an enemy of Ford." Worth laughed.

"You should stay anyway. Even if you don't participate in any of the other contests," Mother said. "It is your land, after all, and we'd enjoy your company."

"I think I'll stay for the night at least," he said. "Though I'll need to wash for dinner. We all reek. I'm surprised you're able to stand so close to Shipley, Mrs. Newbold." Worth smiled and Mother returned the grin.

"He looks so handsome in his overalls I can hardly help it," she said. If any of this—the outfit, the mountains, the fish—made her melancholy, I couldn't tell. "We'll see the two of you at dinner. I'd better get back to the tent. Sylvia will be waiting to dress me. Belle, she'll be by your tent after."

I nodded and they departed arm in arm. I watched them go. If I hadn't known that the man in the overalls was Papa, and if it had been a bit dark, I could have thought the vision was my parents, together again.

"Is it peculiar to see your mother with someone else?" Worth's question seemed to come from somewhere far away. Had he read my mind or simply noticed my attention on them?

"Not much anymore," I said.

Behind me, Marie Austen was still speaking loudly, and her voice echoed over us. Worth didn't seem to mind her at all. His gaze remained steady on me.

"Cider, Mr. Delafield?" The waiter materialized with another tray of steaming drinks and Worth took one.

"Yes, thank you. In fact, may I have two?" He took another and handed it to me, then removed the other mug from my hand and set it on the waiter's tray. "They're better warm. It seems yours has chilled."

The waiter departed toward Marie Austen. I watched her take another and discard her empty mugs.

"It occurred to me that I shouldn't have handled your cider. I haven't even washed my hands. They're filthy."

I took a sip, this time expecting the bite from the rum that accompanied the sweetness.

"I'm not bothered by it. I used to clean fish often." The moment I said it, I regretted it. I thought of Carolina Elkhorn, Boss Elkhorn's daughter who had been sent to boarding school and whose life had been nearly as charmed as my new one. Everyone thought my old life was like hers. There was no way she'd ever touched a fish, much less filleted one.

"You did? Why?" he asked.

"I was an inquisitive child." That much was the truth. "I often watched Mr. . . . . Mr. Coleman prepare our meals, and he eventually taught me." I looked at Worth's face, realizing a part of me was waiting for him to react, to tell me he knew Mr. Coleman was really James Coleman, my father, but of course, he'd never heard his name. None of them had.

"And your parents allowed it?"

"Of course. It was a small town and there wasn't much to keep me occupied."

"You should have joined in the contest." He smiled and took a drink.

"I wanted to." I glanced at the buckets still half full of fish at every station but Worth's and Mr. Carver's. Back home, I'd been known for the way I extracted every bone—even the small ones—and I wondered if my hands still knew the way of it.

"Can't believe we got all these from your streams, Delafield," Mr. Burroughs said, breaking away from Edsel.

"My streams?" Worth asked.

"Yes. You said there were plenty of fish in them, and though we tried the French Broad earlier today, it seemed the current was running too swiftly, so we returned."

"Oh. I . . . I gather you found the streams easily. Whereabouts did you go?" Worth's voice was tense and his face displayed panic. "I could have directed you had I known."

"North, I believe. We crossed the bit of valley behind you and entered the woods that way, passed a small cave, and drew left at a large birch there. The stream was just beyond."

Worth seemed to relax.

"Yes. Good. There's a nice hole there too."

"Yes." Mr. Burroughs snapped his fingers. "That's where I had the most luck. Edison even took a little swim. Said it was warm."

"It is. In the winter steam rises from it. It's a bit of an illusion, though. It isn't a hot spring by any means."

I recalled the feel of the water in a swimming hole, the way the minerals softened my skin and hair and made me feel altogether alive. Perhaps I could find my way there and bathe. Washing with a pitcher and a towel was supposedly more sophisticated and proper, but often the film of sweat and grime remained on some surface of the skin.

"I doubt we'll need to cast a line again with the success we had today, but if we do, I wager you could show us some other spots around this place. Are there many streams to the south? The terrain looks a bit less steep to that side."

Worth took a long sip of his cider.

"No, actually," he said finally. "It's the least impressive side of the property." He tipped his head back, gesturing to the woods behind him, and my heart quieted. His expression and the way he discouraged the exploration of it indicated the fire had happened there, in the section of forest I'd ventured toward our first night.

Mr. Burroughs went on about the flora and fauna he'd found, but my mind was fixed on Worth. I couldn't comprehend how everyone seemed to know that Worth had suffered a terrible tragedy, yet no one, including Papa, seemed privy to the specifics of it—even that it occurred here. Surely if they knew, they would be more sensitive to Worth's facing the site of it. Then again, everyone else had moved on and there was always the assumption that because time had marched along and others had returned to life, the sufferer would do the same. That was how mines were reopened after horrific explosions, sending the same men into the same place that had stolen their friends.

"I suppose I'll go locate my tent now," Worth said to Mr. Burroughs. "I'll see you at dinner," he said to me. He lifted my hand and kissed it, then turned to walk toward his tent.

I watched him tip back the mug as he went, and when it was finished, he let the handle swing in his hand. An imagined vision of the fire startled me, and I swallowed hard and forced it away.

Everyone else had gone. Marie Austen was likely already situated in our tent waiting for the Kipps' maid or Sylvia to appear and do her up for the evening—or possibly she'd convinced Edsel to kiss her, though I hoped she wasn't that daft.

Two servants appeared from the cooking tent and walked toward the fire. They gathered the fillets and the whole fish. My eyes shifted to the woods. I wanted to go there, to stand in front of that clearing and verify that what I'd come across had once been Worth's home. It wasn't inquisitiveness that drew me. I wanted to take his pain, to absorb the magnitude of Worth's sorrow so I could understand all he'd lost, so I could heal it, but I shouldn't. I'd come across it first in error, but now that I knew, that site was as sacred as a cemetery, and visiting it without him seemed underhanded.

"Do you need help cleaning those?" I asked the servants, who were now both carrying two buckets each. I ought to go to my tent, to wait for Sylvia like the society lady I was meant to be, but I suddenly couldn't bear the idleness of it all. I needed to work with my hands, to divert my mind with a task that required concentration.

"No, ma'am." One of the servants, a boy who couldn't be older than fourteen, stared at me, a peculiar expression on his face.

"I meant to say, can I please help fillet those?" I asked again.

"Dinner will be served in two hours, miss. We don't have time to teach you, I'm afraid, and you'd ruin your dress," the other, older servant said.

"I already know how, and I'm quite good at it. I'd be another hand."

They looked at each other and shrugged. I knew they didn't quite believe me.

"Very well," the younger one said. "Right this way."

I followed them around the back of the cooking tent to the fire I'd seen earlier, now occupied by five different pots and at least a dozen people. The aroma of butter and frying fish, lima beans with bacon, and a sweet smell of boiling peaches washed over us and I inhaled deeply. Inside the tent were long tables lined with half-constructed courses and empty silver platters. Servants bustled back and forth, cutting orange slices and mixing sauces, arranging dessert platters and decanting wine. The sun was nearly gone now, and oil lamps were scattered here and there, casting the tent in a glow.

"We clean the fish around the side here," the older servant said, walking past the warmth of the tent and the cooking fire to a dim spot around the side of the tent. There, the mouthwatering smells of our dinner were extinguished and the earthy stink of fish hung in the air. Even though it was barely spring, flies buzzed from a large galvanized bucket set up beneath two wooden tables equipped with fillet knives and cutting boards.

"You can go back to your tent if you wish, miss," the younger man said, clearly aware of my distaste at the sound of flies. I loathed flies. They'd always enjoyed our small home in the summer, sneaking in the windows and finding the smallest scraps of fried potato or fish before buzzing about my head and waking me up. "I'm afraid it's messy work, and we don't have smelling salts—"

"I grew up filleting fish," I said. I set my portfolio on the ground and reached into the bucket they'd just abandoned. I grasped a knife and slid the tip into the fish's stomach near the anal opening. Moving the blade swiftly along the body to the head, I was horrified to find that the act made me sick. I gagged, though thankfully it was a silent sort, and spread the body open. I'd done this same thing thousands of times, but now, having been absent the necessity of it for seven years, it seemed awful to cut open anything that had been alive.

I knew why. Being catered to instead of barely surviving made all food seem the same. We never harvested any of it. Whether it originated on a vine or a tree or a farm or a stream didn't matter. What did society know of canning, fishing, and hunting so that when the money ran dry food was still available? People like Marie Austen or Mrs. Firestone or Mrs. Edison had never sent their men off to a shooting contest for pigs' feet. Mother had. And when Father had returned with them, the hideous vision had seared into my mind because they had been so needed, such a blessing.

"I'll bet that's rare in your set," the older man said. He was standing on the other side of the young man beside me, his hands swiftly removing the entrails of his first fish. I did the same to mine and then lifted a small pitcher of water between our cutting boards and rinsed the cavity.

"I didn't grow up in this set." I left the head on and placed the finished meat in a waiting clay bowl.

"You mean to tell me there's a chance I'll wind up as a guest at a table such as these someday?" The young man shook his head and tossed his cleaned fish into the bowl with mine.

"There's a chance, though whether it's a better life than the one you've got, I can't say," I said.

He laughed. "I'd trade these ten-hour days of serving and being disregarded and disrespected in an instant. I can't imagine what it would be like to be waited on hand and foot."

"It can be quite boring," I said. "And there are unspoken rules, things you can no longer do that you were free to do before. But you'll never wonder if you'll starve again, and that is why I'll never risk returning to the life I had."

"How do you suppose you avoid that? Isn't even Mr. Ford a few steps away from where we are? One unfortunate business deal, one mistake, and everything he's worked for could crumble," the older man said.

I reached for another fish.

"Yes, but doesn't that seem like an incredible long shot? It would take a disaster, multiple disasters, for his fortune to even notice."

"You'll marry a man like him then?" the young man asked as I opened the body of a second fish.

"Yes," I said simply.

We cleaned the fish in silence, and though I'd been honest, I felt like suddenly there was a great divide between us.

Despite knowing that what I was doing was the right decision, a match like mine would be impossible for men like them, and because of that, they would view it as unfathomable, wrong. The men and women they knew married for love or married because they had loved and the result of that required a commitment. Those were the only reasons. Sure, there were a few women who would view a specialized laborer as a prize—the wages were slightly higher and their work more certain—but marrying them hardly came with a fortune.

"Belle . . . what . . . what are you doing?" Worth materialized around the side of the dining tent. He'd said he'd departed my company to wash and dress, but that clearly hadn't been the case. In the near hour since I'd last seen him, something had come undone. His hair, typically tidy in its pomade, was wild and unkempt and his shirt was untucked and wrinkled beneath his jacket. He held an empty crystal glass, and the etching along the sides kept twinkling when it caught the oil-lamp glow. It had somehow stolen the light from his eyes.

"Cleaning fish. I told you I wanted to see if I could still do it."

He lumbered forward, stumbling a bit. Whatever had befallen him, likely the memory of his tragedy, had completely eclipsed the person he was, and the sight was unnerving.

"Your mother is looking for you. Sylvia is waiting to dress you for dinner and do up your hair." His voice sounded almost as if he'd fallen ill with a cold. I tipped the fillet I'd just finished into the bowl and reached into the bucket for another.

"I'm helping these men right now, and it will take but twenty minutes to make me presentable," I said.

I glanced at him and he stopped suddenly, still a distance away from me. I couldn't quite see his face, cloaked in night, but he stood a bit straighter.

"You remind me of Mother. You have since I first met you. I'm only realizing it now."

I busied myself with the fish. I didn't know how to respond.

"Is that why you accepted when Papa wrote back to tell you I was willing?" I asked, forcing my attention to the fish and not to Worth, who somehow felt foreign, like the stranger he was instead of the man who had begun to feel like family.

"Perhaps," he said.

"Miss Newbold!" Sylvia appeared behind Worth. "It is nearly dinnertime and you are a sight. Not to mention, Marie Austen is . . . Well, she's indisposed, and I was hoping you could help me. I'm afraid in this state, she may ruin everything."

I set down the knife and sighed.

"Thank you, men. Do you happen to know where I could procure a strong coffee?"

# CHAPTER FIFTEEN

Efforts had been made for the women's entertainment tonight by request of Mrs. Firestone, so as not to restrict all nighttime activities to the men. As nice as the thought had been when the request was made, the actual materialization of it on a night like this was a mistake.

Dinner had been horrific. Despite the best efforts of a cup of coffee so strong it looked like sludge, Marie Austen had not come back to herself. In fact, the fusion of caffeine and alcohol actually seemed to accentuate her erratic behavior. She'd run from our tent in her shift twice, both times blabbering on about how Mr. Thorp was to meet her at the edge of the forest, forcing Sylvia and me to run after her. She was swift, and the only way we caught up to her was because her legs began to wobble.

I'd barely had a moment to change into my dinner costume—a figaro jacket formed of jetted satin over a gauze blouse, finished with a skirt of black satin with jet-black embroidered tabs—and certainly hadn't had a chance to have Sylvia do up my hair. I'd simply tucked it as best I could back into the pins on my way to dinner.

We thought we'd convinced Marie Austen that it was nighttime and she should sleep. She had reclined on her cot. I'd seen her do it and Sylvia was to keep watch, but sometime between the filet de bass sauté and the salade verte, Marie Austen joined us.

I hadn't noticed her at first. I was situated at the far side of the table beside Worth—whose alcohol-induced stupor had thankfully shifted to a noted silence at this point—and Mr. Firestone, with whom I'd been deep in conversation about my meeting with Mr. McKibbin. Our discussion had paused when the servants entered the tent with trays, and a wail erupted, followed by a full platter of salads flying into the air, the Bibb lettuce, haricots verts, and radishes landing on the ground, along the table, and atop Edsel, Toots, Mr. Gibbins, and Mr. Carver.

"I am *not* soused," Marie Austen had screeched at the top of her lungs. "I am heartbroken." The whole table, already startled by her intentional overturning of one of the salad platters, had silenced. "Don't tell me how to behave, Mr. Gibbins. I am not your wife yet, and even when I am, I will not listen to a word you say. Do you understand me?"

Mr. Kipp finally rounded the table to where she sat, snatched her wrist, and attempted to drag her away, but she evaded him and lunged for her wine goblet. She tipped it to her mouth as her father's hand found her arm again, and the liquid sloshed down her face and her white pearl-beaded bodice.

"Get her under control, man! Her behavior is ruining our party," Mr. Burroughs had bellowed from the end of the table across from me. Mrs. Burroughs had tipped her head back and laughed. The sound was like a fuse ignited.

"And your behavior has ruined my life," she said to her husband. I recall glancing at the empty wineglasses then, wondering if perhaps the copious amounts of cider had been pressed upon us much too early.

At once, it seemed everyone was shouting, everyone but Worth, who under typical circumstances would have been the one to speak sense to the group. As it was, he simply remained silent, likely trapped in his remembrances, staring glassy-eyed at the oil-lamp flame flickering in front of us.

Finally, Mr. Kipp snatched a water glass from Mr. Gibbins and doused Marie Austen's face with it. She'd sputtered and gasped, then stumbled from the tent, her father and Mr. Gibbins on her heels.

The aftermath of the row had rendered everyone silent through dessert. That silence had carried over to the evening's entertainment. Whether it was exhaustion or anger or disappointment, I really couldn't say. Mine had to do with Worth.

I'd tried to talk with him privately after dinner concluded. I'd pulled him aside outside the tent and told him I knew he was greatly bothered. I'd asked if he wanted to return to Mr. Seely's and said Mr. Leslie would surely be happy to take him, but he'd only shaken his head and slurred something about having a cigar with the men. He attempted to kiss the back of my hand but missed entirely and then, as though he hadn't noticed, let my hand go and walked away. I'd asked Papa to look after him and he'd agreed. I hoped he was keeping his promise.

"Champagne, Mrs. Newbold?" Mother reached for a flute, and I declined when the tray was extended toward me. I was shocked alcohol was being served at all after the events of this evening, but then again, the servants held no power to exercise that restriction.

"Don't worry about Worth," Mother said under her breath. I looked at her, wondering how she knew my thoughts. "Tomorrow all will be well. Shipley says he's never known him to imbibe to excess. He'll remember himself tomorrow. It's the recollection of his parents' death—a terrible fire two miles or so south of here. Papa told you of it, didn't he? I told him you needed to know."

"No," I said, "but Worth did."

"It is a sensitive matter. Perhaps Papa thought it best to let Worth tell you himself," she said.

She took a sip of her champagne and cast her gaze to the flame in front of us. The light made the diamond pastes embedded in her pink satin sparkle. I knew I shouldn't ask her, that I should let Worth tell me the full story of the tragedy in his own time, but the desperation to know suddenly couldn't be contained.

"Did Papa . . . Did Papa tell you how it started? Were Mr. and Mrs. Delafield the only ones lost?"

"An overturned oil lamp. I didn't hear of others, though I suppose there could have been siblings or servants," Mother said. She leaned back against the canvas chair and sighed. "Now that I see the two of you together, my only hesitation to your match is that you are both deeply feeling. You were in quite a state when we first arrived here, as he is tonight. Given the right circumstances, one of you could become inconsolable, withdrawn, inattentive—"

"We have both lost parents; both of our families have been shattered. It would be unnatural if we were not affected." My tone was sharp. I recalled the way she looked even months after Father's death. She was ashen and frail, reduced to nearly a skeleton because she refused to eat. She'd slept most of the days, leaving the cooking and washing and cleaning to me. It was only when Father's bereavement money ceased that she revived, and even then it was only a superficial enlivening so she had the energy to work.

"Yes, and that is my point. If you are both this wretched over the death of your parents, how do you suppose you or he would fare if tragedy befell either of you? The death of a person bound to your soul is a horror." She turned the stem of the flute around in her hand.

"I'm not in love with him, and he's not in love with me. Our souls will never intertwine. I have determined that love will not be a part of my life. I respect him and enjoy his company as he enjoys mine, but if I were to die, he'd mourn me as a friend."

A servant was withdrawing what appeared to be soft meringues from a tin and began prodding them with skewers. Mrs. Firestone clapped in delight around the fire as if she knew what this odd display indicated.

"And if you find that you love him despite your best efforts?" Mother asked.

"I will not. I have sworn it to myself. But if I ever did and lost him, I suppose I would move along as you have and soon enough, I would be affected by nothing at all." I said the last part on purpose. Not that I thought for a second I'd allow myself to slip into adoration for Worth, but because Mother's coldness when we'd arrived had been bothering me for days.

Mother tensed and her eyes jerked to mine.

"Have you ever considered that I cannot think of it? I refuse. I must live as though he never existed," she whispered. "It is the only way."

Her eyes blurred, and the reminder of the person I could become if I fell in love reemerged, startling me, pouring terror over my spirit. Her hands shook as she tipped the flute up, draining the remainder of the champagne.

"Have any of you had roasted marshmallows?" Mrs. Firestone shouted. I was thankful for the distraction for Mother's sake. Of course she'd been ignoring Father's memory for her own preservation. I knew that, and yet the idea that he was being forgotten on purpose made my heart ache.

"No," Mother replied to Mrs. Firestone. "Is that what you're doing there, young man?" The servant, a boy no older than fifteen, nodded.

"It's quite a delightful treat," Mrs. Firestone went on.

"Would you like to roast yours yourself, ma'am, or shall I do it for you?" the servant asked her.

"I prefer mine scorched, so I'll do the honors," she said, rising from her chair. The servant handed her the iron skewer, the end of which boasted a small white confection. Mrs. Edison followed suit, and then Mother rose to obtain a skewer.

"How is Marie Austen?" I whispered to Mrs. Kipp, who was on my other side. "I went back to the tent to check on her but she wasn't there."

"She's under the care of Mr. Gibbins and my maid, Bertha. He said he would sit with her while she drank some coffee, and when she was back to her right mind, he said he'd take her for a moonlit stroll and return her to your tent."

"We tried coffee, Mrs. Kipp. It didn't work before—"

She silenced me with a wave of her hand.

"It doesn't matter. If he'd like Rues D'Or, Marie Austen's airs are his trouble now."

It was no wonder Marie Austen treated me the way she did. It was the same manner in which her mother treated her.

"You may think us horrible, but Mr. Kipp and I did what was

necessary for her future. Mr. Gibbins is wealthy and smart, a perfect match. She is not suited for life with that newspaperman, Mr. Thorp, as much as she thinks herself in love with him. Marie Austen is the star of her own life. We thought her tremendous beauty and high intelligence would render her countless matches, but so many simply selected the low-hanging fruit, the quiet sort."

Mrs. Kipp's eyes settled on my gown, then on my face, and I knew I was the low-hanging fruit she was referring to. I didn't think myself quiet, but in comparison to Marie Austen I was.

"The men in Gas City are too dull for someone like her," I said. For as horribly as she treated me, she was also my greatest ally at times—when it suited her. "I know it's not my place to say so, but Mr. Gibbins is as well. Perhaps she should have been presented in New York too. Don't you have a sister who lives in the city?"

Mrs. Kipp laughed.

"It's much too late for that, and of course, Mr. Kipp and I have thought of every friend and acquaintance we know, considering all the eligible men for our Marie Austen, but she refused each suggestion. She said she wanted to fall in love. We've given her three seasons and she did not. Now she's getting older, and if her father and I did not intervene, she would wind up either impoverished or an old maid. It doesn't look well when an eligible woman remains unattached year after year."

She beckoned for another glass of champagne.

"You would have been in her same position if it hadn't been for the good fortune of your father knowing Mr. Delafield."

"My match is quite the same as hers, only I'm amiable to it."

"And why wouldn't you be? His fortune is well beyond that of any other man who would agree to marry you—a young woman existing in a world that isn't truly her own without future security from her father's will."

I knew well enough what was said of me. The uncertainty of my breeding and the exclusion from Papa's will had been a frequent topic of conversation among the parents of the young men who occupied the ballrooms in Gas City. What I couldn't fathom was why Mrs. Kipp believed me to be naive to society. Of course, I was, but even Papa Shipley seemed to think I'd been groomed in some sort of wealth.

"What do you mean by—"

"I've been through the coal fields, Belle. The sort of circles you were accustomed to had to have been more . . . shall we say, primitive . . . despite the fact that you were town nobility."

"They were fine people. Finer than any I've come across in—" I stopped before I ignited another row. We didn't need it tonight, yet I meant the sentiment. Since leaving Red Dragon, I'd come across only one person as kind and warm as our friends there, and that was Papa.

I looked up at the sky, sure I'd find a full moon. Full moons were magical, foreboding things. The illusion of bright beauty was a mask cloaking the oppositional tension of the sun that truly gave people over to panic. Thankfully, the moon was a thin sliver, a tiny crescent that barely allowed any light.

"I'm sorry for my tone," I said to Mrs. Kipp. "It's been a strange evening, has it not?"

"Indeed," she said.

The servant roasting the marshmallows walked over to us.

"Would you like to try one, ladies?" he asked.

"Yes," I said, and he handed a skewer to me. The confection smelled a little buttery, almost like the vanilla Mother used to get from the company store right before Christmas for cookies.

"Just slide the marshmallow off and eat it. I'll fetch you a moist towel for your fingers."

I did as I was told and took a bite of the marshmallow. The outside of the candy had been hardened a bit by the fire, while the inside was gooey, nearly liquid, and tasted like pure sugar. I loved it.

"That is horrid," Mrs. Kipp said. "And my fingers are sticky."

The servant hastened back to us and wiped my fingers, then Mrs. Kipp's. Mother, Mrs. Firestone, and Mrs. Edison were still standing by the fire, holding their skewers over the flame, roasting their third or fourth marshmallows.

"Shall we do this again tomorrow night?" Mrs. Firestone asked.

"I'd rather another option," Mrs. Ford said from beside Mrs. Kipp. "If I never smell woodsmoke again, I'll be overjoyed. I woke smelling of it and I'll go to bed tonight smelling of it. There's no way to expunge it from my hair." She huffed. "Henry says Edith Vanderbilt has already gone to Newport, which is a terrible shame. If she hadn't, I'd write to her to beg a bath at Biltmore. I'm sure she has wonderful oils and warmed towels."

"You could always take a dip in that swimming hole like my husband," Mrs. Edison said, laughing.

"Imagine," Mrs. Ford said. "I'd likely drown."

Once again, the memory of dipping in water so cold that it shocked my body and cleared my mind emerged, and I longed for it, for the way it felt to slide my clean legs into crisp sheets, for the way it amalgamated human and nature, eliminating the need to think of anything but the wonder of creation—myself and the water and the trees.

I would go tonight. Once the whole camp was slumbering, I would find my way to it. I closed my eyes, already imagining the way it would feel—the worry and the memories and the anticipation completely lost to peace.

# CHAPTER SIXTEEN

When Marie Austen hadn't returned by the time Sylvia came to undress me, I began to worry. Regardless of the Kipps' unending trust of Mr. Gibbins, I wasn't of the same mind. It wasn't that I found him ominous necessarily, but they'd given him charge of Marie Austen at a precarious time, and I knew for a fact that though he might have developed some affection for her, the truth was that he was primarily interested in Rues D'Or.

"Marie Austen hasn't turned up. Have you spoken to Mrs. Kipp's maid? She was supposed to be chaperoning Marie Austen along with Mr. Gibbins," I said to Sylvia.

"She's asleep in Bertha's tent—that's Mrs. Kipp's temporary maid. I heard commotion as I passed by to ready your mother for bed but heard only snoring on my way here. I pray she's finally settled down." Sylvia sighed. "Excuse me for saying so, but that girl should never be allowed to take another drop of alcohol."

"I agree."

Sylvia slipped the pins from my hair, letting my full waist-length waves cascade down my back.

"Nevertheless, I hope she finds happiness. Everyone deserves that," Sylvia said as she undid the laces at my back.

"I hope so too," I said. "Though it seems she doesn't quite know the way there." I shivered when the last of the fabric was discarded and I stood completely naked from the waist up. The night was more winter than spring, and the cold air seeped in between the cracks in the canvas tent.

Sylvia dug into the armoire and emerged with my nightgown. Thankfully, we'd brought an assortment of fabric weights and the one she selected for tonight was a heavy cotton edged with lace. I ducked as she put it over my head and did up the few buttons at my neck.

I sat on the edge of the cot, and Sylvia walked to the washbasin. She dipped a cloth in the water and rubbed a bit of soap on it, then grasped the gold hairbrush from the side of the little table with her other hand.

"When you're married and I'm not there, don't forget to tell your maid that your face cannot bear more than three days of cream. Older ladies require it daily, but your skin will appear like a greased pig if it is applied more often than I recommend," she said.

I laughed at the insinuation that I could easily appear as beautiful as swine.

"You surely know how to make a girl feel beautiful," I said.

Sylvia shook her head and smiled. "I am only telling you these things because I'm afraid I'll forget. Your mother is one of the nation's great beauties, and you take after her."

I knew she was right about Mother. I'd always heard people speak of her loveliness, but when Papa pulled his auto over in the middle of nowhere, interrupting his quest for the luxury of The Homestead to speak to the woman whose face had enchanted him, I finally understood how beautiful she really was.

"Thank you," I said.

"Are you enjoying your writing?" she asked as she ran the cold washcloth over my forehead and cheekbones. "And spending time with Mr. Delafield? I do hope he's a good man like they all say he is." Her lips pursed. She must have taken note of him tonight. It wasn't a wonderful first impression.

"I'm over the moon with my writing. It has been years since I've done it, and I feel as if I've been reawakened." I eyed the tip of my portfolio beneath the pile of my clothes. Even now I wanted to read over my interview notes again, to write Mr. McKibbin's portion of the story already, though I knew it would be a waste of time. A story was shaped by the collection of all the facts, and I would need to gather all of the interviews—each person's personal story along with the particulars of their work on the inn—before I could possibly understand a theme or a thread that might tie them all together, much like an architect plans his build.

Finished with my face, Sylvia hung the washcloth on the hook next to the washbasin and then returned to run the brush through my hair.

"I do enjoy Mr. Delafield as well. He is courteous and very kind." I hesitated. "Tonight is not how he ordinarily behaves. He is . . . He is reeling from a tragedy."

"Oh." Sylvia's eyes clouded in the mirror. She'd lived half her life in and out of our home in Gas City, and I had never asked her about her life, about her family. In the six years I'd known her, I'd been hiding my own past and had therefore never thought to inquire of others' lives unless the information was volunteered. I was suddenly ashamed that I'd never asked. If she didn't wish to discuss it, I'd not press further, but she should know I cared about her personal life as well as her professional post with us.

"Are you all right?" I asked.

"Oh yes." She said the words quickly and began braiding my hair. I wanted to tell her to stop. It would be a terrible waste of time considering I was planning to go for a dip in the swimming hole, but of course I couldn't confide that to her.

"I understand how Worth feels. It is a gutted sort of sensation. I feel it even now, and my father died years ago," I said. "I can't blame him for leaning into the bottle tonight, though of course, it isn't a solution. It only—"

"It makes the pain more severe," Sylvia said. "I gave my husband scarlet fever. I was working cleaning the offices at the gasoline wells. He was a drilling engineer. His post was primarily solitary, while I was tasked with going 'round the buildings. I contracted it and brought it home to him. I recovered and he . . . he died."

"I'm so sorry." I turned and clutched Sylvia's hand.

"It was twelve years ago. I thought to move away, to go to California or New England, somewhere that didn't remind me of him, but

I hadn't the money. I couldn't bear to be at the wells anymore, so I resigned. Then your stepfather asked if I would consider working as a lady's maid to his wife—his former wife, I mean. I told him I had no experience in that role, but he was unfazed. He paid for me to train under Mrs. Kipp's maid for a few months."

"I'm glad for it. You've been a blessing to Mother and me," I said.

"And you to me. The former Mrs. Newbold barely spoke to me, to anyone really. It was rumored that they only wed because their parents were peers, and I believe it. They lived separate lives," she said. "It made me incredibly happy to realize that Mr. Newbold would have a chance at love after all."

Perhaps she couldn't tell that Mother wasn't in love with him because the contrast of his former wife's coldness made fondness look like love.

She finished with my braid and gestured for me to lie down. I did as I was told, and she spread the hide blankets over me.

"Get some rest, Miss Newbold. You'll need it for your work in the morning."

I nodded and thanked her, and then she was gone. I lay there for a while, listening to the sounds of the night—the crickets and the wind. I imagined the transformation that was happening in the forest—the little crocus and tulip shoots emerging, the new leaves dancing, celebrating their new life in the breeze. Then I threw the hides off, stood, and walked over to my armoire. I withdrew the plaid cape and fixed it over my nightgown, then slid my feet into my boots and painstakingly laced them.

Outside the tent, the woodsmoke hung thick in the air, and vapor dense as a cloud had settled in the valley. As a child, when the mist made its home in our holler, I imagined our town was special, that from time to time we lived in the sky, in the clouds.

I could barely see more than a few feet in front of me as I walked north through the tents until the last bit of canvas fell away. I kept my hands stretched out still, despite knowing there was nothing but a slight grassy incline until the woods.

Finally, my feet crunched leaves and the vapor dispersed, giving way to tree cover. Even though it was spring and the leaves were still small and new, the forest canopy was nearly impenetrable. I blinked, willing my eyes to adjust, scanning the landscape for the small cave Mr. Burroughs had mentioned. A dogwood tree was blooming early, its dainty white flowers a substitution for the moon and stars in the darkness. Beside it, only a hundred yards away, was a cave. Its mouth was minute, perhaps able to shelter only a squirrel or family of mice.

As I approached it, the white birch came into view, its pale trunk stretching up to the canopy. I circled left around it, hearing the soft burbling of running water beyond. My whole body tingled in anticipation, and I released the top buttons of my cape. My shoulders ached—oh, how they ached. My feet hurt. The band of tension that often constricted my lungs in times of panic was there, though it didn't squeeze my insides. I'd been carrying all of this around without awareness, but now, moments from washing it all away, I saw my need for release with absolute clarity.

Rhododendron gathered in heavy groves, like sentries posted down the stream channel. I followed, listening for evidence of still water, waiting for the babbling to die away. Soon the noise dropped to a whisper and the rhododendron thinned. In front of me was a magnificent swimming hole. Boulders bordered much of it on my opposite side, and a thin stream of water dropped from its ledge— there clearly hadn't been much rain. Where I stood was mostly dirt and grass and a few scraggly mountain laurels.

I shed my cloak and shivered. Steam rose from the water and despite Worth's comment that it was an illusion, I imagined that the moment I submerged I'd be warmed through. I pulled the nightgown over my head and then discarded my drawers. *Freedom.* The word lodged in my mind and I smiled. I lowered myself into the water, my breath catching at the first feel of the chill.

My legs churned in the frigid depth, desperate for some sort of warmth. I took a lungful of air and then submerged. The pressure of the water rang in my ears as I let my body drop down. I pointed my toes, waiting to reach the bottom, to feel the sandy loam or sharp prick of rock, but I didn't. It was deep here. As I swam back toward the surface, my hair webbed around my arms like a soft blanket, and every inch of my skin prickled with goose bumps. I laughed when my face broke through the surface, and the sound echoed over the rocks.

I lifted my body and floated. A small sliver of sky was visible between the trees and I could just make out the tail of the Big Dipper. The swimming hole in Elk Run had been wider than this, the tree limbs unable to merge across the expanse. In the summer I'd sometimes float there for hours, watching the clouds pass by. I'd gone through a phase when I was about ten where I'd been absolutely gobsmacked by clouds. I'd read every encyclopedia I could find in our small library and had been the foremost—annoying—expert on every variety. I'd even written a book on them. Father had bought it for five cents, and I'd swiftly spent the earnings on a Coca-Cola—located right next to Grove's Chill Tonic—at the company store.

I thought of Mr. McKibbin, how he'd spoken of his mind seeing things in measurements and units. I didn't have a mind that evaluated things in bits, but rather as a whole. To create a hotel, one would have to have both—to see the glorious outcome and all the necessary pieces required.

I forced my mind to silence and my body to relax. It still remembered the exact way to float so I could drift off and slumber a little. My eyes were heavy, and I let them close.

"I . . . I told you I can't."

A voice drifted through the trees. *His* voice. I jolted upright in the water and froze. He wasn't close, but he wasn't very far either. Perhaps I was hearing things.

"You can follow me, but I told you I will not."

He was coming closer, and I could hear footsteps crunching over dried leaves.

Despite the whole body of water being covered in shadow, I would be noticed in the middle of it. I swam to the side, beneath a rock jutting into the water. The space between the surface and the rock was only large enough for my head to remain out. I thought of my clothes beneath the mountain laurel on the bank and prayed he wouldn't see them—if he came this far.

Then I saw him.

His eyes settled on the water and swept over me.

I barely breathed.

And then he whirled. So quickly I feared he would tumble in.

A pale hand snaked around his neck, followed by the sound of parted lips suddenly pressed together, the click and silence of a kiss deepening, and a woman's soft sigh.

I gasped and covered my mouth, my body washing with heat despite the chill of the water. I couldn't see her. She was still among the mountain laurel, her face shrouded in darkness and covered in his shadow.

"No," he said, his voice still slurred with drink. "I told you to go back, that I wouldn't permit your advances."

# CHAPTER SEVENTEEN

**B**reakfast was served around the fire, and Mrs. Ford had reached her breaking point.

"I'll take my oatmeal in the dining tent," she pronounced loudly to the group. The servants had clearly worked hard to extract the large table from the tent before sunup, and the setting was lovely—a Brussels lace tablecloth adorned with purple redbud sprigs in blue glass vases. Above, the sky was the color of a robin's egg, and the chill was all but gone.

"Smoke follows beauty," Mr. Ford attempted as his wife shook her head and rose from her chair. The unfortunate thing about the position of the table was that it was directly in the path of the wind, and gusts of woodsmoke kept piping toward us.

"Coffee?" a servant asked, the question ending in a squeak as the heat and the scent temporarily took our breath. When we could both breathe again, I looked at her and smiled.

"Yes, please."

I yawned and covered my mouth as she poured another steaming cupful. I hadn't slept at all. Even though the sheets had felt heavenly against my just-washed skin, even though my hair smelled like home and the delicate earthy fragrance of a mountain stream attempted to coax my slumber, I could not. Despite my best efforts to forget about it, my mind kept bringing up Worth—the odd slur of his voice, the woman's hand gripped to his neck.

I'd braced myself to see him at breakfast, but he wasn't about. Perhaps he was still sleeping. It wasn't what he'd said that gnawed at me or even that another woman had kissed him. It was the implication of what he hadn't said. He had begged her off. Told her to go, that he couldn't engage her. What he hadn't said was that he didn't want to.

I hadn't heard the exchange that led to the woman following him into the forest. Surely she'd thought him amiable to the idea. Desire brought forth action. Perhaps he hadn't taken her into the forest to take liberties with her in the same manner as Mr. Thorp had taken Marie Austen to his tent, but the next time he might. I didn't need to be the object of his affection, but I was to be his wife. I would not be made a laughingstock. I would not sit by, pitied, raising his children, while everyone whispered about his mistress.

"Everything tastes and smells of campfire. It is unbearable," Marie Austen muttered beside me. I breathed through my mouth and took a bite of oatmeal, concentrating on what I should taste—the cinnamon, the blueberries, the brown sugar.

"You're still bothered. I can tell." Marie Austen sighed. "I told you it doesn't matter. They all have them or will soon enough. It would do you well to make peace with it. I have."

When I'd finally returned to the tent, freezing and dripping, Marie Austen had been snoring. She'd snored the entire night, a terrible whistling snort won by her intoxication. Sylvia had come at sunrise, and after she dressed us, fixed our hair, and departed, I burst into tears. It was unlike me. In fact, I didn't think I'd ever cried in front of Marie Austen. I could hardly help it. By that time, nearly eight hours after I'd encountered Worth in the woods, I'd worked myself into a bit of a fury.

I told Marie Austen what I'd seen. For some reason I'd expected her to sympathize with my anger, but she'd just taken me by the shoulders and said, "*Oh, darling, it was probably just his lover or a girl he chose for the occasion. It has nothing to do with you. All men of our class have mistresses, which is why I don't feel at all bad about taking a paramour myself.*"

I'd been appalled. Of course I knew of Mr. Burroughs's young mistress—everyone did—but I hadn't heard of others. I'd asked if her father had one, if Papa did. She said her father had had the same one for years, but she didn't know about Papa. I'd gone silent then, simply stunned. In Red Dragon, one of Father's friends, Stanley Perdue, had been caught in bed with Boss Elkhorn's unmarried secretary. His wife, Valerie, had promptly expunged him from their home and he'd been nearly excommunicated by the town. I'd always been taught that marriage was sacred and that those who found love outside of marriage were engaging in a grave sin.

"I will not make peace with it. It is wrong," I whispered before shoveling a bit more oatmeal in my mouth. It tasted like smoke, regardless of my most earnest attempts at concentrating on the flavor.

"I don't agree. As I said, you'll still have the comfort, the money, his name. She'll have nothing but a few moments here and there. You will still be his wife, the picture of propriety and loveliness that he can take to dinners and soirees." Marie Austen plopped a sugar cube in her coffee and twirled her spoon in the warm liquid to dissolve it. "You already fit that bill swimmingly, unlike me."

"He told me last night that I remind him of his mother," I said under my breath, ignoring Marie Austen's reach for pity. I'd never seen Worth's mother, but having a man say a woman reminded him of a person who was his flesh and blood, a woman who raised him, indicated that she was not at all an object of desire.

It had occurred to me that Worth's taking a mistress would eliminate any feeling of love that could bloom in my heart or his. Perhaps if I allowed the possibility, I could know without doubt that I'd have exactly what I set out for—a family, security, and friendship . . . Even so, I regarded myself as a woman with higher standards. I would never follow Marie Austen's quest for a paramour. It would be cheating Worth and my children of my devotion. I hadn't grown up in this world where the lines so often blurred, and though I understood there was much wrong about our way of life in Red Dragon, there was much right too.

"Yes. It's what all men desire for their children, if their mother was a good one," Marie Austen said. She beckoned to the servant cooking eggs in a skillet over the fire, and he hastened over to deposit one on her plate. "The fortunate thing for me is that Mr. Gibbins's mother died in childbirth. He doesn't have one to compare me to. I think that's why he's so irritatingly patient. Still, the moment we wed and return to Indiana, he'll find someone to truly share his life with. Someone who won't be me."

Marie Austen's fingers snaked around the handle of her coffee cup. I stared at them. Did they match the hands I'd seen around Worth's neck? But of course, she'd been asleep at the time of the incident. I'd been doing the same thing to every woman in camp—young women, older women, servants, and my peers—examining their hands, as though I'd been close enough to see any distinguishable markings. As it was, I couldn't recall much beyond their shade, and all but a few women in our company boasted pale skin.

"I think I'll have to adjourn to the dining tent with Mrs. Ford. Even if it means I'll have to sit on the ground," Mrs. Kipp said from Marie Austen's other side. She looked at us after she stood. "Would you like to join me, dears?" Marie Austen nodded and stood, taking her plate of eggs with her, while Mrs. Kipp charged the servants with preparing another plate entirely and bringing it to her in her second location.

"Ready for whittling today, men?" Mr. Ford asked. "Finish up your breakfasts and I'll round up the autos. We're going to get some instruction from a man in town called Duvall, a woodworker Grove knows, and then come back here. You'll have to harvest your own wood from the forest and whittle a wooden knife. First to craft one proficiently wins." He grinned.

"Can I come?" Toots asked. I glanced down the table at her as she daintily dipped her sausage into her egg yolk as if a gust of woodsmoke wasn't engulfing her. I found my gaze fixing on her fingers and quickly refocused on Mother, who batted the cloud of smoke with her napkin. Toots was much too lively to have been up at the hour required to be cavorting in the woods with Worth.

"Miss Newbold." A servant appeared at my left shoulder. "I'm sorry to interrupt your breakfast, but when you're ready, Mr. Leslie and Mr. Delafield are situated in the auto just there." He pointed and my eyes shifted to the edge of the group of autos, where the engine chugged beneath the hum of our voices. "Mr. Delafield asked that I tell you that he's made an appointment with the Grove Park Inn's construction foreman, Mr. Oscar Mills, for eight thirty sharp."

"It's the first I've heard of it," I snapped, tossing my napkin on the table and rising with more fervor than I'd intended. It wasn't this man's fault, after all. "I apologize. It's only that I would appreciate Mr. Delafield communicating my itinerary to me the day prior and he has not." I smoothed the olive-green capes of cloth at my shoulders, edged in ecru and gold, that had turned in and flipped up in the process of my eating. "Please tell him I'll be right there."

By the time I'd gathered my portfolio and started back to where the auto was idling, my nerves had begun to fray again. I'd excused Worth's indulgence yesterday because of the knowledge of his grief and panic, but his behavior had been an embarrassment. Even Sylvia had commented on it.

I walked around the breakfast table still occupied by my parents, Mr. Kipp, the Firestones, Mr. Carver, and the Edisons and then skirted the fire. Worth saw me approaching and stepped out of the cab. He looked like himself, dressed trimly in a black suit—a shade he seemed to wear daily. I evaded his gaze and his greeting as I stepped past him through the auto's open door and into the back seat. When I was situated, I stared straight ahead over Mr. Leslie's shoulders as Worth's weight settled beside me. I heard the door click shut.

"Good morning, Miss Newbold. How did you sleep?" Mr. Leslie asked. His question was innocent enough, but it was the strike of flint against steel.

"I didn't, actually," I said.

"Belle." Worth said my name gently.

"I'm sorry to hear that. Is there anything we can do to make you more comfortable tonight?" Mr. Leslie asked.

"Could you propose that the servants refrain from serving liquor until dinner has been consumed?"

"Yes, I understand how that can tear a stomach to shreds," Mr. Leslie said. "I'm sorry you're feeling unwell."

"It's not me—"

Worth grasped my hand suddenly, and I yanked it away.

"To the hotel, please, Mr. Leslie," Worth said, clearly hoping to turn the conversation.

"I embarrassed you last night," he whispered. "I embarrassed myself. I'm sorry. I thought the drinks would help soothe my spirits."

His voice was normal, warm, and for some reason, the return of it, as though the person he'd been last night hadn't been him at all, made me furious. All the restraint I'd attempted finally collapsed and I turned to face him. I wanted to ask him straight out about the kiss. Who she was, why she'd done it, but I couldn't here in front of Mr. Leslie. Even so, I wanted Worth to know I'd seen him, that I knew what had transpired, and that regardless of his pushing her away, she must have deduced she had a chance to trap him at some point prior to her reaching for him.

"When you do propose—if you're still set on it—I'll require a ring with a blue sapphire. I do hope you can acquire such a stone in the coming days. I have always loved the water for one, and for two, I like the meaning of them—honesty, loyalty, and trust—which, I'll be forthright, I'll require of you as my husband," I said evenly.

Worth blinked at me, confusion playing on his face, as if nothing I'd said—not the water, not the honesty—reminded him of the night before in the slightest.

"Yes. Yes, of course. I'll get you one. Anything you wish." He swallowed and whispered my name again. "And I'll expect the same of you," he said in a tone so low I could barely hear him. "I know I was horrid, awful, inebriated. I woke outside my tent on the ground. Will you forgive me for humiliating you? I swear I'll not do it again."

"Your actions last night were nearly understandable. I defended you and sympathized with your pain, but when I saw you in the forest . . . To demean our agreement in such a way, I—"

His eyes widened and he reached for my hand again. I placed it in my lap and scooted toward the window.

"I didn't go into the woods. Surely you know I wouldn't. Not after . . . Not after what I told you. I could barely stand to be here in the valley, Belle. I wouldn't. You must have been mistaken. Even looking at the tree line made me feel as though I would expire."

"You were there," I said plainly.

"I woke on the ground. There was a time, later in the night, perhaps in the morning, when I lost my head. I can't figure where I was or— Please, Belle. If I was in the woods, it was not my intention, and I don't recall it at all. What did you see?" He closed the gap between us and took my limp hands in his.

I'd heard tales of people losing their memories to drink. Back home, it had happened often on account of homemade moonshine. But I also knew the occurrence was easy to utilize as a way to dismiss regrettable behavior. In the short time I'd known Worth, I'd thought him honest, but there was no way to tell whether he had truly taken leave of his person in those hours or he was lying about his condition to prevent my anger. I wouldn't have my concerns dismissed so easily and I couldn't discuss them openly here.

"Nothing," I said.

"Belle."

"Nothing," I said again.

We were silent the remainder of the drive to Grove Park Inn. His hand stayed clasped on mine and I allowed it. I didn't entirely know why; it just seemed like the right thing to do. After all, he had dismissed the woman, he had pulled away when she kissed him—at least that I could tell by the brevity of the noise and the swiftness of his rebuke. Perhaps it was only Marie Austen's talk of lovers and mistresses that made me question his honor.

"Ah, here we are," Mr. Leslie said as the ground leveled and the side of the inn came into view. The sight still took my breath and I couldn't help smiling as I beheld it. Men crawled across the sharp sweep of roof, carrying wires or red clay tiles. Some of the tiles had already been installed, and it occurred to me that the color would echo the sunset guests would enjoy from the front porch.

"We must find a moment—no, hours—to speak alone," Worth

whispered. "There is much to say on both sides. I cannot bear holding the weight of what I must tell you and wondering what I've done to upset you so." He paused. "There will be times when we will anger each other, but we must speak of it. We must be forthright about our fury or our sadness or whatever emotion arises, because if we do not, if we give in to the temptation to hold it close and let it burrow into our hearts, you will resent me, and I will resent you, and we will both be miserable indeed."

"I don't want to resent you." I looked at him then, and his gaze settled on mine. I meant it. I wanted a happy life, not one filled with romance but a life filled with comfort and ease, with peace. I hadn't truly felt settled in years. It suddenly dawned on me that I had grown to resent Mother. It wasn't that I didn't agree with her choice to marry Papa—it had given us a better life—but the way she refused to remember Father, the way she ignored not only her pain but mine as well, was a rage I'd buried deep. It had kept me from confiding in her, and in many ways it had separated us, strained our relationship when I needed her the most. "I don't want you to resent me either," I said. "I want to be happy with you."

He smiled, and even though I'd seen it plenty of times now, the way it brightened his face and warmed my soul still struck me.

He squeezed my hand.

"We will find time together. Perhaps if we conclude early today. I promise you," he said.

"Mr. Mills looks eager to greet you," Mr. Leslie said as the auto veered around the circular drive to the entrance.

Mr. Mills was a mustache. Somehow I hadn't noticed last time, but as we stopped in front of him it was all I could see. It was an English sort, plump with turned-up wings, that fully eclipsed his lips and most of his cheeks, and as a spring breeze skittered over him, he swiftly lifted his hand to smooth it.

"I'm not sure that's the case, but I appreciate the confidence, Mr. Leslie," I said. Mr. Leslie exited the auto and hastened to my door.

"Something's gone wrong," Worth said, likely noticing the red wash to Mr. Mills's face and the way he held his hands in fists at his sides.

I grasped my portfolio and exited the auto.

"Wonderful to see you again, Miss Newbold," Mr. Mills said as I approached. "Thank you for taking the time." His tone was clipped, but he attempted a smile. Teeth appeared beneath the mustache.

"Thank you," I said. "I'm sure you're an incredibly busy man."

"Indeed," he muttered.

"How are things going for you today, Oscar?" Worth asked when he reached my side. He grasped Mr. Mills's hand in greeting. "You look a bit tense."

"I am. Just found out the mule shipment is delayed from Salisbury on account of a track issue, and the animals we're using now are unacceptable. They're exhausted. Two slipped and broke their legs this week. Not to mention three of our section heads are unwell, as well as twenty-four laborers—some sort of cold coursing 'round." He shook his head and sighed.

"Seely and I have a long history and I love the man, but his insisting on a July first opening makes any misstep seem monumental. It's not that I don't understand the need for swiftness—there are new sanitoriums being proposed to the town daily, and Asheville is reluctant to deny them until this fine inn is complete. The town cannot transition to an economy centered on tourism before then. But the quick timeline is quite a lot of pressure."

"The progress you've made already is wildly impressive," I said. "I know it's due to your efforts."

Mr. Mills made a noise of disagreement.

"She's right. You've been on the project night and day since ground break," Worth said.

"You're correct on that point. I'm ready for July so I can return home to Atlanta. I'm not sure who I'll be more pleased to see, my bed or my family." Mr. Mills laughed. "Seely did procure me a mattress, but it's too refined for my liking—the feather variety." He turned to me.

"I figure we'll start on the north side of the inn with the roof and tile, Miss Newbold. Your intention is to see a bit more of our process here, correct? I know you've already been shown around a bit by Mr. Pierce and Mr. Delafield, so do tell me if I start speaking about something you already know."

"Yes, I'm interested in the entire construction process, but I also want to know more about you. A building is only as strong as the men who construct it, and a story on a wonder such as this inn can't be told without your story too."

"The articles I've read often focus more on those funding the place, like Grove and Seely," he replied. "The papers already say they're the ones building it. Suppose you tell their tale instead."

"Everyone already knows who they are and what their contribution is," I said. "You are an invaluable part of this build, and it would be remiss to exclude you from the history books. Mr. Seely and Mr. Grove agree." I didn't know about the truth of that last part. I hadn't had a discussion with them to find out, but from what I knew of their characters, I figured I was speaking truth.

Mr. Mills laughed. "Seely and Grove are brilliant men, both inventors who, through their inventions, have saved thousands, millions of lives." He started walking around the side of the hotel, down a small channel between the rock walls and the mountain face, and we followed.

"I am an orphan from outside of Atlanta. To my knowledge, I've saved no one's life." Mr. Mills pushed his hands into the pockets of his gray overcoat, a normal gesture against the spring chill, but it was also a movement that indicated unease. I'd watched the men in Red Dragon shift their weight and still their hands in the pockets of their dungarees around Boss Elkhorn for years. Mr. Mills didn't think himself worthy of any sort of feature.

"To your knowledge." I echoed his words as the side of the building gave way to the mountain view. "You might deal in lumber and stone and concrete, but you also deal in the hiring and managing of men and the selecting of companies for sourcing. I hear work is rare these days, that a man is considered fortunate to obtain a post at all. You're helping these men survive. Their families too." I lifted my hand to my eyebrows to shield the sunlight so I could see the view. The brim of my picture hat seemed to block the light from only one side.

The mountains were still blue today, though the clouds were gathering in the distance, cloaking them in gray. Whether that would make for a rain shower later, it was hard to determine.

"Aren't you also sourcing your materials as locally as you can?" I continued. "Mules from Salisbury, you said, and the tile roof and glass ceiling are from factories in Tennessee, the concrete from Southern Ferro in your hometown? A project such as this one doesn't come around often, I imagine, and would keep a company afloat for a long time. And those companies often employ others as well."

"You have quite a way of making a person feel worthwhile, Miss Newbold," Mr. Mills said.

"It is her greatest gift," Worth said. I looked at him and he smiled.

"It is easy to consider yourself ordinary, worthless even, when you mistakenly think of your contribution as small. No one's life is small, and to be part of creating an inn this breathtaking is an accomplishment to be proud of. That's why I intend to write my story this way."

"Mr. Mills!" A man called down from the top of a five-story wooden ramp held up by scaffolding. He leaned over the flimsy beams, one hand on the roof, and my stomach swam with nerves. One inch and he could fall to his death. Above him, dozens of men crawled atop the pitched surface, their hands fixed to hammers, sprigs of wire, or a tile. The same pounding, crashing sounds I'd heard in the rafters with Worth echoed over us, but this time it wasn't atop my head, threatening that the roof could cave in on us.

"Morning, Burke. What can I do for you?" Mr. Mills called.

I breathed deep, trying to dispel my worry for the men. I could hardly make out the sweet smell of the mountains for the heavy woodsmoke coming from everywhere—from fires outside the workers' tents, fires outside the inn.

"Do you suppose they could attach the men to the roof with

something to prevent injury in case they fall?" I whispered to Worth. I kept my eyes fixed on the mountains or on the ground.

He laughed. "No, but these men are versed at their balance. Most have done this sort of work for years."

"More gloves," the man named Burke called from the roof. "We're cutting our hands on the wires and it's slowing our progress significantly."

"I have a few pairs, but I'll have to order more. I'll bring them 'round in a bit," Mr. Mills said, then turned to me. "Burke Hayes is the supervisor over the roof. In case you'd like to put him in your story."

I pulled my portfolio from beneath my arm, opened it, extracted a pen from its space in the crease, and wrote his name.

"How exactly are they fixing the tiles to the roof?" I asked. I forced myself to look up and found that Mr. Hayes had already scrambled back to the top of the roof. "I'd inquire of Mr. Hayes, but it appears he's occupied." There was a mechanical method to the way they were working. A man next to an open window on the fifth floor handed tiles to another man outside of the window, who passed the needed tile to a worker who'd just affixed one.

"The inn is constructed of much concrete, and the roof is no different. Mr. Seely is adamant that the whole place be made entirely fireproof, so the base of the roof is continuously poured concrete. If it was poured in pieces, the slope wouldn't be smooth enough to obtain the look or the hold required of the design." Mr. Mills pointed to what looked like a metal grid beneath the kneeling men. "Then we secured a horizontal lathe made of rebar across the concrete, and the tiles are attached to that in parallel rows with copper wire. Each row overlaps the row below it to exclude rainwater and to cover the wires."

I recorded his answer and glanced back up at the roof. It had been only two days since my first visit, but the tile already covered a full section of the inn.

"They're making tremendous progress. Even since we were here a couple of days ago," Worth said as though he'd read my mind.

"Indeed," Mr. Mills said. "Work does not stop, even into the night and early morning. Mr. Seely has provided electric lamps for when it's dark."

Mr. Mills led us across the front lawn of the inn, where we'd gathered for luncheon before. Since we'd been there, pillars had been sunk into the ground.

"We're about ready to make headway on the terrace here," he said as we walked past.

"It will be quite a place for sunsets," I said.

"It already is. I had occasion to come up here with Fred right before they broke ground, and the view was breathtaking." Worth smiled.

"My favorite time of day," Mr. Mills said. "Now we're going to go inside to the office washroom. The first plumbing is being installed today. Mr. Seely required that all piping be concealed completely, save the faucets and showerheads. It's unique construction."

We walked through the doors to the Great Hall. I gaped at the completed stone fireplace that had, two days ago, boasted only a few rows of stone.

"How in the world do you figure it all? How much material to order? How many men to hire?" I asked, still gazing at the artistry of the fireplace. On the other side of the Great Hall, closest to the flight of stairs that led to the guest rooms and the atrium, at least thirty masons were at work on another matching masterpiece.

"Same way Delafield here figures the particular dimensions of his land, I suppose. I walk it."

Worth laughed. "I wouldn't compare my ambling around with a cartography chain and a notepad to the tremendous amount of thought it must take to orchestrate a project this size."

"Stop," Mr. Mills said and stretched an arm out in front of me in case I didn't comply. We were crossing the hall on the side of the completed fireplace, but a boulder at least ten feet in width was suspended high in the air by a pulley. The boulder itself was bound by a metal chain and kept from swinging by a frame of timbers. A group of men gripped the other end of the boulder's chain, straining against the weight, while a man with full white hair and old-fashioned spectacles yelled instruction.

"We had a man perish here in February," Mr. Mills said. "Nat Purdue. It's best to stay back while the rock is lifted."

"Did . . . Did the rock fall?" I asked as chills washed over my body. I recalled the tile setter, Mr. Woods, mentioning something about a casualty when we'd spoken in the atrium.

"No, thank God. That would have been worse. A beam came loose of the frame around one of the stones and struck him as he was walking beneath it. At first we thought he might pull through." Mr. Mills shook his head. "He was an older man, seventy. It was a tragedy indeed."

"Have there been any other fatalities?" Worth asked.

"There have not," Mr. Mills said. "It's quite remarkable. On a project like this, one might lose a dozen men. It is a terribly risky profession."

The boulder was now shifted to the side of the room, descending midway down the wall of the fireplace.

"That man over there, the one with the white hair, is John Corbin, our head mason. Worked for Biltmore for many years before going to partner with Samuel Bean, the premier stoneman around this area. He just retired last year," Mr. Mills said.

"Do you suppose I could have an interview with Mr. Corbin?" I asked. "With the stone being so vital to the inn, I want to know how he figures the way they fit together."

"Certainly," Mr. Mills said.

We walked across the hall to a northern corridor and then up a small flight of stairs and into what would be a guest room, though now it was only an empty space framed in wood.

"Mr. Corbin?" Mr. Mills called.

We stepped into a narrow opening and a small room equipped with drywall. Pipes and fixtures were set in a pile on the rough wood floor, and the wall boasted one precise hole at the bottom where I assumed sewer or water piping would be installed.

"Looks like he's taken a break." Mr. Mills shrugged. "I suppose we could wait for him?"

"Can I ask you some questions in the meantime?" I asked.

Mr. Mills hesitated, then finally nodded.

"Earlier you mentioned you were in the business of roofing at first. How did you get into that, and how did that post encourage you toward this sort of work?"

He cleared his throat and ran a finger along his mustache.

"I suppose I have to start at the beginning. I was orphaned at birth. My parents eloped to Atlanta—Mother's parents didn't approve of my father, an Italian immigrant, and disowned her for running away with him. They both contracted cholera from the tenement they were living in and both perished from it. I was born prematurely right before Mother's passing."

He stopped for a moment and looked away. "I've never forgiven my mother's family for disowning her. Society does that, though. They leave their disappointments, their embarrassments, for dead."

"Mr. Mills, we don't have to discuss this. I didn't mean to upset you," I said, my voice strained. "But if you'd like to tell me, I'll listen. I'd like to hear about your life."

Tears sprang to my eyes and my body tensed, but I blinked and forced the emotion away lest Worth and Mr. Mills see. There were so many stories like this one, too many to count. Every time I heard one, the possibility that Mother and I could be next haunted me. I didn't think of the fear every day, but it always lingered in the recesses of my mind. I knew it always would. Papa and Worth could never know the truth. I ran my hands over my leather portfolio, taking the time to feel the grain, bringing myself back to the moment, to a story that wasn't about me.

"I know," Mr. Mills said, his feelings now tempered, like my own. "You're a kind woman, Miss Newbold, to take interest in a stranger and encourage a man so."

"Too many people aren't celebrated when they're alive," I said. "I think that's wrong."

"Very well," he said.

I could feel Worth's gaze and knew he'd likely seen my momentary distress, but I kept my attention fixed on Mr. Mills.

"My life ended up well. I was eventually adopted by an unmarried aunt of a missionary." He paused. "I am grateful. She was in her sixties and worked as a bookkeeper for Atlanta Roofing. From the time she brought me home, I went to work with her. I was raised around figures. It was her responsibility to order enough roofing tiles for each month. She taught me how to estimate just the right number of supplies. I didn't have enough time with her. She died from an unknown illness when I was only thirteen."

His voice broke a little on the last word.

"She sounds like she was an incredible woman," I said.

He nodded.

"I'm not the only one who had to grow up fast. Older I get, the more I realize a lot of people have the same kind of story, but—"

"They don't have your story," I said.

I'd bargained with myself when I first moved to Gas City. I'd hear others' stories of sadness and convince myself that theirs was worse, and because of that, I needed to let Father go like Mother had. It was a lie—lives were shaped and maimed and put together again in all different ways—but I'd let him go all the same. And now I was still holding him to myself as I encouraged someone else to speak of their hardship if they wished. I wanted to talk about Father, to speak aloud about the person he was and about the person I'd been, but I had Mother to think of. I had myself and my livelihood to think of. It was one thing for Mr. Mills to talk of his impoverished past and another entirely for Shipley Newbold's stepdaughter to speak of hers.

"After her passing, her boss took me on as a roofer and later promoted me to a position that combined roofing and ordering—a roofing foreman was what he called it. My first project was for a city hall. I was tasked with the entirety of it. The cost figures, the staffing figures, the management of the shipping, and the management of the people. When it was finished four months before schedule, I developed a bit of a reputation around town for my proficiency, so I opened a small shop independently. I went on to have quite a fruitful career. I met Mr. Seely when I was managing the building of his newspaper facility, which I finished with two months to spare." Mr. Mills laughed. "My wife and children were the cause. It was my eldest's birthday and she wanted to visit the shore." He paused. "All that to say, I do know without doubt that my propensity for early completion is why I was hired for this space."

"All businessmen are known for something. How wonderful that you are known for something so positive," I said.

"Mills, I know you wanted me to start on this today, but—" The plumber, a slight man wearing overalls and carrying a wrench, walked into the room and lifted his hand to us. "Morning, folks."

"Yes, Geoffrey, this is Miss Belle Newbold—she's writing a story on the building of this fine place for Mr. Seely—and Mr. Worth Delafield, a friend of Mr. Seely and Mr. Grove," Mr. Mills said. "We were hoping to catch your work today to be included in the story, but perhaps we'll have to see if Miss Newbold would have time another day."

"That would be best, unfortunately. I need a smaller saw for the holes, and it seems we don't have the correct size. I checked with Paul in the lumber tent."

"Actually, we might. William was using a small one in the Great Hall when I walked in this morning. If you'll excuse me, Mr. Delafield, Miss Newbold, for just a few moments, I'll walk over with Geoffrey to see if that one might suffice. Then you'll be able to see our vision, Miss Newbold, without another trip."

"Of course," I said.

The two of them walked away, leaving Worth and me standing alone in the unfinished washroom. I looked at him, at the vibrant blue of his eyes that had returned since we arrived at Grove Park Inn and at the strong set of his jaw—determination to make something beautiful out of a life that had already endured much.

"I want to know everything about you too," I said. "Everything. Will you trust me with it?"

"Yes. I would have told you anyway, but after watching you with Mr. McKibbin and Mr. Mills, I've seen that you don't offer false compassion." He stepped toward me. "I am a marred man, a scarred soul. I'm afraid I have nothing to offer you in terms of innocence, but in terms of joy, I want to pour it over you. I want to see nothing but delight in your eyes for the years we have." His hand lifted to my cheek, and I leaned into his touch, his fingers tracing the corner of my eye. My heart skipped, and I stepped back, the movement so sudden his hand remained suspended.

"Excuse me . . . Lunch has just been brought to Mr. Mills's office. He sent me to collect you." A worker had materialized in the space adjacent to the washroom, startling me.

"Thank you," Worth said. "We'll be along." His gaze settled on my face, on the place where his thumb had just been, and then, as though he could see inside my mind and understand it, too, he walked out of the room, his hands at his sides.

# CHAPTER EIGHTEEN

I'd adjourned to my tent immediately after dinner, forgoing the dessert and coffee the rest were taking around the fire—much to the horror of Mrs. Ford. Even though it had been an entertaining hour, to say the least, with the men insisting they use their hand-whittled wooden knives to slice their porterhouse steaks while the photographers' cameras popped, my mind had been fixed on the notes on Mr. Mills in my notebook. I wanted to organize them, to take the time to read over his story fully as I had Mr. McKibbin's.

After our conversation in the would-be washroom, we'd taken lunch in his office where he'd gone over his methods of converting square footage to the needed figures of lumber and tile and concrete and rebar and steel and stone. Order too much, and Mr. Seely and Mr. Grove could possibly be saddled with thousands in extra material—there was a time frame for returns that the inn's building would inevitably go past—but order too little, and the project could be delayed and even halted until shipments arrived.

"Mr. Leslie is asking for you, Miss Newbold." Sylvia walked into the tent, holding a tray of what appeared to be the dessert—apple pie and wine jelly with whipped cream—and coffee I'd left behind. She glanced at the portfolio open on my lap, then at my hair, which I'd undone on my own. Half of it was still up, but I'd relieved myself of the pins closest to my scalp, the ones that pinched and scratched when I tried to concentrate.

"Whatever for?" I asked.

"He said you were unaware of the departure time this morning, and he wanted to set a suitable hour for tomorrow."

She set down the dessert tray with a clatter on the bedside table between my cot and Marie Austen's.

"Yes. That would be much better." I knew we were going to witness the stone extraction tomorrow behind the inn on Sunset Mountain and that we were to be told of the process by a man named Mr. Smith at nine o'clock, though we hadn't discussed the particulars of when we would leave.

"Let me fix your hair so you're at least suitable to be seen," she said. "Everyone is still about—Mr. Delafield too. I saw him taking a cigar with your father and Mr. Firestone just now."

Sylvia started to sit behind me on the edge of the cot, but I stopped her.

"Don't waste the time. I'm going to be gone only a moment or two, and it's dark besides."

"I don't think that's wise, Miss Newbold. It's important to make impressions that—"

"I appreciate your care, Sylvia, but I don't think Worth is the sort of man to back away from a match because of the state of my hair." I was quite lucky in that regard. There *were* men who insisted their women be done up to perfection at all times. I'd even heard Mother and Mrs. Kipp speak of one of their friends in Gas City who slept in her hairpins and rouge.

I closed my portfolio and rose from the cot.

"At least let me fetch your cape." Sylvia crossed to the armoire and extracted the thick wool garment from the back before I could stop her. Her fingers recoiled and she dropped the cape to the floor of the chest.

"It is freezing, wet." She looked at me. "What happened?"

"I don't know." I couldn't think of an excuse. The truth was that my hair from last night's swim had thoroughly soaked the wool. I'd expected it to dry quickly, like my nightgown, but I'd forgotten that wool often took days.

Sylvia pursed her lips and stared at me. "I find that difficult to believe, but perhaps it is the fault of one of the other servants. I'll ask Mrs. Kipp's maid if she mistakenly washed this instead of one of Miss Kipp's garments." She turned back to look in the armoire. "I suppose you'll have to wear your velvet and mink again until your cape dries." She reached for the overcoat I'd worn to the Grove Park Inn and held it out to me. I threaded my arms into the sleeves.

"Where will I find Mr. Leslie?" I asked.

"Down past the dining tent. The horses have just arrived for the gentlemen's trek tomorrow, and given the absence of a barn, the valets are being made to watch 'round the clock for any wildcats or bears that may find them appetizing."

"I'm sorry for them. It seems like it's going to be a chilly night, possibly rainy too," I said. A front was coming in. The clouds had piled over the mountains all day.

"I hope for all of us it doesn't rain. I suppose these tents keep the elements out, but I've never been in one to know for sure," Sylvia said.

"I imagine it will sustain for a sprinkle but not a shower. Once it's saturated, I assume it will drip in places," I said. "Hides would have been better for the elements, but given we're here only for a week, I suppose the trouble wouldn't have been worth it."

I'd never seen the villages of the native people on the Great Plains, but my grandfather had. He'd gone out to California to hunt for gold before returning to what was then Virginia at the onset of the War Between the States. He'd told Father about the artistry of the tepees and the genius of their construction. Once, Father and I had tried to build one from deer hide, but the hide was too thin.

"You're so cavalier about the possibility of being doused in your sleep," Sylvia said as she fastened the buttons at the top of my neck.

"What should my reaction be? There isn't another choice for shelter." I laughed.

"I guarantee if there's a storm, we'll find the likes of Mrs. Ford asleep in the autos by morning," Sylvia said, a grin lifting her lips.

"I'm certain of it. Can I please have the pie?" I gestured to the tray and Sylvia's nose scrunched.

"Now? You'll be walking through the camp."

I shrugged. "I'm hungry."

She walked to the tray and handed me the small plate of pie. The smell of cinnamon and butter wafted over me, and my stomach growled.

"Thank you," I said, but she made a disapproving noise and plucked the plate from my hands. "I've changed my mind. When you return," she said. I sighed.

She lifted the tent flap for me, and I ducked out.

Most of the ladies must have just retired from the fire. The channel between the tents was bustling. Maids scurried out of their tents and toward their employers, their hands clutching vials of oil and tubes of cream.

"It's the witching hour—hurry!" I heard one young maid whisper to another before they fell into a fit of laughter. I'd heard the term used when it came to small children, but I knew without a doubt the maid had been referring to the hour they spent readying their ladies for bed. By the end of the day, society women were cranky, tired, and exposed to dinner drinks, which made for horrid attitudes.

"Belle, there you are. I was just coming back to the tent to ready for bed." Marie Austen materialized from around the last tent before the walkway to the fire. She'd been solemn tonight. Not in a sulking way, strangely enough, but quiet, measured in what she said. I hadn't had time to ask her what she'd done in my absence today, but perhaps something had transpired.

"I'll be back in a moment," I said. "I've just got to speak with Mr. Leslie about tomorrow's transport."

"Good. I . . . I need to discuss something important with you when you return," she said.

"Is everything all right?" I asked.

"I suppose it'll be up to you to determine that."

My heart quickened at her statement, but I had to speak with Mr. Leslie. I couldn't forgo arranging our departure.

"Sylvia was in the tent when I left. Have her undress you and fetch you a cup of tea if it will help, and I'll return momentarily."

She nodded and stepped around me and I kept on, past the fire where Mr. Burroughs and Mr. Carver lingered, past the dining tent.

The horses were gathered, tied to several temporary hitching posts in a circle, while Mr. Leslie sat in front of a small fire in a canvas chair. In the flames' light, absent his smile pasted on for us guests, I could see the exhaustion in his face.

"Can I get you a coffee, Mr. Leslie?"

He lurched from his seat.

"Miss Newbold, I apologize," he sputtered. "I didn't hear you approaching. And no, I'm afraid coffee keeps me awake all night if I drink it at this hour, though it's very kind of you to ask."

"Not to worry, Mr. Leslie. Please sit. It's been a long day."

"I couldn't," he said, attempting in vain to press the wrinkles from his jacket with the palm of his hand. "I don't have a seat to offer you."

"Well then, let's make this conversation swift, shall we? What hour would be suitable for our departure in the morning?"

"It will take us quite a bit of time to get up the mountain. I proposed eight o'clock to Mr. Delafield when I saw him after dinner," he said. "I would have sent word with your maid, but I wanted to ask you personally if that time was best for you. It is your work we are traveling for, after all."

"It was kind of you to consider my feelings on the matter," I said. "But that time works fine. I do hope you're able to retire to your tent soon."

"One more hour and I'll be relieved," he said.

I smiled and started to walk away, but he stopped me.

"I hate to ask you for a favor, but if you happen past your mother's tent, would you mind terribly to tell her that I'll be back here around nine o'clock to chauffeur her and Mrs. Kipp to tea with Mrs. Grove? Oliver, their normal chauffeur, has taken ill."

"Certainly," I said, though delaying my discussion with Marie Austen was torture. Her words had been haunting, and the knowledge that something was amiss, something that would affect me, made my stomach ache.

I hurried down the opposite aisle between the servants' tents and the elder guests'. Most were still aglow with lantern light, and the soft hum of lowered voices chattering joined with the slight cry of a few brave crickets in the night.

"I think I've made a terrible mistake."

I froze at Worth's voice, just outside of Mother and Papa's tent.

"What is it?" Papa responded.

"I shouldn't have agreed to the arrangement with Belle."

I heard my mother gasp. My breath caught.

"Whyever not? You seem more suited to each other than I thought possible—and I knew from the start the match was a good one. If it's the permanence of matrimony you're worried about, it's just fear," Papa said. "You'll—"

"I don't know if I can find the ring she requires in the days remaining," Worth said evenly.

I'd forgotten about my asinine demand for a blue sapphire and at once wanted to burst into the tent and tell him the request had only been made in anger.

"And beyond that, I . . . I can't provide her what she deserves. She is a wonderful woman, but I think it best we dissolve the arrangement. I wanted to come to you first, Shipley. I cannot offer her—"

"You will not dissolve the arrangement." Papa's voice roared from the tent. My hands were shaking, my whole body quaking with Worth's words. I flipped through the day in my memory—the pleasant conversations, the tender way he'd touched my face. We'd even laughed on the ride back to camp in the auto. There was nothing I could recall that would merit his doing this, his going back on his word to marry me.

"I have to, Shipley. I cannot marry her knowing—"

"Knowing what?" Mother joined in. "Knowing what? She is beautiful and kind, smart and undeniably loving."

"Yes. She's all those things." Worth's voice was quiet. "She must marry someone better than me, someone who can give her the life she ought to have."

"You will forget about this foolish conversation. You will take

Belle as your wife. And if I hear another word of this nonsense, I will tarnish your name. Your father was like a brother to me, and you are like a son, but Belle is my true daughter. Go through with your plan, and I will reveal it all," Papa snarled.

I stopped breathing. My lungs constricted and my head spun. I tried to focus on the tent fabric, to smell the woodsmoke, to feel the sensation of the velvet cuff I'd gripped in my palm to steady myself, but it wasn't working. Worth was concealing something awful, something horrible, something he'd been trying to tell me, but now it was clear. It was the only thing that made our match possible. The murkiness of my past matched his.

At once, the handful of wealthy men who had once considered me for marriage and disappeared shortly after discovering that I wasn't, in fact, Papa's flesh or heir flashed in my mind. They'd all been unfavorable to behold—old or pockmarked or rotund—and they'd all fled. Of course, this was why I, a woman of paltry breeding and empty pockets, had obtained the hand of one of the most eligible bachelors in the country. There was something terribly wrong with him.

"Reveal what? What is there to reveal? You know the truth, and I was going to tell her everything."

"From the outside, things can look different," Papa said.

"It won't matter what lie you tell her. She won't believe it," Worth said.

"She might not. But others will," he said. "Abandon Belle and you'll never have a family again. Not with a suitable woman, anyway. I'll make sure of it."

The tent flap was flung back and Worth emerged and paced toward his tent. I shrank back into the shadows and sank to my knees. A sob wedged in the back of my throat, but I swallowed it. Worth didn't want me. Papa was blackmailing him to take me.

I would refuse his hand. I would have to now. I clutched my chest and closed my eyes. A vision of myself at four emerged. Mother had deconstructed the pants I'd just outgrown and was sewing them together again, larger this time, with bits of a potato sack. That night, we each had two fingerling potatoes for dinner and my stomach had felt hungry and hollow all night. My stomach had felt hungry and hollow most nights in Red Dragon.

When I thought of home with longing, it was only missing Father. Otherwise, I knew I could never go back to a life like that, where my basic human needs had barely been met. Worth was my only chance, my only hope, and Papa knew it. I would have to find a way to accept him knowing it wasn't what he wanted.

I stood slowly and walked the opposite way, around the servants' tents and down the aisle of the younger guests' toward mine. I would have to tell Mother of Mr. Leslie's arrangements in the morning. I didn't have the strength to face them now.

I wiped my eyes and lifted the tent flap. Marie Austen sat on the edge of her cot in her nightgown. Her hair was neatly plaited, but her eyes were watery and red, like mine.

"You know, don't you?" she said, her voice full of emotion. "I was angry and sad and drunk—my fate sealed—and he was so handsome."

I stared at her blankly, my mind still fixed on Worth's words.

"If you leave me forever, Belle, I'll die. I need you and I've been the worst friend, the worst cousin," she sobbed.

"What are you talking about?" I asked. My tone was a whisper, an indication of the strength that had been stolen by Papa, by Worth.

She rose and clutched my elbows hard. Tears poured down her cheeks.

"I was going to hide it from you forever. I was going to take it to the grave, but then Mr. Gibbins pointed out that you are the only one who truly loves me, and I can't. I have betrayed you. Belle . . . I . . . I . . . kissed Worth Delafield."

# CHAPTER NINETEEN

There are three options when a woman is ignited into fury. She can fight, she can let it consume her, or she can flee.

I held onto the reins and the horse's coarse black mane for dear life, my portfolio gripped with equal fervor beneath my arm. My legs ached and my feet were going numb on account of the fact that I hadn't any stirrups. I'd been riding for half an hour and was now—finally—ascending the road to the inn.

I straightened atop the horse and tried to raise my knees to pull my light green skirt farther over my legs. I'd put on a pair of cotton pantaloons beneath my dress for the occasion, but it still was far from proper to be seen riding astride at all, even if my ankles weren't in danger of showing. I breathed deep, inhaling the crisp, early morning air and the heady woodsmoke from the workers' quarters.

It was only me and the workers and the words now. I was miles away from Marie Austen and Worth and Mother and Papa and everyone else. The mere thought of them made me want to keep going, to ride farther, to disappear, but where would I go? I wasn't resourceful enough to make a life on my own, and even if I was, I couldn't. I couldn't stop telling this story now. I knew for a fact that another writer, another newspaperman, would write the facts of the build clinically, without heart and without giving the builders praise. Without my story, the legacies of these men would be all but forgotten, like Father.

I crested the hill, and the side of the inn came into view. I pulled back on reins gently and the horse stopped. A team of men was scattered across the roof, bathed in the pink-gold of sunrise, their limbs spread like spiders' as they worked to attach the tiles. They were in the middle of the building now. I wagered another day or two and they'd have to stop to let the masons catch up on the south side. Their voices—their yelling and laughing and talking—echoed over the valley and over me, joining the soft chug of the steam shovel below. The noises seemed to wake me a bit, shake my insides in the same sensation as Sylvia rousing me from slumber.

I hadn't spoken since Marie Austen told me about her kissing Worth. She'd come looking for forgiveness when I'd already been emptied. I'd extinguished the oil lamp and lain down on my cot in the dark, the echo of Worth's words and the wail of Marie Austen's sobs my companions.

At first, I wasn't angry. I felt hollow, depleted, as though this revelation wasn't a revelation at all but a conclusion I'd been expecting. After all, when I'd been presented, I'd never thought myself destined for a man like Worth—I'd never wanted a man like Worth. He had been a pleasant surprise despite his attractiveness. I'd thought him kind and thoughtful, but most of all, I'd thought him trustworthy.

He'd confided in me and I in him. I'd thought our match a true miracle. I hadn't bargained on him falling in love with my friend. Of course that was the reason he wanted to break our arrangement. He hadn't said it, but there was no other explanation. Marie Austen had repeated over and over that she was sorry, that she had only come upon him on her way back to our tent that night and begged him to take her on a midnight walk, and then later, to kiss her. She'd said he had refused her, but she'd kissed him anyway, and he'd kissed her back.

A shout ricocheted over me, and I glanced up in time to see a man catch another man's wrist and hoist him back up on the roof. I gasped and nudged the horse forward, following the drive snaking behind the inn. The possibility of a man falling to his death made me tremendously uneasy. I couldn't look at it again.

*"I'll never even look at him again,"* Marie Austen had said after

her hysterics gave out and it was clear I wasn't planning to respond. *"I don't even find him appealing in the slightest anymore. Do you know he acted like he had no idea that anything had transpired between us when I pulled him aside after dinner? What a cad."*

At least Worth was keeping his story consistent with us both, that he had no recollection of a rendezvous in the woods. Even so, there were other things to consider. Papa hadn't known of his tryst with Marie Austen when Worth begged to end our arrangement. Whatever secret he claimed he held over Worth's head wasn't this one.

I nodded at a group of masons staring up at an incomplete rock wall on the southern edge of the inn.

"Could you point me in the direction of where the men are harvesting the granite rocks today?" I called. I ran a hand down my braid, sure I looked a fright.

"Follow the road 'round past the housing and up the furthermost mountain trail. Keep going until you find them," an older man in overalls yelled back. "Your horse spook easily?"

"I don't know," I said. The decision to set out on my own had come suddenly with my anger. I'd been mired in thoughts of Marie Austen kissing Worth, Worth's affection for her, and Worth's secret, the majority of the night, but in an instant, my mind shifted to the implication of it all for me.

Unless he actually told me he was dissolving our arrangement, I would have to pretend I knew nothing of his desire to walk away. I'd have to marry him anyway. I couldn't risk a future filled with poverty. I couldn't risk a future without a family, without children. The realization of it all made me furious, and though I knew I'd have to face him eventually, I didn't want to have to endure the auto ride up the mountain, the way he'd mask his disdain for me in pleasantries and kindness.

"Might want to know," the older man called out. "Trucks are loud. Squeal of the axels from the wagons on the way down the mountain are too. The first shipment is due in"—he extracted a pocket watch—"twenty minutes, so they're already on the way."

I glanced down at the face of the bay mare. She seemed calm.

Then again, what did I know? When I was young, I'd ridden my grandparents' old horse bareback often, but that had been fifteen years ago. I knew nothing about the temperament of horses. I'd chosen this one because she was the farthest from the chair where Mr. Solomon, the valet lookout, was snoring.

"How many miles to where they're working?" I asked.

"Seven or eight, most likely," he said. "If you're asking to consider the walk, I don't think you'll make it. What is it you need up there?"

I stared at him. I knew what he saw when he beheld me. Regardless of my hair, he saw a fine dress. What he didn't figure was that I'd once walked five miles into town and back again daily.

I swung down from the horse, my arm still clutching the portfolio.

"Do you suppose there's a place I can house her while I walk up? I'm writing a story for Mr. Seely."

"Miss, I told you, it's quite a way and uphill. The whole of it is muddy and dusty and—"

"I'm aware, sir," I said, leading the horse down to where they stood.

"There's a makeshift barn down the way between the two workers' quarters. Suppose you can put her there 'til you're through." He eyed the horse without a saddle while a few other men turned away from their work to do the same.

"Thank you kindly," I said.

By the time I settled the horse in a stall and made my way up the winding, wooded hill to the top, I was sweating profusely, and my dress and shoes were covered in earth, rendering the green a light gray.

I knew I was getting close. Up ahead, I could hear the screech of pulleys, the rattle of chains, the occasional clang of metal hitting rock, the braying of donkeys, and the voices.

I followed the path up a steep shoulder, my heart pounding with exertion, as the road leveled on a small ridge. The wagon train headed by a Packard truck was stacked high with boulders, idling on the path in front of me. Two men in corduroy jackets and trousers with knotted neckerchiefs sat behind the wheel, while others in similar attire clambered into each wagon, settling atop the rock.

"Where are you headed, miss?" one of the men at the wheel asked me, but I barely heard him. The view was breathtaking from here, mountain upon mountain in the distance. My gaze broke from the horizon to skim along the view just below me. Here, the lush forest plunged downward, leveling in an expansive valley washed near emerald green, and on the far edge, a wide creek bent its way through. Hundreds of men dotted the acres, some freeing the stone from the encasing dirt, their shovels gleaming and shadowing with each effort, some working steam pulleys, some hoisting boulders into wagons powered by teams of donkeys.

"Miss?" The man's voice interrupted my wonder and I turned.

"Hello there. Yes, I'm here looking for a Mr. Smith. I'm Belle Newbold, a writer for Mr. Seely," I said.

"And daughter of Shipley Newbold, the gasoline magnate. Yes, we've been told of your arrival, though I must say, it couldn't come at a worse time. We're short near fifty men today and quite behind," he said.

"I don't intend to get in your way, and it isn't my fault you're short fifty men," I snapped, my anger at Worth and Marie Austen emerging in my tone. "Where can I find Mr. Smith? I'm a bit early for our appointment."

The man sighed. "I know, Miss Newbold. It's just that this illness going 'round threatens to set us back significantly, and Mr. Mills has been clear that if we don't harvest the granite in a timely manner, the operation will suffer and our pay will be docked. I can't afford that, see. None of us can afford that." He lifted the flap of his neckerchief and wiped the dirt from his face.

"You can find Mr. Smith down at the creek's edge. He's instructing the extraction there." He pointed down across the valley to the banks of the creek where a few men stood in a group while a scattering of others were bent over extracting rock from the earth above the water. "Quickest way down is the donkey path just there." The man tipped his head at a thin, worn path that dipped to my right.

"Thank you. I hope your peers get well soon and that you stay well yourself," I said. "It's clear you men are some of the most important people on the project. You're doing vital work for Asheville too."

The man chuckled. "I doubt we're as cherished as you make it seem, but it's nice to hear."

He whistled and the truck's engine whined as the wagon train was set in motion. I made my way down the steep path toward the valley, leaning against the solid ledge of the mountain so as not to risk tumbling off the precipice. I wiped a bit of sweat from my brow and my breathing eased as I reached even ground.

"Pull!" someone shouted. A gust of steam burst forth from a pulley gathered beside a natural rock pile in front of me, and the squeal of a metal chain followed as a stone at least five feet wide was lifted from the top of it. The donkeys, hitched to wagons, idling beside the pulley, didn't seem to notice the noise either from the chain or from the gathering of men beside them working pickaxes in the dirt around the boulders.

"Ma'am," one of the men said, before helping direct the suspended stone into a waiting wagon.

I tipped my head at him and hastened past three other near identical operations to the creek's edge. Here, most of the large stones had been taken away, but up a bit higher on the bank, there were trees and untouched boulders ripe for sitting. Perhaps after I spoke with Mr. Smith, I could write there. Something was mesmerizing about the sound of burbling water winding its way through the mountain and the harmony of birdsong in the tree canopy above me. It could settle me.

I looked around for the right man. The group of men the engineer of the wagon train had identified as containing Mr. Smith had since dispersed. Usually, the supervisor had a certain distinction. It might not be a different manner of dress, though it often was. Downriver, more donkeys and their wagons stood beside the water while lines of men extracted rock from the shallow floor of the creek and the banks beside. In front of me, a few workers were on the opposite bank, knee-deep in the water, their picks working either side of a boulder.

"Why, Belle Coleman, as I live and breathe."

I whirled, the sound of my real name like the shock of a lightning bolt.

Willie Smith was standing there, all white-blond hair and freckled skin just like I remembered, just like I thought I'd seen the day we arrived. He threw his arms around me, and I nearly fell back. My body teemed with conflicting feelings all at once—joy at seeing him and the horror that followed the implication of his seeing me.

"What are you doing here, Willie?" I asked, breathless, as he let me go. He was bony, unnaturally so, and his blue eyes appeared sunken in, but then again, it had been six years and we were older now.

"I could ask you the same, Belle. One day you're next door; the next day you and your mother never return from your holiday away. The whole of Red Dragon wondered about you for months. Finally, everybody just assumed your mother found work in—Indiana, was it?—and that was that."

"What happened to our home?" I'd wondered for years, and in the moment, it seemed the most important question to ask. "I didn't know I wasn't coming back, and we left all of our things, all of Father's things. Do you suppose anything was salvaged?"

Willie's face sobered and he shook his head.

"A new family moved into your house about two months after you left. I suppose they got rid of everything, Belle. There was an awful lot you left behind."

My eyes filled.

Willie shoved his hands in his moleskin trousers. The bottom half of each leg was soaking wet and stained with earth. His iron-shod clogs too. "What brings you here?"

At once, the desperation to know if anything was left of Father in Red Dragon wore off and the remembrance of who I was, who everyone here knew me to be, set my nerves to quaking.

"I'm Belle Newbold. I suppose you're the Mr. Smith I'm supposed to meet."

His eyes widened.

"What? Your stepfather is Shipley Newbold? Belle, how—"

"Promise me you'll not speak my former name," I said without preamble. "Please, I beg you. They all know where I'm from and that I had a father, but they think he . . . they think he was a mine operator."

Willie squinted. "Why?"

"I don't know. Most simply assumed and Mother never corrected the assumption, I suppose. But don't you recall Boss Elkhorn's first wife? What happened when she was found to be a pauper? I can't let that happen to Mother, Willie. It's my greatest fear, and I—"

Willie nodded.

"Yes. I do. How could I forget? Father was the one who found her that day. I'd not wish that fate on my greatest enemy, and I know what danger you'd be in if word got out. I'll not say anything, I swear it." He turned and started walking down the riverbed toward where the water pooled in depths of only a few inches. I followed.

"Why are you here in Asheville now?" I asked. "Not at home, I mean."

Willie stopped and shrugged.

"I never took to working underground and, well, when Mother . . . When she . . . We needed to come here to take . . ." His voice trailed off and he shook his head. "It comes down to that I didn't want to die in the mines." His mouth pinched and he nodded quickly, as though he'd just decided that was his reason.

"Are your parents well?" I asked.

"Most certainly. We're all living just down the holler, only a mile from here, in fact." He paused and smiled at me. "Why don't you join us for dinner tonight?"

"I'd love to come, but I don't think it wise. It would be—"

"Belle . . . Miss Newbold. There you are." Worth's voice came from behind me, his tone gruff and angry.

Willie's eyes widened, and he immediately stuck out a dirty hand as Worth appeared at my side. My heart raced, thankful Worth hadn't appeared a moment earlier to hear our familiar pleasantries.

"I'm Worth Delafield, Mr. Smith," Worth said, his amiable polish emerging swiftly. He grasped Willie's hand. "Did I hear an invitation to dinner? How kind of you to offer. If there's room for one more, I'd be happy to accompany Miss Newbold."

"Yes, of course, you're welcome as well. Mother doesn't make the sort of fare you're likely used to, Mr. Delafield, but if a bit of vegetable soup and bread is to your liking, do join us," Willie said.

The thought of facing the Smiths with Worth by my side made me sick to my stomach. I couldn't figure why Willie didn't immediately withdraw his invitation. Surely he understood that dinner with his parents and Worth would be exposing me to the very danger he'd promised to help me avoid only moments earlier. Then again, perhaps he felt that propriety dictated he keep his invitation extended when it involved people of a certain caliber.

I felt as though I might collapse. I'd stepped into a nightmare.

"Surely—" I started to protest that we didn't have the time, but Worth interrupted me.

"I'm particularly fond of vegetable soup." Worth smiled. He hadn't looked at me, not once, and I could tell he was avoiding doing so on purpose. My mind raced and my skin prickled with heat.

"As I had begun to say, Mr. Smith, I'm not sure we'll have the time this evening," I said, my voice shaking. "There's much going on with the others in our party, and—"

"The evening's festivities aren't until much later," Worth said, interrupting my third attempt to avoid a meal that could be my undoing. "We'd love to dine with your family, Mr. Smith."

Tears sprang to my eyes, equal parts frustration and fear, anger and betrayal. Neither Worth nor Willie seemed to notice. I wiped my lids with the back of my hand. It wouldn't do to fall apart completely, not yet. I had a story to write and there was always the chance we would avoid dinner after all, that Mother and I would remain safe despite our closest friends from home materializing from three hundred miles away.

"Wonderful. Well, I know we have much to discuss for Miss Newbold's story, but I'm going to need to fetch a new crowbar from the shed for Mr. Roberts there," Willie said, pointing to a young man who was trying to free a boulder with a shovel. "If you'd like to settle yourselves on the bank somewhere, I'll return momentarily to answer your questions, and then I'll show you around this operation." Willie walked down the shore toward a small shed tucked beneath a tree just up from the creek bed.

"It would be impolite to decline his invitation," Worth said under his breath.

I didn't respond. I could feel Worth's fury, the tension radiating from his body suddenly matching the feeling that reignited in my chest.

I spun on my heel and walked quickly up the bank, toward the trees and the grass and the boulders. I could contain myself if only I could breathe for a moment, I was sure of it.

Worth followed after me, his long stride catching mine in a matter of seconds. We dipped into the forest, and as if the shade broke some sort of spell, he grasped my wrist and pulled me toward him.

"Don't ever do that again," he growled. His jaw bulged and his fingers tightened on my skin.

"I'll do—"

"No one knew where you'd gone. No one. I . . . We looked everywhere. I never figured you would come here alone, but I'd exhausted all other options. Do you understand the panic you caused? Mr. Leslie followed me here in another auto and is on his way back to camp with word you've been found. I was prepared to drive these hills and then walk them. Whatever it took to find you." He took a breath, his eyes cutting into mine. I tried to pull my wrist away, but he held it fast. "I envisioned the worst. You could have been hurt. You could have—"

"Why would you care?" The question came out in a whisper; otherwise I would have screamed it. I held his gaze. The top of my nose itched, and I blinked to stop the impending emotion. I'd thought us friends. I'd thought we were the same. He'd betrayed me.

"If something had happened to you . . ." His fingers trailed down from my wrist to my hand. "If something had happened to you, I—"

The tenderness in his voice raked down my spine, and I jerked my hand away.

"You would have proposed to Marie Austen. I know you've fallen under her spell. I know she was the woman with you in the woods," I said evenly. The blood drained from his face. "And I heard you last night with Papa. I know you want to dissolve our arrangement. I will grant it." The moment I said it, panic clutched my lungs and a weight settled on my shoulders. I would die penniless, childless, alone.

"Belle, I know it is unforgivable, but I promise you I wasn't lying to you. I didn't recall it. I didn't recall her taking me into the woods. You know how I was avoiding the forest. I only heard of what transpired when she told me last night. And as for my plea to Shipley, you don't understand."

I ignored the way his fingers reached desperately for my hands.

Willie appeared over Worth's shoulder. "I apologize for the delay, Miss Newbold, Mr. Delafield. Shall we begin?"

# CHAPTER TWENTY

I gasped when I saw the Smiths' home. I'd imagined something similar to our small houses in Red Dragon, something tiny but neat.

"What is it?" Worth asked, as though he couldn't see the gaping holes in the roof and the rotting wooden siding, splintered with damp and termites. We had spoken minimally after our confrontation in the woods, restricting conversation to our interaction with Willie.

"This is horrid," I whispered as Worth drove to the front of the home and shut off the auto's engine. The home was barely more than what people called a lean-to. It was tucked, quite literally, between two great mountain cliffs, and I was certain that despite getting the light for an hour at most each day, the home's windows had never seen a ray of sunshine because of the trees. The only consolations were a tiny stream trickling beside the home's left side and the fact that the brick chimney—currently piping smoke and missing several blocks—hadn't yet caved in.

Nerves rattled in my stomach, and I felt my head swim. I was about to face the Smiths with Worth. I was about to face the Smiths in their undeniable hardship while I resided in luxury. I was about to face the fate I could easily be subjected to again. Willie had said he was going ahead of us to tell his mother to set two additional plates. He'd looked at me pointedly after he said it, and I prayed the look meant he was going before us to warn his family about the person I'd become and to tell them that to speak of Father or my life in Red Dragon could risk my welfare and Mother's too.

"At least there's a roof of some sort, and their land isn't a sewage wasteland like those in the slums of great cities," Worth said, his eyes meeting mine. "That is the worst fate, I think."

"Neither should be allowed." I stared at the home in front of me, and even as Worth opened the auto's door and started around to collect me, I didn't move. Getting out of the auto felt much like beginning a walk to the gallows. My throat tightened.

"I suppose we should go in," Worth said, opening my door and holding out his hand to me. The air smelled damp beneath the woodsmoke, as though it had rained for days, instead of a brief shower the day before.

"I told you I didn't want to take dinner here at all." Panic lodged in my throat. I'd tried my hardest to get out of the meal again after the interview with Willie, feigning exhaustion, but Worth had insisted. He'd reiterated that it was impolite to decline, and dining with him would help with my article in any case—wasn't I interested in a full profile on Willie Smith too?

"They're still people like you and I," Worth said softly, as though the reason I was hesitating was because I hadn't been exposed to poverty.

"I'm aware. You forget I was raised in a mining town," I said, refusing his hand and getting out of the auto. "It's only that despite the state of it right now, I'm wearing a fine dress—a dress that costs more than Mr. Smith makes in a month—and even though I'm Shipley Newbold's stepdaughter, I haven't any money to give them to make their lives better." Though I'd concocted the sentiment as an excuse for my hesitation, it was also the truth.

"But I do." Worth sighed as we walked toward the front door. It was cockeyed, the top hinge having given way to rot. "You must also be aware, Belle, that at times, charity isn't welcome. Mr. Smith is a hard worker, someone who might be acutely proud of the way he cares for his family, that he earns enough to afford this modest house and provide food for his parents and any guests he may see fit to invite."

I'd forgotten about the pride of the people in Red Dragon, but

Worth was right. Once, when the miners were on strike, Mr. Samuelson, the manager of the company store, had tried to sneak some families some potatoes and bread—just a bit of something to get them through—but the men had refused. They thought it shameful to receive anything for free.

I knocked on the front door. My palms were clammy and my heartbeat roared in my ears. Inside, I could hear the distant clatter of plates and the scrape and squeal of chairs being rearranged. I thought to knock again, but before I could, the door creaked open and Mrs. Smith appeared in the doorway.

My breath escaped my lungs. She was nearly unrecognizable save the mop of gray-red curls.

"Oh, Belle—" Mrs. Smith exclaimed, nearly throwing her arms around me. Then she remembered herself and forced them down at her sides. "Miss Newbold, Mr. Delafield." The sound of my new name was a great relief, but the sight of Mrs. Smith was not. She had once been a plump lady with a merry countenance won by both her spirit and her full cheeks. Now she was skeletal. Her eyes were sunken in, much like Willie's, and she grasped my hand and looked from me to Worth and back again. Was it a lack of sustenance or another sort of terror that had caused this change in them?

"Thank you for inviting us into your home, Mrs. Smith," Worth said in time for my shocked silence to go unnoticed.

She laughed, a merry sort of chuckle just like I remembered.

"It's not anything like what I imagine the two of you are used to, but Willie insisted you both wanted a bowl of my soup, so I'm happy to oblige."

"It is the best," I said. "I've heard," I amended. Cold fingers squeezed my hand. I'd forgotten she'd retained mine.

"We'll take dinner in the garden," she said matter-of-factly. "Willie has gone to help Mr. Smith out of bed and will be along shortly. We've all come down with a bit of ill health these last months—like everyone it seems, according to Willie—and Willie said some men on the job are of the mind that it's spread 'round in close quarters. I wouldn't want the two of you taking to your beds when you're needed so. I hear you've been tasked with writing a story on the grand inn, Miss . . . Miss Newbold."

She turned and led us through the small house. Metal buckets filled with old rainwater lined the warped wood floor, and two rocking chairs I recognized as those that had occupied their old house sat in front of the fireplace where a cooking pot was suspended over the flame. A doorway to a bedroom was to the right of the fire, and I could barely make out a quilt lying on the floor and a dry cough coming from the pile of linen.

"Yes, the Grove Park Inn is such a wonder of a build, and I'm thrilled to be able to catalog it," I said, pushing thoughts of calamity and poverty away as we emerged from another small door at the back of the house and made our way down the steps to a set of five ladder-back chairs gathered around a worm-eaten table.

"Do have a seat," Mrs. Smith said. "When Willie comes out with Mr. Smith, I'll return to pour our bowls. I admit I'm looking forward to reading your piece, Miss Newbold."

We sank onto the chairs, Worth with particular care. Like the rest of the house, the wood was soft and damp, and one of Worth's stature never knew if such a structure would hold him. I wished it would collapse.

"As am I. She is doing a remarkable, thorough job of it," Worth said. "She's quite perceptive and talented. Mr. Seely will be pleased, I'm sure."

"She always was—" Mrs. Smith stopped cold and shook her head. Worth glanced at me. "What I meant to say is that Willie said her questions were unique and would lend to a lovely story indeed. He said the inquisitiveness reminded him of our neighbor in our hometown who used to write up pieces on all sorts of things. He was never a newsman, mind you, but he had the sort of curious brain that makes a good reporter. Sometimes he'd let Mr. Smith or me read the stories he'd write. They always made you see the world a little differently. I imagine Miss Newbold's story will be quite the same."

My hands balled in my filthy, dusty skirt, and I kneaded the fabric between my fingers. I smiled at Mrs. Smith and she grinned back. She remembered Father's stories despite his never having achieved a byline. Father had been a loud man, a boisterous soul who was known for his love of fishing and jests and Mother. When there were plenty of other things to recall about a person, the small loves could be lost in memory.

"I think you're absolutely right, Mrs. Smith. By the time a person is finished reading her article, I reckon they'll be packing their trunks to take a visit to see the wonder of the inn for themselves, hoping they'll glimpse Mr. Mills or Mr. McKibbin or Mr. Smith when they do," Worth said.

Mrs. Smith laughed.

"To think that my Willie, a boy raised up by a coal miner, would rise to such a prominent post as to be featured in a news story is thrilling." She shook her head and pulled her wool shawl around her shoulders.

"Coal, you say? Whereabouts did you come from, Mrs. Smith? Miss Newbold was born in a coal town herself." Worth's gaze drifted to mine and he smiled. I forced myself to return the pleasant expression, but my stomach was churning.

"I can smell the soup," I said, hoping to dispel talk of origins and coal towns.

"I'm sorry to keep you waiting." Mrs. Smith hazarded a glance at the empty doorway. "It's been on the fire for these past five hours made from vegetables gifted to us by some of Willie's stonemen. There's even okra, canned last summer. Nothing much grows here, I'm afraid, so we've been relying on the kindness of peers with land in the sunlight."

"How many years have you resided here?" Worth asked, circling back to her history despite my trying to thwart the effort.

"Near five now. My mother had taken ill around then and there'd been another fall that claimed the lives of eleven in the mine. Stephen and Willie couldn't go back after that. I wouldn't allow it."

Our neighbors in Red Dragon flipped through my mind. I wanted to ask her who had been killed, whose lives had been cut short and whose lives had been changed forever. I wanted to ask her how my friends fared, if any had married or moved away, but I couldn't.

"We heard there were many opportunities here, and—"

"Mother, could you give us a hand?"

We turned toward the doorway and my blood ran cold. Mr. Smith and Father were the same age, had the same build—both tall, hulking, mountain-bred men. But Mr. Smith was now as thin as Mrs. Smith, hunched near to her height as well, balanced on a branch cane. His face was gaunt, though his lips seemed to lift in a smile when he saw me. As though Worth could sense my horror, he reached for my hand and I pulled it away. Why he continued to attempt to comfort me, I couldn't say. I had freed him from his obligation to care for me.

"Belle." Mr. Smith's voice was a hoarse whisper and the uttering of it immediately sent him into a coughing fit. Willie grasped his father's arm.

"Try to breathe," Willie instructed as Mrs. Smith reached his other side. They held Mr. Smith's arms and guided him slowly down the steps to the ground and across the grass to the arrangement of chairs. The moment he was settled in the chair at the head of the table opposite Worth and Willie beside him, Mrs. Smith disappeared into the house for our soup.

"It's just the dirt I bring home from extracting the stone," Willie attempted to explain. "It settles in the walls of the house and makes the illness worse. I—"

"I told you it's from the mine. Same as everybody else. Belle, you remember how your father used to cough—"

I froze.

"Father, this is Belle Newbold, the gasoline baron Shipley Newbold's stepdaughter, remember?" Mr. Smith's eyes widened, and he nodded. "There was a neighbor we had back home, a girl named Belle who had the same sort of hair. He's been a bit confused as of late," Willie said, mostly to Worth, who seemed to buy the lie.

Mrs. Smith emerged from the house with a tray of steaming soup bowls. My stomach rumbled. It was rare that we were served hot soup, and if we were, it was always a cream base. Mrs. Smith set an earthenware bowl in front of me, then Worth, then Willie, and I leaned over the steam and breathed. Chicken stock and tomatoes, onion and garlic. Mother used to make the same sort of soup. Everyone did, especially in the summertime when vegetables were plentiful.

"I hope this makes you feel better, Mr. Smith. A crock of vegetable soup always soothed me when I was ill as a child," Worth said.

"I've quite given up feeling better," he said as he slurped a bit of broth from his spoon. "We left home on account of the danger of work in the mines, but there ain't been nothing but trouble since we . . ." Mr. Smith stopped and coughed so heartily his eyes watered.

"We heard there was work to be had here. One of the miners back home heard tell of a new rail line coming into Asheville after Mr. Vanderbilt built his mansion and that they were in need of a great number of workers. When we arrived, we found he was right, and all of us—Father, me, my friend John Connolly—got hired right away on the rail," Willie said.

I took a bite of soup, savoring the flavors I hadn't tasted since we'd left home. I looked from Willie to Mr. Smith and back again. Though Willie wasn't nearly as emaciated as his parents, his face still had that same pale cast, the same inset of the eyes.

"Then the rail pulled out on account of the city council's emphasis on welcoming new sanitoriums," he said. "I was out of work for near four years. We both were."

"Seely and Grove are adamantly fighting against that fate for this town," Worth said.

"I couldn't be more thankful," Willie said. "I am finally able to provide again, especially with Father in the state he is."

"We shouldn't have left. We've withered away here, and what for? True, I could've died in the mines, same as James, but I'm dying now."

I set my spoon down with a clatter, the mention of my father's death, the vision of Mr. Smith on the verge of it, too much to bear.

"Why would you bring that up? In the presence of Miss Newbold," Mrs. Smith said. Her voice sounded far away as she settled in the chair across from me.

I swallowed hard. Mrs. Smith was hazy in my sight, her waiflike frame suddenly more like an apparition.

"I'm making more than I ever would have back in West Virginia," Willie said. "And soon enough we'll shake off this little house and I'll buy you a place in the sun."

Suddenly, the purpose of his invitation was certain, the reason he'd not rescinded it when he knew I would be in danger of being found out—he wanted me to help; he thought my pockets full.

"We'll be gone by then," Mr. Smith said matter-of-factly. "I dream of home every day. We didn't have much, but those little homes on the side of the hill were paradise, weren't they, Belle?"

I stood abruptly, nearly unsettling my bowl as my arms hit the table.

"Th-This has been l-lovely," I stammered. "I . . . Worth . . . We have to go."

# CHAPTER TWENTY-ONE

I couldn't stop crying. I didn't try. I let the tears soak my cheeks and run down my face unchecked. Outside the window of the auto, darkness consumed. It felt appropriate to the moment, to the way my heart had shriveled.

It was cowardly to leave that way, to push back from the table and flee, but there was no other option save crumpling to my knees in front of people who were already on theirs. It wasn't just the sight of them, their bodies wasting away, becoming something unknown. It was that I had to pretend I didn't know them or I would become like them, and I had chosen the former to save myself.

The Smiths had been a part of our every day, people I'd shared life with for seventeen years. Our reunion should have been one of celebration. I'm certain that was what Willie had in mind, a familiar face to lift their spirits. Instead, the meeting had been stilted, terrible, foreign, and Worth had discovered the truth anyway. There was no way he hadn't, though he'd said nothing.

I hugged the portfolio to my chest and angled my body farther from Worth, my face fixed toward the window. I'd lost myself. On one hand, I'd done the abandoning, and on the other, I'd been abandoned, betrayed. An unbearable ache settled in my heart. I had no true home, no true family to bind up my wounds.

The tears ran out, but the shuddering and convulsing in my chest did not. I wiped my cheeks with the back of my hand and sniffed. Up ahead, the gas lamp headlights swept over the drive up to camp.

We were almost back. It had to be said, lest my mother's life fall to ruin. She wouldn't be able to survive it this time.

"As I said earlier, I will tell Papa that I refuse to marry you," I said, my voice gravelly, as though I hadn't spoken for hours. "I will be the one to end the arrangement, and whatever it is you're hiding will be safe. Just please . . . Just please, I beg you, Worth, don't tell anyone about tonight, not even Papa. I know you understood it. Perhaps not all, but enough to gather who I truly am and who I came from."

Feet before the turn, the auto jerked to the right, to the side of the road, and stopped. I turned toward Worth, stunned at the sudden movement of the auto.

"I have let you cry because I have no right to comfort you. I cannot take the pain away besides." His voice was low and he kept his gaze fixed out the windshield. "But hearing you plead with me after I've listened to your heart break again, knowing now that all this time it's not been welded but taped together . . . I cannot bear it, Belle."

He turned to look at me and even in the dark, I could see his eyes pooling.

"I promise I'll not say a word of tonight. The knowledge of your past doesn't change my view of the person I've come to know. I have cried as you have, until the well has run dry. I have felt the searing pain and the deep ache, the realization that what I've gone through has rendered me entirely and completely alone in this life."

He reached across the seat and found my hand. He drew me close, and his fingers drifted across my cheeks. I closed my eyes to relieve the burning. I could feel the warmth of him, smell the light sandalwood from his soap.

His lips swept mine. At first I thought I was mistaken, that it had only been his fingers wiping away the last of my tears. But then his hands lifted to cradle my head. His fingers threaded the hair at my nape, and his mouth found mine. My lips parted to his, surrendering to the rush of want sweeping through me, to the relief of his acceptance, to the way his tongue took my grief, and I touched his neck and willed him to give me his as well.

When our lips finally broke, I opened my eyes to his face, felt the grip of his fingers still tangled in my hair, and lurched away from him.

"I'll never love you," I whispered, forcing my gaze from his. "Never. I have sworn I'll not, that I'll not fall in love."

The silence was deafening. I could hear only our breathing and the pounding of my heart.

"Then perhaps it is destiny that we marry after all," he said softly. "I have sworn the same. It's the reason I begged to have the arrangement broken. Of course it's not that I love Miss Kipp. I don't even think her attractive. I was honest with you when I said I didn't recall the kiss at all. The problem is that I find you remarkable, and in that I thought . . . I thought you deserved, perhaps in time you would want love."

"No," I said simply.

I turned back to face him.

"Are you certain?" His gaze found mine and stayed.

I nodded.

"Then I promise I will care for you as a tenderhearted person ought, but I will never . . . I will never allow my thoughts to linger on you, to long for you—or for any other," he said. My eyes drifted to his mouth, to the lips that had just been on mine. I could feel the echo of his kiss, the hum of my quickened heartbeat in my veins. "There will be times when I need your touch or you mine," he went on, his voice low, "but we won't idle there."

I forced my gaze away from his, cleared my throat, and straightened.

"I desired a match only for comfort and stability, for a family of my own," I said. "I never want my children to taste the bitterness of poverty or the trauma of a family torn to shreds by the heartache of parents in love."

"I'm of the same mind," Worth said. "I find it truly miraculous that out of all the people in the world, we have found each other. You can trust me, Belle. And I know without doubt that my confidences are safe with you." He smiled at me, shifted the auto into gear, and steered us back onto the road.

Relief was a balm to my heart, and I smiled back, before realizing he had yet to tell me of all the confidences he trusted me to keep.

# CHAPTER TWENTY-TWO

I was tired of listening for the northern saw-whet owl. It was late, nearing ten in the evening, and we'd been walking in a section of pine forest adjacent to Mr. Vanderbilt's property for almost an hour, listening to Mr. Burroughs discuss the elusive, nocturnal nature of the bird in whispers, requiring us all to clump together on the path. He'd been on the hunt for one for years—at least that's what I overheard him say to the newspaper writer—though the sentiment could have been said simply to excite.

"Was that it?" Toots shouted in response to a faraway scream. She was in the front of the Vagabonds throng, right behind Edsel, who was right behind Mr. Ford and the writer, and they were behind Mr. Burroughs. Her lantern swung, set to motion by her enthusiasm, and Mr. Burroughs made a noise of frustration.

"No," he said under his breath. "As I've said, Miss Edison, the owls we're searching for have a distinct *too-too-too* song, a series of whistled notes on the same pitch at a rate of two notes per second. That sound we just heard was a barn owl."

I yawned and rubbed my eyes. Despite most of the women having forgone this expedition to remain at camp, I'd been convinced to join the moment Worth and I arrived, primarily out of guilt born from the distress I'd caused by running away. We'd seen the autos readying when we came down the hill. Mother had been walking around the fire toward Papa, who was waiting for her by her door. When she saw me emerge from the auto, she ran toward me, crying, and Marie Austen also hastened to my side, looking as I must have when she'd failed to turn up in the tent that first night. Both of them said I wasn't permitted to be out of their sight. I hadn't thought of how my disappearance would affect anyone; I'd just needed to go.

I yawned again and this time the gesture ended in a slight squeak. "What was that?" Worth whispered. "The rare green-coated West Virginia owl?" He chuckled quietly. We'd walked at the rear of the group behind Mother and Papa, neither of us apparently keen to fight the others for the prime position near Mr. Burroughs.

Nevertheless, I'd thought the night walk extraordinarily peaceful. The lanterns each of us carried glowed gold warmth while the darkness and Mr. Burroughs's demanded quiet were calming. It was a welcome ending for such a day, when there was much to think over—the bleakness and beauty of life, the redemption.

I'd thought to tell Mother that I'd seen the Smiths but swiftly changed my mind. The news would only engulf her in fear of being found out and sadness at the horrid state of our friends, and in a way, it would discount what Willie had done. Despite the terrible reality of his parents' illness, he had risen to the ranks of a leading foreman. I thought of the notes I'd written before we adjourned to dinner with the Smiths. They were inspiring, and Willie's knowledge was vast. I wouldn't let calamity overshadow that.

"Yes, it's quite rare, rarer than the northern saw-whet, they say," I whispered, forcing my attention away from the Smiths. I breathed in the sharp woody scent of the pine all around us. The ground was coated with red needles shed from last fall, and when the needles were broken by a heel or a shoe, the scent deepened.

"I do hope we're nearly through," I heard Papa say. "It occurred to me on the way over here that we were being prevailed upon to search for a bird in the dark. Even if we hear its call, we won't be able to view it."

"I don't know about that, Shipley. John said some nest at eye level. Perhaps if we hear one and lift our lanterns, we may spy its face," Mother said. "And even if we don't, I've quite enjoyed this walk with you." Mother leaned in for a moment against Papa's shoulder and then they parted. They often walked this way, close, but not touching. Father and Mother had always been arm in arm, their limbs clasped together, unwilling to let the other go, even for a moment. They had truly become one person when they fell in love.

I felt Worth's presence beside me, the solid steadiness of his body at my shoulder. It was a nice sort of sensation, the knowledge of being cared for while retaining the autonomy of your heart.

"Do you smell that?" Worth asked. "That bit of sweet?"

I inhaled and a vanilla-almond scent joined the pine.

"Yes. It's heavenly. What is it?"

"Night-blooming jasmine. It must be growing on a nearby trunk."

Up ahead, Marie Austen proclaimed that she heard the *too-too-too* call, and the group paused to listen. Before we'd set off, when the company was gathered at the trailhead, the sight of her in the same assembly as Worth had lured my mind to imagine their kiss. I'd felt the prickle of anger rise in my chest, but I would have to dismiss it and trust the man I was planning to spend my life with. Forgiveness was the only choice. I wasn't planning to abandon either of them.

As though he'd felt my apprehension, Worth had tucked my hand in his. Marie Austen, similarly, had been with Mr. Gibbins since the start of the walk. I couldn't figure what had come over her, why she suddenly seemed to stop fighting the course of her life and embrace it, but she seemed changed, more mature. Perhaps she simply realized she didn't have a choice.

"When I was young and we had just started our travels, we wound up on an old farm in the Tennessee mountains. I didn't have any siblings or friends, so Mother took it upon herself to make up games for us to play at the end of Father's workday," Worth said. "One of them was that we had to go into the woods at night and, using only our noses, find the jasmine, pluck a flower from the vine, and bring it back to her. I always won."

"With such a talented nose, perhaps you should have gone into the business of colognes," I said.

"Perhaps you're right," he said, laughing. "Anyway, I think back on those nights often. It was before Father got so busy that he was rarely home. Mother was happy. I was happy. Later, there was bitterness. Mother felt as though he'd abandoned us."

"Were they in love? Your parents?" I glanced at him, at his face barely lit by the lantern flame.

"Not particularly. But there was fondness and we were a family. They did well to acknowledge the strengths of each other and mine as well."

The lights from the other lanterns ahead were growing fainter. I could tell by the faraway chatter that there had been a verified call and the rest—including Mother and Papa—were chasing it, but I couldn't force my legs to carry me any quicker.

"Then what was it that turned you away from love?" The question deadened in the night air and I wished I could take it back. I could feel his unease, and when I turned to look at him once more, his shoulders were squared, his posture rigid.

"I should have waited to ask until we had time," I said. "I suppose it's only that it's quite unnatural, this stance we share, while the rest of the world pines for it."

He said nothing.

I went silent too, listening to the crickets and our footsteps and the gravelly hoot of a great horned owl.

"When my father died in the roof collapse, my mother died too." I spoke under my breath, mostly to myself, but it occurred to me that though I'd mentioned the reason for my trepidation, I'd never elaborated so he understood. "I can't quite put into words the way her scream sounded when they came to tell her. His friends came to our front door with Father's hat. I remember the dull thud of it hitting the ground and then the scream.

"It tore through the mountains and made my legs give out. My knees hit the wood so hard I had bruises for weeks after. His death maimed me. He had been my best friend. But his death killed Mother. She took to her bed for eight months. She had bed sores and refused to eat much. The only thing that eventually got her out of bed was me. Father's pay eventually ran out and she knew Boss Elkhorn wouldn't hesitate to evict us if she didn't pay. She took a post as a model for the company store and some money trickled in, but even then, she barely spoke to me or anyone else.

"She would work and then come home and immediately fall asleep. In her sleep she would cry or call Father's name or claw her hand across the bed to where he used to lay. She did it until we left for Indiana. She might still."

Worth said nothing. A part of me panicked at what I'd just revealed. He could retract his promise. He could tell Papa of the Smiths and who he knew us now to be.

"She loves Papa, but she loves him differently. He is her family, not her heart. The moment I understood that a marriage could be one of care and friendship instead of passion and heartache, I knew that was what I wanted for myself."

Worth's footsteps slowed and then stopped.

"I know I need to tell—"

"Please don't," I whispered. "Please don't tell Papa about my father, about our past. He could turn us out. He—"

Worth grasped my free hand with his and shook his head.

"Shipley loves your mother, and I know she loves him too. If there was a chance he'd been taken advantage of by an evil woman with greed in her heart, I would want to reveal it at once, but this is not so," he said. "And even if I wanted to, I've given you my word that I'll not."

His fingers ran across my knuckles.

"I began to say that I know I need to tell you of my reason, and I will. I will tell you all of it and I will answer your questions, but tonight . . . tonight has been riddled with heartache, and to speak of it would be more than I can carry."

His eyes held mine and I nodded.

"I understand," I said, though now, with all of my past laid bare for him, I wanted to know of his too.

"She died." The words came in two punctuated noises that sounded as though he'd been stabbed.

I set the lantern at my feet and reached for him. I wrapped my arms around his back and held him fast. Worth didn't move.

"I'm sorry." It was all I could say. His hands lifted slowly to my back, and I let my head rest on his chest. Then he stepped away and knelt on the pine needles. His fingers reached for mine and our eyes met.

"Perhaps this is a strange time, but here, in the quiet, in the dark, I feel it's right. I have no doubt that we were intended for each other. We value the same things, and you care for me as I care for you. You are selfless and your heart is unmatched," Worth said. He smiled and I grinned back. He was proposing and I was about to swear my life to him, and yet my hands didn't quake, my soul didn't shudder. My heart felt as though it could burst from my chest, as though I could suddenly take to flying. Surely the feeling was the sensation that came with all of my fears relieved.

"Will you marry me?" he asked. The answer was simple.

"Yes, of course." I couldn't look away from his face. It was radiant, like his spirit, and I had the sudden urge to touch him, to verify that he was real and not an apparition. He reached into his jacket and withdrew a box. He opened the lid. Inside was an enormous oval sapphire ring bordered with diamonds. I laughed. "When I told you I required such a ring, I was angry. I wasn't serious, Worth. And I heard you tell Papa last night—"

"This is the ring I planned to propose with all along," he said, smiling. "I've been carrying it since I arrived in Asheville, thinking I'd be able to ask you whenever the time was right. I suppose it being a sapphire is quite a coincidence. It was my grandmother's." He slipped the ring on my finger and rose. For a moment, we stood there, inches apart, and my mind fell to the kiss in the auto, to the way his mouth felt on mine.

His eyes drifted to my lips, and I lifted my face to his, my body strangely quaking. I thought he might kiss me again, but he simply stepped back and squeezed my hand. An immense calm settled on my shoulders.

"You will never be alone again," I said. "Nor will I."

"I know, though I can hardly believe it. It has been my greatest prayer to have a family again, and I am overwhelmed with gratitude to have found you." Worth's eyes drifted above my head to the path beyond me.

"I suppose we should catch up to the others." He took my hand and then one of the lanterns. I picked up mine as well. "Let's tell the others of our news. With any luck, they'll throw off the hunt and insist we return to camp to celebrate."

# CHAPTER TWENTY-THREE

"It's much like solving a puzzle, Miss Newbold, or perhaps like designing a fine dress." John Corbin, the head stonemason, shook his head at a fellow mason who had prematurely jabbed a cylindrical stone between two boulders and snatched a trowel to infill it with the mixture of stone chard and red clay.

"Remove that please, Gerard. The height of that stone is much too low to install here. I don't think it was Mr. Seely's intention to send his guests to the infirmary with gouged eyes," Mr. Corbin said. The young man's face immediately reddened, and he jerked the heavy stone from the wall with such fervor that he nearly fell under the movement and weight of it. "Now, don't be sore at me. The idea was a good one. It's dimensional and interesting, but try it again up the wall a bit." He turned to the rest of the group. "Only a few more hours, men, and we'll be toasting—"

"'Til we begin again tomorrow," one of the older men said, laughing.

They were completing the final internal wall today and everyone's spirits were quite jovial. I'd pretended mine were the same—smiling, laughing at their jests between writing—but the truth was that I was troubled. I hazarded a glance across the room to the doorway, to the spectacular view of the mountains, and to where Worth stood, his back to me. I wished he would go back to camp, but he refused. I turned the ring on my finger. It felt too tight.

"Have Harry and Daniel bring more stones," Mr. Corbin said to no one in particular. I looked at the enormous pile of granite that had been placed in a makeshift wooden box wheeled in on a dolly.

"How many carts do you go through building a wall like this one?" I asked.

"Can't have them bring more. They didn't report today," a man with an enormous mustache said to Mr. Corbin. He had just placed a small rock in the crevice between two large ones, and the older man snatched the trowel and filled the space between the rocks.

"Hold it here, Gerard," the older man instructed, and Gerard complied, though his face suggested he was less than enthused at the task.

"Then go instruct whoever is out there that we need another cart. The options are lacking. I need several large stones and these are all small to medium," Mr. Corbin said. "Apologies, Miss Newbold. It's quite irritating, these staffing changes. To answer your question, we usually use about seven or eight carts of granite for one wall. Different from the work we did on Mr. Vanderbilt's place. There it was swift building. The limestone was cut to large flat pieces and the goal was to lay them evenly for a smooth finish."

"I'm sure this build has been much more difficult," I said.

"Yes. Some days, I'm thrilled by it—it's one of the more challenging things I've done, and the completion of each wall makes me realize that I am capable of such a task—but other days, it is exhausting work, especially if I can't seem to see the build clear. At times I go home and barely have the strength to speak to my wife."

"I imagine it is a feat of both physical and mental exertion."

"Most certainly. I've tried posts where less is required, and I can't stand it. I was a tool dresser with Samuel Bean—Mr. Vanderbilt's head mason—and foreman during the build of Mr. Vanderbilt's nursery at Biltmore before that, but those only entailed the strength of the body," he said. "My favorite projects are those where construction serves as an answer to a problem, like this one, and isn't just a structure. That interest started early. I was raised by corn farmers over in Jackson County and started building silos of concrete and stone to help prevent rot when I was but fifteen." He paused and pointed at Gerard. "You can let it go now." He cleared his throat and turned back to me.

I wanted to ask what problem he supposed Grove Park Inn was solving, but he answered my question for me.

"When this inn is complete, this town will come alive again," he said. "It is Mr. Seely and Mr. Grove's mission to help Asheville survive this tuberculosis epidemic that continues to insist on settling here."

Despite hearing these sentiments expressed many times, despite understanding the need to retain industry for those who were well here, I still found it strange that men so ardently devoted to restoring the health of others would be so vehemently against rehabilitation facilities for some of the sickest in our country.

"Is it so rampant?" I asked as I wrote the rest of his answer in my notebook. "I have no doubt that when this inn is finished, Asheville will be one of the most sought-after tourist destinations—and I plan for my story to help further the news of its wonder—but is consumption as widespread here as they have made it seem?"

"It is everywhere," Mr. Corbin said, his face sober. "Especially these last months. I've not known anyone to be infected personally, but they're recording tallies in the papers. I've only seen the faces of the sick on the balconies and porches of the sanitoriums, but they are springing up all over town. It has come to the point where I fear my daughters and my wife interacting with others, and that is not a life to live." He paused.

"You should be mindful of exposure yourself. When we adjourn to the masonry tent where they're preparing the boulders, remind me to fetch you a tincture we've made. Seems to be effective at warding off many illnesses, including the one going 'round the workers here."

"Thank you," I said. "I'm sorry you've had to shoulder the worry of such a devastating illness coming to your family."

Beside him, the older man who had been prevailed upon to order another cart hadn't yet departed and was instead searching through the pile of existing stone.

"I'm beginning to think you'd like to live in the workers' tent permanently, Christopher. I've asked you to go fetch another cart and you're idling. The longer it takes us to construct this wall, the longer the project will delay, and returning you to your home in Georgia will be prolonged as well," Mr. Corbin said.

"I suppose I got distracted," Christopher said. He turned toward the open doorway behind us where a steam shovel chugged and the shouts of men unloading boulders from the wagon train were heard.

"Mr. Seely has had to reach outside of the area for workers as of late to fill in for the workers catching ill, and Christopher is one of them. Complains about the housing every day, though he has a down mattress on which to lay his head. Most projects don't even provide a tent for shelter. His enthusiasm for the post leaves much to be desired." He shook his head as Gerard tried, yet again, to place the cylindrical rock.

I looked across the room at Worth's silhouette in the doorway. Talk of housing had ruined our engagement celebration the night before and was ruining our day today. We'd returned to camp at thirty minutes to midnight, but the late hour hadn't stopped the group of explorers from waking a few servants and inquiring after champagne. The glasses had been poured to the brim and as we'd gathered around the fire, everyone toasting in hushed voices so as not to wake the rest of the camp, I'd been perfectly happy.

Worth had played the part of doting fiancé, his palm finding its place on the small of my back or clasped to mine, and Mother had been beaming as though every worry she'd ever had about me had suddenly departed. Marie Austen and Mr. Gibbins had been merry too. I'd even seen her lean into him when he kissed her cheek.

The trouble had occurred after my second glass of champagne. My insides had been thoroughly warmed with contentment, and I'd tipped my head up against Worth's back toward the stars. The view had been so spectacular, and the smell of the fire and feel of the spring nip so enchanting, that I'd turned to Worth and asked if he'd been serious that night at Mr. Grove's. I'd recalled him saying he would consider settling here in the mountains if I so wished, and at that moment, I did.

His reaction to my question was immediate. He hadn't responded but let me go at once, downing the last bit of champagne in his flute. I'd tried to go after him, to ask him what I'd said to upset him, but Toots detained me, asking to see my ring again. By the time I was able to break free, when the rest of the night owls were ready to turn in, he was nowhere to be found.

He'd materialized after breakfast this morning, his countenance pleasant, as though last night's disappearance hadn't occurred. His sudden absence had been embarrassing. I'd continued to toast our union while others asked where he'd gone. Of course, I didn't know. I loathed being made to look like a fool. When he came to fetch me for our auto ride to the inn, I allowed him to drive me but refused to speak. After minutes of unbearable prodding, I told him I was angry that he'd walked away.

Worth had erupted then, his knuckles white on the steering wheel. *"You vanished just yesterday, sending everyone into a frenzy. It is acceptable for you to disappear, to hide your melancholy or fury from me, but I am not permitted to do the same?"*

I'd settled for a moment then, acquiescing to the fact that he was right, so I asked him why he'd been bothered. He said he didn't wish to discuss it as the auto settled in front of the inn, and my anger was reignited. For as much as we'd promised each other to be forthright, we were not. I'd overlooked the questions he had yet to answer because I understood the worry that the past could irrevocably tarnish the perception of even the purest hearts, but now, with my past laid bare, he had no reason to conceal his. My mind drifted to Papa's threat. Of course, he'd threatened Worth with a falsity—that was clear in the words I'd overheard—but perhaps even the truth of Worth's past would change what I thought of him, cause me to question swearing my life to his.

"Thank you, Christopher. It looks like these boulders are much more suited to my vision for this wall," Mr. Corbin said, interrupting my reflection on the morning's unpleasantness. "Gerard, we'll need the pulley for the first window frame. Please fetch it. I've selected this stone here for the head." He pointed at a light-colored oblong stone that looked to me much like the rest.

"I'm amazed at your eye, Mr. Corbin," I said. "I admit I haven't the same vision, and to witness what you've done here is incredible." I glanced around at the other completed walls, at the delicate balance of large and small, light and dark displayed in the stonework.

"Ah, that's kind of you to say, Miss Newbold. Like I said, I enjoy a puzzle, and this is an enormous one." He glanced at my portfolio. "I don't have the gift of the written word. Wouldn't be able to accomplish much of anything if everyone had the same skill."

"How's this one, boss?" Christopher asked, lifting a darker stone with some effort to a space at the window apron.

"That'll do." Mr. Corbin looked at Gerard, who was disentangling a set of chains from the pulley. "Make sure he doesn't injure himself, will you? I'm going to take Miss Newbold here down to the masonry tent. I'm sure she's had her fill of this nonsense."

He smiled and Christopher grunted. "Sure, sir," he said.

I followed Mr. Corbin out of the room, down the two concrete steps, and onto the dusty path that led down the hill to the construction tents and, beyond, the workers' dwellings. Wagons full of stone idled from the mouth of the inn all the way down to the first canvas structure, our destination. It occurred to me as we cleared the side of the inn and started along the crest of the hill that I hadn't alerted Worth that I had finished my survey of the wall and was moving on. Perhaps it was for the best. We were not of the same mind right now and he would only distract me.

"Good day, Carl, Barton." Mr. Corbin tipped his head at a few men loading granite into waiting wagons outside the masonry tent. On the opposite side, the wagon train was stalled, depositing another load. I hoped Willie was faring well today. I'd prayed last night and envisioned the whole Smith family well. I'd told myself a story about their healing and their move to a house with sunlight and a garden. It was only a fiction, but I had to believe it was a possibility too. Only then had I been able to fall asleep.

219

Mr. Corbin held the canvas flap open for me and I walked inside. The space was dim and packed with men. The heat of so many perspiring bodies was at once stifling. The smell of oniony sweat and the earthy metallic scent of dirt and rock permeated the air. He led me to the far end of the tent, where a sliver of light punctuated the dusk. A giant of a man was reaching into the wagons loitering outside and flinging boulders onto long tables as if they were as light as kindling. Opposite him, an assembly of at least fifteen men lined the worktables, some with rags, others with pickaxes and chisels.

"Bear, this is Miss Belle Newbold. She's writing an article on the building of the inn for Mr. Seely. Would you please show her around and explain what you're doing here?" Mr. Corbin asked.

Bear cast a glare my direction, made a noise of disdain, and shook his head.

"Thought you said we wasn't supposed to stop for nothing," he boomed. He could hardly help it. It must take quite a bit of effort for a man that size to speak in a normal tone.

"It won't take but a few minutes," I said.

"I give you permission to hand off your duties to whoever you see fit for as long as Miss Newbold requires your assistance," Mr. Corbin said.

"Then would you like to require my assistance for the remainder of my eight hours, Miss Newbold? Sure would be nice to let Andrew here finish the granite for me today," he said, elbowing a much slighter man next to him who looked as if he could use a break himself. Sweat rolled down his neck in rivers and his eyes held the same sort of gauntness I'd seen in Willie's. He started to reply but coughed instead, a rattling noise that startled me.

"Sounds like you might need that tincture, Andrew. Do obtain some before your shift concludes," Mr. Corbin said.

"I ain't takin' it again," he said. "Made me lose my lunch the last time. Nobody's been taking it."

"I suppose I'll have to call a meeting then. We cannot afford to sit by while the whole of our force takes ill. If you enjoy your employment, Andrew, you'll have a nip of the tincture. It isn't any more pungent than the shine you're keeping in your flask," Mr. Corbin said.

Andrew's eyes widened.

"I wasn't born yesterday." Mr. Corbin laughed. "I'll be getting back to the inn now. Bear, if you will?" He gestured to me and Bear nodded. He mopped his face with a dirty rag and stepped around the metal tables and the stone he was working on. Mr. Corbin paused at the entrance to the tent. "Get Miss Newbold some of that tincture too."

"All right," he barked. He looked down at me. "So what is it you want to know?"

"I would like you to tell me what you're doing here," I said, sweeping my hand across the tableau of men. The first three or four stood next to buckets of water, and as a new boulder was placed in front of them, they wiped the surface—only lightly—with rags, removing the loose dirt from the stone. Beyond them, men worked with chisels and hammers as new stone was shifted into their work-space. The noise was deafening.

"I suppose we're doing a bit of fabricating, though we've been ordered to keep the moss on the stones," Bear said. "Down yonder where I just was, we're cleaning the dirt off. Then these other men chisel off splinter fingers, those little bits comin' off the ends of the boulders."

I walked to the line and wandered down slowly, greeting the men and watching their progress. They all looked tired, emaciated, and the sounds of coughs and grunts filled the air.

"Should the tent flaps be lifted?" I asked Bear when we reached the end. "Perhaps some fresh air would do these men well." I fanned my face with my portfolio.

"Can't," he said. "Behind the carving men, those two are collecting the stone chards to be mixed with red clay for mortar, and we can't afford moisture getting in. Wish we could. We're losing men by the dozen each day to that illness going around, and they're remaining out of work for days and weeks, some. Most of us will work through it. Can't afford to take a day to sleep."

"Are you well?" I asked.

"So far," he said. "Missus tells me to eat every hour and drink a bit of that horrible drink Mr. Pierce has made up for us." He paused. "Are you hungry?"

Before I could say no, he withdrew two packages covered in wax paper from his overalls.

"Livermush. Want some?"

The name sounded unappealing, but the aroma coming from the packages made my stomach growl.

"I couldn't. You have a long day ahead and will need those for your strength," I said.

He shook his head. "She packs me five extra for the other men. She came up here once and saw how skinny they all were. Insisted I share them."

"I'm well fed," I said. "Please do share them with your fellow workers here. It's not that I don't appreciate the gesture, but—"

"You're like the missus, always thinking of others," he said, placing the packages back into his pockets. "Now about that tincture Mr. Corbin told me to give you. I think it works. It's awful stuff, but I haven't been ill once."

I thought to refuse it, but one glance at the men inside the tent had me reconsidering. If I was rendered ill, I'd never finish my story.

"Very well. I'll take it. It can't be any more pungent than the tea my grandmother used to make us from wild ramps. She claimed it would keep our lungs clear, and I still believe it worked," I said.

Bear chuckled. "This is quite the same, it seems."

He led me toward the back of the tent where the two men were hammering discarded stone into a powder and depositing it into large metal basins. A clear bottle boasting a murky brown liquid was propped against the tent pole with a stack of clean metal cups beside it. Bear reached down and grabbed the bottle and uncorked it with a *pop*. Beside us, one of the men coughed so hard he gagged.

"I apologize, miss," he choked out. I waved my hand at him but reached at once to the cup Bear was holding out to me and lifted it to my mouth. It tasted of apple cider vinegar with a lemon and

222

lavender infusion that didn't make the taste any better. I breathed through my mouth and swallowed the entirety of the liquid in a long drink.

"Do you know about how long it takes to recover from the illness befalling these men?" I asked Bear, handing the cup back. "Is there anything else to aid them in it? I have a friend whose family is ailing, and—"

"Afraid I don't," he said. "Most of us don't seek the counsel of physicians. It's too costly."

A mighty groan came from the far side of the tent, and a thud followed.

"Bear! Bear! Come quick—Roger's dropped a stone on his foot," someone yelled.

Bear hastened to the tent flap, and I heard a cry as Roger's foot was released.

"Is it broken? Can you move it?" Bear asked.

I heard a meek yes and watched as Bear resumed his position next to the wagon.

I walked toward him. "Thank you."

He nodded, and I pushed my way out of the tent flap, relieved to be washed in midday sunlight.

I recorded the activity of the masonry tent in my notebook and then made my way up the hill. The chill in the spring breeze made the sweat that had gathered beneath my corset in the sweltering tent feel extraordinarily cold.

"Have you finished?" Worth called to me.

I looked up to find him in the exact place I'd left him nearly an hour ago, still standing in what would be one of the doorways to the terrace from the southernmost wing of the building. I couldn't figure what he'd been doing all this time. Staring out at the mountains could occupy very few people for as long as it seemed he'd been occupied. Then again, I'd done the same on countless occasions when there was much on my mind.

"Yes!" I yelled back, wincing as a man placing rebar on the roof nearly lost his balance. I forced myself to look away as Worth jumped down from the doorway's considerable ledge—a height of at least six feet—and then made his way across the lawn to me.

"I've been doing a lot of thinking," he said when he reached me. He offered his arm and I took it. "First, I apologize for departing so suddenly last night. I should have considered how it would make you feel since I'd so recently been the recipient of your going away."

"I apologize for that too," I said.

"I'm not bringing it to the surface to fish for another apology. You've already done that. I'm only mentioning it because you will be my wife and I your husband. I want to earn your respect, and I made no strides with last night's escape. My walking away had nothing to do with you, by the way, but I have no doubt it made you wonder. The next time I need a moment to myself, I promise to tell you before I go."

"I don't want us to feel that we have to depart each other's company when we're troubled," I said. "I want to be able to tell you why I'm grieved or irritated. I want to be able to walk through it with you. Otherwise, there will be spaces of our lives where we are still quite alone."

His free hand came to rest atop mine as we walked toward the auto parked beside a grove of trees in front of the inn.

"Yes, you're right," he said. "And in that spirit, the honest truth about last night is that your request to live here caught me off guard. The last time I lived—"

"Worth Delafield." A voice came from beyond the auto, from the wing of the inn that included Mr. Mills's office, and in short order, a thin gentleman with an equally thin mustache—the sort that looked as if it had been penciled on—appeared around the front.

Worth's face brightened.

"David White. How are you, man?"

"I'm as well as I can be." The man glanced around. "Hoping to secure a contract with Seely for quite a bit of furniture to outfit the guest rooms here. Have you seen him today?" He stopped looking over the building and grounds for a moment and his attention steadied on us. "What a place."

"It certainly is. A wonder," I said.

Worth cleared his throat.

"Forgive me," he said to me, then turned to Mr. White. "David, I'd like you to meet my fiancée, Miss Belle Newbold. Belle, this is David White. David owns one of the finest furniture companies in this part of the country, White Furniture, out of Mebane." Worth paused, then addressed Mr. White. "Fred's in St. Louis with Edwin dealing with some business. He should return within the week. Mr. Pierce is here somewhere, however. He might be able to evaluate your proposal on Fred's behalf."

"It's nice to make your acquaintance, Miss Newbold." Mr. White sighed and ran a hand across his face. "I suppose Fred's business travel must have come up suddenly. He sent a telegram just last week saying this would be an opportune time to pop in." He glanced down at the leather bag in his hand, a bag that likely contained a week's worth of preparation to suggest the correct furniture to Mr. Seely. "And you know Fred. Despite his respect for Pierce, he's unlikely to allow anyone else the option to approve anything related to this inn. This was a waste of time, I'm afraid."

"Perhaps show what you've brought to Pierce anyway. At the least, he could put in a word when Seely returns," Worth said.

"I suppose you're right," Mr. White said. "Are you back in Asheville now? It occurs to me that I haven't seen you in years, since right after the fire."

He said it so plainly, so nonchalantly, that it took me a moment to register his words. Worth's body tensed beside me and his face paled. I squeezed his arm beneath mine, sure that if I didn't do something to tie his conscience to the here and now, he'd faint.

"You're looking well. I'm glad you've recovered," Mr. White went on as though he was blind and couldn't see the way his bringing up Worth's calamity was affecting him.

"Yes, he is quite well indeed," I said. "We must be going. Good day to you, Mr. White."

The man nodded and scampered down the drive with his bag, likely after an audience with Mr. Pierce. Worth didn't move. I could feel his pulse thumping against the inside of my elbow. I led him slowly around the side of the auto, where the woods shielded us from passersby, and put my arms around him.

I held him tightly, my cheek against his chest, my palms on his back, and suddenly, his arms enveloped me in turn, his fingers threading in my hair, his thumb against my cheek. My skin prickled and warmth spread through me at his touch. I was relieved that the rift between us had been mended.

I could feel his body trembling. It was a feeling I knew well, a feeling that always accompanied the remembrance of Mother's screams and the sight of the other men walking home from the mine that day. Worth had been thrust toward the memory of his terror, a terror he would not share, though sharing it was the only way to break free of it. I lifted my face to his and found his eyes closed. The color still hadn't returned to his skin, and his jaw was strained.

"I'm sorry," I whispered. His hand still cupped my head and his eyes opened as a breeze blew over us, making me shiver.

"Belle," he said. "I can't . . . I can't do this anymore."

# CHAPTER TWENTY-FOUR

My stomach growled and I pushed my hand over it to stop the sound. Worth looked at me, but Mr. Pierce, sitting opposite Worth on the scaffolding, did not.

"We should have gone back to camp for dinner and returned after," Worth said.

The moment we'd settled in the auto, Mr. Pierce had materialized from his office to tell us Mr. Mills had instructed the concrete men to pour the last bit of roof this evening, and he'd asked if I would find it advantageous to watch. I'd immediately declined. Worth had just confessed he was expiring under the weight of his past, and we were alone in the auto. We would finally have occasion to discuss whatever had transpired without interruption, without Worth changing his mind.

Worth, however, had disrupted my refusal to Mr. Pierce and told him we would stay, that seeing this bit of construction completed was vital to my story. I didn't know if he'd been earnest in his reason or if he'd simply decided he didn't wish to speak of the fire. Either way, we'd disembarked the auto and followed Mr. Pierce to a tent just beyond the masons' tent where great piles of concrete powder idled next to barrels of water.

For the next hours, we watched workers prepare to pour the roof—pushing wheelbarrows of powder and rolling kegs of water from the tent to the roof via a scaffolding walkway that concluded at a steam mixer at the roof's edge. By the time the materials were prepared and the pouring was ready to begin, full wheelbarrows and barrels of water lined the steep incline to the roof. Once they started, there would be no time to idle, to go back for more powder or water. The roof had to be poured continuously to suit the design work and later hold the tiles.

"I'm nearly certain the state of my stomach would be the same had we returned to camp," I said as my stomach growled again. "The Vagabonds were off on their wilderness stew competition, remember? We were to eat their creations for dinner this evening."

Worth laughed and Mr. Pierce leaned around him.

"Surely the cooks would have mercy on all of you and assist the men with their stews," he said, though his smile indicated he'd had enough interactions with Mr. Ford and his challenges to know otherwise.

Worth shook his head.

"No, unfortunately. I've had Mr. Ford's wild stew before. It tastes like the weeds from which it is made. I suppose the only fortunate side effect is that it cleanses the body quite nicely."

I scrunched my nose and Worth shrugged. Mr. Pierce withdrew his pocket watch from his coat.

"It is a quarter past eight. No wonder you're starving, Miss Newbold," Mr. Pierce said. "Let me go see if there's anything I can procure from Mr. Mills. He often takes dinner here and the cook is known to bring him too much." He started to rise and I felt my arm reflexively lurch to steady him. I pushed it back to my lap.

"There's no need," I attempted. "I'll fetch something later." But Mr. Pierce waved me off.

We were perched on a platform of scaffolding seven stories high, on level with the roof, and though we were surrounded quite securely by a solid floor of wood and a five-foot slatted railing, in order to disembark the roof Mr. Pierce had to make his way across a narrow walkway guarded only by a simple one-beam railing. I'd nearly fainted when I looked over the side at the drop, and even when the sunset painted the sky and mountains in gold and orange, I'd barely been able to hazard a glance.

Mr. Pierce walked away from us down the narrow path. He

ducked under the large electric light that had been installed with an extension cord earlier in the day and skirted around several lanterns that had been scattered across the roof to provide additional illumination.

"I feel quite useless just sitting here," Worth said. Nearly fifty men were lined up and down the scaffolding pushing the wheelbarrows of powder and rolling the water toward the carrier to the mixer, which looked like a wheelbarrow that had been affixed to a pulley instead of wheels.

One young man tipped the contents of his wheelbarrow into the carrier and the gears clicked as it rose to the top and deposited into a chute attached to a great drumlike hopper that chugged and sighed with the efforts of the steam engine. Another man stood at the end of another narrow chute, his wheelbarrow filling with cement. When it was full, he pushed the contents across the roof while balancing on a wooden beam to avoid sinking either the wheelbarrow or a foot in the just-poured concrete.

"You are not useless in the slightest," I said to Worth. "If you hadn't been with me, I wouldn't have had the courage to climb to such a height." I placed my hand on my open portfolio, feeling the indentation of my writing on the pages. I'd filled nearly ten today. "Or to watch these men risk their lives." It had taken quite some time for my nerves to settle enough to watch the operation on the roof without wondering at every turn if someone would fall to his death.

One of the men poured the concrete in front of us, letting it flow over the rebar. He lifted the metal carrier back to level and in the process upset a nearby lantern. The glass fell on rebar and shattered, the blaze extinguishing immediately.

Worth's head snapped up and his body went rigid.

"It was just a lantern," I said, assuming his reaction owed to the fear that someone had fallen.

Worth's hand grasped mine and he took a heaving breath and looked at me.

"It was an overturned lantern that killed them," he said.

My heart dropped. His eyes welled, but he blinked and cleared his throat. "I've never spoken of it to anyone before, not the particulars at least. I tried to tell Shipley everything once but couldn't get through it. I managed to tell him the outcome, but the events leading up to it . . ."

I turned to face him, looking away from the roofing men as he took a deep breath before continuing.

"My parents moved to Asheville five years past. Father had respiratory troubles and his doctor knew we had holdings here, so he recommended they relocate. Mother had always . . . She'd always loved the woods. Father had cleared land down near the French Broad, but she asked if they could build a home atop the mountain on my property, nestled in the trees. Of course, I agreed. Father was in such ill health that I commissioned our architect to build two homes—one for my parents and one just down the hill for me and my . . . my family so I could be nearby."

I thought of the foundation I'd come across in the woods. It must have been the start of Worth's home.

"Father had a nurse, Eliza, who was with him day and night. Naturally, I was around her often as well. Our attraction was instant, and our love was swift, and I'd proposed before I knew her two months." He paused and looked away. "That love brought nothing but destruction. It stole everything. I'll never allow it again." I felt the warmth of his hand fixed to mine, and a feeling welled up inside me and my heart began to race. I breathed in deep to calm it.

"Their house was completed in April of '09 and we all moved in while mine was started—just in time for Father's health to take a turn for the worst. No one knew why he was ailing, Eliza included. I went up to Boston to speak to a doctor there on his behalf and took Eliza with me, hoping for a solution, anything to help him. When we returned without an answer only one week later, Father's condition was startling. In a week's time, it seemed he'd diminished to a shell of himself.

"It was painful to see and Eliza said she couldn't bear it. She said seeing him that way reminded her that she'd failed to make him better. She told me she wanted us to leave, to marry and move away immediately, hopefully to Richmond, where she was from. As appealing as it seemed to run rather than face my father's slow death, I couldn't. I wouldn't leave my parents knowing the state they were in, and I told her so, but she was adamant."

His voice dropped to a whisper, and I could barely hear him over the steam engine. His eyes were heavy, his mind far away from this roof at the Grove Park Inn.

"Before, I'd been convinced she was a kind soul. Otherwise, my heart wouldn't have intertwined with hers, but when she became enraged that night, nothing could calm her. We had a terrible argument in the dining room. She accused me of trapping her in the woods, of caring for my parents above her and placing their well-being over hers . . . My father was dying, Belle. I . . . I thought my abandonment the wrong choice." Worth looked at me and I gripped his hand.

"It would have been," I said.

"Yet if only I'd acquiesced, perhaps he would have survived. Perhaps we would have found a treatment and—" He stopped talking, and for a moment I thought he may not go on. "Belle, I need you to know that what happened has made me a dead man inside." Worth ran a hand across his face.

"That night, after the fight, I called Father's doctor to the house to evaluate him. I loved Eliza. I told her if the doctor confirmed that Father had time, we'd marry the next morning and move that day. We'd find a house in Richmond and settle there. But the doctor confirmed what we already knew. Father's body was failing, and we had months at best.

"I told Eliza I needed to stay, but we could move after Father passed away, so long as we took Mother with us. She lost her temper entirely. She threw a lantern at me from across the porch, and as I moved toward her to try to calm her, the flame ignited a pile of varnish-soaked rags gathered behind me, next to the front door. Our foreman had treated the porch and interior floors earlier that day, and when I turned around, the house had already begun to blaze." Worth's voice faltered and he closed his eyes.

"I ran inside toward my parents' bedroom at the back of the house, and Eliza followed, but several of the walls were completely engulfed, including the one that separated their room from the dining room. My parents were trapped behind the closed door. I remember striking the burning wood with broken window frames, with iron beams, but I couldn't find my way through.

"Eventually, I was able to lift a bit of the collapsed door to their room with the leg of a broken chair and was sure if I kept at it long enough, I could free them. In the midst of my struggle, Eliza said she was going to see if she could reach them from the front parlor. I told her not to, to stay with me. I could tell by the noise and heat that that side of the house was about to fall, but she refused to listen and disappeared into the hall.

"A few moments later, after it was clear I wouldn't be able to lift what was left of the door, I followed her, but the flames surrounded me. Every square inch of the house was ablaze. I kept calling my parents' names and Eliza's name, but there was no answer. Then I heard the ceiling scream and I ran outside.

"To this day I don't know why I didn't let it consume me. Regardless, I emerged on fire, my skin burning."

I disentangled my hand from his and ran my fingers up his arm until I found the puckered skin. He didn't stop me. He opened his eyes.

"It haunts me that I left them in there. The moment I got out, the roof collapsed, every bit of the house swallowed in flames. A few minutes more and only ashes remained. They were gone.

"If I had told her to run, if I had gone through my parents' window instead of trying to get through the door, perhaps—"

"Worth." His name was all I could say. I scooted toward him until I was nearly in his lap, and I wrapped my arms around him. The horror of what he'd experienced was unfathomable, and I could do nothing to take it away. My father had died, but I hadn't seen the roof collapse on top of him. I hadn't played a role in his final moments. I couldn't imagine the pain I felt intensified. At times it already felt like an endless darkness.

"When you overheard Shipley threaten me with something, it was the suspicion that surrounded the fire. When everyone you love goes up in flames and you emerge alive, there's always the skepticism, the notion that perhaps it was your fault, that you started it. I suppose he planned to circulate that idea should I break our arrangement. No one—not Shipley or anyone else—knew of Eliza or my engagement. She was in our employ, an orphan far removed from the circles we revolved in, so I never told anyone the particulars of that night. I could barely speak my parents' names after, let alone hers." He paused.

"Their faces are always before me. I loved my parents deeply, and despite knowing I should hate Eliza, I cannot. She didn't set out to do what she did. Still, because of her, my family is gone, she is gone, and I am—"

"No." I didn't know exactly what he was planning to say, but I knew it was despairing. I couldn't blame him and yet I needed him to hope—as much for himself as for me. "You are not alone. You have me now."

He stared at me. "You don't wish to dissolve our engagement?"

"I wish you'd felt able to tell me sooner. You've held this terrible tragedy all alone for over three years. I can't fathom the weight of it, Worth." My eyes blurred.

"You don't question my account? You don't wish to interrogate me? I expected it, and I welcome it, Belle. Surely you have doubts."

I had questions about Eliza, about how he could love a woman whose selfishness demanded the abandonment of his sick father while her profession demanded his care, but I wasn't going to ask them. They weren't important. The heart was fickle, and she was gone. *Bless them all.*

Worth's eyes searched mine. A tear had fallen and its path glistened down his cheek in the lamp glow. I knew he was telling the truth. It wasn't his emotion that told me; it was the way I saw myself in his grief, in the way he refused to remove the misplaced remorse that had settled atop his heart. The guilty were often keen to throw off the shackles; the guilty found excuses for their actions. Worth blamed himself in his innocence, and it had ensnared him for years.

"I believe you. Everything you said."

"Why?" he asked, his face displaying something akin to shock. I knew the exact way he felt, the disbelief that another could possibly accept the truth of who he was, of where he'd been, when for so long he believed the truth would destroy him. It was a mercy he'd extended to me first. He'd given me a safe space. I wanted to do the same for him.

"Because I know, somehow," I said. "And I trust you." I lifted my hand to his cheek and drew my finger down the path of his tear. "Now that I know all of you, now that you know all of me, we must promise to confide in each other whenever we are melancholy or furious or happy . . . I do wish greatly for the last in abundance."

Worth smiled and took my fingers from his face and kissed my knuckles. His touch lingered. I couldn't look away from his lips, suddenly entranced by the way the sensation of the coarse hair around his mouth prickled not only the point of contact but also the base of my spine.

"As do I," he said.

"I was able to locate some crackers, grapes, and a few slices of sausage," Mr. Pierce said as he approached. Worth let my hand go and I blinked, feeling altogether jarred by Mr. Pierce's presence. He teetered toward us holding a platter. He settled back beside Worth and extended the plate to me. I placed a grape in my mouth, focusing on the burst of sweetness and the activity of the workers in front of us. "I apologize for my lengthy absence, though I suppose I've come just in time to see the last of the cement poured. I do love to see a project settled."

I watched as the worker tipped the waterfall of cement over the final section of exposed rebar.

"This roof is now completely fireproof," he went on. "Seely was greatly afraid of a blaze overtaking the guests at his hotel. He will be relieved to know it's been accomplished."

I waited for Worth to tense, but he only reached over and clapped Mr. Pierce on the back.

"He will indeed. It is a gift worth much, to find your fears eased."

# CHAPTER TWENTY-FIVE

I hadn't ever been to a baseball game, not a proper one anyway, with uniforms and concessions. A man walked by on a sidewalk between the field and the section of stands where the group of us had been deposited to take in the sport. He was juggling a tray of hot dogs topped with chili and mustard, wrapped in wax paper. My stomach growled.

"Belle!" Marie Austen charged from my left side, as though I could help the noise.

"Would you like me to fetch you something?" Worth asked from my other side. The concession men had continually passed us by. Whether it was an accidental omission or intentional in order to avoid having to converse with the famous Vagabonds — some flocked to them while others balked — I couldn't tell.

"I appreciate the offer, but I'll survive," I said, smiling at Worth. He was dressed in black again despite the day feeling quite like the beginning of summer. Sylvia had insisted Marie Austen and I dress in the lightest fabrics we had — two nearly matching Grecian costumes made of silk. Mine was a light blush with a white bodice lined in pink ribbon, while Marie Austen's was silver with a black belt adorned with beaded pink roses. Neither matched the colors of the home team — the Asheville Mountaineers.

The team lined the immaculate spring grass in the outfield, passing the baseball back and forth. They wore white shirts with peculiar sleeves that ballooned at the elbow and were embroidered with enormous cursive blue As on the left breast and their numbers at the collar matching their blue ball caps. The opposing team, the Philadelphia American Yannigans, occupied their set of bleachers next to home plate in maroon-and-white uniforms, while their coach shouted encouragements and instructions. Mr. Ford stood on the sidelines next to the Mountaineers' manager, Mr. Mack, as he waited to throw the first pitch to mark the beginning of the game.

"No, you won't. We barely ate two bites last night, and before that, your most recent meal was yesterday's oatmeal." Worth rose and made his way down the line, past our group's knees to the open stairs that rose up to the roof of the grandstand. The game had sold out today—twelve hundred tickets—and I'd overheard, as we were ushered in, that the businesses and schools in town had granted a half workday so people could make it to the two o'clock start. Most of the attraction was the weather and the excitement of opening day, but another draw to the park today was the spectacle of Mr. Ford and the knowledge that he'd promised spectators a look inside his autos following the game. The entirety of our procession to camp had felt like a parade, but the drive to the ballpark felt even more so. People lined the streets and cheered as we passed.

"Would you like any concessions, Mrs. Newbold?" Worth asked Mother when he got to the end of the aisle. "I'm just going to acquire some for Belle."

"Perhaps a box of Cracker Jacks, Worth. It's so kind of you to offer," she said.

"And a Coca-Cola if you can balance it for me, son," Papa said.

"I'm sure I can manage. I was a guest performer with the Ringling Brothers once when I was four, you know," he said, laughing. "Truly. They called me down from my seat to juggle."

I wondered how he felt when Papa called him son. He'd done it a few times since our engagement. Worth didn't seem to mind. Perhaps he found it nice. Papa had been his father's best friend, after all.

"I do wish they'd all quit staring at Mr. Carver," Mrs. Firestone said to her husband. "It's so uncivilized." They were sitting in front of me. I glanced at Mr. Carver in the front row of our group next to Mr. Burroughs and Mr. Kipp. I hadn't noticed anyone ogling him, but I had heard Mr. Carver's sharp retort to the man who'd been assigned to lead us to our seats when he'd attempted to direct Mr. Carver to a different area of the stands designated for Black guests. Why people of all skin shades worked amiably side by side at Grove Park without issue but were forcibly separated only a few miles away to take in sport, I found difficult to understand. It was a terribly ignorant, unfair practice.

"Mr. Carver does not pay them mind, and neither will we," Mr. Firestone said. "He is a genius inventor well beyond his years. He is well aware he will leave a mark on the world. Perhaps some of these beholders are simply in awe of him. Those who aren't are buffoons."

Just then, the electric organ began a loud piping of "Where, O Where Has My Little Dog Gone?" from its perch just behind first base, and Marie Austen let out a sigh.

"What a dreadfully sad song. Why not start with something cheery, like 'You Beautiful Doll' or 'Let Me Call You Sweetheart'?"

"This isn't a ball, dear; it's a ball game," Mr. Gibbins said dryly from her other side.

"You're right. How silly of me," Marie Austen said, her tone void of the sarcasm I was used to.

"What is going on?" I leaned into her and said under my breath, "Your behavior is rather—"

"Strange? Changed?" She looked at me and pursed her lips. "Yes, darling, it is. I realized after I nearly lost you to my folly that I couldn't lose another, and . . . and I wrote to Mr. Thorp at his residence in New York." Her voice dropped to a whisper. "I know he's likely not there, but surely whoever is looking after his place will know where to forward the message." She smoothed her sleeves and looked out at the players who were running in from the field to either their designated bleachers or a small seating arrangement with a shelter I'd heard someone call the dugout.

"I am engaged and I will marry Mr. Gibbins, but I have proposed

Mr. Thorp another arrangement." Her lips lifted in a grin. "As I told you I would. It settled me greatly to make such a plan."

"But, Marie Austen, what if your letter is intercepted? What if Mr. Gibbins finds out and calls off the engagement? Then what will you do? Your father will surely disown you as he threatened, and—"

She made a noise of dismissal and waved her hand at me.

"I insinuated my proposal delicately. No one would suspect anything untoward," she said. "I didn't tell you before because I know you disagree with my decision, and I don't wish to disagree with you when it doesn't matter."

I nodded and watched as she accepted Mr. Gibbins's outstretched hand. Nothing I said would change her mind.

The organ struck the first notes of "The Star-Spangled Banner" and everyone in the stands rose. The metal creaked with the strain of the crowd, and for a moment I braced myself on the seat I'd just abandoned, thinking it might collapse. A player with a curled mustache stood on the pitcher's mound waving a large American flag, and I put my hand over my heart. When the anthem concluded, everyone continued standing as Mr. Ford paced to the mound with a new baseball in his fist. A catcher, looking much like an armored knight, ambled to his position behind home plate.

Edsel whistled.

"Go, Father!" he yelled while the rest of the crowd hollered and clapped. Two of Mr. Ford's photographers huddled behind their cameras on the sidewalk, their bulbs flashing, while the new reporter scribbled hurriedly on his notepad from a chair beside them.

"Does he know what he's doing?" I heard Toots ask Edsel.

"Quite. He used to play, though not as proficiently as your father, I'm told." Edsel shrugged.

The organ played a suspenseful sort of tune and then Mr. Ford wound up and threw the ball. It was a respectable, even pitch, and it stoked the crowd's enthusiasm.

Worth appeared from somewhere beneath the stands, and I couldn't help but laugh at the sight of him. He carried four glasses filled with Coca-Cola in a tray-like contraption with a handle and had balanced two hot dogs and four boxes of Cracker Jacks atop the mouths of the beverages.

"I take back what I said about his appeal being squandered by my horrid betrayal," Marie Austen mused. "You truly have it all, don't you, Belle? Not only is he handsome, but he has made quite an effort to make sure you are cared for."

"He always does," I said, choosing to believe Marie Austen's sincere tone. I smiled at Worth. His eyes swept mine, and he grinned back. We'd had our rows and would certainly have them again, but the fact that my life had intertwined with his was a miracle.

We'd held hands the whole way home from the inn the night before. He'd asked me several times if I had any questions for him, if I was certain I believed him. Even then, in the midst of his wondering, there was a comfortable sort of way about us. I'd asked him where his parents' house had been—on the southern crest of the hill—if his house had been slated to have been built farther down, if I'd seen the ruins—I had—and if his scar ever hurt—it did.

He'd pulled to the side of the road then, removed his jacket and unbuttoned his shirt. *"I'd rather you see it now than be startled by it on . . . later."* He'd not said "our wedding night," but I knew that was what he meant, and as he pulled his right arm from his sleeve and edged the fabric back from his shoulders and his chest, I felt not horror but a tingling in the pit of my stomach. The scar was extensive, encompassing the whole of his arm and his right side to his nipple and down to the base of his lung. It was purple, raised, thick in places and thin in others. *"If I'd had it treated, I'm sure it would have been more favorable to the eye. I healed it myself,"* he'd said. *"If it disgusts you, you'll never see it again. I'll wear a shirt always."*

I suppose I'd been too quiet, too fixed on the sight of his chest—the lean muscles despite the scar—the heartbreaking thought of him salving his wound alone. *"Can I touch it?"* I asked. I recalled in that moment Mr. Dalfonzo, a man in Red Dragon who'd lost his leg in a rockfall. I remembered his wife speaking of how important it had been for her to touch the place where his leg ended, to let him know she wasn't put off by it, that she still saw him, not his injury. Worth had balked at my request, insisting it wasn't necessary. He'd started to put his sleeve back on when my palm landed softly on the largest section of puckered scarring on his lower chest.

He'd drawn a sharp breath then, and I thought I'd hurt him, but he shook his head when I asked. *"The pain comes from inside, not out, if that makes any sense,"* he'd said as I moved my hand from his chest to his shoulder and down to his wrist. *"It's the nerves, I think. Sometimes it's numb, sometimes it tingles, and other times pain shoots from my chest to my wrist."* I'd removed my fingers and he'd threaded his arm back in his sleeve.

"Here's your Coca-Cola and your hot dog or Cracker Jacks, whichever you'd like," Worth said as he sat down beside me, interrupting my memories of the night before. Below us, the Yannigans' most promising hitter had just struck out, swiftly calling the team to the field while the Mountaineers took the plate, and the umpire was trying to calm the coach, who was making a terrible racket.

"I'll have all three," I said. He set the metal carrier on the floor between our feet, then handed me a hot dog and retained one for himself. "How do you eat these?" I asked.

He looked at me peculiarly, held it between his thumb and index finger, and took a bite. Chili dripped over his fingers, and he quickly reached for his handkerchief, dried his fingers, and then handed a clean handkerchief to me.

"If you find the game and the concessions agreeable, let me know. I quite enjoy watching the Charlotte Hornets back home when the weather is fair. We could go together," he said.

I took a bite of the sandwich as I'd seen him do. The taste was wonderful—the salt of the meat, the smoky flavor of the chili, and the buttery bread made me wish I'd requested two at least.

"I'll go with you. Even if I loathe the game, I'll go for this." I thought of the bland meals we were served back home in Gas City, the mild gravies atop various meats, the steamed vegetables with no flavor, and wondered why more fine homes didn't insist on hot dogs.

Directly behind the stands, church bells chimed Westminster from the Presbyterian church's steeple, ringing over the shouts of glee from everyone—Worth and Papa included—as a man named Milliman hit a ball so far he was able to round all the bases.

"It's a home run!" Worth shouted, rising to his feet so quickly he nearly toppled the drinks. I clapped and watched the players rejoice with the spectators. When the crowd finally settled, Worth sat, but remained on the edge of his seat.

"Have the two of you had any discussion as to the particulars of your wedding?" Marie Austen turned to me, her nose scrunching at the way I angled the hot dog into my mouth. Our set wasn't used to foods that didn't require utensils. "The bells reminded me to ask. Robert and I have just settled on a ceremony in Gas City June second at our home, and I'd love for you to be my maid of honor . . . That is, if you won't be married already by that time. If you are, you can be my matron of honor, though doesn't that sound like an old dowager rather than a lively woman in her twenties?"

I glanced at Worth. We had grown so close so quickly that we hadn't spoken at all of our actual arrangements to marry. The particulars of that seemed inconsequential in the wake of his discovering who I was and my discovering who he'd been. I didn't care where the ceremony took place, though I was eager to say the words, to promise I would stand by him and hear him say he would stand by me.

"I wouldn't miss it," I said. Worth stood and yelled again, along with Mr. Burroughs, Edsel, Mr. Kipp, and Mr. Carver this time. They were all in a tizzy about a man named McKeithan being called out at second base. When the sides were switched and the play forgotten, they all sat down.

"We can get married whenever and wherever you'd like," Worth said to me. He tipped his head at Marie Austen. "I heard her ask." Her kissing him had surprisingly not rendered their proximity strange in the slightest. My forgiving them both had taken the power from the event, I suppose. That, and the fact that Worth's true disinterest in Marie Austen was evident. "I'd like a church wedding because it seems to me a perfect place to make a serious vow, but if you don't prefer it that's as well with me."

"Shall we have it in a church in Charlotte, in the town of our home?" I ate the last bite of hot dog and looked at him. "Next month, perhaps? I don't require a fine dress to be made up, so there's no use to tarry, unless—"

"May seventeenth at the First Presbyterian Church in Charlotte," he said. He glanced at me and smiled, then took my hand. "It is my parents' anniversary. Would you mind it?"

"I would be honored." My father's birthday was the nineteenth. I thought May a good month. He squeezed my fingers and let them go to open a box of Cracker Jacks. He dug around in the narrow box filled with caramel popcorn and extracted a red card that displayed a photo of a baseball player and the words *Cracker Jack Ball Players* printed across the top.

"Joe Jackson," he said, wiping the candy dust from the card with his handkerchief. "What a find."

# CHAPTER TWENTY-SIX

The Mountaineers cinched a victory eleven to ten at the bottom of the ninth inning. By that time, the stands were in a frenzy, save for our section's women. Even when a player named Barbare hit a grand slam to win the game, Marie Austen only yawned, and I overheard Mrs. Edison muse that she preferred polo. In contrast, I was captivated.

I'd watched a baseball game before, but never on a true baseball diamond and never with professional players—only the miners challenging each other to a game on a rare day off. When Barbare struck the ball, launching it over the fence to the place where our autos were parked, I'd jumped up with the others. Worth had taken me in his arms and swirled me around, nearly launching my legs into the Firestones, and when he'd made a full rotation, his attention had shifted from the field to my face, and he didn't let me go.

We stood there holding each other for what seemed like minutes.

*"Belle,"* he'd said, and his hand had lifted to my cheek. He'd leaned down, and I thought he was about to kiss me, though the truth of that was preposterous. We were in public, in the midst of over a thousand people, and we were not yet married.

*"Isn't it wonderful?"* Mr. Firestone had interrupted, turning to us and jolting Worth out of his trance. He'd released me quickly and slapped Mr. Firestone's hand, then told me he had to go into town to send a telegram, that there was a bit of land he was in the process of purchasing and he'd be back to camp late.

We'd all poured out of the stadium after the final congratulations died, our group mingling with men who'd come from the lumber-yards, women who'd come from a seamstress shop, and children who'd been released from school a few hours early. Despite the game's conclusion, it seemed no one was going home. They'd all crowded around the autos, keen to take a turn at the wheel as Mr. Ford had promised, while our group of women adjourned to the bleachers, accepting the ballpark manager's offer of tea and more boxes of Cracker Jacks.

The final driver was nearly finished as the sky turned gold.

"I've never been to Charlotte," Mother said. We'd been discussing my wedding, and even though I knew she was elated and my moving off was what one did when she was married, we would be a two-day train ride apart. "I'll be excited to arrive early and get acquainted with your new home. Perhaps I could convince Shipley to buy a little bungalow nearby."

"If not, we will see you often still, I'm certain. Worth travels around the country frequently, and though he's sworn he's planning to settle down, I'll go with him when I'm able," I said, leaning into her. Mother had started wearing Lilas Blanc perfume when she married Papa, but even with the green leaves and lemony notes wafting from her costume, today she still smelled like she always had, like warmth. She put her arm around me.

"We've been through so much," she whispered. "But for most of my life, I've been happy. I hope the same for you." An auto drove to the foot of the bleachers and stopped. Papa Shipley emerged and smiled at us.

"What a lovely sight. My girls," he called. "I was hoping you'd take a drive with me, Belle. There's a country road down the way that Mack says is quite beautiful this time of year."

He leaned against the polished black metal and put his hands in his pockets. He was in his sixties now, and his face had wrinkled and his hair was graying, but in this moment, I could imagine him young.

"Of course," I said, rising from my place next to Mother. "Would you like to come along?" I asked her. She shook her head.

"No. I'll remain here until your return, or perhaps I'll take a ride back with the Kipps. There are some things Papa would like to discuss with you in private," she said. I nodded, wondering if the conversation would reveal something dire, but her face was pleasant.

"Very well." I bunched my pink silk skirt in my hands and made my way down to Papa.

"I'm surprised you wish to drive anymore after today's exposition," I said when I reached him. "How many turns have you taken around the grounds these last hours?"

"Too many to count." Papa laughed and walked around the front of the auto to open my door. "On our way home, I'll gladly accept one of the chauffeurs. I must admit that nothing makes a person question the invention of the auto more than sitting beside a person who hasn't a clue what they're doing. You realize swiftly that you're risking your life."

I climbed in and he closed my door.

"You've done Mr. Ford a great service in participating. I'm certain those men all went home determined to own a Model T of their own," I said when he was settled beside me.

"I'm sure they did. And today was nothing compared to the favor Ford's doing for me," he said. He drove around the back of the outfield and onto a little dirt road through the woods. Mr. Mack had been right in saying it was a pretty drive. Even in the first moments, the evening sun dappled the forest in gold, and the redbuds and emerging dogwoods were plentiful, eclipsing much notice of the new green leaves.

"So he's agreed to the gasoline stores then?" I asked. "I'd say the idea is as much an advantage to him as it is to you."

"Yes. Fifty to start, though where the first will be we're still debating, as you know." He smiled, then cleared his throat. "Things have been so busy as of late that I haven't had occasion to tell you how proud I am of you." He glanced at me. "I know I'm not your father by blood, but it has been my honor to stand in his place these past six years. I hope when I meet him someday, he approves of my hand in your life, that he knows your mother only changed your last name to make things easier for you."

"He would be thankful for you. For the way you love us," I said and meant it, disregarding the matter of my name. It was true that assuming the name of Newbold had made it easier for suitors and friends and acquaintances to connect me to Mother and Papa. I had never been certain whether Father would have been angry or understanding about that. "You have been so generous and kind. You've never treated me like a stepdaughter." Father and Papa Shipley couldn't have been more different on the surface, but underneath, their hearts were similar.

"You will always be my girl. Your mother is the love of my life. I married my former wife, Hartley's mother, because it was prearranged. We weren't happy. At times I've regretted my part in her never having experienced love." He paused. "Are you satisfied in your engagement to Worth? You seem as though you are, and yet I wanted to be sure. I know you never said it, but I knew what sort of arrangement you were seeking." Papa looked at me. "I am sorry that my will cannot include you, that my fortune must go to Hartley and Eunice. The stipend will care for your mother, but on my former wife's deathbed, I promised—"

I reached over and patted Papa's shoulder.

"I understand, and all is well. I'm more pleased than I thought I'd ever be with Worth. He is caring as you are and will make me very happy."

"I'm glad to hear it. He's like a son to me. Certainly more interested in my well-being than Hartley, and I quite like the way I've seen him encouraging you in your writing. His parents were the same way—always the most supportive friends." Papa slowed the auto and his eyes met mine.

"Speaking of Miller and Florence, did Worth tell you of his calamity? It is not my place, but if he hasn't—"

"He has," I said. "He told me everything and encouraged my questions." I felt my eyes prickle with emotion and I sniffed it away. "It is the most horrible thing to endure, and it has marred him terribly."

"Yet you understand it," Papa said. He didn't have to explain why. He may not have known who my father was, but he knew the particulars of his death.

"I understand the grief, the sharp pang of loss, but I was not there when he died. I didn't see the rock fall atop him and wonder if I could have stopped it or if the rockfall was my fault," I whispered, somehow unable to lift my voice higher.

"Lanterns topple frequently. I've reminded him of that even when he hasn't asked," Papa said. Of course, he didn't know about Eliza, that the lantern had been thrown.

"He said some question his story and wonder if he set the blaze intentionally. He could never, Papa. He wears the badge of guilt in spite of his innocence. I hope to remove it and set him free," I said.

"If anyone can, it's you, Belle. He's a good man. Otherwise, I never would have agreed for him to have your hand. I hope you know that."

"I do."

The woods were dense and the road suddenly narrowed. Beyond the trees, I could see a sizable white house. It had a porch that stretched all the way around and a widow's walk on the second story.

"I don't know how we're going to turn around." Papa chuckled. "I figured when Mack suggested we come this way that he'd know we needed to come back too."

"You could drive off the road, through the trees just there. The trunks are distant enough and there appears to be a clearing right before that house." I pointed and he steered the auto in the direction I'd instructed. Branches screeched as they slid across the doors. I knew they would leave scratches in the polish that the chauffeurs would be asked to buff out later.

The trees gave way to a grassy lawn and Papa began to turn the auto around. As we neared the house, I saw the people on the porch. They were arranged on rocking chairs, clothed in white infirmary gowns. Their bodies were skeletal, their faces bruised. Even through the closed auto windows, I could hear the strangled rattle of their intermittent coughs. They all looked exactly like the Smiths, like the men extracting stone and the men in the mason tents and the men on the roof.

"Another tuberculosis sanitorium," Papa said as we came to face the other way, back toward the road that would lead us to the ball field. My skin washed cold and my heart raced, and at once I thought I might faint. "I'm sorry you had to see that, Belle. Those poor souls."

"Take me to Worth," I said, my voice hoarse. "I must speak to him at once."

# CHAPTER TWENTY-SEVEN

*B*lood struck the white linen handkerchief I held to my mouth, and a sob lodged in my throat. I had it now, of course I did. It was inevitable. The whole town of Asheville had been closed to the outside world, made a tuberculosis colony. Wasted bodies lumbered around me in an endlessly long room, and I balled the bloodied handkerchief in my hand, balking at the sight of my fingers reduced to the hands of a skeleton.

"If only we'd caught it earlier, we could have removed the infected to receive treatment and the inn's construction wouldn't have halted." *I whirled to find Mr. Mills, gaunt, in a hospital bed. His face was gray, matching the blanket that covered the whole of his body to his chin.* "But now the town is closed, and Grove and Seely are gone to St. Louis. All hope is lost. The disease doesn't discriminate. Even Worth Delafield had to sell his land to a man who's building another sanitorium."

*Worth. Despite the terror of knowing I was wasting away—I could feel the weakness in my bones, in the clammy feel of my skin that had endured drenching night sweats and in the tightness of my lungs— the thought that I didn't know where he was ignited a sort of desperation and I yelled his name.*

"Belle." *His answer was soft, tired, and I looked beside me to find him gathered in a matching chair. The sight of him immediately made me cry, and even in his own distress, he reached a hand toward me.* "Belle," *he said again.*

"What's happened to us?" *I asked. Instead of answering, he said my name again, louder this time, and someone pushed my shoulder. I jerked back and suddenly felt myself falling from the chair.*

My eyes flew open in the dark, my hand drawing up to swat at whoever had struck me, but I was in my tent at camp, in Worth's arms. He was crouched beside my cot and grinned down at me in the dim.

"Whatever were you dreaming about?" he whispered. "I tried to wake you gently, but you lunged at me and fell from your quilts."

I sat up. My nightgown was damp. Embarrassment burned my cheeks and I stood. He followed. I stared at him for a moment, trying to figure if the vision of him wasted by tuberculosis had, in fact, been a dream. I suddenly thought of the proximity I'd had to the infected in close quarters—particularly in the mason tent—and was at once relieved that he had only been exposed in open air. I was terrified I might be infected.

"Let's go outside to discuss it," I said, my voice gravelly. I walked to the armoire and opened the door slowly so as not to wake Marie Austen, who was snoring.

"Shipley saw me as I was coming into camp. He said you'd been looking for me and wanted to have a word," he whispered. "I know he meant in the morning, but I couldn't sleep. There are things I need to discuss with you too." His expression, humored by my actions when I was dreaming moments before, sobered. "I hope you don't mind me waking you."

I fitted my cloak over my shoulders and shook my head.

"Of course not."

Worth withdrew from the tent, and when I'd fastened the buttons at my neck, I followed. Outside, the crisp smell of almost frost made me realize the air inside the tent had been stale, smelling of bourbon seeping from Marie Austen's skin, the result of the three nightcaps she ordered to accompany the bedtime story she demanded I tell. I'd spoken of a woman who longed to be a baseball star—proximity and ease had evoked the topic. With the sight of the tuberculosis sanitorium occupying my mind, minimal creativity was a requirement.

"What is it you wished to discuss with me?" I asked Worth. We stood side by side a distance from the tent, looking at the half-moon overlaid with wisping clouds.

"I purchased a home for the Smiths," he said simply. "That's where I was off to today after the game. I didn't want to tell you until I was certain the current owner would agree, but it's settled now—a little white house on Hickory Tree Road within walking distance to where they're harvesting the granite but situated with quite a bit of sun and an acre of land. I couldn't bear the thought of them living in such a place when I had the means to help."

"Of course you would do such a generous, wonderful thing." I took his hand and squeezed, alight at the news of my friends' situation improving, but he didn't return the gesture. Then the realization of their illness dawned on me. "Worth, Papa took me for a drive to—"

"The deal was settled within half an hour of my arrival in town today," he said, his eyes settling on mine. He took my other hand. "But I couldn't return to camp. I needed to sort out something, Belle, and it required several hours alone to realize that what I suspected was true."

He paused and looked away from me, and he ran his thumb across my knuckles over and over again. An owl called in the distance in a too-too-too call. The northern saw-whet. Mr. Burroughs would be disappointed he'd missed it. When Worth didn't go on, I squeezed his hand.

"Worth, what is it?"

His gaze met mine again and lingered.

"I'm falling in love with you, and I cannot. I promised myself, I promised you, and I will not let both of us down. Damn it. I nearly kissed you today, Belle, in front of everyone."

I felt light, weightless, hearing his confession, but his face was stony, his hands gripped tightly to mine. In the seconds it took for the implication to settle on my heart, my soul went from soaring to sinking.

We couldn't go on like this. I couldn't let him love me or I him.

We would end in ruin. Our hearts would shatter, and we would be left a shell of ourselves, forever mutilated by heartache. Panic wrapped like iron around my lungs, and I let go of his hands.

"They have tuberculosis—the Smiths and at least half of the workers constructing the inn. Papa and I took a drive today and concluded by accident at a tuberculosis sanitorium. The patients are emaciated and bruised, mere bones like the Smiths, and the coughs—the coughs are the exact same sound I heard on my surveys. The workers are drinking some vinegar concoction, some tincture they said would ward off the circulating illness—which is, of course, actually consumption. The drink is horrid tasting and some refuse it. I drank some when I was in close proximity of several men. I worry I've been exposed myself, and I don't think the tincture is truly working. If it goes on, I'm afraid the entire force of them will be ill, and Seely's hotel will never materialize after all, and the town of Asheville will be given over entirely to the sanitoriums." I was blabbering, speaking whatever thoughts came into my brain save the ones involving his declaration. It was the only thing that kept me from reaching for him.

"You'll not fall ill. I'll not permit it," he said. "First thing in the morning, I'll take you to a physician I know in town, and after, we must draft a telegram to Seely. He must know the dire state of things here. His infected workers must obtain proper treatment and immediately withdraw from the healthy. Lives and his inn are at stake."

"Let me speak to Willie first. Before we telegram Seely. I am nearly certain of what I saw, but we should have it confirmed, should we not? I pray I'm mistaken, that the illness among the workers is something less dire," I said.

Worth nodded. "Yes. No reason to alarm him if we find that it's a benign virus."

"Tomorrow then."

His eyes searched mine as I began to turn away to my tent. I knew he was wondering if I'd respond to his confession or allow it to linger unresolved.

I stopped and faced him. My fingers found the sapphire on my left hand and gently pulled it off. I held it out to him, and he took it, then wrapped his hand around mine, the silver and stone trapped between our palms.

"You could have kept it, even though—" he started.

"We will help these people together, and then, in another few days, I will take the train back to Indiana and you will go back to Charlotte or wherever your work takes you. If you ever call on Papa, I'll not be there. After these days, we will never see each other again." I forced a smile at him, though my spirit throbbed and ached at my words. This was necessary. One way or another, we would save each other. "In time our hearts will forget this love," I said.

He let go of my hand and held the ring in front of him.

"I hoped for a wife and a family," he said. "I'll not give up on that dream. Someday I'll marry, but she won't have this ring." He looked at me. "Without me, you'll not have the security of my pockets. Perhaps you'll make a match with someone equally suited, but even if you do not, you'll have ample income. I'll make sure of it." Worth put the ring in his lapel pocket. "You'll never find yourself destitute, Belle."

"I couldn't allow that," I said. "Dissolving our engagement was our mutual decision. You don't owe me—"

"I'll not permit discussion on the matter." His voice deadened and his face held a heaviness that I knew mirrored mine. I touched his cheek in spite of myself, letting my thumb remain while my fingers threaded in the gold-brown at his nape. Something about the finality of us emboldened me, allowed me to lean in to him, to draw his mouth to mine, but the moment our lips met, he stepped back.

"No," he whispered. "We cannot. It would only make this worse."

# CHAPTER TWENTY-EIGHT

I'd gone to Mother and Papa as soon as the sun had risen. The comforting smells of coffee and woodsmoke permeated the air but did little for my nerves.

I'd gone over it and over it in the night, how I'd tell them that Worth and I were not to be, but the preparation didn't still my heart. I'd known then, clearly, that I'd been falling in love with him too, that the ache I felt was but a small bit of the feeling I'd possess in an avalanche if we'd gone on—if we'd married and had children and lost each other then. Worth had been wise to recognize it before it was too late.

Without him, I knew I would possibly never have the family I always wanted and could face poverty despite the funds he'd send. I'd refuse them, of course. It wouldn't be right to accept. I didn't want to return to a life of scarcity, but at least I was familiar with hunger, with the way hours of labor made a body collapse. Destitution was a poison, but it was a poison I understood, that I could manage. The depletion of the soul that came with true heartbreak was a near fatal dose.

Mother and Papa weren't awake when I entered their tent. I'd found them holding each other, Papa's body tucked behind hers, and for a moment I considered leaving and returning later, thinking I'd come upon a scene too tender for a daughter to see. But I could hear the clatter of trays outside the tent, the servants hustling to serve their employers coffee and ready them for the day, and I knew if I didn't wake them, I'd not find them alone for some time.

They'd startled when I called their names and tapped their arms, balked at the way I came right out and told them that I'd dissolved my engagement to Worth. I knew I had to take responsibility for our conclusion. The fault had to rest on me and me alone, lest Papa's fury ignite and his threats of spreading lies about Worth materialize.

I'd lied and told them I didn't feel for Worth, that my ride with Papa yesterday made me realize anything short of a love match was a mistake. Mother had tried to argue with me, while Papa remained silent. When it was clear Mother wouldn't convince me to reconsider, Papa sighed and shook his head.

*"I understand and yet, Belle, I must caution you. I am familiar with men of all kinds, and most are brutes. Worth is a rare gentleman, a man who would love both you and your children, a man who would provide for you. If you go on without him, I fear the possibility that you'll find yourself alone, and in that place, exposed to much—loneliness, poverty."*

His words made me feel hollow, and I was thankful for the morning dim. I told him I understood the risk, but I was willing to take it. Mother, still seething, found her voice again then. *"You might not see it, but you do love him and he you. It is obvious, Belle."* I'd said no and turned away, disappearing from the tent before they could see me cry.

After breakfast when I'd composed myself, I'd told them Worth was going to drive me to my next interview at Grove Park—I couldn't tell them of my being examined for consumption first lest they truly explode with worry for me—and they'd both encouraged me to take the time with him to reconsider. Of course, I could not.

"How are we going to do this?" Worth asked. We were driving along the ridge where I'd first encountered the wagon train toward the hill that would lead to the Smiths' holler. The screech of pulleys and the shouts of men were close by, near deafening, but the entirety of the valley and the creek bed was covered in a misty haze, eclipsing any sight of the workers. The wagon train stretched out beside us, half of the cars filled with stone.

"I'll go to their door alone first," I said. "They trust me. I'll simply tell them I've been concerned since I saw them and ask."

"Very well, but you can't go inside, even if they invite you. You heard Doctor Jebens. You must prevent close contact with the infected," he said. I nodded, accidentally meeting his gaze as I did. I'd been avoiding his eyes, the red veins and the bags reflecting mine. Neither of us had spoken of last night. On the way to be examined for consumption, we'd discussed possibly going to see the inn's electricity being installed later today for my story, and after our exam, we'd focused solely on our plan for speaking with the Smiths.

"You must write and tell me if you fall ill," I said suddenly. Doctor Jebens had declared us both healthy but said tuberculosis crept up slowly, often going undetected for three to nine weeks. We would be separated long before knowing if illness had befallen either of us.

"I'll write to Shipley," Worth said. I understood. Writing me would encourage me to respond, would encourage our connection to grow despite our distance, thwarting our plan to become strangers again. Even so, my leaving meant he'd be alone, and I couldn't bear knowing he was suffering without anyone to care for him. He waved to a man in overalls standing next to the final wagon on the train.

"What shall we do if one of us is taken down with it? I know we've promised we'll not speak again, but—"

"You will not be taken ill. I forbid it," he barked in the same tone he'd used when I first told him of the possibility the night before, as though his saying so held some authority over providence. "If I come down with it, I will obtain a place in the most reputable sanitorium I can find, and you won't worry for me. If it is my fate to perish, I will be surrounded by capable nurses. You will not come for me and risk your life in the process."

I remained silent as the gray light on the ridge gave way to the dim of the forest and the auto started down the hill.

"Promise me," he said as a redbud branch slid across the windshield and rain began to drizzle through the trees.

"I can't," I whispered. "Surely you know I couldn't stay away if I knew you were dying."

"Then I'll not write to Shipley and tell him if I'm ailing," he said. "It's just as well. Whether I live to be one hundred or die the day you leave, we aren't supposed to know it anyway. We agreed that we'll never see each other again."

"I'll know if you're gone," I said, not understanding quite where the sentiment came from, but I knew it was true.

He nodded. "I know."

The auto steadied at the base of the hill. In the shade of the mountain cliffs on either side and in the gloom of a rain shower, the light was all but extinguished and it appeared nearly night. Up ahead, smoke rose from the chimney of the Smiths' home, while water overflowed the banks of the little creek beside it, sweeping dirt from the base of the house.

"I'll beckon to you when I'm through speaking to them so you can explain the particulars of their new home," I said. "I still can't believe you bought them a house, Worth. It was—"

"Nothing. It was nothing for me. I'll do more when they're settled. I'll look in on them when I'm about, Belle. I know what they mean to you."

I reached across the seat to his free hand resting on the leather. My fingers grazed the back of his, but he quickly pulled it away.

"We must not. A few days more and you will not be there when I reach for you," he said softly. "Stopping it now will make it easier for both of us to get on with our lives."

Worth silenced the auto's engine in front of the house. The rotten wood drooped in a frown that only seemed to deepen with the saturation of the rain.

"Perhaps you should let me go speak with them. We didn't think to bring an umbrella. You'll be soaked and chilled through," Worth said. I hadn't thought of the consequences of standing in the rain. Before we moved to Indiana, I'd gone out in the rain on purpose sometimes, even taken dips in Elk Run during a shower. It was magical, really, and wonderfully cleansing. Perhaps being caught in a storm was exactly the sort of medicine I needed to wash away the melancholy.

"I quite enjoy the rain," I said, opening my own door and disembarking before Worth could argue with me. I hurriedly unpinned my wide-brimmed straw hat and tossed it into the auto as raindrops began to saturate the sky-blue silk-satin dress studded with paste diamonds—Mother's favorite of my spring wardrobe—and my hair. Thankfully, Sylvia hadn't done much with it this morning, simply gathered the unruly waves loosely and coiled them low.

I walked toward the house, the heels of my patent leather boots sticking in the mud, and finally reached the two steps to the front door. I knocked and, noticing the material of my dress had become completely stuck to my body, pulled the fabric away from my skin. Voices came from inside, muted by the rain and the door, and then Mrs. Smith appeared.

"Belle! Child. Whatever are you doing here in this weather?" she asked. Even though I'd seen her recently, I was still taken aback by her emaciated figure. In my mind she would always be plump and rosy, happy. "Do come in," she begged at my silence. I remembered myself and waved my hand.

"I can't, I'm afraid," I half-shouted over the beating of the rain on the old roof. I wiped water from my face. "Ever since I saw you and Willie and Mr. Smith the other day, I've worried about your health. Have you been seen by a doctor, Mrs. Smith?"

Mrs. Smith shook her head and her eyes clouded.

"No. And we won't be either," she said.

"Why? I have . . . I have reason to believe you are all stricken with tuberculosis, Mrs. Smith, and unless you receive treatment, there's a high chance you'll perish. I—"

"Yes," she said. My skin prickled, the chilly rain suddenly icy with what I gathered was her confession. "We know what it is that's ailing us. That's why I was so opposed to Willie bringing you here for dinner that day, why I set up the meal outdoors."

"But there are places that can help. If it's money you need, my friend Worth—"

"No. We won't go waste away in one of those sanitoriums," she said, cutting me off again. "Willie says half of the people that go to those places die anyway and there's no cure. We'll either survive or perish right here."

"Please reconsider. Even if the two of you refuse, surely you'd allow Willie. He's so young," I said. "Mr. Seely would—"

"No. You must not tell a soul, especially Mr. Seely or Mr. Mills or Mr. Pierce or any of the men in charge at the inn that we are — that any of the workers are — infected with consumption, especially Willie," she nearly shouted, pitching forward so swiftly that she barely kept from tumbling over the threshold. Then she wheezed and turned her head to cough. "Mr. Grove and Mr. Seely fear consumption more than near anything else. You know that. There are many infected, so many, but if we are found out they'll all lose their jobs. They've joined together and sworn that they'll not say a word of it."

"But if they keep on, they may infect the well, and those already infected may not be able to work much longer anyway, Mrs. Smith," I said. "Think of Willie—"

"He has a mild case," she said. "Most do. You haven't been subject to seeing the disease as I have. He is going to be all right. And as far as infecting the well goes—" She shrugged. "They are exposed no matter where they work. It is no different in the factories and in the lumberyards. Every operation has a large number of sick among them at this point." She paused and stared at me. "As I said, Willie will be fine."

"I'm certain we can obtain some beds at a sanitorium nearby. It seems there are many," I said, ignoring her pleas to do nothing.

"You must promise me you'll not say a word of our condition to anyone. If you do, if the news spreads and near half of the inn's workers are let go, hundreds of families will starve." She stood as straight as she could. I heard the whistling in her chest when she spoke, and the noise was unnerving.

"It's clear you've forgotten what it's like when your family depends on a check each week." Her eyes drifted over my fine gown, now soiled by rain. I wanted to argue with her, but I knew she was right. I recalled the way Mother had to beg for work in the wake of Father's death, the way families had accumulated so much debt at the company store when a man was injured that at some points they were refused food.

"Promise me you'll not say a word of our condition," she pressed.

I nodded. "Very well." I looked at her. She was withering away. I turned to the auto and motioned to Worth.

"You brought that man with you again?" Mrs. Smith charged. I didn't know how she hadn't noticed him before. Perhaps she figured I'd driven myself, though I didn't know the first thing about driving.

"Yes. He has something to tell you."

"If you're planning to have us drug away, taken against our will, I'll throw myself from the auto," she said.

"Nothing like that," I said. She began to cough again and I turned away. Worth walked toward us. He'd removed his black jacket, and his white shirt had become translucent in the rain. I couldn't help but stare when he came close, as the shirt settled in the lines of his stomach. I recalled the way his skin had felt against my hand, and when I looked at him, he was staring at my dress. He jerked his gaze away and I did the same.

"Good to see you again, Mrs. Smith," he said when he reached me. "I'm here to tell you that someone we know has seen to it that you have a new home. There's a little white house up the mountain here on Hickory Tree Road, relinquished recently by a family who has moved down to Florida. Perhaps you know it? It sits on an acre of land in the sunshine. You're welcome to move in whenever you like."

She stared, gaping at Worth, and then suddenly shook her head.

"Of course I know the house. It was Willie's friend Johnny's place. I don't believe it. Who would do such a thing?"

Worth shrugged.

"The man desires to remain anonymous, but there are many well-to-do men in this town, and some are keen to reward those who they believe deserve a better situation." Rain drizzled over Worth's face, over mine too, so there was no way for Mrs. Smith to see that I was sobbing as I watched her lips turn up in a smile.

"Well, I . . . Well, I . . . I don't know what to say, but of course we're much obliged. Much obliged indeed. William!" She hollered into the house and nearly began to walk inside to tell Mr. Smith the news, but then stopped. "Does he know?" she said, looking at me, and I knew what she was asking. I nodded.

"You have to promise you'll say nothing about the Smiths' consumption, about any of the workers' either," I said to Worth. "You know as well as I do that it would cost them their posts."

"Nothing at all, please. I beg of you," Mrs. Smith said.

"Are you certain Belle can't persuade you and the others to seek treatment?" Worth pushed his soaking hair away from his forehead.

"Yes," she said.

Worth said nothing for a moment but kept his gaze fixed on Mrs. Smith.

"Very well. The home is yours and can be claimed at any time," he said.

"Please thank the giver of such a gift. From the bottom of my heart," Mrs. Smith said, her eyes glassy.

"I will." Worth smiled and looked at me. I tipped my head to the sky, letting the drops fall on my eyes, my cheeks, my forehead, feeling the rain wash away the sadness and leave joy.

"This rain reminds me of when I was a girl. We'd dance in it, splash in the puddles and laugh and laugh," Mrs. Smith said. "There's magic in rain, I've always thought, and today's good fortune confirms it. If I could, I'd join the two of you and spin and spin and thank God for this hope today."

I stepped away from them and spun around once, my arms flung wide.

"Like that?" I asked, laughing, knowing I looked foolish but realizing she was right. Suddenly, my soul felt lighter.

"Exactly like that," she said. "You looked just like your mother right then, and—" Mrs. Smith froze, her face awash in panic. "I only meant that you looked like a friend I had once," she said quickly, her eyes jerking to Worth.

"It's all right, Mrs. Smith. He knows who I am."

She grinned and nodded.

"Then as I was saying, your mother was one of the ones who used to dance in the rain with me. She grew up across the street and your daddy next door. From the time your mother was a little girl, your daddy would wave to us out the window every time, looking at her the same way this man is looking at you."

I sobered and glanced at Worth, whose gaze was now fixed to his boots. Country folk didn't hold back as cultured society people were taught to do. Little was left to silence and most thoughts were expressed in honesty. Mrs. Smith smiled as though she couldn't see the blushes on our faces. Perhaps she thought it was the chill.

"Mother always told me you could see love plain in a look, though the beholder and the beholden would never see it. It's a gift, perhaps from God, to show us that true love isn't just a phantom," she said.

For most, the sentiment would make hearts warm, confirming a love that was wanted, but for me it was an alarm, the sharp clang of trip bells shouting for a blaze to be snuffed out.

"That's a wonderful thought," Worth said, his voice sounding withdrawn. He, too, had been pulled from the trance of the rain by Mrs. Smith's words.

"If you change your mind about the treat—"

"We won't," she said swiftly, cutting me off as I came to stand beside Worth. "But please tell the wonderful man, whoever he is, that we're forever grateful for the new home. It will make me . . . It will make William . . . endlessly happy."

"I'm glad." Worth extended his arm to me. "Shall we, Belle?"

# CHAPTER TWENTY-NINE

"Oh good grief. I hope they're careful. Mr. Kipp is a horrid shot," Worth said as we cleared the tree line and made our way down the hill toward camp. An echo of someone shouting "Pull!" and then the boom of a rifle disturbed the peaceful mountain sounds of birds chirping and the wind flowing through the trees.

I shielded my eyes with my hand—I hadn't bothered to attempt to affix my hat back to my ruined hair that had only barely started to dry—and squinted into the descending sun. The shooting was taking place across the valley from the tents, and despite the distance, I could see the speck of clay pigeon remain untouched in the blue sky and then fall to the ground, unshattered. When we reached the even plane, Worth drove past the campfire and tents toward the group of men.

"Do you suppose it would give me away if I joined in? Father and I used to win shooting contests all the time back home. We'd win duck and pig and even chicken sometimes. We ate well for a week after," I said. A bit of cool air made its way into the auto, and I huddled deeper into Worth's dry jacket. I hadn't said much on our drive from the Smiths', save a thank-you for their house and the warmth of his coat. He hadn't said much either.

"Not at all," he said. "In fact, some Englishmen train their daughters to shoot. It would be entirely proper."

"Is it strange that I'm disappointed? I was hoping to cause a stir," I said.

He eyed me. "We would for sure in these ensembles. The two

of us coming back from who knows where soaking wet. We should change first."

"And miss the shooting? No," I said. "I can bear the discomfort of a damp gown. As to the particulars of why we were caught in the rain? Well, everyone knows you're helping me with my story, so we were likely just off doing something for that. Not to mention, they all think we're still engaged."

"Everyone?" he asked.

"Except for Papa and Mother. Unless they've told others, they're the only ones. No one asked about the absence of my ring at breakfast, and I didn't wish to bring it up."

"How did he take it, Shipley?" Worth asked. He ran his hands along the wheel and slowed the auto as we neared the men. We hadn't discussed the particulars of what I'd tell Papa.

"He was perplexed but supportive. I told him I changed my mind, that I wanted to marry for love after all and that I didn't love you." I glanced at him. "It is obviously the opposite of what I wish, but I couldn't have him assume it was your fault. I couldn't risk his lying about the particulars of—"

"You have been my greatest ally," he said softly.

"Thorp! You're up!" Mr. Ford shouted, and my attention shifted as Peter Thorp materialized in front of the group with a rifle. At once, my throat felt tight. What was he doing here? What if he'd come back to tell Papa, to tell everyone, that Mother and I were but the family of a poor miner? I glanced at Worth and my panic settled slightly. If the worst happened, surely Worth would defend us.

Then again, I recalled Papa's fury when Worth had attempted to dissolve our engagement and knew I couldn't count on Worth's influence tempering any sort of betrayal or anger Papa might feel at the revelation. I tried to breathe, but my lungs felt like iron. Across the field, one of the servants held a bronze clay pigeon thrower at his side, waiting for the signal.

"What's Thorp doing back?" Worth asked. I swallowed hard.

"Marie Austen wrote to him at his New York residence asking for a . . . for a particular favor, but I don't think he would have had time to retrieve the correspondence and return in a matter of days," I said. He also wouldn't have had time to traverse the mountains of West Virginia to locate our town. Travel to Red Dragon from nearly anywhere required at least three rail transfers and a few days, and he'd not known the town I was from besides. This realization filled me with a great sense of relief.

Worth shut off the engine and I followed and climbed out of the auto as Mr. Thorp missed his first shot. Mr. Grove had also joined the party and stood next to Papa, who immediately recoiled at my appearance.

"Delafield, Belle, what in the world has happened to the two of you? You look as though you've been plunged into a river," Papa bellowed, well into whiskey most likely. He was holding his flask at his side. The entire group turned to look at us, and I heard a photographer's bulb pop.

"Don't be ridiculous, Mr. Wheeler," Mr. Firestone scolded when he saw the lens fixed on us. "You're here to catalog the Vagabonds' contests. Focus on the shooting, will you?"

"I needed to survey the place where the men are extracting the granite again and we walked quite a distance into the valley. We got stuck in the rain," I explained. That seemed to satisfy everyone, and they went back to watching Peter Thorp miss his next five clays.

"I'll tell them you'll go next," Worth said to me before departing into the throng of men to where Mr. Ford stood at the front.

"Belle and I saw one of those dreaded sanitoriums yesterday just down by the ball field," Papa said to Mr. Grove. "What an awful sight."

"It most certainly is," Mr. Grove replied. "That one is one of the largest, a smudge on Asheville indeed. I've tried to buy it several times in order to demolish it, but the owner refuses. I keep telling the town council that containment is necessary, that we cannot keep allowing these sanitoriums to spring up all about town, but they won't listen." He took a long draw from his own flask.

"In St. Louis there are but two and they are well situated away from the main centers of commerce as they should be. I went past them on our latest visit just yesterday." He shook his head. "In contrast, yet another sanitorium is set to break ground here in Asheville in a week's time, offering one hundred thirty new beds. I have offered the developers two times the purchase price of the property and thus far they have declined. We are racing against the clock. We will finish Grove Park Inn just in time to prevent the town from being swallowed up entirely."

I thought of all the workers I'd seen eaten away by the disease he so feared. Mrs. Smith had a point. If word got out, they would all be let go—hopefully required to seek treatment—and the building of Grove Park Inn would be halted. Perhaps for months. By then, if Mr. Grove was right, the whole of Asheville would be completely overtaken by consumption, and no one would want to risk their lives to visit the town, no matter how beautiful.

"You're up," Worth said, returning to my side. He handed me a Remington rifle, similar to Father's old one, though his had been trimmed in brass, not gold.

"Belle, you don't know the first thing about shooting," Papa protested as I handed Worth his jacket.

"Oh, but I do," I said, smiling.

I heard whispers as I moved through the crowd to the front of the party.

"Pull!" Mr. Ford bellowed, and I cocked the rifle and pulled the trigger. The clay shattered and I heard a gasp behind me. "Again!" And again, the bullet met the clay with a *crack* that rang out through the mountains. I didn't miss any of them. All five. When I was through and handed the rifle to Mr. Firestone, he whistled.

"Shipley, you have quite a daughter," he called to the back of the group where Papa had stopped talking with Mr. Grove to gape at me.

"Indeed," he said.

Worth grinned next to him.

"Shall I attempt to match you?" he asked when I reached him. I nodded and he made his way back through the men to the front.

"I believe your mother is right," Papa slurred as Worth left me. "There's something between the two of you."

I didn't answer but watched as Papa wandered off to the dining tent, no doubt to inquire of more whiskey to refill his flask.

"Miss Newbold, there you are." Mr. Thorp appeared at my side, a glower on his face as he appraised my unkempt appearance. "As you can see, I've returned and am now able to continue all of the assignments neglected in my absence. Mr. Grove says you're the one who's been collecting notes for my article on the inn."

# CHAPTER THIRTY

"No!" The word burst out in a forceful gust. If it had come from my limbs, it would have been a shove. "It is my story." I was vaguely aware of the sounds of gunshots and clay shattering and of Mr. Grove standing beside Mr. Thorp to my right.

Mr. Thorp laughed.

"Writing is my job, Miss Newbold, and it was my assignment to begin with, only I was—"

"Ushered away for indecency?" His face reddened and I was glad for it. "Whatever are you doing back here in the first place? I thought Mr. Ford and Mr. Kipp had requested you leave."

"The reason for my departure is inconsequential now. It's been resolved," he said.

"Has it really?" I asked. I could feel the tingling in my fingers, the blood draining from my face, the constriction of my lungs. My body was steeling itself for something terrible. I tried to breathe.

"Now, Miss Newbold, don't be so upset," Mr. Grove said. "You've done such a favor for us, collecting colorful information on the whole scope of our wonderful inn. I'm sure your article would have been delightful, but when we ran across Mr. Thorp in St. Louis, I asked him back." He paused. I expected to feel relief at the fact that Mr. Thorp had been in St. Louis and not in West Virginia digging up my past as I'd feared, but my dizziness only intensified, and my breathing came in short gasps.

"I didn't presume he'd be welcome here at first, but Henry

extended the olive branch when I said Thorp was about," Mr. Grove went on. "He's a wonderful talent."

Of course Mr. Grove would presume Mr. Thorp better than me. In many ways he was—he had much experience, was respected by editors of papers the nation over—but in one crucial way he was not. He had no heart. He would not tell the stories of the men I'd hoped to highlight. They would be forgotten, overlooked, just like Father. I'd wanted this piece for his legacy more than mine—to right the world a bit, to shine light on the men who toiled without acknowledgment like he had, to snatch back a bit of his dream to write that had been stamped out by the clutches of duty. But the chance was being ripped away. I felt tears sting my eyes, and anger ignited in my heart unlike anything I'd ever felt.

"You can write the article," I said. "But I'll not give you my notes. They won't be useful to you anyway."

"You've taken exceptional notes, I've heard. Mr. Mills and Mr. Pierce have raved of your depth, of the amount of time you've taken to understand every facet of the work," Mr. Grove said. "I imagine Mr. Thorp can make much of them."

"I wrote about the people too," I said. "The men who are actually building the inn, the men whose hands place the stone and pour the cement and affix the tiles and extract the granite. They are skilled craftsmen, the very top of their fields. My piece was going to highlight them. It would have been a story about the humanity behind the building." I meant to win Mr. Grove to my side, to have him see that my ideas were different from Mr. Thorp's, but I could tell neither man heard me.

Another clay shattered, mimicking the way I felt inside, and I glanced toward the sound of new rifle fire, trying to fix my attention on the particulars of the back of Worth's shirt—the wrinkles, the way the rain had left rings on the white fabric, the crisp fold of his collar. Taking stock of something I could see or smell always helped slow my breath and my panic.

"I'll include those bits too," Mr. Thorp said. "It would be a rather boring story otherwise."

"How? You don't know the men. You've never spoken to them. How would you know how to portray them accurately in your article?" I asked, inhaling the always prevailing scent of woodsmoke and the metallic overtones of exploding bullets.

"You underestimate Mr. Thorp's proficiency, Miss Newbold," Mr. Grove said, chuckling. "He could write an article about watching paint dry and make it compelling."

He didn't understand my resistance to Mr. Thorp's taking over my story. No one would—save perhaps Worth. I'd never made any sort of declaration that I wanted to make writing my profession. It hadn't even occurred to me that I wanted anything of the sort—that had been Father's dream—and women like me didn't involve themselves in any sort of commerce.

When I'd arrived in Asheville, my sole ambition had been finding a match that would win me comfort, a family of my own. But now, the thought of the story slipping from my fingertips felt like Father slipping away all over again. I tried to envision his face, the way he'd looked when he turned to tell me goodbye in the doorway the day he died. The sunrise had been beaming behind him. I could see his frame, the yellow-gold surrounding him, but his face was unclear. Two days later, his obituary was published, heralding his contribution to the community, to the mine, but he'd never seen it.

Darkness loomed on the periphery of my vision and my knees weakened. At once the faces of the men I'd interviewed flipped through my mind one after another, and my imagination conjured an image of them all in the shadow of the mines as the roof collapsed—their legacies never celebrated in their lifetimes, just as Father's wasn't.

"I . . ." A cry burst from my lips before I began to sob.

"Miss Newbold!" Mr. Grove's eyes widened, and he began to reach for my elbows, but I stumbled back.

"What's happened?" Worth's voice reached me, panicked and breathless, as my vision turned Mr. Thorp to a cloud of fuzzy gnats.

And then everything went dark.

# CHAPTER THIRTY-ONE

"**D**on't say a word. She's in a fragile state."

My eyes opened and I found myself in my tent, my body wrapped in countless layers of hide blankets up to my chin. Worth sat beside me in a rigid dining chair someone had undoubtedly selected in a hurry.

"Thank you," I said to him. My voice was gravelly. He nodded and I watched his jaw tighten.

"I never should have let you go out in the cold like that with your dress as damp as it was," he said. "Your body must have gone into a bit of shock. We've been terribly worried."

"I don't recall it being your choice." I smiled at him and edged my arm out of the hides to pull the collection down to my chest. I was roasting.

"You must be more careful," Mother said. I hadn't realized she was there, seated on my other side in a ladder-back chair that looked like it matched Worth's in its discomfort.

"I didn't faint from the cold," I whispered. I tried to envision Father's face, failed again, and lifted my palm to shield my tearing eyes.

"What in the world has happened, dearest?" Mother asked, her voice concerned. "Mr. Grove said you were speaking to them one moment and the next you collapsed." She pulled my hand to her and clutched it. Fury mingled with melancholy, and I sat up, startling everyone with my sudden movement.

"Lie down, Belle," Worth attempted, but I shook my head.

"I'm not unwell, Worth. At least not physically. They . . . They took it from me. All of those men I interviewed, they'll not be . . . they'll not be . . ." I wasn't making any sense. I knew that from the looks Mother and Worth were exchanging, but for some reason, I couldn't make my words plain.

"And I can't recall Father's face, Mother. I tried, and I . . . It's like he's dying all over again, and I . . ."

"He's not. He's not dying all over again, Belle, and you can't imagine his face because you're trying to conjure it. It doesn't work that way, I've discovered, but you'll always be able to see him, hear him especially," Worth said quickly. His hands moved toward me, then stilled on his knees. His gaze was heavy.

"I know," I whispered, my panic suddenly calmed in the presence of another soul who understood. "I know that, and yet it startled me when I tried to recall him and couldn't. For some reason when they took the story from me, the grief struck me tremendously. I suppose I'd thought if I couldn't tell of Father's many contributions to this world, at least I could herald the gifts of these other men. But now—"

"What do you mean they've taken the story from you? No one said a word of it to me," Worth said. His fingers fisted and he glanced at the tent flap.

"That's what Mr. Thorp and Mr. Grove were doing when you found me, asking me to hand my notes to Mr. Thorp so he could write the article."

"I know you've spent so much time on it, dear," Mother said, her voice intentionally leveled and calm to temper me. It was usually effective. Not so now. "But I suppose it makes sense. He has returned, and he's a professional writer."

"He'll not have the story. You've worked much too hard," Worth said bluntly. His eyes drifted beyond Mother to the other cot. I hadn't thought of Marie Austen until now, and I followed his gaze to where she sat, silently crying and holding her knees. "You had something to do with Thorp's return. That's why you appeared in the tent demanding to speak to her alone. You knew he wasn't only back to cover Mr. Ford's goings-on."

Like a dam abruptly bursting, Marie Austen choked out a yes that sounded much like a wail.

"It is all my fault, Belle. All my fault. I am a horrible, horrible cousin, a horrible friend. I had no idea he'd receive word so quickly, but I suppose his maid reads his letters. She sent him a telegram." She sniffled and I stared at her, numb. I knew she'd written to beg him back to her side, but I'd had no idea her sentiments had involved my story. I recalled the way she reacted when she found out I was writing it, the jealousy over the attention it won me, her jealousy over the attention my relationship with Worth awarded me too. She wanted me to be miserable like her.

"What did you say to him?" Worth growled, rising from his chair. "You're not a horrible friend—you aren't a friend to begin with. You are an enemy, a parasite, whose sole goal appears to be breaking the only person who has continually forgiven you . . . loved you, even."

"It doesn't matter what she said. He's here, and I—" I started to say I was done this time, finished placating poor Marie Austen, when she interrupted.

"Belle will be happy, and I will not!" she shouted. "Do you understand the torture of staring at the two of you and pretending to be content with my horrid match while the man I love is banished? I wanted him back. I *deserved* him back. I told him all was settled and that Father was pacified. I told him I'm to marry Mr. Gibbins and that he should return to camp, that Mr. Ford had hired an elderly writer with little vivacity and that because of my being tucked away, promised, he'd take him back in an instant. Perhaps you don't understand it, but this assignment was once in a lifetime for him."

She took a breath, then continued, "I didn't know he was in St. Louis with Mr. Grove and Mr. Seely at the time. I had no idea where he was. It wasn't my intention for him to take the Grove Park story. You . . . You have to believe me, Belle." She flew into a fit of sobs and Mother leaned close to my ear.

"Like mother like daughter," she whispered. "She tried to have the papers smear my name when I was first married."

I stared at Mother, at the mischievous gleam I hadn't seen in seven years. I hadn't heard the first of Mrs. Kipp attempting to have Mother discounted, but it made sense. Mother was a great deal more beautiful—smarter too—and had married Gas City's wealthiest resident.

"Why do you still tolerate her?" I whispered back as Marie Austen let out a howl.

Mother shrugged. "I don't know. I suppose because we're family, and she keeps asking me to accompany her to things."

"I cannot bear the presence of such selfishness," Worth said suddenly. "If you're able to remain by Belle's side, Mrs. Newbold, I'll go have a word with Thorp. Grove, too, if he's still here."

"I'll not leave her," Mother said.

Satisfied, Worth nodded, then glanced at me. A strange look passed across his face when our eyes met.

"I was there to catch you today. I won't be next time," he said, then departed the tent.

I watched the canvas swing shut. He was gone. In a matter of a few days, I'd see him for the last time. It was right and yet I suddenly wished I could call him back, that I could ask him to stay with me every moment until it was time. But that would only make the ache become a wound.

"What did he mean by that?" Marie Austen asked, her voice curiously steady for a person so distraught.

"We have dissolved our engagement," I said plainly, and just as she gasped, shouts disturbed us, and the sharp *pop* of a rifle made my skin flush cold.

# CHAPTER THIRTY-TWO

It had been only a few days, yet the leather portfolio boasted scratches and oil smudges. I turned it over in my hand. It was a mirror of myself, of my time here. I had been healed and broken and restored and stained. At times I felt decades older or possibly that I'd returned somehow to the girl I'd been in Red Dragon. Regardless, I would never be the same. I found that curious, that mere days could alter a person forever. Yet Asheville had changed me.

I opened the portfolio and ran my hand over my writing. I'd held the lantern over the pages and read the notes over and over through the night, the words recalling the memory of every day I'd spent in the company of these remarkable men, every day I'd spent in the company of Worth.

Marie Austen had snored as I'd extracted a clean notebook from behind the filled volume and copied the entirety of my work. By then, I'd known I'd have to turn my notes in to Mr. Thorp, that Worth's pleas had fallen on deaf ears. Despite his fury, despite his telling me to refuse to hand the notes over, I knew refusing would only make me appear cynical. It wouldn't award me the article.

By the time my lamp flickered and the light extinguished, I was on my last sentence and my mind was so exhausted that I nearly fell asleep—before I was jolted awake by the remembrance of Worth's gunshot. I'd lain awake the rest of the night going over the latter part of the evening, recalling the way we'd been spurred out of our tents, my fainting spell forgotten by the pop of the trigger—Worth's attempt to stop Mr. Gibbins from murdering Mr. Thorp.

The fallout from the altercation had lasted nearly an hour. It started during before-dinner cigar selections. Mr. Thorp was offered the box first, selected a Honduras, and then, when the box was offered to Mr. Gibbins, changed his mind and swiped the final Cuban—the same cigar Mr. Gibbins had been eyeing. Quite a metaphor for their relationship with Marie Austen.

That had likely been the catalyst to Mr. Gibbins punching Mr. Thorp and beginning the row. Worth had been having a word with Mr. Grove beside the skirmish, and when it became clear that Mr. Thorp intended to render Mr. Gibbins unconscious, he obtained the rifle always primed next to the fire—intended for protection against coyotes, bears, and the like—and fired a warning shot.

The diversion would have worked if not for Marie Austen, who'd shrieked and run toward Mr. Thorp, who had rolled off the bloodied Mr. Gibbins, who was lying, groaning, on the ground. Mr. Kipp roared a warning at her as she fell to her knees beside Mr. Thorp just as Mr. Gibbins gathered the strength to rise.

*"You choose him?"* he'd sputtered, his gaze fixed on the two of them. *"To think I've been bamboozled by the two of you, and by you too, Augustus. I—"* Marie Austen had come to her senses then and stood, immediately putting on the sniveling act of a woman whose concern for both men had her out of sorts.

*"Tell him the truth."* I'd spoken without thinking, but the sentence was a bomb. The night concluded with a forfeited dinner, Mr. Gibbins departing with Marie Austen's engagement ring, and Mr. Thorp declaring he wanted nothing to do with her. She'd cursed me and tried to run away, but Sylvia and Mr. Kipp had detained her, forcing her to ingest a tincture from the nurse designed to severely quiet a raging spirit. By the time they carried her into our tent, she'd been drooling and snoring.

"Shipley, shall we wager the location of the first gasoline store on the outcome of the round?" Mr. Ford bellowed, disturbing my focus on my notebook and the horrid recollection of the night before. All the women had been directed to sit beneath a row of white umbrellas in uncomfortable slatted wooden chairs facing the men, who were all gathered on Asheville Country Club's first tee box wearing knee breeches and newsboy caps. "We're near the same handicap. I think it would be a fair contest," Mr. Ford continued.

"I suppose it would," Papa said. He'd been on the side of the green practicing his swing for at least ten minutes.

"He is quite good at this game," Mother whispered beside me to elude the ears of Mrs. Ford two seats over.

"Here we are again," Marie Austen sighed on my other side. "Two destined spinsters. Both engaged and disengaged in the course of the same week. Of course, I've lost Rues D'Or, a fiancé, and a lover while you *chose* to lose Mr. Delafield, so I suppose it's not truly the same in the slightest."

She didn't look at me as she spoke, but kept her gaze fixed to Mr. Thorp, who was swinging beside Mr. Carver. He hadn't cast so much as a glance her way all day. He couldn't if he wished to retain his post. He stopped his swinging and extracted a small notepad and pen from his pocket, likely writing down that Mr. Ford had made a wager with Shipley Newbold so he could include it in his catalog of the day's excitement later.

"I find it peculiar that you suddenly wish to find love. You've been set against it for years." Marie Austen twirled a ringlet that had come loose of her coiffure. I'd used the same excuse with Marie Austen that I had Papa. There wasn't an alternative answer that would render Worth innocent.

"I told you, you inspired me," I said.

"And yet I'll never have love again thanks to you," she sneered under her breath. It was the first bit of anger she'd expressed today. She'd woken with an eerie sense of calm. She had been so even-tempered, in fact, that I'd wondered if she was still under the influence of the medicine administered last night.

"It wasn't my intention. I told you I was sorry," I said.

She scoffed.

"It was absolutely your intention. You did it in retaliation for my inviting Mr. Thorp back. I admit, I didn't think you had it in you." Marie Austen paused to wrap her fingers around the crystal goblet full of lemonade sitting on a wooden folding table between us. "Since I'll be deprived of true love my whole life, so will you. I'll see to it." She looked at me then, her eyes filled with the rage made plain in her words.

"You don't have that power," I said. "And I have forgiven you over and over again for your missteps. You can't forgive mine?"

She said nothing but took a long sip of her lemonade, licked her lips, and glanced behind her to where her mother sat and Grove Park Inn loomed. I hadn't allowed myself the luxury of examining the progress made in the days since I'd visited. The view of the inn now only reminded me of what could have been, and the people toiling, riddled with disease, who would choose to die working rather than acquiesce to a sanitorium's bed.

"I'll only forgive you if Mr. Thorp will admit he was lying about not caring for me and take me into his arms once again," she whispered. "Speak to him for me, please. He's alone now." She tipped her head toward Mr. Thorp, who was standing alone beneath a tree, writing in a notebook, his golf club propped against the trunk.

"Very well." I agreed only so I could depart from her company. I rose, clasping my portfolio to the soft salmon-pink taffeta against my chest.

"Whereabouts is Mr. Delafield?" Mrs. Firestone called to me as I made my way toward Mr. Thorp. The breaking of our engagement hadn't been announced. There was no reason to do so. The news of it would be clear enough after we departed camp.

"He promised Mr. Seely he'd attend to some business at his residence today," I said. "He'll join us later." When Worth told me he would be absent from golf today, I'd almost wondered if he was telling the truth or if he'd orchestrated an alternate activity to avoid me. I missed the steadiness of his presence. Perhaps I would always miss it.

"We'll make our way down to Florida day after next—agree, men? I have summer in my bones and would like to see the wildlife they say can be found in LaBelle, on the Caloosahatchee River," Mr. Ford said as I neared Mr. Thorp. "That course won't be suitable for the ladies, naturally, but if any of you would like to venture down with Edison and me, consider yourselves invited."

"Here," I said. Mr. Thorp startled at my voice and stopped writing. I opened my portfolio, extracted the copied notes, and thrust them toward him. He stared at the papers as if he hadn't any idea what they were, then seemed to realize and reached out to retrieve them.

"Thank you. They'll be vital indeed." He sighed. "I do apologize for swooping in like I did. It occurred to me later that you might have thought my sudden presence my way of enacting revenge against you for . . . for waking Mr. Kipp that night, but I assure you it was not. Marie Austen told me her scream woke him, not you." His voice lowered at the last bit. "I initially intended only to retain the Ford assignment, but when my presence was found out by—"

"It isn't your fault," I said, realizing I meant it. "It was simply coincidental. I wasn't even angry about you writing it necessarily; it's just . . . it's important to me to give credit to these men." I turned then and pointed up at the inn. Save a few echoes of distant hammering, the construction seemed quiet today. Perhaps work was confined to the inside now.

"So often the creation of something wonderful is credited to the person with the idea and the pockets to manifest it, but the completion of a marvel such as this couldn't be accomplished by Mr. Seely or Mr. Grove alone."

"Indeed." He smiled. "You're quite a champion of the average man, Miss Newbold. One might even suppose you're well acquainted with people like me."

I laughed, but my heartbeat began to quicken, reminding me that Mother and I were still very much in danger of being cast away by Papa if we were found out. In the wake of Worth's acceptance, that fear had eased, but since we'd dissolved our engagement, it had reemerged twice as strong. My palms began to sweat, and I pushed them flat against my skirt.

"You are hardly one of the average men. You are known by the great industrialists, the great inventors, the great editors of our time," I said, hoping flattery would turn the conversation away from me. "I'm speaking of the—"

"I know. The stonemasons, the plumbers, the tile workers, the masons, the maids, the butlers, the factory workers, the miners."

I blinked. It seemed as though his voice stilled on *miners*, but then again, it was the end of his sentence. Perhaps he knew of my past after all and was planning to use it against me at some opportune point in the future. I took a breath, forcing myself to believe it was but a coincidence.

"Yes," I said.

"I will be sure to give them their due in my story." He snapped his small notebook shut, put it in his pocket, and placed my notes in a compartment inside his golf club bag.

"Thank you," I said, then hesitated. "I also wanted to ask you, beg you really, to be honest with yourself about Miss Kipp. She . . . She loves you, I think, and I thought at one point you felt the same."

Mr. Thorp chuckled.

"I suppose I felt a certain way about her, though I'm unsure love is the sensation," he said. "Surely you understand—she must understand—I cannot risk the professional implication of any sort of entanglement with her. I came dangerously close to losing everything I'd worked so hard for the last time, and—"

"But she is the one who told you to return," I said. "If it wasn't for Miss Kipp, you never would have been given another chance at this assignment."

He shook his head.

"And if it wasn't for Miss Kipp, I wouldn't have been excommunicated the first time." He lifted his golf bag to his shoulder. "Do enjoy your day, Miss Newbold."

I nodded and began to walk back to where Marie Austen sat on the edge of her chair, her hands clasped so hard I could see the whites of her knuckles.

"Miss Newbold! Miss Newbold! Can I have a word?" Mr. Pierce broke from his group of Mr. Burroughs, Mr. Edison, and Mr. Kipp idling behind Mr. Ford, Papa, Mr. Thorp, and Mr. Carver, who were set to tee off first.

"Of course," I said. He was out of breath by the time he reached me, only a few steps from where he'd originated at the tee box. My mind shifted to the rattle of lungs brought about by consumption, and I forced the memory of the sound away.

"Mr. Grove came by early this morning. He was to be off on the train back to St. Louis today but wanted me to extend an offer to you. You see, he's noticed—we've all noticed—your diligence in cataloging the story of our dear inn, and you might be privy to the knowledge that Mr. Seely once owned a successful paper in Atlanta, the *Georgian*, that he recently sold to Hearst."

I nodded. "Yes. I've heard."

"Though he's no longer the owner, his opinion still holds incredible sway," Mr. Pierce said. "The paper needs a writer to craft articles about women's interests. Mr. Grove telegrammed Mr. Seely yesterday to see if perhaps you may be a fit for the role, and he returned the correspondence right away, saying the paper would be much obliged to . . . to offer the post to you." He was speaking quickly, glancing toward the group of golfers and then back to me every few seconds.

"Only you must begin in three days' time. There is a large textile factory opening there and the paper is keen to catalog the thoughts of the female workers before the competitor paper, the *Sentinel*, has a chance." He paused. "I've had occasion to speak to Mr. Newbold about it—you are a woman, after all, and certain people have certain thoughts about the fairer sex entering the working world— but he said the decision should be yours." His face reddened. "And though this might be a delicate matter, I must say straight out that I also know you're no longer promised to Mr. Delafield. The decision is truly yours alone."

I stared at him, shocked. I'd never been to Atlanta, but I'd heard it was a big city. The thought of living in such a place was both exciting and terrifying. But then I thought of the women. Working women, women in general, were rendered nameless by history much more often even than the workingman. No one was keen to tell their stories. If I took the post, I could change that—at least for some. My mind reeled. It would mean leaving Mother and Papa. It would mean setting out on my own. But wasn't that what I'd figured my life would be anyway after Worth and I fell apart?

"The Seelys are still in Atlanta for months at a time. In fact, Mrs. Seely and the children are planning to go there directly after St. Louis, and I'm certain she would have you stay with them for a bit until you're settled. She would ensure you made all the proper connections—with friends, with potential suitors," he said. "And if you prefer to keep your identity secret—I imagine the idea of their wife being a professional writer might be a stumbling block to some men—you could write under a pen name."

"I'll have to . . . think it over," I said, tripping over the words. "The pseudonym, I mean. The post, I'll take." I knew the acceptance was mostly a compulsion, but it felt right. I'd come to Asheville having not written a thing for six years, and now it seemed I'd discovered a purpose much different from the course I'd set for myself.

It was a dream planted by Father, shared by Father, and now it was being handed to me. It would be a terrible blunder not to accept the post. Through it, I could give voice, acknowledgment, to those who had none. Father's legacy would be honored in my work. Still, I couldn't imagine myself setting aside the dream of a family altogether, and though a part of me wished to write under my own name and tell any naysayers I didn't want to consider them anyway, I knew my prospects would be immediately limited. If I wrote under a pen name, I could at least get to know a man and let him get to know me before I told him of my profession.

The thought of another man made me recoil, but I knew I would need to consider others if I wanted stability, a family. It would be difficult to avoid comparing every prospect to Worth. I hoped the impulse would dissipate quickly.

"Wonderful!" Mr. Pierce exclaimed. His face seemed to relax and his body with it. "Just delightful," he said again. "I admit I wasn't sure you would accept. It's quite a big decision for a woman to shift her life to an unknown city, to venture on the path of commerce when so many find it deplorable—"

"Are you attempting to talk me out of it?" I asked, laughing.

"Of course not. You are a clear talent, and to know it and seize the opportunity is something I greatly admire," he said, glancing over as Papa struck the golf ball with fervor, sending it rocketing down the fairway. He whistled. "What a shot."

"There are some things you feel you cannot decline. If I were to say I wouldn't take the post, are there other prospects?" I asked.

"No. I imagine not," he said. "I'll find you after the round and speak to both you and Mr. Newbold about the particulars of the post, but as I said, I'm certain Mrs. Seely would be happy to have you at their home until you're settled, and Mr. Newbold said sending your things by train from Indiana wouldn't be a problem."

Papa was making his way down the fairway now, and as I watched him walk side by side with Mr. Ford, I considered his comment about caring for me as his own flesh and blood. When he'd said it, I'd been promised to Worth, the problem of my future settled, removed from his hands. In the aftermath of our crumbled engagement, my well-being had once again been Papa's concern. Returning to Gas City wouldn't remedy anything. I'd been introduced to every suitor he could fathom. If I returned with Papa and Mother, I'd never marry and eventually I'd be turned out of their home by Hartley and Eunice. Though they were settled in Chicago, Papa's estate was a showpiece, a place I knew Hartley would be keen to obtain even if it wasn't his permanent residence. Atlanta was my most promising choice for marriage, for purpose, and Papa knew it too.

I thanked Mr. Pierce and walked back toward my seat. My head spun and my legs felt weak. I stared up at Grove Park Inn, focusing on a lone man climbing out one of the attic windows to the roof. I recalled the moments in the rafters with Worth, the way watching the construction of such a wonder, the way being in the company of a man who encouraged me to marvel, had suddenly urged the pen back into my hand. I would have written the whole story for just one worker. And I would move to Atlanta and cover the new factory opening even if the story gave a name to only one.

"Well?" Marie Austen urged the moment I reached her. I glanced at her still perched on the edge of her chair, her fingers gripped, white-knuckled, to the arms. "What did he say?"

I gathered my skirts and sat.

"He's determined to stay away from you," I whispered, placing my hand on the back of hers. "I know it's not what you want to hear, but I know he feels for you. It's only that he worries for his career—"

She ripped her hand from mine and her cheeks burned.

"I'll never forgive you. Never speak to me again," she said sharply. "You will pay for what you've done."

I sighed. "I'm moving to Atlanta to take a post with the *Georgian*, Mr. Seely's old paper. I'll not be going back to Indiana with you, and I'll likely never see you again," I said.

"What?" Mother's voice struck me. I hadn't realized she was listening to our conversation, but then again, she was sitting right next to me and that was what mothers did.

"Mr. Pierce just asked me if I'd like a position as a writer, covering women's interests, and I accepted."

Mother's eyes immediately teared and she shook her head.

"You're too hasty," she murmured. "You can't move to Atlanta alone, assuming the role of a woman of commerce. What will become of you? Working is not suitable for . . . for any sort of life you should be living. You will struggle."

"Papa gave Mr. Pierce his blessing to ask me. He thought it was a good idea. I'll live with the Seelys until I'm settled, and then I'll find a place of my own. Evelyn Seely is a kind woman and I know she'll be keen to introduce me to eligible men and her own peers—"

"You'll have no support but your own pockets. You'll be . . . You'll be poor," she whispered. "I swore you'd not be that. Not again."

The reality of her comments made my skin wash cold. The naked honesty of my fate as a writer had been masked by Mr. Pierce's insistence that the Seelys would take me under their wing, but Mother was right. I couldn't take advantage of their kindness forever, and when I set out on my own, I would undoubtedly fall unless I made a match.

"I will write under a pseudonym," I said. "And I will earnestly try to find a suitable man that I'll love the very moment I arrive, but I cannot decline this post, Mother. It is too important. Without me, these women will never be truly recognized for their work, and they'll go their whole lives thinking they are worth nothing. Father dreamed of doing something like this. He also died without knowing what he meant to everyone else." Father's face suddenly materialized clear as day in my mind. I could see him after all.

"He knew how important he was to us," Mother said. She clutched my hand. "And he would swell with pride to see you now, the woman you've become, regardless of whether you accept or decline this assignment."

"Yes, but he had no idea of the impact he made on the community. He worked his whole life for us, yes, but for all the others too, and he never saw what he meant to . . . to . . ." My voice faltered.

"I know. I think about that sometimes. Your father was larger than life, more important than—" She stopped, whether because she was surrounded by people who knew nothing of him or because she realized she was actually discussing him after she'd sworn she'd not, I didn't know.

I glanced beside me, noticing Marie Austen had disappeared sometime in the minutes I'd been talking to Mother. I thought to ask Mrs. Kipp if she knew where she'd gone but found that I no longer cared. She would have to learn to live without me—the one person who had always supported her.

"Fresh tea, Miss Newbold?" A waiter in a crisp white shirt and black pants held out a tray of iced tea to me, and I nodded and took one.

"Thank you," I said after I'd taken a refreshing sip. The tea here was sweet, the sugar always providing a comforting lift of spirits.

When he'd gone on to Mrs. Kipp and Mrs. Firestone, a silence fell over Mother and me. Both of us stared out at the empty fairway, watching the sun strike the green in beams through the cloud cover.

"If I don't find a match within a year, I'll come back, Mother. I'll—"

"I'll give you my blessing so long as you do one thing for me," she said. She met my eyes. "Speak with Worth about this post." She lifted her tea to her lips and took a long drink. "You claim you dissolved your engagement because you don't love him, but I believe you do. Speak with him about your moving to Atlanta, and if in the course of your conversation you can earnestly say you don't feel for him, fine. But if you do find that you love him, perhaps he'll go with you. He's clearly not perturbed by your writing."

"I can't." It was clear that Worth was drawing away on purpose, that he'd gone to the Seelys' to avoid spending the day with me, and if I was honest, he was right to do it. The sting of his absence would heal more swiftly if we withdrew from each other now.

"Then I'll not give my approval, and I'll voice the same to Shipley," she said. "If you'd like to reconsider, I'll send a servant to summon Mr. Leslie right this moment and have him bring an auto around. He could drive us to the Seelys' so you could have a quick word with Worth."

"A conversation will not alter my feelings for Worth," I said, vaguely amused that the statement was a true one. "And aren't we supposed to wait here for the men to finish their round?"

"I will be more than happy to adjourn from this boring perch. They will be at it for at least four hours," Mother said, waving a servant over. "As far as your feelings for Worth go—humor me anyway, Belle. Consider your future when you speak to him. Be absolutely sure that you'll not regret passing him by."

# CHAPTER THIRTY-THREE

The Seelys' house was just down the road from Mr. Grove's, which was just down the road from the inn, and it looked similar—a two-story Craftsman with an enormous porch that wrapped around the entirety of the home. Clear stained glass lined the top of the polished oak front door and a comfortable-looking pair of rocking chairs beckoned on each side of it.

"Should you like us to idle in front or come back in a certain time, Miss Newbold?" Mr. Leslie asked as he turned onto the crushed limestone circular drive and stopped behind the Model T Worth had set off in this morning.

"We should give them a bit of time, Mr. Leslie. Perhaps an hour or—"

"This will be a swift discussion. You're welcome to stay and wait for me to return," I said, cutting Mother off.

As much as I craved a lengthy conversation with Worth, it was clearly not wise, nor what he wanted.

"But, Belle, there is much to say to him, and you'll not want to rush," Mother pressed. She glanced out the window, then adjusted the brim of her straw hat, adorned with a redbud sprig. I was suddenly struck by her beauty. Perhaps I simply hadn't noticed until now, but a slight pink had returned to her cheeks, and she'd gained a bit of needed weight. The mountains suited her as they suited me.

"I'll have ample time, Mother. Don't worry."

Mr. Leslie opened his door and walked to the other side to open mine. I took his gloved hand and stepped down from the auto. Most of the shades were drawn, and I hesitated in front of the door. It made sense that the windows were dark since the Seelys weren't home, but still it seemed like an intrusion to knock on the door and disturb the silence, Worth's solitude.

I raised my fist and tapped my knuckles on the door, hoping he'd not answer. No sounds came from inside—no voice, no footsteps. I turned and shrugged.

"Suppose he's not here," I said to Mother and Mr. Leslie, though the presence of his auto made it clear that he was.

"Try again," Mother called.

I sighed and did as I was told.

"See? I told you—" I startled as the door was flung open and gaped at the sight of Worth in the doorway. He was wearing his black suit and his hair was neatly combed back, as it always was, but his eyes were streaked with red veins and his face was a sort of pale I'd only seen on people like Mother when they were told their loved ones were gone.

"Belle."

"What's happened?" I breathed at the same time he said my name. He stared at me as if he didn't truly see me. "Worth." He continued in his trance, and when I stepped toward him in a motion to indicate I was planning to enter the home, he pulled the door to his shoulder and stopped me. The gesture was a cold one, an intentional blocking meant to shut me out, and it made me furious.

"I know we are to depart each other in two or three days' time, and I understand you wish to separate from me as I do from you, but I must speak to you," I snapped.

"Very well," he said under his breath, but he didn't move to let me pass.

I sighed. "You would prefer to have this conversation on the porch?"

He nodded.

"Wonderful," I said, my voice clipped. "Mr. Pierce—or rather, Mr. Seely—has offered me a writing position for his former paper, the *Georgian*, in Atlanta. A consolation, I suppose, for allowing Mr.

Thorp to take the article from me. Mother is forcing me to tell you before she'll give me her blessing, so here I am. I am taking the position and moving to Atlanta." I started to turn, but suddenly the door was forced open, its hinges squealing, and a little girl no older than three pushed past Worth and onto the porch.

"Doll?" she asked me, her blonde ringlets still bouncing from the velocity with which she'd propelled herself through the door.

"Josephine!" Worth shouted at the same time as a woman's voice behind him. In the barely opened doorway, I could see just enough of the woman to know she was beautiful. Petite with blonde hair that matched the little girl's, she cowered in the hallway, her shock at my gaze the only unfavorable smudge on her appearance.

I knelt in front of the child. It was the only thing I could do to keep from sobbing. Whoever she was, Worth clearly hadn't wanted me to know of her. It was a natural thing, inevitable, that we would both move on, but it had been less than a day. And a woman with a child no less. Perhaps knowing he had someone else would make it easier to forget him.

"I haven't seen a doll. I'm sorry," I whispered.

She shook her little head and started to whimper. I reached out and hugged her without thinking.

"Eliza, she . . . she didn't perish in the fire." Worth's voice silenced everything—the way the wind was rushing across the porch, the shrill sound of the child's cries, the desperate call of the mother— Eliza, Worth's former love, the woman who had started the fire.

I let the child go, at once recognizing the full lips and sharp slant of the nose. She was Worth's. I had no doubt at all. I rose swiftly, my body tense, my mind staggering, and reached to clutch the railing.

"Oh." It was all I could manage.

"She just found me here, only moments ago, and I haven't . . . I haven't made sense of it . . . I haven't . . . I haven't sorted any of it or figured how she found me, but—"

"Goodbye, Worth," I said, shocked at how calm my voice sounded when my insides insisted I'd be retching over the railing momentarily. I wanted to ask Worth what he was thinking, how in all creation he'd allowed the woman who'd killed his parents inside, but I knew why—his child and his heart. Regardless of the horror she'd inflicted, he must still love her. I turned and tapped the little girl on the head.

"Go see your mother," I whispered. "Perhaps she can find your doll." I heard the hurried footsteps of the child and then the door shut with a solid *thud* behind me.

I blinked and forced the ache down deep, burying it like I'd done before, like I'd watched Mother do. I balled my hands in my skirt and forced my lips into a smile.

"It's done," I said to Mother when I reached the auto. "I've told him and nothing has changed."

"Who is that child?" she asked, not hearing me.

"I don't know," I said honestly as Mr. Leslie opened my door. I climbed inside and settled next to Mother on the seat I'd so often shared with Worth. As much as I wanted to tell her everything, to punch the seats until my hands were numb, I could not. Even now, I couldn't betray his trust. "Perhaps a friend of the Seelys."

# CHAPTER THIRTY-FOUR

Worth hadn't returned to camp. Not that I'd expected him to after Eliza's materializing with his child, but his absence had been acutely noticed. Papa and Mother and I had spoken openly about my moving to Atlanta over dinner, and the disapproving silence had been deafening. Everyone had seemed to rally behind my writing about the inn for Mr. Seely, but when they were presented with my continued scribbling—for income, no less—the prospect seemed outrageous.

"*Are you certain it's wise?*" Mr. Kipp had whispered to Papa from his seat next to him. The braised Bradenham ham with champagne sauce had just been served and Papa had set his knife on the china with a clatter.

"*Yes,*" he'd said in a sharp tone. "*If you're insinuating that it would be a wiser decision to force her back to Gas City to endure the possibility of men who have already considered and denied her—for some ridiculous reason or another—you are quite more dull than I thought you to be. She is going to be presented to a new set of suitors in Atlanta while doing something she enjoys. Perhaps you should consider expanding your horizons for Marie Austen.*"

Mr. Kipp had turned red and would have argued if doing so wouldn't have cast him in an unmannerly light. Worth would have said something firm but diplomatic to smooth over the conversation, but without him, the dinner went on in awkward silence at our end from the spring lamb with mint sauce to green peas to plum pudding.

Marie Austen had kept her promise never to speak to me again and remained focused on her plate across the table through the dinner, only looking up periodically to ensure that Mr. Thorp still occupied the seat between Mr. Carver and Mr. Ford at the other end.

"This must be it, Mr. Leslie," I said, forcing my mind away from the night before and motioning toward the only white house on Hickory Tree Road. It really was a pretty little house. Mature apple trees dotted the flat acre of lush green grass, and though the paint held a bit of mold from the spring moisture, it still looked rather clean—especially compared to the rotting wood and crumbling brick of the homes around it.

"I'd like to get out and say goodbye. This man was quite essential in helping my research along, and I'd like to tell him that—even if my story is never to be."

"Yes, very well. I'll wait," he said, cutting the engine off in front of the house. He got out of the car and I yawned. I'd risen early, dressed myself in a simple ceil-blue shirtwaist and skirt, and found Mr. Leslie taking coffee by the fire. I asked if he was available to take me somewhere. When he said yes, I told him I wanted to thank one of the Grove Park workers. Though Mr. Leslie was privy to much, he didn't know of my past and I intended to keep it that way.

"Thank you," I said as he opened my door. I stepped out onto the pillowy grass. It occurred to me then, standing in front of this house by myself, that my life would be like this most of the time from now on. I'd be alone. In two days, Papa and Mother would board the train to Indiana, and I'd get on a different track bound to Atlanta. Papa had made arrangements via telegram last night. Mrs. Seely's driver would meet me at the station. From there, I would be escorted directly to the new textile factory to interview the women alone. The prospect was both nerve-racking and thrilling.

The sun was bright today, and the beams fell on my face as I walked toward the porch, warming the chill that had seemed to settle just beneath my consciousness since seeing Worth yesterday.

A squirrel chattered in a nearby tree and swallows flew overhead. From somewhere in the distance, the smell of woodsmoke and frying bacon joined with the scent of new grass and spring blooms on the breeze.

The Smiths didn't appear to be heating their home with a fire this morning. Back in Red Dragon, Mrs. Smith had always been the first to stoke her fire in the wee hours of the morning, and Mother often took me over to their house when Father went off to work so we could warm while our own house expelled the chill.

I knocked on the door and the sound seemed to echo inside the small home.

"Mrs. Smith?" I called. "Willie?"

I knocked again, and when there was no answer, I stepped down from the porch and looked into the windows flanking the entryway. The house was vacant. There were no chairs, no beds, no tables. I turned around, confused. Perhaps they hadn't had time to move yet. Perhaps Mr. Smith was too ill.

"I suppose I've gone to the wrong place, Mr. Leslie. I apologize. Would you have time to take me to another house? I know the men are to set out to canoe the Swannanoa this morning, but—"

"Yes, of course," he said. "I've been assigned to the women today anyway." He smiled.

"Who're you looking for, ma'am?"

A ragged man emerged from a tumbledown clapboard home next door. He shoved a piece of bacon in his mouth and then thrust his hands in the pockets of his worn overalls.

"Oh. Just some friends who were set to move in here. I suppose they haven't yet," I called.

"Well, a family started to move in there yesterday," he said, pausing to chew. "But late yesterday evening, one of those hospital vans showed up and loaded three of them inside. The man was hollering that he didn't want to go. I felt mighty bad for them."

My heart dropped into my stomach, and the familiar prickle of panic flooded my brain.

"Was one of them a young man with white hair?"

"Yes, and the other two were a couple, about my age I suppose," he said.

I reached out to steady myself on the auto door Mr. Leslie had just opened for me. I recalled how adamantly Mrs. Smith had refused treatment. It seemed unlikely that she would have accepted it regardless of how sick she felt, but perhaps Mr. Smith's illness had taken a severe turn and she'd reconsidered. I thought of our conversation in their doorway the day their consumption was confirmed, the day Worth gifted them this house.

At once my body flushed cold. I had promised Mrs. Smith to keep the news of their illness quiet, but Worth had not. He'd deflected the vow by asking for the third time if she was sure they couldn't be convinced to convalesce at a sanitorium. Worth had gone to Mr. Seely's yesterday citing business needs. The timing matched and the Smiths had already mentioned that the sort of illness the workers were battling was known among themselves, that they'd all sworn to keep it quiet. They'd gone undetected for months. It was unlikely that their illness had been found out otherwise. Worth's involvement was the most likely explanation. If I was right, he'd betrayed my trust. He'd betrayed the Smiths.

"Thank you," I managed.

"Are you all right, Miss Newbold? Do let me help you sit. Your face is quite pale," Mr. Leslie said.

I obliged, forcing my limbs onto the seat.

"Will you take me to the inn?" I asked. I must have looked quite panicked, because Mr. Leslie nodded and practically ran around the front of the auto to the wheel.

"Is it an emergency?" he asked as the engine roared to life.

"Yes," I said. I prayed Mr. Mills or Mr. Pierce was there, that they would know the particulars of where the Smiths had gone. Had they been the only family detained, or had the breadth of tuberculosis among the workers been made plain? My stomach swam with nausea as Mr. Leslie accelerated, barely braking around the mountain curves. I closed my eyes and tipped my head back in an attempt to keep myself from vomiting.

"Just a few moments more, Miss Newbold," Mr. Leslie said.

My palms were sweating, but I was freezing. I balled my hands in my skirt and my teeth began to chatter. The dream I'd had in which I'd been trapped in a sanitorium edged to the forefront of my mind, only now I knew it was a reality for people I loved. As much as I'd hoped they would seek treatment, their lives weren't my own, and the reality that they'd live out the few remaining days they had within the clinical walls of a sanitorium, instead of at home like they'd wished, was devastating. Even if they did make it out, Mrs. Smith was right. They wouldn't have any income saved to live on or a post to return to. Thanks to Worth, they'd have a roof, but food required income.

The auto came to a sudden halt, jerking my head forward. My door was swiftly opened, and Mr. Leslie's hand was extended for mine. I took it and stepped out of the auto, thankful my knees didn't buckle.

"Would you mind escorting me to Mr. Mills's office? I'm quite unsteady," I said.

Mr. Leslie held my arm, and we walked together past the entrance, around the curved edge of the hotel, and into the door at the side. The pounding of hammers and scraping of saws echoed from the Great Hall, down the smaller corridor, and the heels of my boots clicked on the newly polished stone floor. I was right yesterday, I thought vaguely as we made our way to the closed door of Mr. Mills's office; all of the construction was now confined inside.

"Mr. Mills," I called, tapping on his door.

I heard a muffled greeting and entered the room. He was sitting at his desk, a telephone receiver grasped in his palm. He looked gray, like he'd aged a decade in a matter of days since I'd seen him last. His hair was disheveled, his mustache too, and he was hunched over a stack of papers.

"Miss Newbold," he said softly. "To what do I owe the pleasure?"

Mr. Mills ran a hand across his face in an attempt to revive his clear exhaustion and stood to hang the receiver back in its place next to the telephone on the wall.

I opened my mouth to speak and realized I didn't know what to say. Suppose it was only the Smiths who had been taken away? I couldn't expose all of the workers if they hadn't been found out already.

"I'm looking for Willie Smith, the foreman over the stone harvesting," I said. "I went by to see him at their new home—I wanted to thank him for his time before I departed—and a gentleman said they'd been taken away to—"

"A sanitorium," he said. "Yes. It seems that near a quarter of our workers are stricken with tuberculosis. It is the worst sort of nightmare. Mr. Pierce is attempting to place people, but there are not enough beds around here, and there are not enough workers to fill the places of the ill, and furthermore, I'm not permitted to speak a word of it to Mr. Seely or Mr. Grove. They will think it my fault when the construction is delayed, and I won't be allowed to speak the truth of why."

"I'm sorry," I whispered. My eyes teared. "How was the illness found out? Do you know which sanitorium Mr. Smith was taken to?"

"No. I've spent the last day calling and sending telegrams to all the facilities within the state. I've been up all night. There were only eighteen beds available here in town, and we're in need of near seventy." Mr. Mills looked at me. "I should have seen it earlier. I suppose I did, but my mind didn't allow me to truly register what I was looking at. I fear for these men and their families. It's my fault they're in such a bad way."

"No, it's not. They didn't want to be found out. They hid and discounted their illness. They feared what it would mean for their families if they were let go."

"Was it that obvious to you?" Mr. Mills shook his head. "How did I miss it? Why didn't you alert me to it immediately?"

"I didn't detect it. I believed it was a virus, like you did. But I grew up in a mining town before Mother married Papa, and those men would pull themselves out of their deathbed to work. It was hard enough . . . for them when they were employed, but the sort of poverty that befell a family out of work was horrific."

"I know and I understand it," he said. I recalled what he'd said of his life, his adoption, the illness of his mother that had left them destitute. "Even so, without treatment they'll never work again and many will leave their wives widowed." He glanced down at the papers in front of him. "These seventy or so have been walking around the streets of Asheville. They have not been containing consumption, and the exposure of the healthy population is obvious. I am going to be hard-pressed to find workers who are well." Mr. Mills sighed.

"It seems a bit hopeless now, this striving toward the completion of the inn, the transformation of this town into something brighter than a colony for the sick. I can't understand how I didn't see it. If only I could have caught it before I—"

"Who did? Catch it, I mean," I asked. My heart drummed, the beat skipping in my temples. I needed to know if it was Worth, if my intuition to trust him, the feeling that I'd truly known him, was wrong. I knew Mr. Mills spoke the truth—that without treatment many would leave families destitute by death, but many would also pull through. Either way, the choice to receive treatment should be made by the individual, not their employer.

"Pierce, I suppose. He came bursting into my office yesterday morning in a frenzy, saying someone had pointed out that the circulating virus echoed the signs of tuberculosis."

He'd known before the golf outing yesterday. No wonder he'd seemed so out of sorts. Worth had departed camp early yesterday morning too. The need to know if he was involved was insatiable.

"Did Mr. Pierce say anything about Mr. Delafield speaking to him? I only ask because he seemed concerned about the virus when he accompanied me," I said.

"No. Whoever it was, they were adamant that Willie Smith and his family seek treatment, though, so perhaps it was someone who worked alongside him. It was said that his illness, or perhaps that of someone in his family, was quite advanced."

"I'm sorry," I said, attempting to sound as empathetic as I truly was while my fury burned unchecked. Sometime in the hours between our last visit to the Smiths and yesterday morning, Worth had decided he couldn't stay silent, that he needed to tell someone of the calamity befalling the inn workers—and he'd chosen not to tell me.

# CHAPTER THIRTY-FIVE

The men were readying for their canoeing outing when we returned to camp. Despite a constant urge to strike something, I had to laugh at their ensembles. They all wore fine suits and polished leather boots. Clearly none of them—even Mr. Ford and Mr. Burroughs—had any experience navigating a river while teetering down rapids in a canoe. They would most certainly topple out at least once.

"I don't see Mr. Delafield among these either," Mr. Leslie said. We'd driven past the Seelys', hoping to find Worth so I could confirm if he'd alerted Mr. Pierce about the illnesses, but the drive was empty and the windows were covered. He was gone, reunited with Eliza somewhere.

I could still see the weathered agony on his face in the doorway, the way he'd panicked when his little girl pushed past him to materialize in front of me. I knew his feelings for Eliza had to be complicated, but I also knew he'd not deny a child. A family was what he'd wanted after all, and now he had one. The betrayal I felt deepened and blistered at the thought. He hadn't known of his child—that much was plain in his eyes—and we'd planned to separate anyway, but none of it mattered to my heart. He'd betrayed me and forgotten me in the matter of a day.

"No. I suppose he's been called away," I said.

Mr. Leslie pulled the auto to the side of the line readying to leave camp and shut off the engine.

"Is there anywhere else you'd like to go before I depart? I'm afraid the moment I emerge from the seat, I'll be asked to make tea or gather water for a bath—something that will occupy me," Mr. Leslie said.

"No, though I wish you could obtain a break. You've driven me around for hours."

"It's my pleasure," he said. "I hardly consider it work." He grinned and got out of the auto, walking around to my door.

"Belle!" Marie Austen's shrill voice cut through the hum of the men's tones as they settled in the autos.

I stepped out and walked around the bumper to find her sitting by herself in front of the fire, her hands clutching a glass filled to the brim with an amber liquid and a telegram.

"There you are," she slurred. Her mouth turned up in a smile that made my blood run cold.

"What's happened?" I asked, rushing toward her.

"Oh, nothing," she said, tossing the telegram in the fire. She laughed as it burned and then looked at me. "I'm no psychic, but I'd say there's about to be a terrible row in your parents' tent. I suspected you were not quite who you claimed—I have for some time. I overlooked it, but the other day, I decided to confirm my suspicions. I asked Mr. Newbold where exactly he'd met your mother, and he was obliged to tell me it was a town called Red Dragon.

"Funny, it took only a telegram to the Red Dragon Mining Company to verify the truth. Soon enough you'll be back in your hovel where you always should have stayed. I'd hasten over there if I were you . . . Belle Coleman."

The whole world stopped.

I couldn't feel the breeze that moments ago had been tousling my hair. I couldn't hear the chug of the auto engines or smell the stifling smoke from the fire.

My name echoed in Marie Austen's voice as I stared at her, and then her words sank in, and I ran. The few yards felt like miles as I skirted the first two rows of tents and made my way down the third.

I could hear Mother sobbing before I reached their tent.

"Shipley . . . I . . . Shipley . . . I . . . Shipley . . ." She kept starting and stopping, starting and stopping. I threw back the canvas and found her huddled on her cot, her knees gathered to her chin, her face streaked with tears. Papa knelt on the ground beside her, his hands searching for hers, but she kept pulling them away. "No. Belle." Her eyes found mine and she shook her head and closed her eyes.

"Mother, what's happened?" I asked, though of course I already knew. Our poverty, our hardship, our grief, the way we'd covered it up, was now exposed.

"Darling, what is it? Surely you can tell us," Papa pleaded, his fingers finally stilling their search for Mother's.

"I . . . I haven't been honest with you, Shipley," she said. The final notes of his name were uttered in a squeaking sob. "If I don't tell you, Marie Austen has threatened to tell Mr. Ford of my . . . of our past and embellish it so he'll not deal with you. Your gasoline stores will cease to exist, and the wells will dry up, and—"

"Grace, is there someone else?" Papa's voice was soft, barely a whisper, and his gaze didn't fall from her face.

"No!" she nearly shouted. "Of course not. It's only . . . Shipley, I have betrayed your trust." Mother sniffed.

I stood frozen, unable to speak, to help her in her unveiling of who we were. She took a deep breath and sat up straight.

"When we met, I was modeling dresses for the Red Dragon company store. I wasn't wearing it about town as you assumed, and I wasn't widowed by the mine operator. My husband, James Coleman, was a miner, the regular sort. Not a manager or an operator. When you stopped by the side of the road that day, I hadn't eaten in two days."

Papa said nothing. He didn't move or shift his focus.

"When you began to tell people that my former husband operated a mine, I simply went along with the story." I watched her body stiffen and her jaw clench. "I should have told you your story was wrong, but the moment Belle and I got off the train in Indiana, I couldn't bear the thought that you'd leave me or that I'd have to go back to misery when I thought . . . when I thought I'd found happiness again."

Papa remained absolutely still.

"I watched a woman get turned out by her husband because she'd lied to him, because she said she was from a wealthy family and was not," Mother went on. "She died alone in the woods from starvation and the elements. Perhaps she deserved it." Mother began to cry again. "I can bear being punished, being banished, for the lie I've told you now for years, but I cannot bear the thought that I would be the reason Mr. Ford abandons your gasoline stores. You've worked so hard, Shipley, and I'll—"

"Damn the gasoline stores. Damn the wells. Damn the money, Grace." Papa stood suddenly and Mother jerked back on the cot. "Don't you know I'd throw it all away for you?" He began to cry and dropped back down to his knees next to Mother.

This time when he reached for her hands, she allowed it. "I never asked of your husband because the depth of his pockets didn't matter. He was tremendously wealthy." He heaved a breath. "I am a greedy man. You may have considered yourself poor, but I saw in your eyes wealth that I never had. It was an exact mirror of my father's eyes when he lost my mother. Until the moment I saw you, my life had been formed by careful decisions made with great consideration. My marriage had been amiable but gray, and though this may sound terribly strange, I wanted a love so consuming that if lost, it would turn my eyes hollow like yours when I first saw you, like my father's. I knew you had the capacity for deep love because you'd had it before, and the moment I saw you, I wanted to be the one to set sparks in your eyes again." He paused and his thumb ran across Mother's hand.

"What is life if not filled with love to set your soul alight? I don't pretend to think it is the same for you, but you have revived my life, Grace. You have set my heart ablaze with love, and I pray every moment that I perish before you, but if I do not, I will treasure the grief because it will mean that I obtained a wealth far more important than riches, and I will be thankful."

Papa drew Mother toward him and kissed her. I was taken aback by the calm I felt, by the mercy extended to Mother, to us.

"I loved James. I always will," I heard her whisper. "And even though James told me he didn't want me alone if something happened to him, I never wanted to love again. I fought against it until I couldn't any longer, until my heart became yours. Even so, I have lived most of our marriage overwhelmed by fear that it would happen again, that I would lose you and feel that terrible sensation of my very soul being ripped from my body and the void that follows. I have let the terror hold my heart captive, let it reign with a rigid grip that refuses to let go. These past days, I have felt it easing, and though I will always be scared, I will try—" She threw herself into his arms. "I love you. That's all I truly wanted to say. I never thought it possible twice, but I have been blessed indeed." Papa kissed Mother's forehead.

Her heart's words were my own, though mine were still shackled to a millstone, safe onshore, but sure of a swift drowning if tossed into the swell and crash of love. Mother was braver than I'd ever thought her. Perhaps love didn't permanently break us after all.

"I meant what I said, Belle," Papa said, and I turned to him. "I consider you my daughter, and I love you as such. This revelation, a knowledge I suppose I already assumed, does nothing to alter that."

"I love you, Papa," I said.

"It is up to you if you'd like your past known or kept between us," Papa went on. "I'm not bothered by it in the slightest and will stand up against anyone who dares question us. But I know—"

"I'll speak of it more now, between us, but I'd like to keep it safe here. Out there, there will be questions I don't wish to answer and a divide where once there was none," Mother said.

"Very well, my dear," Papa said. He squeezed Mother's hand.

I felt comforted looking at them, and a warmth settled over me like a fur coat. Father's face appeared in my memory, as clear as if he were standing in front of me once again. This time, he was smiling.

"Father is smiling on you both," I said abruptly.

"I know," Mother said. "I can feel his love. That, and you have his smile." She turned to Papa. "I hope you don't mind."

"Not at all. As I said, his love has made me the wealthiest man in the world." Papa leaned in to kiss Mother again, longer this time, but she withdrew quickly as the kiss deepened.

"I'm going to go for a walk," I said. "Perhaps even tell Marie Austen that my papa loves us and we'll be staying right here."

"No," Papa said. "Allow me to have a word later—with Augustus. Her behavior is reprehensible. Especially given she is family." He began to stand, but Mother grasped his arm.

"Later," she whispered.

"I'll see you at dinner," I said. "I have never been more thankful to be both a Coleman and a Newbold."

"Indeed," Mother said, her attention fully fixed on the man whose heart held hers.

# CHAPTER THIRTY-SIX

I was lost. I'd wandered into the woods intending to clear my mind, intending to let the relief of Papa's acceptance and the confusion of Mother's confession and the pain of Worth's betrayal and likely hand in the Smiths' banishment to a sanitorium manifest in whatever way they willed.

I'd been vacillating between anger and peace when I walked away from the creek I'd been following for at least an hour. I'd spied a pink lady's slipper flower poking through the old leaves. The blooms were rare, and I needed beauty at that moment. I was thinking about Mother's admission of her love for Papa.

Though Mother's words about her heart should have set mine free, they did not. In fact, I felt as though I'd been deceived. I'd lived years believing I should avoid love altogether, that love was a poison that would burn my soul to vapor. I'd assumed Mother felt the same. Would my life have been different if I'd allowed love? Would I be happy? Settled? Instead, I'd closed off my heart along with the possibility of what accompanied love.

Moments before Mother's words shattered my perception, I'd accepted the likely outcome that I'd be alone, my course that of a professional writer, an unmarried working woman. I knew I'd find fulfillment in writing the stories of these women, yet my mind couldn't help fixating on Worth's face despite my anger, on the way his mouth had felt on mine, on the way, if I was honest, I yearned for him. But it wasn't only the commitment I'd made to myself that stood in our way. It was his too. He didn't want love either. Perhaps

Eliza's return had changed his mind, since her presumed death was one of the reasons he'd avoided love.

The sun was golden now, washing the new leaves and the little swallows and the wild redbuds in its shimmering light. If not for my being completely turned around and the slight panic that accompanied that fact, I'd sit down on a rock and watch the day celebrate its conclusion by turning the forest orange and red and deep purple.

I'd been climbing up. That was the only direction I could accurately tell. The moss signaling north and the branches stretching south wouldn't do much for me, since I hadn't taken note of which way I'd come.

"Hello!" My yell echoed over the mountain, doing nothing but startling a doe and her fawn a few yards away. I shivered and crossed my arms. The night would be cold. I looked around for a cave, but I hadn't passed any. There were a few small rock formations, but nothing large enough to provide me any sort of shelter.

And no one would come for me. They wouldn't know where to look. The camp had been quiet as I'd crossed the valley and entered the woods. This section of woods was farthest from camp, a wilderness that held no horrid memories of fires or of Marie Austen's betrayal, a wilderness that was free to endure whatever feelings and thoughts I needed to work out beneath its branches.

I started to panic. I thought of Boss Elkhorn's first wife. What if I perished in the woods regardless of Papa's acceptance of us?

I breathed deep and tried to encourage calm. I'd find my way out. I had to.

As I continued walking, my fingertips brushed the soft leaves of an ostrich fern just unfurled. Beside it were a dozen or so fiddleheads, their thin, papery brown scales still intact. I leaned down and plucked as many as I could from the ground. Father had sometimes picked them when we were wandering the woods in Red Dragon. They tasted like asparagus or broccoli, and I knew they'd sustain me. I pushed the stems into the neckline of my bodice, against my collarbone, and kept walking.

Rocks appeared up ahead in the distance. Their jagged profile nearly made me cry with relief. Surely there was a cave at their front; there had to be. If I could find a shelter, I could eat the fiddleheads and rest for the night, then find my way home in the morning when my vigor was restored.

The wind shifted, pulling my hair from its coils and pins, fluffing the strands around my face. A rattling, like the shaking of nails in a tin can, sounded above me somewhere, then stopped. I kept moving. I was hearing things. The forest could do that, make you believe you heard an auto engine in the middle of the woods, miles away from the nearest road. It was a survival mechanism designed to instill hope. Otherwise, it was much too easy to believe the message of despair—that there was no way out, that you would perish.

I wandered higher, toward the rocks. The sky looked brighter there, and my heart began to skip with the hope that I'd find a cave or even an auto.

I extracted one of the fiddleheads and crunched the curled shoot, enlivened by the burst of water and flavor. I reached for the trunk of a small birch and pulled myself up the sharp incline and then reached for another. By the time I crested the hill, I was out of breath and sweating. The rock face loomed in front of me, and I skirted around to the front of it.

My eyes welled as I stared at the solid tower of rock. There was no cave. There was no overhang to burrow under, away from animals and cold.

If I perished, would my parents know I truly loved them? Would Worth know I'd cared for him? I'd find the next large tree and settle beneath it. I'd try to sleep while it was still light so that when night came with the sounds of coyotes and owls, I'd be able to guard myself as best I could.

I ran my palms over the cold, jagged rock and walked beyond, through a grove of pines along the top of the ridge, breathing in the sharp scent of evergreen. The moment I cleared the grove, I gasped, my heart nearly exploding with relief and joy. A worn dirt drive overgrown with weeds stretched through the woods below me. It must have been an auto I'd heard, and the road had to lead somewhere.

I made my way down the hill and followed the road as it twisted to the right. If I could find a person with an auto, I'd beg them to take me back to camp. Perhaps I'd return by dinner as I'd promised Mother and Papa.

The drive took a sharp curve to the left. I followed and then, at once, any sort of relief, any sort of joy, was completely stolen by the scene in front of me. Charred skeletons of wasted trees stood like cemetery spires around a blackened depression of ash and fallen leaves. My tongue curled in the back of my throat, suppressing a scream, and my soul urged me to run, but I could not.

Instead, my knees buckled and I fell to the ground. I began to sob, my eyes blurry as they focused on the singed cornerstone in front of my hands, the gray licked with black.

"My God," I whispered. "My God," I said again, realizing that prayer was the only way to encounter such a place. "Give them rest," I choked out, my voice barely audible. "Give him peace. Let him know this is not . . . this is not where they reside. Let him know this is not his fault, that he will never know a moment when he is not loved."

"What are you doing here?"

His voice was low, but it startled me, and I lifted my head to find him across the expansive footprint of the home's foundation. He was leaning against the side of one of Mr. Ford's autos, it and his body cloaked in the shadow of several charred tree trunks and the growth of new leaves overhead.

"I . . . I didn't mean to," I stumbled over the words, rising slowly. My presence felt wrong, as if I'd intruded on something holy. In many ways I had.

"I took a walk in the woods and got lost. I thought I'd take shelter in a cave just over there." I pointed in the direction I'd come from. "But then I saw the road and thought I heard the sound of an engine." I couldn't look away from Worth. Even in the shadows, I could see that his frame was hunched and his face haggard. His shirt was untucked beneath his suit jacket and his hair was disheveled.

"I thought I would find someone to help me. I . . . I'm sorry," I said.

When he didn't reply I forced my gaze away from him. I forced my body to turn and walk past the scorched trunks, back the way I'd come, though my knees were weak and threatened to buckle again with each step. Tears streamed down my face and I let them. My heart was pulverized, shattered beyond repair not only because of the horror I'd seen, horror he'd endured, but because he was alone, because he was without me.

"Please don't go!" The sentence was shouted, a sob punctuating the last word.

I turned and ran to him, my soul feeling the heaviness of every footstep over the ground his family had once called home. Our bodies met with such tremendous force that it stole my breath. My arms strained to hold him closer, and his fingers pressed into my back, as though if we absorbed into each other, perhaps together we could bear the pain.

"Worth." I whispered his name and his body heaved.

"Four years ago today, they moved here," he said. "It feels like a hundred years or a day." His head was bowed to the top of mine, and I could feel his breath in my hair. "Eliza too."

I pulled back slightly at the mention of her and met his swollen eyes.

"Eight months later they were gone. I thought all of them were gone." He sniffed and looked over my shoulder at the sunken ground. "But when she said she was going to try to help my parents from the parlor, she was lying. She ran instead. She fled and let me believe the fire took her too." His voice was still low, but it harbored an edge, a growl that sliced through my spirit.

"All this time, I told myself that perhaps it hadn't happened the way I remembered, that perhaps my mind was playing tricks on me, that I could have been the one to throw the lantern, that I could have killed them all."

"No," I said. "You would never—"

"Do you know she's been following me for weeks?" His jaw

bulged and I could feel his hands fist behind my back. "She followed us everywhere. To the inn, to camp, to the Smiths', trying to . . . trying to find the right time to apologize, she said. But even in her waiting, she wrought destruction." He paused.

"She is a nurse. She works at a tuberculosis sanitorium in Virginia, Belle. She saw the Smiths, and she saw the other workers at the inn, and she told Mr. Pierce. She had them all taken away despite their wishes to the contrary." His eyes teared again and so did mine.

"I know," I whispered. I was ashamed when relief washed through me. I hadn't trusted him when he'd always proven himself to be a man worthy of my confidence. "I went by to see them settled and was met with an empty house."

"We will find them," he said. "I'm sorry. I . . . I told Pierce this morning, after he made me swear not to tell Grove and Seely of the outbreak among the workers, that I intend to pay the salaries of all the men let go while they convalesce. It is the least I can do. It is my fault—"

"No, it isn't." I touched his face, smoothing the tears away with my thumb, and he closed his eyes. "It isn't your fault just as this fire was not your fault."

"She told me she still has nightmares of it, that she carries the burden of guilt with her every day, and that these last weeks she knew she needed to confess, that she couldn't keep her mind from fixating on what she'd done. She said she can still feel the fury of the anger she felt toward me that night, and see the lantern strike the wood." An owl called somewhere nearby. "I forgave her. Mother would have wanted me to."

"Where is she now?" I asked. He was here alone, holding me. The image of her standing there in the hallway behind him haunted me; the memory of his child standing in front of me made me step back.

"She's turned herself in. She'll serve much time in prison, I'm certain, once a judgment is made." Confusion played on his face at my separating from him.

"Justice will finally be served as it should have been years ago. But what of your child?"

He shook his head and took a haggard breath.

"She'll reside with her father. She's not mine. She couldn't have been mine. Eliza was pregnant by another man—a decent, kind man, in fact, but a man without much to his name. Eliza had always desired riches. That was why she was so adamant that we marry quickly and move. She thought she could trick me into believing the child was mine if the marriage was consummated swiftly."

My lips turned up, my spirit lightening at the revelation, but his countenance didn't brighten.

"She killed my parents, and she never loved me," he said. "And when I came face-to-face with her, I realized in the wake of you, I never loved her either."

I didn't know what to say, so I remained silent. The same owl I'd heard earlier swooped over us, following the setting sun behind me. I turned to watch it.

"Please don't go," he said again and grasped my hand to pull me back to him. "Don't go to Atlanta. I know you've sworn not to love me, and I've sworn not to love you, but I have made myself a liar."

I leaned into him. I could hear the echo of Papa's words, of Mother's too. I could risk my heart. I had to. Only then would I truly be set free. Only then would I truly be alive. Love hadn't ruined Mother and me. Love hadn't ruined Worth. We'd made it the scapegoat, but in truth, love was the reason we'd all kept on.

"I have to go to Atlanta, Worth." Emotion balled in my throat as I beheld him. He was a treasure, my treasure, and yet I couldn't abandon the women whose stories I was destined to tell.

"Very well." His touch disappeared and the chill of impending night suddenly made me quake.

"I love you too," I said quickly, realizing he'd taken my words to mean I didn't love him. I shivered, desperately empty and cold without him. "I love you, and I'll keep falling in love with you. I swear it."

Worth stepped toward me and gathered me in his arms once more, then his lips whispered against mine as if in question.

"Worth," I said, my mouth inches from his.

"Do you mean it?"

"I love you," I said.

He wound his hands into my hair and kissed me. His lips parted mine with a desperate hunger that matched my own, and when my tongue sought his, when my hands went inside his jacket and my fingers clutched his back, pulling him closer, I felt him tremble. His hands dropped to my hips, and his lips fell to my neck, but I grasped his chin and led his mouth back to mine, sure that his lips, his tongue, the feel of his body against me were now as vital as the air I breathed.

"I'll go with you," he said suddenly. He brushed my hair back from my forehead and kissed it. "If you want to go to Atlanta, I'll go too. I just don't want to be without you." He let me go and put his hand in the pocket of his jacket.

"Then we'll go together," I said. "I don't want to be without you either. You brought me back to life." It sounded dramatic, but I was sincere. The way he loved me, the way he cared for me, had sewn up the hope that grief had shredded.

"You did the same for me," he whispered. He held the sapphire ring between us. "I couldn't part with it. I haven't even been able to put it in a drawer. I've been carrying it in my pocket as if I was carrying you with me." He paused. "My soul was crushed the night we decided to end our engagement. At the time I thought it meant we'd made the right choice, the noble choice, that we were saving each other, but now I realize—"

"I would have loved you always and missed you as much," I said.

Worth took my hand and dropped to his knee.

"Belle, will you marry me? Truly this time."

"Yes. At once," I said. As Worth slipped my ring back on my finger,

I felt the chains around my heart, the fear that had become a part of me, dissolve.

He stood and I kissed him again, this time softly, our lips doing a slow dance as though we had all the time in the world.

"I came here to tell them I loved them," he said when our mouths parted. He looked over my shoulder at the ruins cast nearly entirely in the hazy gray of dusk. "I'd avoided it for so long, but when Eliza confirmed the truth I knew, that it wasn't my fault, I thought I could face it again. I couldn't." Worth's fingers brushed my lips, then swept across my cheek.

"Before you materialized like an angel sent from God himself, I wasn't sure I could move. I wasn't sure I could continue to breathe with the scene before me. But then, there you were, and at once I wasn't alone."

"I thought I was lost," I said. Goose bumps rose on my arms.

"No," Worth said. "You were sent to find me."

Over his shoulder, a redbud bloomed in brilliant sprays behind the charred trunks. I let him go and walked toward it. I bent a branch and broke a length from it, then carried it back to the place right beyond him where the ground began to dip. I knelt on the carpet of old leaves, letting my eyes wander over the expanse of where the home had once been, where the people he loved had once lived.

"Thank you," I said simply to the audience of trees and Worth behind me. "Thank you for loving him. We will always remember you."

Worth knelt beside me and took my hand as I placed the redbud blossoms on the sunken earth.

"They would have loved you," he said.

I smiled and kissed his cheek.

"If I do nothing else in this life, I hope my love for you reminds you of theirs," I said.

We stood.

"Shall we go?" he asked.

I nodded, taking one last look at the ruins as the last of the sun dropped behind the trees.

# CHAPTER THIRTY-SEVEN

A fiddle whined in the distance, its shrill notes echoing over the mountains, and Mr. Ford laughed and spooned the last of his peach ice cream into his mouth.

"I have a surprise for all of you. A farewell gift, I suppose, since tomorrow's festivities will doubtless be restricted to packing trunks," he announced, standing from his chair at the head of the table. He dabbed the corners of his mouth with his napkin before placing it atop the empty crystal bowl.

"If it's a contest of musical acumen, I'm going to pretend to be ill," Worth said under his breath beside me. "I don't enjoy losing, but my playing any sort of instrument sounds like a chipmunk lamenting its every misfortune, and it would be a terrible embarrassment for you."

"I'd hate to forfeit it altogether. I suppose I could try to win it for us." I grinned at him, and he smiled back, his whole face lighting up. He was wearing a blue jacket tonight, a royal color that matched his eyes.

We'd returned in time to ready for dinner, and when I entered the dining tent and saw him in a shade other than black, in a shade that mirrored my own delicate costume of silk and lace, I'd nearly melted into a puddle. The troubled paleness had left his face, replaced by a warmth I hadn't seen in days, and when I'd taken my place beside him, he'd held my hand beneath the table, his fingers finding my ring.

"*This jacket was my father's,*" he'd whispered. "*I knew you'd won-der. I'd begun to doubt I'd ever wear it.*"

"*It couldn't suit you more,*" I'd said.

"What instrument do you play?" he asked.

"Oh, I don't. I said I could try."

Worth chuckled and squeezed my hand.

"We're going to adjourn in a moment and engage in a bit of dancing beneath the stars," Mr. Ford continued. "I've procured a band of men whose families have been in the hills here for near four generations to teach us a bit of North Carolina folk dancing. They've promised they'll be gentle with our ordered formality." He paused and subdued groans rang out from most of the party.

I glanced down the table at Marie Austen sitting between her parents. She'd hardly looked up from her plate the entire meal, not even to gaze upon Mr. Thorp across from her. Papa had had a word with Mr. and Mrs. Kipp while I was gone, and her parents' favor had been with him. They had threatened to withdraw their funds from her in the wake of her broken engagement with Mr. Gibbins, but nothing had been concrete until now. Following our departure, Mr. and Mrs. Kipp were sending Marie Austen away to live with Mrs. Kipp's sister in South Dakota. I still felt sorry for Marie Austen, regardless of her hatred for me and the way she figured my advanta-geous match and imagined meddling had ruined her life. She had no true ally. Then again, she'd alienated the one she'd had.

"Mulled wine will be served during the festivities," Mr. Ford said, and everyone seemed to brighten at that news. "It has been a pleasure to have you all along on the Vagabonds' wilderness adven-ture. I do hope you'll consider joining us again next year. There is nothing so refreshing as a week in the woods to clear one's mind. Wouldn't you agree, Pierce?"

Mr. Ford had invited Mr. Pierce to join our dinner tonight after they'd struck up a friendship on the golf course. He nodded agree-ably.

I thought of Mr. Ford's words. He was right. How desperately I'd needed this week. Our arrival felt like years ago; the memory of my panic at the sight of the mountains, decades. I'd come expecting to endure days of angst as I remembered Father and days of decorum as I accepted my place by the side of a man I'd not known. Though the week had brought anguish, it was redeemed by tremendous hope, by purpose, by a profound love that infused my heart with life.

My thumb swept Worth's and he lifted my hand to his mouth and kissed it. The feel of his lips on my skin made me want to close my eyes and raise my forearm to his mouth and beg him to continue.

"Shall we?" he asked instead, as everyone rose from their seats.

"Yes," I said, forcing my mind away from the sensation of his touch. "Though I'm not proficient at playing, I'm quite versed at dancing."

"They won't be playing waltzes," he said as I threaded my arm through his and we walked out of the tent into the cool spring night.

"You've forgotten where I came from."

Mother and Papa joined us as the crush made their way toward the players and the roaring fire.

"You'll soon realize that Belle and I were luminaries at Red Dragon barn dances," she said to Papa and Worth, laughing.

"Well then, we'll certainly have a time," Worth said. "Father took us to every celebration we were invited to growing up, and Mother forced me to learn the steps to every local dance. The mountain reels were my favorite."

"It makes me happy to see the two of you settled," Papa said, appraising us. "I admit I was terribly worried for you both."

"I was worried for me too." Worth grinned and pulled me to the front of the gathering where our peers stood awkwardly in front of three men enthusiastically taking up their banjo, fiddle, and bass to play "Soldier's Joy."

"Do you know it?" I asked him.

He shook his head and I turned to the women in fine dresses and men in tuxedos, people used to the sophisticated cadence of a waltz. They were staring at the players and sipping their mulled wine. I looked around for the caller. Surely Mr. Ford had obtained a dance caller to assist us in learning the steps, but none was about.

"Obtain a partner and arrange yourselves in a circle, every other couple facing along and against the line of dance!" I shouted. I grabbed Worth's hand and people began to arrange themselves as I'd instructed. Though the song was nearly through by the time everyone was situated, I called out the steps anyway—advance toward the opposite side and retreat; advance to the opposite, turn, and retreat; advance toward partner and retreat; advance to partner, turn partner, and retreat. By the time the song concluded, everyone was laughing, breathless, and asking the players for another tune.

The dancing went on for nearly an hour without stopping, the fiddle and the wine loosening everyone's limbs through "Hop High Ladies" and "Sally Goodin'" and "Red River Valley" and others that sounded familiar but whose names I couldn't recall. The camera flashes popped in the darkness, capturing the pompadours ruined by exertion, the laughing faces of the Burroughs, who hadn't been merry together all week, and Mr. Pierce's magnetic attraction to Toots, who seemed to ignore him. No one save the Kipps and Mr. Thorp begged free from Mr. Ford's entertainment, and as Worth twirled me to the music of my childhood under a clear starry sky, I felt nearly weightless.

"Father was right," Worth said when the fiddle bow slowed and the banjo player set aside his instrument to sing. Worth swept me into his arms, and I let my head rest against his chest.

The singer's voice was haunting:

"Of all the money that e'er I had
I spent it in good company
And all the harm I've ever done
Alas, it was to none but me."

It was the harmony to the heartbeat drumming against my other ear.

"Love sets a person free," Worth went on. "Father always said that when he spoke of how he felt for Mother and me, but I never understood what he meant. I do now. My shackles are gone." He sighed.

"I was thinking on the auto ride down the mountain of the day I wrote Shipley that letter inquiring of a wife. I almost didn't send it. I knew how desperate it sounded, but I'd been in Arizona, alone in the desert for weeks, and the memories threatened . . . I was so lonely, I—"

"You were meant to write it just as I was meant to find you today," I said.

Worth smiled and tipped my chin up to his face. He leaned down, but then remembered where we were and righted.

"Come on," he said, stepping away and leading me out of the throng. He pulled me behind the first tent, lowered his mouth to mine, and kissed me deeply. His hands grasped the back of my head, and then his fingers drifted down my collarbone, pushing the fabric away from my shoulder.

His touch filling a space that had once been covered ignited something in me, and my hands pulled at the back of his shirt until it loosened. My fingers ran over his skin, both smooth and marred, and he made a low noise and gripped my waist. My fingertips pushed into his back. Our bodies were pressed together, but we weren't close enough.

"Belle, I love you. I want to—"

"Don't!" A scream tore over us. We stepped away from each other, startled, as the fiddle faltered and the laughter silenced.

"Please!" The second yell was a wail. Worth took my hand, and we ran back toward the fire where the dancing had suddenly stopped.

Mr. Kipp held a shirtless Mr. Thorp by the wrist and was dragging him toward the row of parked autos. Marie Austen hastened behind them, her gown damp and smudged with mud.

"Father, you can't send him away! Not again! We love . . . We love each other," she shouted, so frantic that she didn't seem to notice the crowd staring at the display.

319

Mr. Thorp didn't utter a word. He didn't fight to remain. Instead, he complied when Mr. Kipp demanded he arrange himself in the auto.

"You will never work again. I will tell everyone what you've done," Mr. Kipp growled, loud enough for everyone to hear.

"It wasn't him, Father. Please! It wasn't him," Marie Austen sobbed, falling to her knees at her father's feet in front of the auto. "Peter. Tell him. Tell him what you told me before . . . before . . ." When she was met with silence, she crawled to the open door, but Mr. Kipp jerked her upright and slammed the auto door shut.

"I'm terribly sorry for her," I whispered. Worth put his arm around me and drew me close.

"Ah, I know. Someday she'll find her way." He cleared his throat. "I suppose since Mr. Thorp has been excommunicated again, Mr. Seely might see clear that you're the proper writer for the inn's story."

I wanted to retort that I didn't want to write the piece anyway, but that wasn't the truth. Regardless of my being looked over, I still wanted to tell the tale of one of the great wonders of the world and the men who built it.

"No. She is to be in Atlanta within days. Out of the way." Mr. Pierce's voice intruded, and we looked at him standing stone-faced beside us, staring at the auto.

"What?" Worth asked.

Mr. Pierce's face blanched.

"I was speaking in jest," Mr. Pierce said, laughing nervously in an attempt to alter the tone of his previous words.

"How so?" Worth stepped toward him, and Mr. Pierce stepped back.

"Perhaps I wasn't, but you know my predicament, Delafield. I trust your confidence because I've known you for years, and I know you understand what is at stake, but I do not have the same assurance of Miss Newbold, and she is privy to the information given me by that Eliza woman too. Miss Newbold has seen it firsthand." Mr. Pierce's words came quickly and he took a swift breath.

"If word gets out to Mr. Seely or Mr. Grove about the . . . about the illness among the workers, I'm afraid it would cause them quite a panic. They are adamant the inn will be finished in two months' time and adamant that this town become a place for the well, and if Miss Newbold finishes the story, she'll need to communicate with them both. Furthermore, Mr. Grove insisted that I find her a position at a paper after Thorp returned. He felt terrible. He suggested I recommend her to an Asheville paper first, but I thought it too risky to have her lingering, so I—"

"You are—" Worth's words were growled. His hands fisted and the veins in his neck bulged. I stepped between him and Mr. Pierce.

"You should have asked for my confidence and trusted my word rather than send me away," I said as calmly as my sprinting heart would allow. "I understand that you were attempting to protect yourself from being seen as negligent by your superiors. I would have kept quiet about everything so long as you were treating the workers with the respect they were due, but you have ripped them from their homes without giving them a choice to decide whether they wanted treatment."

"You must understand, Miss Newbold. The call of a newspaper writer requires the promise to inform the public of subjects both sensitive and ordinary," he said, refusing to address the way he'd treated the sick. "If I had secured you a position in Asheville, you would have written of the epidemic we're facing at the inn. You would have felt as though you had no choice, and the article would undoubtedly spread to other parts of the country. Grove Park Inn would be a failure before it was opened, forever connected in print to consumption, to an illness that kills." He whispered the last part and shook his head. "Healthy people would not come rest in its Great Hall. They would not come at all. The inn is Asheville's final hope. If it fails, the town will become what Mr. Seely and Mr. Grove fear—a veritable leper colony."

As furious as I was, I knew he was speaking the truth. Asheville was on the verge of failing.

"Where did you put them? The Smiths? The others?" I asked.

"We were able to situate them at Blue Ridge Terrace," he said. "The others are spread about. There was little to no room." He quieted for a moment. "Before you think me heartless, please understand that I had another motive to usher the sick into sanitoriums as quickly as I was able. It wasn't only to hide them. My wife died of tuberculosis. She begged to be treated, but there were no beds. It is a terrible disease. I could not stand by and watch these men waste away as she had if help could be obtained." He tipped his head at Worth. "Especially when I can tell them they'll be paid while they're receiving treatment."

I took Worth's hand, and he shook his head as though he wanted no acknowledgment for his kindness.

"Now that you know everything, I suppose I'm asking you, quite belatedly, for your confidence with regard to the illnesses. I hope you understand the need. Mr. Seely and Mr. Grove would be beside themselves, and—"

"Asheville would fail," I said. "I understand."

Behind us, the men began to play again, a merry reel I'd never heard. Ahead, Marie Austen had fallen to the ground once more, her father now sitting by her side. "I'll promise my confidence so long as the ill are given a choice in the matter of whether they are treated."

Mr. Pierce nodded. "Very well."

"And the story?" Worth asked. "I know Grove thought Thorp was the man for the job, but I can tell you with confidence that he's not."

Mr. Pierce laughed.

"I know. You're welcome to it, Miss Newbold. And if you decide you'd like to decline the Atlanta post—now that you've been made aware of the reason for it—just say the word."

I turned to Worth, watching his face for signs of relief at the possibility of my abandoning the position there, but he simply smiled at me.

"Were you being honest about the post's focus?" I asked.

"On the women? Yes, of course," Mr. Pierce said.

This new revelation of how the opportunity had manifested made no difference. My writing would serve the same purpose. I would honor Father. I would tell their stories.

"I'll finish the inn's story from Atlanta," I said.

"It will be a grand adventure for us both," Worth said.

Over his shoulder, Papa was spinning Mother and she was laughing, her eyes sparkling like the stars above us.

"Six years ago, Mother followed love out of heartache to somewhere unknown, and it brought her purpose. It brought her joy."

I looked to Mr. Pierce to find him gone, now dancing with Toots.

"It will do the same for us," Worth said, squeezing my hand. "Your father would be proud of you too, you know. *I'm* proud of you."

"And I of you," I said. "The man you are—the sort of man who buys a family a home and pays dozens of salaries he doesn't owe—is a testament of your parents' love for you. Your love for them too."

We stood together watching the ballroom set abandon their cares and dance unreservedly to a fiddle. The scene made me smile.

"People are all the same deep down, aren't they? Industrialist or inventor, miner or mason, they're all looking for something to make them happy and to know they're worthy enough to be invited to dance." I watched Mrs. Burroughs take Mr. Carver's hand and Mr. Pierce take Toots's as they all circled up once more.

"Everyone—every person in front of us and everyone on earth—is living a grand story no matter how small it seems, and our greatest hope, I think, is that at some point it catches another's eye and becomes their favorite. I find that fascinating."

"It is," Worth said. "My favorite story is about a young woman. She was beautiful, absolutely breathtaking, but that part is often untold because what mattered most to her was her voice. You see, she used it to speak strength to others, to tell of their lives. Only one person could actually hear it, though. That was the thing. It was quite magical. To everyone else, her voice manifested in a pen stroke, but that hardly mattered. When she spoke your name on the page, when her words finally reached you, you were transformed. You stood a little straighter, you worked harder, you loved deeper."

"And the one person who could hear her? Who was that?" I asked.

"Ah, well. That was the man who loved her." Worth drew me close. "He was granted the gift for only one reason. She spent her life making much of others, thinking little of her own adventure. His purpose was simple—to tell her story."

I touched his face, unable to look away from the blue eyes that finally seemed so contented.

"Was their love a long one?" I asked.

He grinned. "Indeed," he said as the banjo struck up the opening notes of "Blackberry Blossom," Father's favorite song. My breath caught and I heard his voice join Worth's as clear as if he was standing beside him.

"A love like that goes on forever."

### THE EIGHTH WONDER OF THE WORLD DISCOVERED IN ASHEVILLE, NC: E. W. GROVE AND FRED SEELY'S GROVE PARK INN

**Belle Delafield**
**July 1, 1913**
Sunset Mountain in Asheville, North Carolina, is the site of a marvel. Grove Park Inn, facing the peaks of the Blue Ridge Mountains with a red-clay tile roof and towering walls of granite stone, is a phenomenon rivaling England's Stonehenge and Italy's Leaning Tower. It has been heralded the finest hotel in the world, and upon sight of it, guests will have no doubt.

The inn was built by visionaries, those whose mind's eye is vivid enough to see such an edifice emerge as if it was not built at all but simply uncovered beneath layers of trees and forest floor. Such a discovery is innate to these creatives, these dreamers whose talents were once plucked from their own metaphoric hillsides and utilized by others who have marveled at their minds as they have marveled at the possibility of such an inn.

Grove Park Inn is an enormous structure with four bays in total, the exterior and interior walls formed by reinforced concrete frames cast in a single pour in situ and granite stone, some still covered in moss, obtained from the mountains behind the inn. The red-clay tiles lining the impressive sloped roof are the only craftsmanship visible to the naked eye, yet the five and a half inches of reinforced concrete slab beneath ninety thousand pounds of twisted rebar on top of filler sheet fiber and Trinidad asphalt make the building completely fireproof.

Inside, the Great Hall is the inn's clear showpiece, boasting its constructors' artistry, and is primed to be the epicenter of guests' gatherings. Stretching one hundred and twenty feet with towering twenty-four-foot ceilings, the hall boasts a breathtaking view of the Blue Ridge Mountains through its many glass doors leading out to the inn's covered veranda. In cooler weather guests will find the two stone fireplaces flanking the hall to be their favored places of respite. At thirty-six feet wide, the hearths are wonders all their own. Their creation required one hundred twenty tons of boulders. The New York–based Roycrofters hand-built the furniture for the room, providing comfortable seating arrangements for the many orchestra and choral performances and gatherings set to take place in this striking space.

Lifts installed behind the firewalls will take guests up to rooms arranged in an atrium where quiet and rest will reign supreme. The ground floor of this section was also outfitted by the Roycrofters—as were the guest rooms—and small seating arrangements will encourage hushed conversation or perhaps a game of checkers. Above the space a glass ridge skylight obtained from Tennessee allows natural light to filter down to the five floors of guest rooms arranged in parapeted galleries over the interior court. The guest rooms will be reminiscent of the simple comfort of a mountain lodge. Arranged in suites, the rooms will include two single beds and will be served by a bath and a lighted closet.

Beside the Great Hall, the dining room is double leveled with windows cast east and west and adjoins a kitchen with a Gothic ceiling. Below, in the basement, guests will find billiards, a swimming pool, shower rooms, and a children's dining room.

The idea to build Grove Park Inn came to inventor, pharmacist, and developer E. W. Grove of the Paris Medicine Company, and to his son-in-law, chemist, inventor, and philanthropist Fred Loring Seely, of the same company, with the vision to provide a world-class place of rejuvenation and relaxation to those exhausted by the demands of the world. Grove and Seely are prone to the same fatigue as their guests, taxed by the strain of running one of the country's most respected pharmaceutical outfits, and have both seen the health benefits of a respite in these particular hills.

Seely is the one to credit with the design for the inn. He was particularly struck by the rustic comfort of Old Faithful Inn in the western part of this country, designed by architect Robert Reamer, and desired to create a similar biophilic resting place in Asheville.

To make their dream manifest, Grove and Seely sought the country's most lauded professionals and laborers. Seely's first call was to his friend, architect G. W. McKibbin of Southern Ferro Concrete in Atlanta, Georgia, who has been celebrated for his work on churches, college buildings, and business facilities in that city. Originally from Calhoun County, Alabama, McKibbin was raised in his father's machine shop but soon realized his imagination was better suited to the drafting of structures. He began training under famed late architect Willis Denny, and McKibbin's place in the chronicles of architecture was quickly solidified.

The man charged with obtaining laborers, ordering materials, and orchestrating the day-to-day building of the inn is Oscar Mills, also from Atlanta, whose work was known to Seely through Mills's serving as foreman on the building of his newspaper offices—a project Mills completed two months ahead of schedule. Mills began in the field of roofing, a post obtained at a very young age by the association of his mother as a secretary at the same company, but swiftly his natural talent in organization and his amiable temperament were noticed as assets in managing the overall operation of a construction site, and he was hired to fill that most essential role.

Grove Park Inn's striking walls were arranged and set under the eye of renowned stonemason John T. Corbin of Asheville, whose work has been featured prominently at the Vanderbilts' Biltmore Estate, the Central Methodist Church, and the Buncombe County Courthouse, all of his town. Corbin's masonry acumen was first realized by S. I. Bean during the construction of Biltmore where Corbin was serving temporarily as foreman for the estate's nursery, a role that bridged his upbringing in farming with his natural talent in building. Mills acquired Corbin for Grove Park Inn as a result of the diverse and arresting work he has become known for in his trade.

The construction of such an inn required over twenty thousand tons of rock, and the extraction of stone from the neighboring mountain and creek beds required a man drenched in the specialized knowledge of geology. Mills procured William Smith, formerly of the West Virginia coal mines, to supervise the removal of stone and its transportation from the mountain to the inn by Seely's wagon train made from six-foot Birdsell wagons pulled by Packard motor trucks.

Guests will notice the work of George Woods, a second-generation tile setter originally from Virginia, in the perfectly even blush tiles arranged around the parapeted gallery walls overlooking the internal courtyard.

Throughout the inn, guests will enjoy fine details from pure molded porcelain baths to brass pipes to hammered silverware and Irish linens, hand-selected by Evelyn Grove Seely.

The balance of laborers needed to complete the inn number into the four hundreds, all of them especially selected for their craft by Mills. Their names are listed below, a testament to their contribution to the eighth wonder of the world. When guests visit the glorious Grove Park Inn, may they take a moment to recall the involvement of such men, as well as those listed above. The greatest hotel in the world can only be built by the hands and minds of the greatest people in the world.

# CHAPTER THIRTY-EIGHT

JULY 12, 1913
ASHEVILLE, NORTH CAROLINA

"Oh, isn't it the most glorious day? We couldn't have dreamed up a better one for this occasion." Evelyn Seely leaned back against the auto seat and tipped her head to the blue sky, interrupted only by the lush green of the treetops overhead.

"Indeed," I said, breathing in the sweet mountain air. Evelyn had just picked me up from the train station, and I was home once again, my soul as light as a hawk sweeping over the wild peaks. The velocity of the open-air auto zipping up the hill gave me nearly the same sensation as flying.

"Many on the train were discussing the event and commenting on how urgently they wished to see the inn for themselves," I said, lifting my hand to the brim of my hat—adorned with nearly a dozen pink hydrangea sprigs and white feathers—to keep it from flying off my head in the wind.

"I have to assume that's thanks to you and your wonderful story. We're nearly booked into next year, you know," Evelyn said.

I laughed. "I suppose, but many an article is written about lesser hotels and most never find their rooms in demand. The inn itself—the eighth wonder of the world as people are apt to say now—is the reason for its success."

My article had been published in Asheville but also in newspapers across the country from Florida to New York to California.

I'd received letters from many readers compelled to send comments about the inspiration they gleaned from the workers' lives and expertise, as well as messages expressing wonder at the craftsmanship and amazement that the photo included atop my article was of an actual standing structure and not drafted from a sketch.

"How about we compromise? Its success is due to both the awe won by the structure and your work." Evelyn grinned, and her hand jerked to her own hat, fashioned in the color and detail of a Wedgwood plate, as a strong wind drifted over us.

"Though you must admit your words have become quite influential. Think—if you hadn't taken the post at the *Georgian* and written the article about the factory workers' want of voice, would Georgia even be speaking of giving women the vote? Even the *Atlanta Constitution* is creating a suffrage department now." She paused.

"And your piece on the impact of tuberculosis on a person and a town and the treatment of it was quite thought-provoking. Of course, you know it caused Mr. Pierce—before he left us to work with Mr. Flagler—to suggest we educate our workers on its prevention and implement a periodic screening by a doctor. I can't believe we hadn't thought of that before with consumption so rampant here. Can you imagine if we'd flung open the inn's doors heralding a safe place for the well only to have our guests infected with tuberculosis by those in our employ?" She shook her head.

The Seelys and Groves never had found out about Asheville's near collapse due to the tuberculosis outbreak among their workers. Of course, Evelyn and Fred knew that some in their employ had come down with tuberculosis—it was a foregone conclusion that some would—but they hadn't been privy to the knowledge that the infection was spread in the course of their operation and threatened to halt the inn's progress altogether. Mr. Mills was able to hastily procure eager men from states as distant as West Virginia to continue construction, and with Worth paying for the lost salaries of the sick, none previously in the inn's employ had harbored a complaint. In fact, Mr. Mills was able to take many of them on again once they recovered.

"Are you enjoying Atlanta? I miss the parties," Evelyn said, her voice stopping on a strange note as though she'd intended to go on but thought it unwise.

"I suppose. Inman Park is lovely and our home is spectacular, but I imagine I didn't have quite the same reception you did," I said. Worth had procured us a beautiful beaux arts–style home in one of the finest neighborhoods in the city, and though I loved being home with him and I loved my work, he was gone periodically in order to buy land or sell it, and we rarely entertained. I was lonely.

"I'd forgotten about the old guard being so stodgy at times. It used to be they'd overlook little things like a wife's writing newspaper articles if her husband had pockets like yours does." Evelyn nudged me and laughed.

The auto lumbered past her father's house. A bank of rhododendron was in full bloom beneath its porch, and a servant, more indiscreet than I knew Mr. Grove preferred, beat a small rug on the side of the home.

"They're afraid their factory or company will be the subject of my next story. They're not incorrect to think so." I sighed. "Mr. Pierce told me once that as a news writer I'd feel compelled to tell the truth no matter the cost, and he's right. I'd rather be honest than have friends. It sits better with my conscience." I closed my eyes and tipped my head to the sky, letting the sun strike my face.

"I worry Worth will tire of our being outcasts at some point. I know we've only been married for two months, but I already feel—"

"Then move here," she said. "You already have quite a lovely piece of land, and to Asheville society, the both of you are deeply beloved."

I glanced at the wild around us, at the conglomeration of tree and flower and animal species that came together to make something breathtaking. The mountain landscape was the epitome of beauty created by differences. Of course it would embrace us if we were to claim it as our home.

"I'll have to talk it over with Worth, but I suppose I could convince

Mr. Graves to allow me to travel down to cover certain assignments and write the pieces remotely."

"He can absolutely be convinced. John and Fred are still thick as thieves, and I know him well enough to know he'll want to retain you regardless of your whereabouts. And if he doesn't, you can simply transfer your genius to the *Citizen*." She paused to smooth her white satin dress adorned with blue paste diamonds.

"Or I suppose you could simply be a roaming writer like that scandalous Mr. Thorp. Perhaps that would suit better, actually. You could travel about with Worth and have him travel about with you."

"You've hit the nail on the head, Evelyn. That would be my ideal." The thought of never being separated from Worth, of having him by my side in my work as he'd been from the start, of exploring new land with him, was wildly appealing. "Though I don't suppose I'd want to be anything like Peter Thorp. Do you know Marie Austen has already filed for divorce for infidelity?" The moment it was out of my mouth I realized how ridiculous the sentiment was. I sounded surprised, but of course their marriage was doomed. After Mr. Thorp was driven from camp for the second time, Marie Austen had feigned a pregnancy to trap him into marriage.

Evelyn grinned and I sobered. Even though everyone knew of Marie Austen's humiliations, she was still my cousin, a troubled soul who had at one time been my only friend. I hoped she'd find her way.

"She wrote just the other day saying her former fiancé, Mr. Gibbins, has been calling, and she's planning to accept if he proposes again."

"That's wonderful," Evelyn said. "Now you've made my mission today threefold—celebrate the inn, celebrate the workers, and dazzle the Delafields enough that they'll abandon all thought of Atlanta and move here where they belong." The sun disappeared beneath a heavy tree canopy and the road narrowed.

"Could you slow please, Mr. Wade? There could be a crush of autos up ahead, and I don't wish to be in an accident today."

Mr. Wade nodded and did as she asked. The auto swept around a curve, and at once I could make out the side of the inn, the same view I'd seen upon my first look. The boulders were piled to the tree line, and as we continued, the eye-catching red-tile roof came into sight, a sharp contrast to the equally striking blue sky above.

Abandoned Packards and Fords and a few Rolls-Royces lined the drive as we swung out from the inn and back to face it directly. The finished inn was a wonder indeed. Even though I'd seen it nearly in its completion before I left in April, the dirt at the entrance had been covered by stone along the drive, and grass and flowers had been installed at the base, creating the illusion that the inn had simply always been, a natural phenomenon crafted by nature instead of by human hands.

"I hope Secretary Bryan will have the same reaction as you," Evelyn said as the auto dipped down the small hill toward the expansive double doors flung open to welcome us.

"How could he not?" I asked. Secretary of State William Bryan was to be the guest of honor at tonight's grand opening banquet—a stag dinner of four hundred influential men. At first I'd been put off by the idea of a stag dinner celebration. It excluded the women, especially Evelyn, who'd been essential in the materialization of this magnificent place. But when I realized our exclusion gave us an opportunity to hold a second celebration, a dinner acknowledging the workers, I wholeheartedly embraced it.

"It takes much to impress him, Fred said." Evelyn glanced at the entrance, and I followed her gaze to find a spectacle that stole my breath.

Worth walked out the doorway in his fitted tuxedo and stood beneath the portico, his gaze searching the autos until he found me. He smiled and I grinned back as my heart began to race. At once I recalled my first view of him in the same place only months before, the way he'd bent to greet each guest, the way he'd clasped my hands, the way his face had enchanted me.

The moment the auto stopped, I opened my own door and ran

to him, meeting him in the middle of the drive where he'd started on his way to me. It had been five days, less than a week since he'd departed from me to settle a deal in Florida, and yet it had felt like a lifetime. My arms wrapped around his neck, and he lifted me in the air before setting me down.

"I've missed you terribly," he whispered against my ear and then dropped a kiss on my mouth, his lips lingering just barely longer than a peck.

"At least five seconds, for each of the days you were gone," I said, pulling his face back to mine and kissing him again, longer this time, my heart settling as my mouth found the warmth of his.

"I'll require at least five hours later on," he said, grinning. "I'd insist on starting this second if it weren't for all these onlookers and our dinner appointments."

I laughed.

"I've been trying to convince Belle that the two of you belong here," Evelyn said, breezing past us into the lobby. "It does suit, you must admit. Come along, you'll want time to see it all before we adjourn."

"It is more glorious than I could have fathomed," Worth said, taking my hand as we followed Evelyn inside. "The attention to detail, the craftsmanship, it—"

His words silenced as if he hadn't just emerged from this very room, but I knew why. The sight of the finished Great Hall was breathtaking.

"What do you think of it?" Evelyn asked. Servants in crisp gray liveries scurried about and an orchestra tuned on the far side of the hall, next to doors leading out to the terrace exhibiting a view of the mountains tinged blue in the evening sky. Certain places of magnificence required reverence, silence, and they nearly all felt stuffy. Not so here. Here, the noise seemed right. Here, the tone was set in excited voices and music notes, celebrating the marvel, lending to a sense of warmth and comfort despite the finery.

"It is a masterpiece," I breathed. Perfect stone pillars matching the walls lined the entirety of the one hundred and twenty feet, stretching up to the soaring ceilings where twelve brass chandeliers cast electric light on the space below and on the enormous fireplaces flanking the hall.

"Where did you obtain the fixtures?" Worth asked, pointing to one of the chandeliers. "They're quite unique."

"The Roycrofters crafted those too. Fred adores Mr. Hubbard, you know, and I do too. Their work is unmatched. They hand-hammered each of these chandeliers, which are illuminated by lights that equal one thousand candles. Mr. Edison advised us on the strength of the beams." She walked toward one of the fireplaces, beckoning us to follow.

"The rugs are imported from France," she said as we skirted a row of wicker rocking chairs. There were dozens of them, some arranged in a semicircle in front of the fireplaces, and others arranged facing each other in the middle of the hall. "We considered simply allowing the gray-tile floor to remain naked," she said, giggling. "But with all the stone and tile and brass, we decided it might need a bit of comfort." Evelyn waved at a man in overalls stacking wood in a sizable cart next to the mouth of the fireplace.

"Hello, Mr. Johnson. May I have a word?" The man set the log he was carrying on the cart and turned. "We're going to keep the doors open to the terrace and the entrance throughout the evening. It's quite warm and the mountain air flowing through will promote cool. However, when the temperature dips to a point where the heat from a fire is welcome, please feel free to set the blaze," she said.

"Look," Worth said, tipping his head to the stones above us as Evelyn continued to speak with Mr. Johnson about the evening's plans. "Did you know they were planning to inscribe quotations on some of the rocks?"

The sayings weren't on every stone but mingled along the fireplace in a demure black print that matched some of the granite tone.

*"Be not simply good—be good for something." —Thoreau*

*"Take from this hearth its warmth. From this room, its charm. From this inn, its amity. Return them not—but return."*

*"The sun will shine after every storm."* —Emerson

*"This old world we're living in is mighty hard to beat. We get a thorn with every rose, but ain't the roses sweet."* —Stanton

"I think it's wonderful," I said. "The one by Stanton is my favorite."

Worth squeezed my hand. "Yes. That or the Emerson for me." He leaned down and planted a kiss on my cheek.

"Do you suppose they're too much?" Evelyn asked, coming to stand beside Worth. "The quotations? Father and Fred had a few painted on the stones at first temporarily, simply to motivate the workers, but everyone seemed to enjoy them so they decided perhaps the guests would as well and added more." She paused.

"We hit a bit of a snag right after you all departed, and Mr. Mills said spirits were down. Fred thought perhaps the quotations would remind the workers of the guests the inn would serve, that they were building for weary and celebratory and grief-stricken people who would be coming here for generations for rest and renewal."

"They're perfect," I said.

"I'm glad to hear it," she replied. "I know evening commitments for all of us are looming, so let me personally show you to your quarters to freshen up. Our suites are just down the hall from where you'll be staying, and my maid, Mrs. Craig, will be over to help you dress and situate your coiffure momentarily, Belle. Worth, I'm afraid the men will begin to arrive in less than half an hour for the introductory tours, followed by dinner, but you're already dressed in any case."

She glanced across the hall toward the orchestra and the open doors to the dining room. Even from this distance, it was clearly a spectacular space. Windows displayed views east and west and the area had been furnished with legless tables—mushroom-shaped iron bases supporting polished oak tops—and handcrafted chairs from the same sort of wood.

"Let's take the lift," she said. "It's just here."

We walked around the side of the fireplace to find an older gentleman in a black suit with brass buttons standing next to a door.

"Would you kindly give us a ride up, Mr. Grant?" Evelyn asked, giving the older man a pat on his shoulder.

"Of course, Mrs. Seely," he replied, opening the door and then pulling back the metal grates of the lift so we could step inside.

"I still find the idea of lifts inside the fireplaces remarkable," I said.

"Yes, well, Mr. McKibbin said it was the only way we would have room to provide one to access the atrium," Evelyn said.

"Are you ready for this evening, Mr. Grant?" Worth asked as Mr. Grant pulled the metal grate back over the opening and selected the fourth-floor button. "You certainly look the part."

The older man chuckled. "As do you," he said as the lift rose. I squeezed Worth's hand. I'd been on a lift only a few times in my life, and I'd heard stories of them getting stuck, requiring an emergency call to a fire department for assistance.

"Mr. Grant was a tile setter until a week ago. Most of the work you'll see on the east side of the atrium is his doing," Evelyn said.

The man beamed and I recalled the tile setter Mr. Woods, whom Worth and I had encountered on our first tour of this place.

"It was to be the last post of my life. I'm near eighty and my back can't take the work anymore, though I need the money. When Mrs. Seely here asked if I'd consider operating the lift, I nearly cried." He paused. "I've never worn a suit like this before."

"Well, you look dashing in it," I said as the lift stilled. "Did you work with a Mr. Woods here? Worth and I happened to meet him upon an earlier visit." At once my heart filled with worry and I prayed he wouldn't tell me Mr. Woods had been claimed by illness.

"Yes, we worked together 'til the very end of the project. He'd be here now except that your news article gave him quite a bit of business. He's been asked to serve as the lead setter at a new church build in Boone, just over the mountains from here." Mr. Grant grinned and unfastened the metal grate as the lift door opened to a sitting area with two wicker chairs and a simple oak table overlooking the parapeted gallery. On each side of the sitting area, guest room doors stretched down long walkways, and sunshine from the glass ceiling beamed down on the shiny rose tile from one end of the rectangular atrium to the other.

"I'm so glad it's given him a boost," I said.

"Indeed. Your work gave us all a bit of honor that we can carry throughout our lives," he said as we disembarked. "I'll see you later." The door closed and I glanced at Worth. Unlike the boisterous celebration found in the Great Hall, a hush fell over us here, just as it had during our first tour.

"It's intentionally quiet here," Evelyn said as if she could read my mind. "Sleep is so vital to a restful stay, and Fred believes wholeheartedly that though the inn should be a place of much fun, it should also be a place of much relaxation. The Great Hall is for entertaining, and the rooms are for peace."

I ran my hand along the tile parapet as we walked.

"Your room is just down the way here in the middle," she went on, stopping in front of a door that read 452 in gold numbers. "If you should need us, we're tucked away in the suites behind the lift." She gestured toward the short hallway behind us. "It's easier to obtain a bit of privacy that way since we'll be living here for at least six months while our home is being built."

"Edison is coming to do the electric design for your home soon, correct?" Worth asked. "Fred said it is to be a showpiece, fashioned after a European castle."

"Yes to both accounts," Evelyn said. "It's going to be quite an undertaking, but Fred cannot function without such a project on his hands." She grinned and nodded toward the door. "It's open. The key will be on the nightstand in case you choose to lock up. I'm off to fetch Mrs. Craig for Belle. We'll meet downstairs in an hour, and a driver will take us down to dinner."

"Thank you," I said.

Worth opened the door, but I lingered in the hall. I turned and looked over the parapet to the interior courtyard below, the place where I'd once reclined on scaffolding to look at the sky. The expanse was decorated much as I'd assumed, with intimate seating areas and chessboards and bookcases.

"Shall we ask Mr. Grant to take us down? The carpets are new. I'm happy to lie on the floor with you," Worth said, coming to stand beside me. He smiled. Anyone else would find his comment humorous, but I knew he was serious. If I wished, he'd lay on the floor of this fine inn and stare at the sky with me, just like he'd done on the scaffolding that first day.

"We haven't the time, but I know you would."

I reached for his hand, my fingers threading the back of his set on the tile, and I looked up at the sky. It was a bit hazy today from the heat, but still perfect cyan. Atlanta was a gray-blue nearly all summer because of the humidity.

"You were right when you said this sort of blue can't be found anywhere else," I said.

I sighed and turned away to find our door open and another spectacular scene out our window. I walked into the room toward the mountain view, and Worth followed. The rooms were sizable, the simple oak Roycrofter furnishings providing a comfortable ambience. There were two twin beds against one wall and a chest against the opposite. A dresser stood in the corner equipped with a telephone, and above us, a smaller version of the brass chandeliers in the Great Hall illuminated the room.

"Have you ever seen anything so lovely?" I asked. I heard the door click shut behind me when I reached the sill. The green trees cloaking the distant hills were bathed in gold and blue in the evening light. The window was open and the mountain air breezed over me. I closed my eyes, breathing it in, reveling in the feel of the cool.

"You are lovelier," Worth said, his voice low. I opened my eyes and turned to face him across the room. "Seeing you standing there, your beauty against the view of the mountains . . . It's the view I fell in love with. That day in the rafters I felt it, this incredible yearning, this insatiable urge to hold you, and now that I can, now that I love you, now that you're mine—" He stopped talking and unbuttoned his jacket, shrugging it off and throwing it onto the first bed as he walked toward me.

My heart raced and my breath quickened.

His hands found my waist, his fingers drifting to the snaps and hooks at my back, while his lips found my mouth. My hands shook with need of him as I unbuttoned his shirt.

A knock at the door stilled us, followed by another, more persistent knock and the sharp call of an irritated maid.

"Mrs. Delafield! I am here to help you. Mr. Peterson is out here with your trunks as well. We are both in quite a rush."

Worth started to pull away, but I held him fast and kissed him hard.

"Until we meet again," I whispered, and Worth grinned against my mouth.

"Mrs. Delafield!" Mrs. Craig nearly shouted, pounding on the door again.

"Just a moment, Mrs. Craig," I called, smoothing my dress. I started to walk toward the door, but Worth caught my wrist.

"We can discuss this later, but I want you to know I've been thinking of what Evelyn said when you arrived. We will be happy anywhere, but perhaps we should consider settling here, where we began," he said. "Perhaps a home in the valley on our land."

I glanced out the window at the mountains where I'd always truly belonged, and then at the man who would always be my home.

"Mrs. Delafield!" Mrs. Craig persisted.

"There is little to discuss," I said, smiling. "Of course we should."

# CHAPTER THIRTY-NINE

I'd been standing in the same place for nearly an hour. The immense canvas tent that had been set up outside of the unfinished Sunset Hall—the inn's new servants' quarters—was crushed with guests. I'd assumed upon entering that the priority was on celebrating, that Evelyn's speech of thanks would be short and guests would be keen to see themselves to the long tables set banquet style, boasting the same dinner the men were enjoying at the inn—lobster cocktail, green turtle soup, ramekins of diamondback terrapin à la Maryland, roast stuffed turkey, broiled squab with currant jelly, vegetables, potatoes, alligator pears, and every pie and pudding and candied fruit one could imagine—but I'd been wrong.

Instead, it seemed that every worker I'd had occasion to speak with wanted to speak with me, to thank me for my article. It had seemed rather odd at first to accept praise for simply writing a comprehensive account of the genius that construction of such a place required, but Evelyn had leaned in after the Corbins departed my company and told me to simply accept it, that it was the gracious thing to do.

Alone for a moment, I pinched the pale pink taffeta, fluffing the puffed sleeves at my shoulders, and tried to avoid looking around the room for missing faces, people lost to consumption. Tonight was a night of celebration, not mourning. I glanced at the panels of hand-painted flowers on my skirt, studying the brushstrokes on the peony blossom. I'd worried at first about wearing such a dress. It was an elaborate Bernard. Worth had insisted upon it because he loved the way the chiffon and silk crepe fell on my figure.

In truth, it made me feel the most beautiful of all my dresses, but I didn't want it to draw too much attention when the evening should be focused on the contribution of the workers. Upon entering the tent, I'd realized my worries were completely unfounded. A few men wore dungarees and overalls, but most wore suits. Some were ill-fitting and out of fashion, but they were suits nonetheless. The ladies wore beautiful handmade dresses that reminded me of the sorts of costumes my grandmother made for Mother. Perhaps they were formed from less costly material than my gown, but their ingenuity was remarkable. And besides, my gown was handmade by someone too.

"Champagne, Mrs. Delafield?" A waiter held out a full flute to me and I took it.

"Thank you," I said, taking a sip. The bubbles tickled my lips and made me blush. The drink reminded me of our honeymoon. Instead of the church in Charlotte as we'd first planned, Worth and I had been married at Wesley Chapel in Atlanta mere hours before I was to report to the newly constructed textile factory.

Consequently, the traditional honeymoon tour was reduced to a week at the Georgian Terrace Hotel, but Worth was determined to make it seem as though we'd gone abroad anyway. He'd employed Atlanta-based chefs from Paris and Budapest and Rome to cook us elaborate dinners in the hotel's dining room, and at the end of the night, when it was just us, he would open a bottle of champagne and kiss me.

"There you are, Belle." Willie appeared from nowhere in a beige suit. It was his father's. I recalled it plainly because he'd worn it to Father's funeral and cried so hard that tear marks had marred the front like rain.

I knew I shouldn't hug him. It wasn't proper, and yet he stood before me—healthy.

"I'm so glad to see you," I said and threw my arms around him anyway. He chuckled and hugged me back.

"Mother will be over in a moment. She has something for you. It's at the table," he said.

"How have you been? I'm so sorry for your—" I stopped myself.

The reminder of it here was likely unwelcome. I knew his father hadn't recovered from tuberculosis. In the wake of Papa learning about our past, I'd told Mother the day of our departure about the Smiths and their whereabouts, of course leaving off the bit about the greater pandemic among the rest of the inn's workers. Papa and Mother had delayed going back to Indiana in order to visit them out of doors at the sanitorium, and Mr. Smith died only hours after. Knowing it was Mr. Smith's wish to be buried in Red Dragon, Papa and Mother had financed the burial and the casket's travel to West Virginia as well as Willie and Mrs. Smith's train tickets. Mother and Mrs. Smith had been writing ever since.

"We're doing all right. We miss him terribly, but we're well situated now, thanks to you. Mr. Seely has given me quite a promotion— I've been appointed lead foreman in charge of the new quarry he's opened. We'll soon be extracting granite for the Seelys' new home. I'm also training with Mr. Corbin to become a stonemason." He grinned. The rosiness had returned to his cheeks, and his frame had regained some of the heartiness I remembered.

"I'm so glad to hear it, Willie. I've thought of you all so much in the past months. When I heard you were shipped to the sanitorium, I nearly lost my mind with worry."

"Oh, well, that was the best thing that could have happened for Mother and me. Father was too far gone, but for the two of us, they cared for us and nursed us, and I know we would have lost our lives if we had remained untreated," Willie said. "I think a part of our healing was knowing we could relax, that we weren't going to lose our home or our money if we took the time to recover." His eyes teared up and he wiped away the moisture with the back of his hand.

"Here's Mother now." His gaze shifted behind me and I turned.

Mrs. Smith was walking toward us carrying something. It was draped in a crocheted shawl.

"Belle, dear," she said when she reached us. Like her son, she'd returned to a person I recognized. Her red-gray hair curled and her figure was full and healthy.

"You don't know how relieved I've been to hear that you're well," I said.

She smiled. "For quite some time, I thought I'd never be well again. I feel blessed daily to watch my Willie grow into a fine man, though I miss Stephen fiercely," she said. "Here." She held a box out to me and I took it.

"What is it?" I asked.

"I draped one of my shawls across it to prevent scratching, but I think you'll recognize it." She reached over and lifted the fabric from the box. The moment she did, I gasped and began to cry.

The top of the cedar box boasted a swirl of the initials JTC—James Thomas Coleman. My father had always called it his hope chest—never mind that a true hope chest was where a woman's dowry was typically contained.

"*Because all of my hopes are in here. My dreams, my stories, my moments of wonder.*" I could still hear his voice when I'd asked him why he called it that.

"How did you get this?" I managed when I could finally speak.

"After we buried Stephen, we went by to see our old house. I looked over at your old place and felt compelled to ask if they'd kept anything of the old tenant," she said.

"They told me there was so much left behind that they'd kept most of it in the cellar in case you returned someday. I went and looked, and many of your things were soiled beyond repair, but this was in a canvas bag, shielded from the elements. I thought to send it to you, but I didn't know the address, and I figured—"

I reached for her, hugging her tightly.

"Thank you. It's all I have of him," I said, clutching the box with one hand and wiping my tears with the other.

"No, it's not," she said, patting my shoulder. "Even if you'd never got this back, you have his words in your head and his smile on your lips and his love in your heart."

I opened the lid, and the pungent scent of mothballs and cedar overtook the warm smells of roast meat and sugary pie wafting from the banquet tables. On the top was a notebook dated

November 14, 1906. The day before he died. I flipped the cover back, expecting the pages to be blank. I was mostly right. Only nine sentences were written on the first page beneath the title, "Today's Observations," but the sentences took my breath.

> *Walked the creek bed home tonight. Looked at the layers of rock — sand, stone, mineral. Thought about how they all told a story about a time and a place. I've seen a house built of stone before. I recall wondering if they knew what they were doing, if they realized they were building a house out of stories, out of the memories of all those souls who walked atop the granite and worked to dig out the stones before them. I'd like a house like that for myself, for my girls. It would talk forever and therefore stand forever. It would warn us of folly before — of anger and jealousy and sloth — and endear us to love — I suppose that is the whole of what we should aspire to give and receive in this life. It would be a structure worthy of admiration.*

I ran my hand over Father's handwriting. There was now no questioning the reason I'd been struck by the inn, why it felt to me like a place of endless wonder or why I'd come to see that a life without love wasn't a life at all. I'd already known it, but seeing his words in front of me verified the truth: Father had been captivated by the same thoughts. He had been with me all this time.

"Good evening, ladies and gentlemen!" Evelyn called, standing atop a chair in the middle of the tent. Mr. Corbin stood beside her looking nervous. She did appear as if she could topple at any moment.

"I looked through the box to ensure it was whole, that the contents weren't ruined," Mrs. Smith said. "There is a photo inside of your parents. When I told you that day that Mr. Delafield looks at you like your father looked at your mother, I wasn't speaking out of turn. The photo is evidence." She patted my hand. "You are a fortunate woman, Belle."

"I . . . I know." The view of the workers all together, the vision of the Smiths restored, Father's box, and Worth's love—it was almost too many blessings to fathom. "I can never thank you enough for this," I said, tipping my head toward the box.

"You already have," Willie said. "You've been a steadfast friend to us and will continue to be. So have your mother and your father and your stepfather and your husband. We are grateful."

The box beckoned. I wanted to abandon the dinner and search through it. I couldn't wait to read Father's stories of Joseph Tominsky, the strongest man in Red Dragon, or Lydia Claire, the county's greatest baker. I couldn't wait to read his discoveries over again. Each day he'd find something remarkable in the ordinary, something new to celebrate, from different sorts of worms churning the soil in our small garden to the way the shifts in the wind could tell the weather to a poem he'd read and found poignant.

I also wanted to find the photograph. I knew which one it was—my parents standing beneath an oak tree beside Elk Run. His arms were wrapped around her waist and his eyes were fixed on her, not the camera as the photographer had intended. I thought of Mrs. Smith's words, and though I'd never be able to catch Worth looking at me to see it for myself, perhaps I could see his love for me in the eyes of my father.

"I apologize for the interruption, ladies and gentlemen, but I want you to be able to enjoy the food before it chills, and I wish to have a word before we begin," Evelyn said. She looked steadier now with the knowledge that both Mr. Corbin and Mr. McKibbin stood beside the chair she perched upon. She glanced at me, and I smiled.

"On behalf of my family, thank you." The tent chatter silenced. "I have no doubt that many of you came to our employ considering it simply another job, but to us, to many for generations to come, your contribution is something monumental, something that is to be celebrated for as long as this inn stands . . . which, of course, we hope will be forever."

A few claps and cheers rang out.

"Mrs. Delafield alluded to an important truth in her article—at times we are all propelled toward something simply because it is the next step, hardly realizing that what we are doing is something spectacular, that what we are doing could be accomplished by the skill of our hands alone. It takes another to speak to our unique genius in order for us to see it; otherwise, for most of us, we would let it go unused and that would be a terrible shame.

"I do hope you've read Mrs. Delafield's story and that someone at one point or another has told you of your worth, but if they have not, allow me to reiterate—you were hired to construct this wonder of the world just beside us for a reason. I will be forever thankful to the person—whoever that is—who believed in you, who encouraged you to pick up the axe or the chisel or pour the cement or cut the tile or draw the blueprints or inspire hundreds of workers or pick up the pen." Her eyes steadied on me at the last and I wiped my eyes. How close I had been to never writing again. Being here, in this place, being here, close to Worth, had forced the pen into my hands and told me I was needed for a specific purpose.

"Your father would be beaming," Mrs. Smith whispered as Evelyn went on. "And your mother and Shipley are so proud of you." She looped her arm around my waist. "She said for years you'd been trying to find your way, and I can see why. But it's clear now that you have, dear. You've found love, purpose. It won't matter where your feet settle anymore. You've found your way home."

I sniffed and nodded.

"She was right that it took some time," I said. "But yes. I am exactly where I'm supposed to be."

Loud cheers rang out and champagne corks popped, and I joined the merriment to celebrate the people standing before me.

## THE END

# AUTHOR'S NOTE

Hi, friends!

First, I want to tell you how honored I am that you picked up my story. I hope you loved it and that it reminded you of how important each and every one of you are—to your loved ones, to your communities, and to the world! If you haven't yet read the book, please don't read any further. ☺ There are a lot of spoilers in the following pages and nothing ruins a book for me faster than knowing what happens ahead of time. I promise you'll appreciate this note so much more after you've read the story!

I've known I wanted to write a book about Grove Park Inn for years. Growing up in Charlotte, I went to Grove Park with my family at least once a year—usually in the winter when the big fireplaces were roaring. One of my earliest memories is sitting in front of the fire as a very young girl with both sets of grandparents, my parents, my cousins, and my brother, listening to a band play in the Great Hall. I can still recall the way the music echoed off the stones, and I can still see the people laughing and dancing as snow fell outside.

I remember being absolutely awestruck by the construction of such a place, even as a child. Each time we visited, I'd always spend a lot of time wondering about how it was made and thinking over the quotes Mr. Seely had painted on the stones. We always stayed in the original part of the inn—my parents love old places, as do I— usually in the rooms on the top floor. The windows there are tucked right beneath the roofline, and the view is amazing—the same view I described when Belle and Worth are exploring in the rafters. My husband and I still request those rooms today. In fact, my daughter's first trip out of town at four months old was to Grove Park, and I remember rocking her to sleep while looking out at the same blue mountain view I've loved forever.

There are countless stories I could have told about Grove Park Inn—its history is rich, filled with glamour and celebrity—but when I thought through the various eras, my mind kept returning to the 1913 construction of the inn as it did when I was a child. To me, Grove Park is truly a wonder of the world, and the idea that something so magnificent was built without today's modern equipment captivates me. Right about the time I settled on the foundation of the story, I decided to do my usual deep dive into newspaper archives to make sure I was making the correct choice—newspapers are a treasure trove for me and the information found in their pages often helps guide my work.

I read through months of newspapers in Asheville, and something struck me that I'd also seen in the New York newspaper research I'd done for my previous book, *All the Pretty Places*. When a remarkable structure was built—whether a home or a hotel or a town hall or a courthouse, the credit went only and always to the financier. At times, a newspaper might mention a general contractor or architect, but they were usually only called out if the person was well known in their own right—like Richard Morris Hunt or the controversial but renowned Stanford White. Though I understood the emphasis on the financier—money and vision are hugely vital to any project—I considered the artistry of these early-twentieth-century buildings, especially Grove Park Inn, and thought it such a shame that the skilled laborers who built these wonders were never acknowledged publicly. That thought stayed with me as I began plotting, and early on I knew the quest to recognize those laborers would be important to Belle.

As I dove into the story, I began to look everywhere for the names of the men who built Grove Park so I could include them all in the book. It was a challenge. I was able to pull some names from historical records, newspaper archives, the amazing works of Grove Park historian Bruce E. Johnson, and even ancestry records. I learned that G. W. McKibbin of Atlanta's Southern Ferro Concrete was the architectural engineer tasked with transforming Fred Seely's vision into blueprints, that Oscar Mills, also of Atlanta, was the inn's construction superintendent, and that North Carolina native John T. Corbin served as the head stonemason—he also worked on Biltmore with his Asheville contemporary, Samuel I. Bean.

However, despite my digging, I wasn't able to locate any time sheets or records to find the names of the four-hundred-person team that built the inn. I reached out to the archives department at UNC Asheville, as well as the Asheville Historical Society, and though they were incredibly helpful, they didn't have time sheets from the era. Eventually, I was able to speak with Bruce Johnson, who confirmed a rumor I'd heard. The employment records from Grove Park's building era had been destroyed in a basement flood. Mr. Johnson was actually the person who inspected all the soaked boxes and salvaged everything he could. We would know next to nothing about the inn without his efforts and research.

Of course, the idea that we'd never be able to find a comprehensive list naming the men who built Grove Park was highly disappointing. I'd hoped to acknowledge the work of everyone who helped construct Grove Park in my book. Still, I knew I wanted to pay homage to their efforts by shining a light on the astronomical undertaking the inn was and diving into the individual skills required for such a project. Belle's eventual reporting career was born out of the desire to highlight the magnitude of the inn's construction, an interest I shared with Mr. Grove and Mr. Seely, who did, in fact, have a comprehensive article written about the intricacies of the inn that was published in countless papers upon its opening.

Many years ago, I read an obituary printed in a Boone County, West Virginia, newspaper archive from the early twentieth century. I'd been doing ancestry research for myself at the time—my family is from the same area. The man who had passed was a miner, a man heralded as a wonderful father and a friend to all, but one line struck me—he'd wanted to be a writer and was known for storytelling. The sentence implied he'd never had the opportunity to live out his dream, but that he was dearly loved. When I started writing this book, the sentiment found in his obituary pushed its way into my mind and held firm. I wondered about the man—if he knew while he was living how valued he'd been. I thought a lot about the people who are celebrated in this world and why, about the fact that most people have no idea how vital they are. Addressing that reality became central to the story.

Later, I found an article during my research that said Mrs. Seely was planning to host a big celebratory dinner upon the opening of Grove Park Inn for the builders to thank them for their work. Though I never found another mention of such a dinner—perhaps it was overshadowed by the fancier dinner with William Jennings Bryan—I was glad to know that the Seelys and Groves wanted to acknowledge the crowd of talent they had employed, to show them they were important.

Since I was never able to find the names of the other laborers at Grove Park Inn, I had to manufacture some of my vital characters. Willie Smith and his family are fictional, but they represent the contributions of real people. They also help bring Belle's past to her present.

Thomas Pierce is also fictional. During my research, I was stunned to learn how prevalent tuberculosis was in Asheville at this time and how many sanitoriums called the town home. Mr. Grove and Mr. Seely were truly desperate to provide Asheville's economy with an alternative and had to persuade the town council over and over again that tourism, not tuberculosis rehabilitation, should be the future—otherwise, the town would fail.

Grove Park Inn was certainly constructed to set the town's sights on a different course. Still, I found it interesting that two men who'd made their fortunes making people well were so determined to eradicate the sanitoriums. I have no idea if any employees at Grove Park Inn were stricken with tuberculosis, but it would make sense, given how common it was in town at the time, and I wanted to explore the tension that certainly would have been present if an outbreak had occurred. Since infection among the builders was a figment of my imagination and not solid fact, I didn't feel comfortable involving Mr. Grove's or Mr. Seely's characters in that part of the plot. Mr. Pierce was created so he could be the one to hide—and resolve—this catastrophe without his bosses' knowledge.

When I started to build the story, I knew I needed to get Belle to the inn, but I didn't know exactly how that would happen. I thought of several other options, but upon rereading the history of the inn, I kept returning to the Vagabonds' visit to Grove Park in 1918 (not 1913 as in the book) and decided to move their appearance back for my narrative.

The Vagabonds, a camping group originally formed by Henry Ford, Harvey Firestone, Thomas Edison, and John Burroughs in 1914, traveled through Asheville four years later and stopped to see the wonder of the inn, built by their friends Grove and Seely. Though the first camping trips—which were always actually luxurious glamping vacations—involved smaller groups, the population traversing the wilderness expanded in the following years to include the founders' families and any others they saw fit to invite, including many scientists and industrialists.

As I looked at photos from these trips—most were carefully documented as publicity boosters for Ford and Firestone—I could immediately envision Belle among them: an accidental heiress who was secretly more like the skilled laborers than she was like the Vagabonds, a girl who was used to the mountains and versed in camping and desperately hoping to reclaim a part of herself. I invented Belle's character—her mother's and Shipley's and the Kipps' too—and thought that, based on who the original Vagabonds invited camping, someone like Shipley Newbold, a gasoline magnate, would be a natural fit. I knew from previous random research that the Gulf Refining Company opened the first drive-up gas station in 1913. (There were a few other gas stations that predated this one, the first in 1905 and the second, opened by Standard Oil Company in Seattle, in 1907, but they were not drive-up stations.) The endeavor seemed a great one for Shipley to attempt to champion with the help of Ford and Firestone.

Worth, though I wish he was real, is also fictional. After the loss of her father, Belle inadvertently loses the relationship she's always depended on with both of her parents, and before Worth comes into the picture, she really has been without a confidant. I wanted to explore how unconditional love heals and empowers. As the inn rises out of the mountain it comes from, so does Belle, so does Worth. As they begin to realize that in each other they are seen and loved, they step into their purpose—a purpose they'd never envisioned before, a purpose that prompts them to empower others, a purpose much bigger than themselves.

Many of my stories seem to emphasize the same truth: There are no small lives. There are no small stories. Strangely enough, this is an accidental theme. I don't set out intending to write novels that underscore this fact, but I suppose I am subconsciously drawn to them. I am daily in awe of others' talents and also people's tendency to discount them. It is my hope that you, my friends and readers, will grasp how vital you are, how loved you are, and how important it is that you realize and live out your gifts. If I could write a story about each of you, I would. ☺

## RECOMMENDED FURTHER READING

Guinn, Jeff. *The Vagabonds: The Story of Henry Ford and Thomas Edison's Ten-Year Road Trip.* New York: Simon & Schuster, 2019.

Johnson, Bruce E. *Built for the Ages: A History of Grove Park Inn.* Asheville, NC: Grove Park Inn and Spa, 2004.

Johnson, Bruce E. *Tales of the Grove Park Inn.* Fletcher, NC: Knock on Wood Publications, 2013.

# ACKNOWLEDGMENTS

Those who know me know I'm a mountain girl through and through. The cool breezes, the breathtaking views, the sweet smell of honeysuckle, and the wonder of the woods all make me feel tremendous peace, and I know when I'm there I'm home. The mountains also point to God, and seeing them always reminds me of his majesty. He has created the most breathtaking things—us included—and allowed them to be a part of his story. Thank you, Jesus, for letting us all be a little, but absolutely vital, part of the greatest book ever written.

Thank you to my parents, Lynn and Fred, for always being so supportive. Thank you for being my road-trip buddies and the best word-of-mouth marketers who ever existed!

To the rest of my family—Jed, Hannah, Reece, Gran, Momma Sandra, Beth, Josh, Mady, Elise, Dianna, Johnny, Jeremy, Aunt Cindy, Bill, Samantha, Jamie, Jancis, Porter, Mauve, Uncle Jim, Uncle John, Becky, Alice Jean, Uncle Billy, Janine, Blair, Davis, Camden, Aunt Sarah, Richard, Ellen, Jeb, Keith, Britt, Jeremy, Ryan, Lori, Randy, Rochelle, Tim, Abby, Jeff, Lisa, Nancy, Kevin, Peter, Kristen, Richard, Elizabeth, Coco, Morgan, Eric, Susan, Judy, Robert, Winky, Lilly, Scott, Bonnie, Alevia, Merci, and Katrina—your support and love mean the world!

To Maggie Tardy (Drew, Ava, and Claire too!), who is the opposite of Marie Austen and the best friend who ever lived, thanks so much for coming to countless tour events, for always grabbing the coffee creamer and Sour Patch Kids when I crash at your house, and for the endless laughs!

I can't articulate how important it is to have a crew of friends who are like family. Thank you to Jessica, Mindy, Julie, Carolyn, Katie, Amanda, Ronni, Brittany, Megan, Elaine, Jodi, Shea, Court, Hollie, Laura, Sanghee, Joy, Michelle, Liz, GraceMarie, Christine, Kasey, Alice, Rena, Rich, Jim, Carrie, Sarah, Arden, Krisha, and Caitlin for being the definition of true friendship and love!

Being an author is crazy, beautiful, and unique. I couldn't do this job without the support of my writer friends who get it. Thank you to Cheyenne Campbell, Sarah Henning, Kim Wright, Erika Montgomery, Marybeth Whalen, Kim Brock, Lauren Denton, Adele Myers, Wade Rouse, Erika Robuck, Kristy Woodson Harvey, Sarah McCoy, Leslie Hooten, Kristy Cambron, Lauren Edmondson, Meagan Church, Jennifer Robson, Meredith Jaeger, Yvette Corporon, Jenni Walsh, Heather Webb, Vanessa Miller, and several others I'm accidentally forgetting! Love you all!

I wouldn't have a career without booksellers. Thank you for championing my books and helping my stories get into readers' hands. I'm especially grateful for Olivia Meletes-Morris and Wendy Meletes of Litchfield Books; Sally Brewster, Sherri Smith, Halli Gomez, and Jamie Brewster of Park Road Books; Kimberly Daniels Taws of The Country Bookshop; Shaye Gadomski of A New Chapter Bookstore; Karen Schwettman and Gary Parkes of FoxTale Book Shoppe; Ashley Warlick of M. Judson Booksellers; Jill Hendrix of Fiction Addiction; Lady Vowell Smith of The Snail on the Wall Books; Dan Carlisle of Taylor Books; Ashley Skeen and Mandee Cunningham of Booktenders; Dawn Nolan and Dawn Hylbert of Cicada Books; Jen Sherman of Bookish Cedar Creek; Lisa Yee Swope and Beth Seufer Buss of Bookmarks; and Maggie Robe of Flyleaf Books.

Thank you to the phenomenal and talented bookstagrammers, bloggers, and podcast hosts for spreading the word about my work! It's always such a joy to see your creativity. Thank you to Annissa Armstrong—the most supportive friend and book lover on the planet—and to Francene Katzen, Renee Blankenship, Julie Chan, Valerie Souders, Cristina Frost, Lisa Harrison, Brenda Gardner,

Bubba Wilson, Jayda Justus, Ashley Hasty, Dawne McCurry, and many others not mentioned here.

For any author, having the best agent in your corner is vital. I'm beyond grateful for the incomparable Kate McKean, for the friendship, guidance, and cheerleading. You're the best!

Thank you to my dream publishing team at Harper Muse — Kimberly Carlton, Amanda Bostic, Kerri Potts, Margaret Kercher, Nekasha Pratt, Jere Warren, Taylor Ward, Becky Monds, Laura Wheeler, Caitlin Halstead, Savannah Breedlove, Patrick Aprea, and Colleen Lacey. I pinch myself every day that I get to work with each and every one of you!

Thank you to Jodi Hughes, the line editor with the sharpest eye in the biz. You make my books shine!

Lastly, but most importantly, thank you to my husband, John, and my children, Alevia and John. You make every day the best day ever. I love you more than you'll ever know!

# DISCUSSION QUESTIONS

1. When Belle arrives in Asheville, she is petrified to see the mountains again because doing so means facing the hardship she's worked so diligently to bury. Have you ever been forced to face something you tried to avoid? How did you feel afterward?

2. Marie Austen is clearly the villain of the story, and yet her interactions with Belle serve a definite purpose. Have you ever had to deal with someone like her? If so, what lessons did you take away from that relationship?

3. The mountains are a heart home to so many. Do you have a favorite mountain spot? If so, what is so special about it?

4. Belle and Worth are both hiding their pasts, scared that they'll be ostracized if people discover the truth. When their pasts are revealed, what struck you most about their transformations?

5. The Vagabonds' camping trips always included a series of rustic challenges. If you had to compete in one of the challenges from the book, which would you choose and why?

6. Belle's career ambitions arise differently than most other people's. At the beginning of the story, she doesn't have a thought about professional aspirations. What do you think prompted

Belle to suddenly realize, when faced with the Grove Park story, that she'd never wanted something so much in her life?

7. If you could have the talents of one of the skilled laborers Belle interviews for her story, whose would you choose and why?

8. Describe Belle's relationship with her mother. How are they similar? How are they different? How does their relationship change over the course of the trip?

9. If you could have dinner with one of the people from this Vagabonds' camping trip, who would you choose and why?

10. What does Belle learn about herself throughout the novel? What does she learn about love?

# ABOUT THE AUTHOR

Photo by Bethany Callaway Photography

Joy Callaway is the author of *All the Pretty Places*, *The Grand Design*, *The Fifth Avenue Artists Society*, and *Secret Sisters*. She holds a BA in journalism and public relations from Marshall University and an MMC from the University of South Carolina. She resides in Charlotte, North Carolina, with her husband, John, and her children, Alevia and John.

എ

joycallaway.com
Instagram: @joywcal
Facebook: @JoyCallawayAuthor